THE VALKYRIE'S BOND

HALF-BLOOD RISING BOOK 1

LUCY ROY

To Mads and Boog

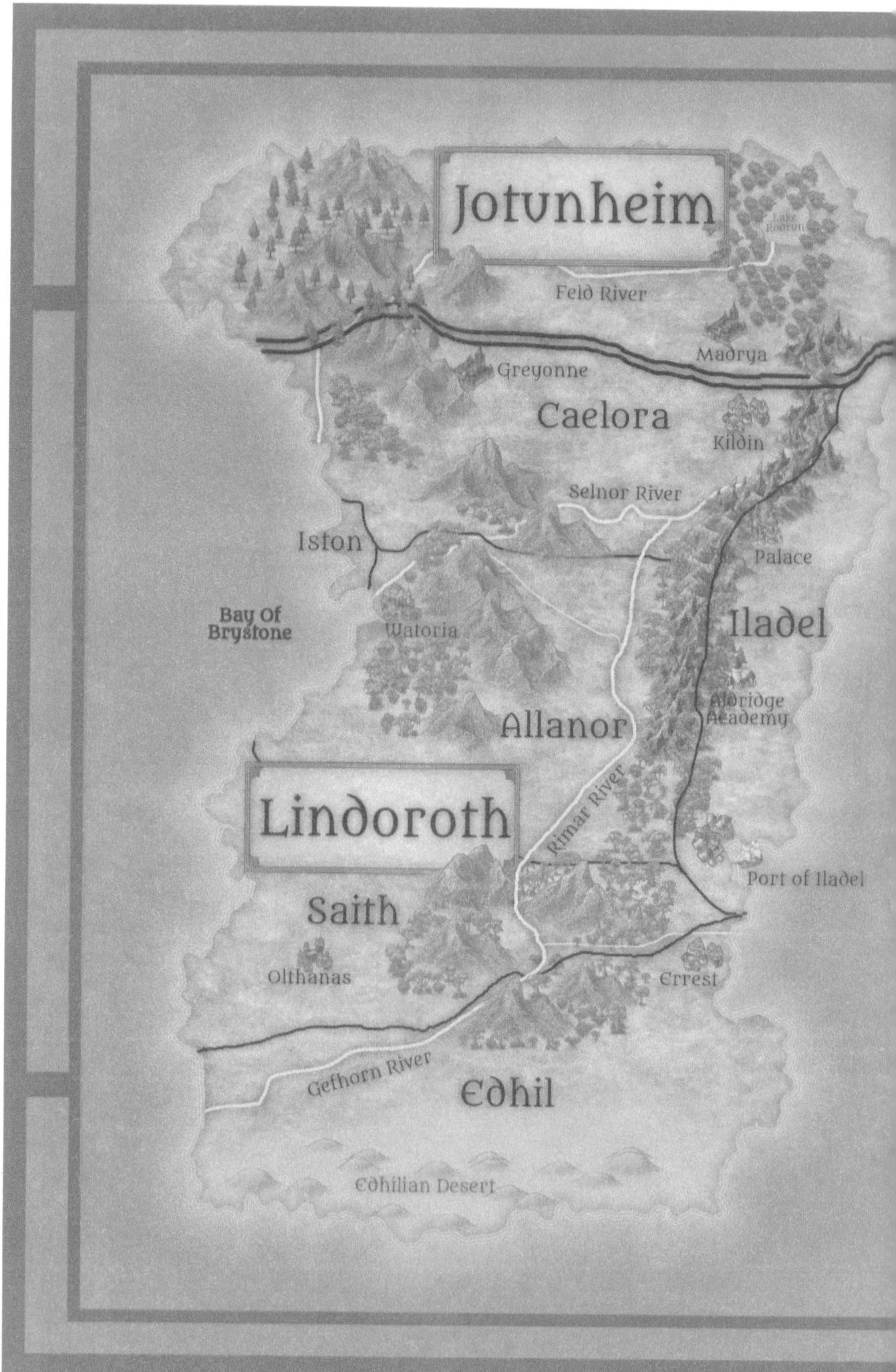

Jotunheim
Feld River
Madrya
Greyonne
Caelora
Kildin
Selnor River
Iston
Palace
Bay Of
Brystone
Watoria
Iladel
Aldridge
Academy
Allanor
Lindoroth
Rimar River
Port of Iladel
Saith
Olthanas
Errest
Gefhorn River
Edhil
Edhilian Desert

Elvish Lands ➝

Dystone

Teid

Port of Caldel

Caldel

Aren

Vindarria

Leford

PRONUNCIATION GUIDE

Freya – Fray-uh
Aerelius – Air-el-yus
Grevillea – Gruh-vil-ya
Lazarus - Laz-uh-rus
Collin – Col-lin
Byrric – Bir-ric
Salazar – Sal-uh-zar
Ordona – Or-doh-na
Myria – Meer-ya
Dystone – Dis-tone
Jotunheim – Yot-un-hime
Lindoroth – Lin-duh-roth

1

Freya swooped over the docked ships in the Bay of Brystone, deftly slipping between towering masts and furled sails as she approached the darkened bulkhead before her. A shadow moved, a thing slithering up the slick wood toward the dimly lit street that ran along the harbor. As the stench of decay stung her nostrils, she let out a muttered curse and closed in.

It had been a slow night so far. Her aerial patrols had yielded little more than a few angry tavern-goers who needed only to sleep off their inebriation at the marshal station before finding their way home in the morning.

When the scent of a Jotnar draug hit her, she couldn't say she was disappointed that her night seemed to be picking up a bit. They always seemed to think coming into Lindorothian lands through the waterways was a surefire way to avoid being seen, yet the one and only reason Freya patrolled the bay was because of the incessant stupidity of the creatures who thought they could pull one over on her.

She slipped on a glamour to conceal her presence, circling wide before setting her feet down in an alleyway facing the bay, then darted toward the bulkhead. As the creature neared street-level, the cloying scent of death became stronger, mixing unpleasantly with the briny odor of low tide and causing Freya's nose to wrinkle.

Moments later, a set of clawed, bile-brown hands covered in pustules reached over the splintered wooden ledge, and a tall, black-haired draug appeared—a creature who'd managed to sneak from the northern lands of Jotunheim to hunt the citizens of Lindoroth.

If he was lucky enough to get past Freya, that was.

Cocking her hip against the stone building, Freya folded her arms across her chest, waiting until the creature found his footing on solid ground before announcing her presence. She forced back the desire to tug on the black vambraces protecting her forearms that itched thanks to the thin film of sweat that had formed underneath.

"Hello, there!" she said brightly, letting her glamour fall as she stepped forward, revealing broad, gray wings and sturdy armor made of thick, spelled leather.

The creature stopped, momentarily startled, then growled, low and guttural, when he took her in.

"You're a Valkyrie," he hissed, his gnarled hands clenching into fists at his sides.

"And you've got eyes," Freya replied dryly. She gestured toward the bay. "You know these waters are infested with kraken, don't you? They aren't so particular about what they eat, so you really should take more care when sneaking about."

"Kraken," he scoffed, the sound a mix between a growl and a hacking cough. His nostrils flared and the thick tendons in his neck trembled with the anticipation of a fight. "I thought your kind kept to the north these days. I'd be rewarded well if I brought you and those fancy feathers of yours back to Jotunheim."

Wrinkling her nose at the offensive odor that wafted toward her, she tightened the cord that fastened her long hair off her face and wordlessly curled her fingers in challenge.

The draug roared and lunged, his claws reaching for her neck. Just as he would've gotten his hands around her throat, Freya struck out, bringing the heel of her hand to his nose in a wet, satisfying *crunch* while the other fist found purchase in his gut. She spun, and the ridge of her wing sliced through the air and to his temple. Blood, black as pitch, spurted from his nostrils and ear as he roared in pain. Before he could regain his balance, she twisted his arm behind his back and pulled him hard against her chest. Plucking a single feather from her wing, she dragged the metallic, venomous tip across his neck, tearing his throat open from ear to ear, sending out a long arc of arterial spray. His gnarled hand flew up to grab her wrist, but he'd hardly gained purchase when he went slack against her. His entire body stiffened, and seconds later, he began foaming at the mouth as her venom made quick work of his insides.

Freya dropped the gurgling body to the ground, wincing as her feather regrew, the burn of venom filling the shaft. It was a sting she didn't think she'd ever get used to. Shaking it off, she wiped her hands, now reeking with blood, on her leather pants, scowling at the scrubbing she—or more preferably, her aunt—would have to do when she got home.

"Gloves, Freya," she muttered to herself. "Get yourself a damn pair of gloves."

With a huff, she hefted the draug's body over her shoulder and took to the skies once again, aiming this time for the wide, deep ravine that ran along the outskirts of Watoria, separating the small capital of Allanor from the dark expanse of evergreen forest that stretched for miles all around. The dark crevice worked well as a means of defense but was also the perfect dumping ground for pesky bodies that stunk to the heavens if burned.

Not wanting to waste time landing, Freya dropped the body into the black abyss, hovering above only long enough to hear the satisfying *thunk* when it landed on the rocky floor before changing her direction back toward the city.

A moment later, her feet came down quietly on the roof of the local town hall, a three-story building that sat in a large public square in the center of town.

The square was a bustling area for shopping during the day, the small shops around it and down the sprawling side streets offering all manner of goods, from foods and freshly dyed fabrics, to talismans and potions imported from the other four realms of Lindoroth as well as the neighboring lands of Jotunheim and Dystone. Now, in the dead of night, it was silent, lit only by the few sparkling pixie lights that dotted the air along the stone sidewalks.

Crouching behind the building's wide brick chimney, Freya watched the street below, the building giving her the advantage of height without revealing her position. A few marshals, oblivious to her presence above them, ambled through the streets, no doubt keeping an eye out for mischief makers. The marshals were in charge of roaming the city streets, but it was Freya's job to climb and fly where no one else in Watoria would or could go.

Satisfied there were no immediate threats in the area, Freya scanned the city, assessing where she'd be most useful. The town hall's rooftop was slick with rain, making any movement a bit cumbersome, so she waited, choosing her next location carefully. Settling on a brighter area toward the north, she took off toward the busy North Ward, a place rife with dancing, drinking, and debauchery. If she was going to find anything more to occupy her time tonight, it would be there.

For the next few hours, she flew low over the roofs, stopping here and there to avoid being seen by any ruffians or other such troublemakers in the darkened streets and alleyways. Despite the usefulness of a Valkyrie's wings, they were, in fact, wings, which were pretty damn hard to miss in the sky, often making the element of surprise difficult to maintain unless she wanted to drain her power by wearing an invisibility glamour for every patrol.

After depositing two more brawling drunkards at the marshal station, she landed on the clock tower of Watoria's secondary school —the school that had been her second home up until a few short months ago—and sat down on the edge, letting her legs dangle over the side. Leaning back on her hands, she looked around the city, watching as the last lights winked off in Watoria's late-night establishments.

She closed her eyes in contentment and tilted her face toward the night sky. *This* was her favorite time of night—when she was on patrol but also able to take just a few moments to enjoy the silence that cloaked this part of the city. Even her home in her own neighborhood in the South Ward, posh as it was, didn't hold the same level of tranquility she found sitting forty-feet above the rest of the world.

Casting her eyes toward the northern sky, she found the large grouping of stars that represented her namesake—Freyja, the goddess and progenitor of all Linds. The triangular shape was low to the horizon, telling her dawn would arrive in just a few hours. She pulled herself to a standing position and yawned, stretching her arms above her head as she took one last look around.

She saw nothing of import in the street, so she spread her wings, smiling to herself as the damp night wind rushed through her feathers. She shot forward, staying as low over the rooftops as was wise, for one final sweep over the city before returning to her quiet neighborhood.

Ana, her aunt and fellow Valkyrie, was waiting in the warm kitchen when she arrived wearing a green silk robe knotted tightly at the waist, a steaming cup of tea in front of her, her chin-length blond hair mussed from sleep. A flame, small and vibrant, floated inside a lantern in front of her, casting a soft glow over the room.

Freya paused at the sight when she stepped through the door.

Ana leaned back in her seat and arched a single, blonde brow as she walked in. "Busy night?"

With a sigh, Freya fully retracted her wings.

"Not so bad," she hedged as she kicked off her shoes and began to divest herself of her leathers, dropping her pants, shin guards, jacket, and vambraces until she was left in her underthings and a thigh-length beige tunic. She dropped down into one of the chairs with a huff, gladly accepting the cup of peppermint tea her aunt offered.

Ana gave her an expectant look. "Well?"

Freya took the tea and sipped before answering. "There was a draug," she said, setting the cup down. "I killed it. Aside from that, a few drunks got a bit rough with one another. They're sleeping it off at the marshal station." She jerked her chin toward her pile of leather. "One ripped a fastener off my jacket, the bastard."

"Then I suppose it's a good thing we've still got your mother's sewing kit. Go get changed," Ana said wearily, running a hand through her knotted hair. "Those clothes will start stinking if you've gotten any blood on them. I'll start them soaking. Once they're done, you can do the fastener repair." She held up a long finger. "And don't even think about asking me to do it, young lady. I told you ages ago you needed a new jacket."

Freya made a face, knowing there was no point in arguing. "Can I at least finish my tea first?" she complained.

"No. Now, go. Your tea will be here when you get back."

Grumbling, Freya made her way to the bathroom, stopping in her spacious bedroom to get a change of clothes on the way. She made a face in the mirror when she saw the messy state of her thick reddish-brown hair and the smudge of draug blood on the tip of one of her ears. Picking up a washrag, she scrubbed at it, wincing when she had to rub extra hard to get the blood off. After changing into a pair of soft silk pajamas, she pulled the tie out of her hair and ran her fingers through, then brushed out the tangles before wrapping it up into a high bun.

She cracked her neck, still a bit sore from carrying the weight of the draug across the city, and sighed.

Then, picking up her dirty shirt and underwear, she went back out to the kitchen to finish her tea.

Ana had just entered the kitchen when Freya returned. As Ana poured herself another cup of tea, Freya saw she wore a pursed expression.

"What is it?" Freya asked, sitting down and sliding her lukewarm tea toward her.

"I spoke with Nadya down the street, who heard from one of the marshals who heard from the commander. Aldridge is expected to send scouts out to gather up any remaining students who haven't yet arrived on campus." Turning, she took a slow sip of tea, her eyes narrowed at Freya over the rim. "Oddly enough, there seems to be just one who hasn't made her way there." When Freya merely stared back, Ana huffed out a sigh. "You were supposed to be on a ship four days ago! Now, Freya, I've been lenient with you, considering, but do you know how it looks—"

Freya rolled her eyes. "The first school term doesn't begin for five days, and I've already booked passage for tomorrow afternoon. Most of my things are packed. The only thing I'm missing out on is—"

"*Four* days, and you're missing out on getting to *know* people, reconnecting with people," her aunt lamented. "Gods above, Freya! Training at Aldridge is a gift most can only dream of and it's important you show your appreciation for it! I thought you'd be happy!"

Freya snorted and turned to gaze out the window. "I'm fairly certain my happiness is the last thing I need to worry about." She smirked at her aunt and circled her finger in the air. "You, on the other hand..."

"*I* will be returning to Iston, where I plan to live out my last few centuries happily with the rest of our kind. As honored as I was when your father chose me to raise you in his absence..." She sighed and smiled at her niece. "I'm eager to return home, just as you should be eager to dive into this new phase of your life."

"I'm going, aren't I? I have no intention of shirking my duties, Aunt Ana." And, as hard as it was for her to admit, she was excited to go back to Iladel, Lindoroth's capital, so she could finally learn and train under experienced professors. The physical training she'd received from the marshals and her aunt, her father's sister and a battle-tested Valkyrie, had been of the highest quality, but the education she would receive at Aldridge Academy, a small, elite university, would set her on another level.

"They won't change you as much as you fear," Ana said quietly. "If that's what's worrying you."

Freya was silent for a few moments, letting her mind wander over her future—one that had been laid out for her when she was just a child. Traveling several hundred miles to Iladel was something that had always loomed on her horizon, getting closer as each day, each *year* slipped past. It wasn't something she feared, but lack of fear did little to quell her anxiety of returning to a place and people she hadn't seen in years.

At the age of thirteen, her nineteenth year had seemed a million years away. Her mother, a general in the Allanorian army that helped protect the western lands of Lindoroth, had just been killed. Freya's father had decided she'd no longer be summering with the royal family, who were long-time family friends. After that, she was sent on her way. She'd trained and fought in Watoria, the capital of the realm of Allanor, earning herself a reputation with the local marshals at the age of sixteen as an ally worth having, while also ensuring she excelled in academics.

Her graduation from secondary school had come and gone three months' past, and since then, a clock had been ticking relentlessly in her mind, counting down the hours until she left her home for good. The obligations she'd made for herself here in Watoria would soon be replaced by those that had been set on her shoulders by others, that would recreate the female she'd grown into.

With a sigh, she drank down the dregs of her tea, wincing at the bitter taste of the leaves that had found their way through the infuser.

"It will be alright, Freya." Ana stared down at her own cup. "When you go... it will be alright."

"I know it will," Freya muttered.

2

———

Freya was woken several hours later by rough shaking and her aunt hissing in her ear.

"Freya, wake up! There's been an attack!"

Freya bolted out of bed, her mind instantly alert as she lunged toward her armoire.

"Where?" She flung the wardrobe's doors open and pulled out a fresh pair of leathers and began tugging them on. "Was it draugs?"

"Yes, at Keranal's," Ana replied breathlessly.

Freya paused in the middle of fastening her jacket. "Draugs attacked a tavern? What in heavens for?"

Ana shook her head. "Not a clue, but the marshals are there now and there are at least a dozen patrons injured. Ashton just called for you. Do you need me to come?"

"No, stay here. If I need any backup, I'll send for you."

"Alright. Be safe, Freya."

Once her protective gear was secure, Freya stepped onto the front porch and let out her wings, leaping into flight and shooting toward the tavern where she'd been dragging raucous drunks toward the marshals' wagon not three hours prior. She did a quick loop around the area to check the side streets for any movement before landing silently in front of the small building.

A marshal stood a few feet from the door, a male called Gideon, who she'd been friends with since she began working with them four years ago.

"What do you have?" she asked him.

He jumped at her sudden and silent appearance. "Freya! You startled me."

She flashed him a quick grin. "Apologies. My aunt said you called for me?"

He nodded gravely, then jerked his chin toward the door. "Ashton is just inside. I think he's waiting for you."

Nodding her thanks, Freya stepped through the doorway and cast her eyes around the darkened establishment. The smell of old ale mixed with death assaulted her nostrils as she stepped further inside, causing her face to scrunch. The stench was forgotten as she took in the scene before her, though. Ana's report had been accurate—there were about a dozen patrons bearing injuries of an attack. A few clutched their heads, no doubt thanks to hard blows, while others were pressing rags against seeping wounds.

"Ah, Freya." The warm voice of Ashton Carinald, one of Watoria's five senior marshals, reached her. She and Ashton had become friends not long after she moved to Watoria when she was thirteen. Three years her senior, he'd been the first to suggest she train with the marshals. Their friendship teetered on the edge of romantic at times, but considering her imminent departure from Watoria, she tried very hard to keep from giving him any type of false hope.

She frowned as he approached. "How long ago was this?"

He dragged a hand through his blond curls and blew out a breath as he gazed around them. "Maybe three hours ago, so far as we can tell."

"Three hours? How—" She huffed out a breath though her nose. "They were entranced?"

Ashton shook his head. "Poisoned. We found a vial of widow

venom on the ground outside and the doors were locked. They're only just waking up."

Frowning, she began to make her way around the room, examining the patrons as she went. She crouched down beside a witch with skin pale as chalk who was clutching her heart.

"May I see?" she asked gently.

The female nodded and pulled her hand away, revealing four vicious claw marks across her chest, the edges hard and blue.

"I didn't see much." Her lips trembled as she struggled to meet Freya's gaze. "I felt the hit, then it all went black."

"These are draug claw marks," Freya said, glancing up at Ashton briefly before continuing. "It may take a bit longer to heal, but give it a few hours and you should be good as new," she told the female with a smile.

The female returned her smile, and Freya gave her hand a squeeze before shifting position so she could get a better look at the male bear shifter slumped on the floor beside her.

She assessed the large gash across his neck and gave him a questioning look. He grimaced, then nodded and tilted his chin up.

Touching a finger to the male's jaw, she nodded. "These are draug marks as well. Slightly different, though. A bit more jagged than hers," she said, indicating toward the female. She winced and lightly touched the edge of the wound. "Have you tried shifting to heal yourself?"

The male nodded. "It was the first thing I did, but my strength still hasn't returned."

Freya gave him an encouraging smile. "Give it time. I know how painful draug venom is."

"A pack was seen roaming the outlands a few days ago," Ashton informed her. "They emptied the till and relieved all patrons of their valuables before leaving."

Freya gave a hum of annoyance and stood, wiping her hands on her pants as she turned to face him. "I killed one earlier. It was climbing over the bulkhead across from the fishery. He was alone, though."

"What did you do with the body?" Ashton asked sharply.

"I dumped him in the ravine." She cocked her head to the side, her lips quirking. "He made a nice *crunch* when he landed."

Ashton ran a hand over his face and shook his head. "Considering how strictly Caelora guards the Jotunheim border, don't you think it would have been wise to report that when it happened?"

Freya's eyes narrowed. "This isn't the first time Jotnar draugs have gotten into our lands. Caelorian knights are strong, but until they agree to send more support to the coast, draugs and their ilk will continue to come in by sea. And as I said, I dealt with it."

"And you're certain he was alone?"

"Yes."

Ashton's brow lifted in question.

"Yes, Ash, I am certain he was alone," she said with a smirk. "They're defensive creatures. If he had others with him, they would've come after me. That and he was talking about dragging me back to Jotunheim in exchange for a handsome reward. It's unlikely he would've been willing to share such wealth."

Ashton chuckled darkly. "I would've paid to see that fight." He scanned the patrons around them. "Is there a chance this could be payback, then?"

Freya's eyes widened at his insinuation. "You think this is *my* fault?"

He shifted his stern gaze back to her, and a small muscle in his jaw twitched. "I think retaliatory attacks are something draugs are known for, *considering* their defensive nature."

Freya blew out a small breath to keep herself from delivering Senior Marshal Ashton Carinald a backhand worthy of his title.

"If that were the case," she said slowly, "they would've come after me and Aunt Ana, not a bunch of people I don't know."

"Maybe. Maybe not. Are you certain you killed it?"

"I stunned it and sliced its neck with my own feather. It's dead as a goddamn doornail."

Ashton's warm brown eyes ran over her face, then he cast a glance toward the door where another officer had just entered and gestured for her to follow him outside.

When they stepped into the cool night air, his expression softened, and he brushed a thumb across her cheek. "You're right. I'm sorry. I didn't intend for it to seem as though I don't trust your judgement."

"Apology accepted." She grinned, then backed away when he tried to reach for her and pull her closer. "I'll do a few more sweeps around the city and let you know if I find our assailants. And, if it will ease that pretty mind of yours, I'll also confirm that the body I dropped earlier remained where I left it."

A smile tugged at the corner of his mouth, one that melted the bit of annoyance she'd allowed to creep in.

Turning, she stormed away from the building, frustrated at the turn the night had taken. With a leap, she was airborne, banking hard to arc over the nearby buildings. She flew down dark alleys and streets, her wings pinned to her body, cutting through the air sound-lessly. Keeping her eyes and ears peeled for any sort of disturbance, she did a thorough air patrol of the North Ward, moving next into the East Ward's marketplace, and, finally, the residential neighborhoods that dotted the Southern and Western Wards.

As she continued her sweep, her concerns seemed to be valid. A few drunks stumbling home, a couple fornicating behind the town hall, and a few vagabonds settling in for the night under a bridge were the only activity she saw. When she glided over the outermost neighborhoods, her worry grew. If the draugs had already fled the city, there was little chance they'd be caught.

When she'd covered the rest of the city, she turned eastward, aiming for the spot where the sun was beginning to lighten the sky. In the soft glow of dawn, the deep ravine appeared like a thick black line drawn in the ground around the city. Banking low, she eyed the surrounding area carefully. It was unlikely any draugs in the area would attempt to recover their fallen comrade, but it wasn't in Freya's nature to assume anything of those creatures, wretched as they were. The Jotnar were, on the whole, quite intelligent and not unlike the

Linds, although the lower strata of their society—draugs, huldra, and their ilk—couldn't make that same claim. They ran on instinct and greed, which was often more than enough to get them killed.

Rubbing her fingers together, she blew on them, forming a soft ball of glowing light that illuminated the air around her as she descended into the darkness. Coming to a silent stop, she held the light at shoulder-height and looked around.

The draug was just as she'd left him—dead, his body broken, the boulders he'd fallen on coated with blood and whatever muck had spilled when his flesh tore on contact with the sharp granite.

Annoyed that Ashton's words had caused her to question her own methods, Freya pulled a vial of accelerant from the pouch at her waist and cracked it open, pouring the contents over the thing's ruined body. She flicked the small light that still glowed in her hand downward, setting the corpse ablaze. After watching for a few moments as the green flames slowly turned the draug to ash, she took to the air for what she hoped would be the last time for the night. She'd check in with Ashton later in the morning, but for now, she wanted—needed—rest.

Freya landed quietly on the cobblestone street in front of her house, keeping her steps silent as she ascended the stairs toward the front door. She knew it would be of little use—if she knew her aunt, Ana had refused to go back to sleep until she knew Freya was home and safe in her own bed. At times, it annoyed Freya that her aunt had fallen so effortlessly into the role of mother after her own had died. But despite Ana's softer nature, she was nearly as good a fighter as Freya, having been subject to the same training regimen in her youth, centuries ago. Unlike Freya's father, though, Ana hadn't followed the same path most of their kind did, by entering the military or law enforcement field. Instead, she'd chosen medicine, acting first as a physician in the field for Lindoroth's royal army, then as a traveling physician in Watoria, a job that kept her aunt busy most days.

Freya turned the knob as quietly as she could, hoping in vain she could avoid the annoying screech that almost always sounded halfway through a full turn. Much to her dismay, the old mechanism squealed, sharply announcing her entry.

When she stepped through the foyer and into the kitchen, she came to a halt, her eyes widening, then narrowing to slits as she took in the scene before her.

Her aunt sat at the table, a look of resignation on her face, her hair rumpled as if she'd actually attempted to get back into bed. A fresh cup of steaming tea sat in front of her. Four males, slender and resplendent in their gold-adorned navy blue uniforms, stood at attention in the four corners of the room, the white epaulets and bronze shields pinned to their lapels identifying them as Iladel's palace knights. The crest of House Harridan, Lindoroth's ruling family, was carved into the metal—two large, golden lynx reared on their hind legs in mid-battle. Each guard wore a longsword at one hip and an onyx-handled dagger at the other.

Freya's nose twitched as she took in their scents, the sharp, earthy smell identifying them as wolf shifters, the type most commonly employed by the monarchy.

A fifth male, tall and foreboding, with dark brown hair shot through with streaks the color of cinnabar, stood beside Ana. His uniform was pitch black with mother-of-pearl buttons. The gold epaulets identified *him* as the commander of King Salazar's Royal Army. The corner of his mouth quirked up when Freya appeared, amusement at her surprise lighting his aged gray eyes.

Freya allowed herself three seconds to recover, then tilted her chin up and folded her arms across her chest. "Commander."

He inclined his head in greeting. "Freya."

"Are you here to drag me off?"

The commander set down the glass of water he'd been drinking and folded his arms, mimicking Freya's pose. "You should have been on a ship days ago."

She walked toward the stove and poured herself a cup of tea from the kettle that still sat there steaming. Ignoring the guard to her left, she busied her hands doctoring her tea with cream and a bit of honey before turning to face the commander again. Leaning against the stove, she crossed her legs at the ankle and took a slow sip of the steaming liquid. She held back a smug smile as the tension in the room thickened, refusing to acknowledge the dirty looks she was sure her aunt was sending her way.

"Is there a reason you couldn't wait until daylight to make this visit?" Freya asked. "It's been a busy night, as I'm sure you know."

"Ah, yes." The commander nodded knowingly, and she winced at the impending barb. "You killed a single draug that was sneaking onto a deserted street, if I'm not mistaken, while twelve of Watoria's citizens were being beaten and robbed less than a mile away." He strode forward, stopping a foot away from her, hands now clasped behind his back. The authority behind the gesture, the kind one had achieved after spending several centuries as a warrior, oozed from him, slapping Freya's own sense of confidence down in a single hit.

"Odd coincidence, isn't it?" he mused. "One draug keeping one of the city's strongest fighters occupied while his comrades attack elsewhere."

Freya ground her teeth together. Commander Balthana delighted in irritating others when they misstepped, and the pleasure he took in goading her, trying to get a rise out of her, was clear in his eyes.

"Yes, I suppose that would be an odd coincidence," Freya said slowly, cursing herself for not considering the possibility when she'd spoken with Ashton. "Although, organized crime has never been their strong suit."

"Quite true." He held up a finger. "But a good warrior knows that her biggest enemies are ignorance and assumption. You allow your assumptions of a creature's behavior to be dictated by what you think you know."

With a sigh, Freya straightened her shoulders. "If you're going to cart me off to Iladel, I'd like to at least get a few hours' sleep before I go. May I have that, at least?"

The commander clicked his tongue and shook his head. "Unfortunately, no. Your disdain for your obligations has caught the eye of those above me. I'm under orders to bring you—kicking and screaming, if necessary—to the capital *now*."

"But—"

He held up a hand at her protest. "No, you may not rest. The belongings you've already packed have been taken to the carriage and will be loaded onto the ship for Iladel shortly. What you *may* do is change out of those filthy clothes and be in the carriage out front in ten minutes. I have an army to lead, and chasing the king's wayward students is preventing me from doing my job." He ran his eyes over her hair and sighed. "And do something about that hair. It looks as though you've been rolling in mud."

She held his stare for several moments before giving him a small smile. "I'll be ready shortly. Feel free to let Ana go back to sleep," she added, glancing down at her aunt, who already appeared halfway there. "She's had a rough night as well."

Not waiting for permission, Ana stood.

"Safe travels, Officers," she said quietly. "Commander."

He nodded a farewell, then turned back to Freya once Ana left the room. "Ten minutes."

Pushing herself away from the stove, she brushed past him. "Make yourselves comfortable."

When she reached her room, she found her aunt perched on the edge of her bed, Freya's repaired jacket draped over the back of a chair.

"Thank you," Freya said softly, picking it up.

"I couldn't very well trust you to do it right, could I?" she mumbled. "Half-witch or not, using your magic to sew has never been your strong suit."

"Are you sure you don't want to come with me?" Freya asked, sitting down gently on the end of the bed. This was a conversation they'd had countless times, and though Freya knew the answer, she needed to ask one last time before she left. "I'm sure there are plenty of opportunities for healers in Iladel."

Ana smiled sleepily and shook her head. "No, my job here is done. I'll come visit when I can, though."

"I know," Freya said with a sigh. She flopped back on the bed and

closed her eyes. "Gods above, why does he have to be so...
tyrannical?"

"Centuries of experience being such? Best not to goad him, dear,"
Ana warned. "It's a long way to the capital from here, and the king
and queen don't take kindly to their commander being harassed."

"Harassed," Freya scoffed. "If anyone's being harassed, it's the two
of us." She gave Ana a small frown. "Shouldn't you be in bed?"

"I'll go to sleep once you're gone," Ana said, sitting up. "I don't
think either of us intend for you to leave here without packing the
rest of your things, so let me help."

Freya grinned. "You couldn't be more correct."

NEARLY AN HOUR LATER, after multiple rounds of Commander
Balthana banging on Freya's locked and spelled bedroom door, she
emerged with a knapsack slung over one shoulder packed with the
few articles of clothing she hadn't had time to stuff in her trunks.

Ignoring Ana's exasperated look and the expression of pure
annoyance Balthana wore, Freya strode down the front walk toward
the first of two large, black carriages that waited at the street's edge.
Each was pulled by a single black stallion and bore the royal crest on
the door. She held her head high as she climbed inside, taking great
care to kick her feet on the sill before sitting on the red-cushioned
bench. Once settled, Ana stepped up to the door and reached inside,
taking Freya's hands.

"Be good, Freya," she said, the warning clear in her tone. "It's been
a long time since you've been in the capital and at court. Things
change over the years."

Freya smiled. "Have you known me to be incapable of adapting?"

Ana gave her a pointed look, her eyes sliding to the left toward
where the commander stood before responding. "Incapable and
unwilling are two different things."

"I am fully willing to adapt to my imminent change in circumstances. I promise." She squeezed her aunt's hands for extra empha-

sis. "I'll get all my brattiness out before we've reached midway, don't worry," she teased.

"Please see that you do," Ana said wearily. "Salazar and Ordona are lovely monarchs, but even they have their limits."

Leaning out, Freya planted a kiss on Ana's cheek. "It will all be fine. Try not to worry. I'll send word when I get there. And, Aunt Ana? Travel safe."

"I will, dear. You do the same."

"Time to go," the commander said.

Smiling reluctantly, Ana stepped away from her. "You be good, Freya," she said in one last warning. "I'll see you at Winter Solstice."

Balthana pulled himself up inside the carriage and took a seat across from Freya.

With one last farewell, Ana waved and stepped back from the road.

Freya took one final look at the house she'd lived in for the last six years, surprised when she found herself struggling against a lump in her throat. Slowly, the carriage pulled away, the tall wheels rattling so loudly on the cobblestone Freya knew better than attempt to sleep on the short trip to the port.

"You'll be happy to know I received word from Officer Carinald," Balthana said. "They located a cadre of draugs in the forest less than an hour ago. The draugs have been destroyed, and the stolen goods are on their way back to their owners."

Freya let out a quiet breath, relieved to know she wasn't leaving the city behind with a mess for the marshals to clean up. "Thank you for the update. I appreciate it."

He gave her a curt nod.

Not wanting to dive into a full conversation just yet, she contented herself with resting her forehead against the cool glass, watching as the rows of familiar houses slipped past, drinking it all in one last time before she left Watoria behind for good.

3

A short while later, Freya found herself settling into a first-class cabin on the ship leaving Watoria for the capital.

A small bed covered in lush velvet the color of new spring leaves caught her eye, contrasting with the carpeted floor in deep colors of autumn. With the white-paneled walls, gauzy curtains in shades of sunrise, and touches of gold in the fluffy bedding, the cabin seemed to encompass all five of Lindoroth's regions in one small space. The beauty of it made Freya feel a bit remorseful about her filthy shoes, so as soon as she sat down on the small bed, she tugged them off and changed them out for her spare boots, ignoring the commander's smug look as she wrapped her dirty boots in a tunic and shoved them into her bag.

Satisfied, she slid her bag under the bed and met his stare, jolting slightly when the ship let out a loud *creak* as it pulled away from the dock and into the Southern Canal, which would take them south through Saith and Edhil, the two southernmost realms of Lindoroth, then east to the capital realm of Iladel.

"Will I go straight to the academy when we arrive, or do you have any stops planned?" she asked.

"You'll be taken straight there," he told her. "Classes start in four days and you'll need to get settled in before then."

"And what about supplies? Clothes?" She gestured toward the simple nature of her outfit. "As much as I'm loathe to admit it, my current wardrobe isn't well-suited for the capital, considering. I'd planned to take one last trip to the markets before leaving this afternoon."

"All of those things will be provided to you. We'll arrive in Iladel in two days' time, so take the third to acquire your supplies and make a trip into Iladel this week to purchase some new clothes. Everything will be billed directly to the capital."

Her brows shot up in surprise. "That's a dangerously long leash to give a girl," she said, smiling. "What if I find a sudden taste for Errestian jewels? I hear Edhil's mines have been quite fruitful this year."

He gave her a dry look. "Your 'leash' consists of clothing, texts, and whatever other supplies the professors at Aldridge require of you. Your roommate will show you the best places to purchase what you need."

Freya wrinkled her nose in distaste. "So I'll have a roommate, then? Have you met her?"

He nodded. "Grevillea Calliwell. A cousin to Prince Aerilius and daughter of Orin Calliwell, the Governor of Edhil. Her mother is the queen's sister."

Freya gawked. "Grevil—good heavens, is that the name she goes by? Please tell me it's not!"

He gave her a warning look. "She goes by Lea. She's quite lovely."

Freya gave a noncommittal *hmm*, unsure if she was ready to trust the commander's version of 'lovely' just yet. It had been her experience that females who lived in the capital could be *lovely* in their own way, but that way typically involved a long look down pointed noses at anyone who wasn't a lifelong Iladelian.

"A schedule of upcoming events you'll be required to attend will also be made available, although some final adjustments are still being made."

Freya rubbed her fingers across her forehead as a small headache began to form behind her eyes. "What kind of events?"

"A few dinners, the annual commencement ball, and the Winter Solstice celebration, among others. I would recommend bringing Lea with you when you're choosing attire for those."

She narrowed her eyes. "Lea..." Freya couldn't bring herself to use the poor girl's proper name. "Should I expect her to act as my shadow, or will she simply be my roommate?"

"That is entirely dependent on you, although the hope is that you'll become friends."

"And is she aware of who I am?"

"She is."

"Lovely," Freya murmured.

He flicked a glance out the small porthole window, then tugged the heavy velvet curtains closed to block out the light. "We'll be on the water for some time. You might as well get some sleep. My cabin is just down the hall if you need anything."

THERE WAS a favorable wind behind them as they sailed, so the trip to the capital took just under three days, much of which Freya spent abovedeck talking with the crew, sunning her wings, and generally lazing about. The commander made appearances now and then, but for the most part he was off doing whatever it was he did. He was a curmudgeonly fellow on a good day, so Freya wasn't overly eager to bask in his company.

When she awoke on the third day to the steady sound of the sloshing water and the call of gulls, the sun appeared high in the sky, and the flowering fields of the southern realm of Edhil were drifting past outside the porthole beside her bed.

There was a knock at her door. Groggily, she rolled out of bed and opened it, then greeted the commander with a tired wave.

"It's nearly noon," he said by way of greeting. "You shouldn't have stayed out so late."

"The crew wanted to wish me well before the start of term," she muttered, ignoring his chastising tone as she flopped back down on the bed. "How much longer until we arrive?"

"About an hour and a half." He stepped aside as a servant set a pot of coffee and a paper-wrapped sandwich on the bedside table. "We passed through Saith and into Edhil about three hours ago. We're just outside Errest now, so pack up your things."

Once the commander and the servant left the room, she began to eat the sandwich, wincing a bit as the crusty bread scraped against her still-dry throat. The roasted chicken was juicy and flavorful, though, and by the time she was done, she felt more alert and less like she'd been up half the night with the crew members.

After packing up her belongs and tugging on a pair of soft linen pants and pale blue tunic, she went abovedeck and spent the rest of the time watching the lush scenery of Edhil slide past.

Her home realm of Allanor consisted largely of grasslands and evergreen-covered mountains dotted through with a few towns, with the largest city being Watoria, the realm's capital. But where Allanor was full of vivid golds, greens, and reds, the region of Edhil that drifted past now was filled with all color imaginable. Far to the south sat the Edhilian desert, a dry, hot expanse of land that spanned most of the southernmost portion of the continent. The waving grasses appeared greener, the trees taller, and even the sun's golden glow seemed to glitter a bit brighter.

The sun was well past its midpoint by the time the captain rang the bell signaling their arrival. As the crew began to prepare to dock, Freya got her first view of the capital, a sight she hadn't seen in nearly six years.

The bustling city spread out before her, rising to the foothills that led up to the craggy peaks of the Aldridge Mountains. Five hundred years earlier, the region had been a shared capital between humans and the Linds, a race of shifters and magic-wielders. When a chain of earthquakes shattered their lands and weakened the humans, the Jotnar, a race of witches and warlocks who lived to the north of Lindoroth, had attempted to take the human territories for their own, taking any opportunity to kill, capture, or enslave every human they could find. After nearly a decade at war, the Linds assisted in negotiating a treaty that allowed the humans safe passage to settle on the eastern continent of Dystone, while the Linds and Jotnar divided the western continent.

Freya cast her eyes upward as the ship slid into the port. From her vantage point, she could just make out the high, sharp turrets of the palace peeking over the lower part of the mountain far in the distance. When the crew dropped anchor and began throwing out ropes to tie down, her attention was drawn down to the busy port, where she saw gray-uniformed guards bearing the official seal of the capital swarming the area.

"Why are there so many guards?" she asked the commander beside her, lowering her voice to a whisper once they disembarked and stepped onto the aged wooden dock.

"Guard presence increased last week when students began arriving at Aldridge. Prince Aerelius will be attending Aldridge this year." Balthana gave her a curious frown. "How do you not know this?"

Freya's heart stuttered a bit and her words carried a sharp edge when she responded. "How would I?"

"Hmm. You received all of your correspondence from Aldridge, correct?"

"Yes, of course," Freya replied, hefting her duffel over her shoulder as he began to lead her up the dock toward the roadway.

The prince had been a good friend of Freya's in their youth—one of her closest—but time and distance had caused that friendship to wane, and now nearly six years had gone by since they'd last spoken. While she knew she'd see him soon enough, she was surprised to hear she'd see him every day.

"Well, had you taken the time to read it," he admonished, "you would've received news of the increased guard presence in the capital and on campus due to the attendance of the crown prince." He didn't bother looking back at her as they quickly navigated the busy port, his purposeful stride and black uniform parting the crowds like water. A long line had formed at the tall gates that led into the city, all passengers who'd just disembarked, each going through the process of stating their business before being allowed through.

Freya quickened her pace to keep up with him, ignoring the glares and grumbles of those queued up beside them. The commander stepped through a narrow door cut into the gate, giving a terse nod to the guards as he passed, then held it open for Freya to step through and onto the paved walkway.

"Why is he attending? That wasn't—surely he can acquire training of equal measure privately and without all the fuss?" Freya adjusted her bag on her shoulder. "It seems a bit unfair to the rest of the students, wouldn't you say? Having a prince on campus, attending classes?"

"Perhaps, although the same could be said for you, considering your background. The assumption, of course, is that he'll find a mate and choose his queen while he's there."

Freya snorted quietly. "A farce, if I ever heard one. Everyone knows the king and queen will choose his betrothed. Will he be living on campus?"

The commander gestured toward a black carriage trimmed in gold and bearing the royal crest waiting at the curb. "No, he'll continue to live at the palace. Come, let's get you settled in."

As was her habit, Freya took in her surroundings as she walked, letting her eyes drift about as she stepped toward the carriage. The city's tree-lined cobblestone thoroughfare stretched away from the station, the foot and carriage traffic neatly separated by a long, narrow flowerbed that bisected the road that stretched off into the distance. Looking skyward, Freya imagined the pale color of the stone would appear as a long, white ribbon from above, stretching from the port clear across the city before splintering off into the rolling hills beyond.

"You know," she commented, turning to face him as he sat down on the bench across from her, "it's quite unprecedented for the royal commander to be escorting one wayward student to school. Might I ask your reasoning?"

He gave her a stern look. "The king and queen don't take kindly to 'wayward students,' especially when an invitation to Aldridge has been handed to her *personally*. As the king, queen, and royal commander are aware of said student's propensity for flying off, they thought it best she have an escort."

"If said parties are so aware of my propensities, they should also know that I wouldn't shirk my duties simply to spite them."

"Certainly, but one can't blame them for being a bit overcautious."

Freya made a face but didn't argue. Her invitation to Aldridge had been written when she was a child by the king himself when her status as a true half-blood—a Lind who inherited equal parts witch and shifter blood—became clear around her sixth birthday. In unions like those of Freya's parents, where one was a shifter and the other a witch or warlock, witch blood always won out. It was incredibly rare for a person to be both shifter and witch, but on the rare occasion a half-blood was born, they were prized, often coveted.

One morning when her father had taken her down to the training yard to learn with the children who were training to become squires, the king came down to check on the progress of the students. After watching Freya hit archery targets thirty yards away and fling knives made of magic alongside the prince and some of the best squires of the king's Guard, Salazar had insisted she attend once she came of age. Her parents and aunt had been proud, as had she, but her pride had faded years later, when her mother, a highly-respected witch who worked for the crown, was killed on a routine patrol of the northern border between Caelora and Jotunheim.

Ever since, her father had become distant, immersing himself in his work and checking in only once or twice a month to ensure both she, the marshals, and her teachers in Watoria were keeping up with her training, continuing to prepare her for life in the Capital. Her aunt Ana had ensured the sums of money left behind when Cina passed were used for housing, food, schooling, and anything else she might have needed.

"You know, I was under the impression you were eager to attend Aldridge," Balthana commented, breaking her from her reverie.

She looked at him. "I was just dragged from my home after patrolling and fighting all night, put on a boat for three days, and now I'm being taken to meet this new best friend that's being forced on me. It's not lack of eagerness that has me down, it's exhaustion and a strong desire to bathe."

"Fair enough." He nodded. "But I trust you'll keep your thoughts to yourself once you arrive. Get it out of your system now because Headmistress Dyren won't tolerate it."

"Your lack of faith in my ability to simper is appalling."

"No one expects you to *simper*, just to behave."

"So long as I get a few hours of sleep before I'm expected to present myself to anyone, I will be the picture of propriety," she said primly.

Exasperated, Balthana shook his head. "A lie, if I've ever heard one."

4

They rode the rest of the way in silence, Freya occupying herself with watching the citizens of Iladel bustle about the city as their carriage rolled along the cobblestone streets. Iladel really was a beautiful place, and despite having been absent for six years, Freya felt a sense of home as they rolled past the people stepping in and out of shops and restaurants. It was nearly three times the size of Watoria and seemed to run at double the pace, but Freya had always enjoyed sinking into the capital's exuberance as a child. She and her mother had taken many trips into the city, wandering the busy streets and strolling past restaurants and taverns, dressmakers and tailors, florists, jewelers, and art galleries that burst with goods and wares from across the realms. As she and the commander traveled now, apartment buildings and homes rose above the din, and when she turned to look through the rear window, Freya could make out the tops of tall masts of ships docked in Iladel's port slipping off in the distance.

When they finally pulled down the shady road that led to Aldridge, Freya shifted in her seat to get a better glimpse of the tall, wooden gates that loomed ahead. Towering oak trees bordered the sprawling grounds of the university, and as unseen magic opened the gates to usher them inside, neatly-trimmed lawns rose away from the main road. A stone path that bisected the vibrant lawn led from the gates to the behemoth stone structure that housed the classrooms of the academy. Some students lounged about on the front lawn, while others walked along the paths in small groups chatting with one another.

She thought it would be rushed, more fitting to the capital, but instead it seemed... serene.

As Freya hopped down from the carriage, taking the footman's hand when he reached out to help, she inhaled deeply, taking in the scent of the woods, the pines and oaks that towered above, and the flower beds overflowing with blooms that waved gently in the breeze along the fence. The unfettered scent of nature was a far cry from the brine-and-soot smell of Watoria, and while she felt a bit homesick being so far from what she'd become accustomed to, she had to admit this wasn't the worst place to call home. Everything about it carried an air of serenity, something she was suddenly eager to explore in depth.

"I take it by your expression you aren't entirely disappointed to be here?" Balthana asked.

Keeping her eyes trained forward, she huffed. "I suppose circumstances could be worse," she admitted. "Although I've never once said I wouldn't like it here."

"Come, I'll take you to your dormitory."

Freya desperately wanted to get a lay of the land from above, but instead chose to follow the commander as he led her away from the carriage.

Despite her skills, her rarity and parentage often caused others to either avoid her entirely or attempt to slip into her good graces. She knew it was only a matter of time before her true identity was revealed, but for the time being, she just wanted to bask in her anonymity. A student eager to succeed, just like everyone else, as opposed to the daughter of one of the fiercest warriors and most gifted witches Lindoroth had ever seen.

Tightening the strap of her bag on her shoulder, she followed the commander through the wide gates and up the path toward the main building. Matching her stride to his, she eyed the busy campus warily.

"Shouldn't I check in somewhere?" she asked when he began to veer off the main path toward a cluster of four stone buildings nestled along the woods away from the academic building that had rose with grandiosity in front of them. Small turrets rose at all four corners of each, the windows tall and arched. If the buildings hadn't been so lovely, the silence and ivy snaking up the walls would've made them seem abandoned, Freya thought.

"That's already been taken care of," he replied. "You're to meet with Headmistress Dyren tomorrow morning to go over your course-work, schedule, and whatever else she feels needs discussing."

"What am I to do with myself for the rest of today, then?" she asked, annoyed. "You were in such a rush to get me here, after all."

"Meet your new roommate, get to know the campus, hopefully make some friends," he said, ascending the three marble steps that led to the glass dormitory entrance. "I'm quite sure those skills aren't beyond you."

Clenching her teeth, she sent him a stormy glare as she passed him and entered the building, where a wide, curved staircase greeted them. On the left, an archway opened into a quaint common area with overstuffed couches and a fireplace, and to the right, a second archway revealed a small study area, the walls lined with shelves of books from floor to ceiling. A fireplace was set in the far wall, and three long wooden tables sat in the center of the room, giving Freya a clear image of students hunched over texts and whis-pering softly. Both rooms were brightly sun-lit through the curtained windows that faced the busy grounds of campus, with gas-fueled lamps installed on the walls to chase away the gloom come nightfall.

As the door shut with a *thud* behind them, Freya noticed it was conspicuously quiet inside.

Freya peered into the other rooms. "Where is everyone?"

He started up the stairs, not looking back as he answered. "On their way to a gathering with the headmistress. I thought it best it not be made obvious I was the one settling you in."

Knowing better than to ask why he hadn't brought her there, Freya followed him up two flights of stairs to the top floor, pausing to look out the large window on the landing of the staircase. The building was laid out in a square with a large central courtyard that appeared to offer outdoor living space that could be enjoyed in Iladel's warmest months.

When they reached the hallway that contained her living quarters, he pulled a large brass key from his pocket and opened the door, then gestured for Freya to go in.

A short entryway led away from the door into a large room. Two wood-framed sleigh beds were pushed against the walls on either side, one already made up with a soft pink quilt and airy-looking pillows. A small stack of books sat on the nightstand beside it. Matching armoires were built into the walls on either side of the window seat that overlooked the campus grounds. The walls were a similar color to the exterior stone—a pale, unassuming gray—and the floors were made of deep brown hardwood that had been smoothed with age. A pale blue rug embroidered with a complex floral pattern covered most of the floor, which Freya hoped would keep some of the chill at bay once night fell. Despite the summer heat that still permeated the capital, nights in the mountains, even as low as the foothills, often turned chilly in the summer.

"Lea should be arriving a bit later," the commander said, hovering at the mouth of the entryway. "So go on and get yourself settled. And Freya?"

Turning to face him, she gave him a questioning look. "Hmm?"

"Be nice."

She feigned offense, pressing a hand to her heart and letting her mouth drop open in an O of shock. "What little you think of me!"

He gave her a chastising look, then left the room.

There was a slightly musty smell lingering in the air, no doubt a result of the building having been sealed up for several months while the academy was closed for the summer holiday. Moving to the window, she pushed the white sheers aside and slid up the sash, letting in a soft, warm breeze.

She dropped her bag onto the unclaimed bed, then groaned when she realized all of her belongings were still on their way from the port and likely wouldn't arrive for several hours. Cursing Balthana for his haste when they disembarked, she threw open the wardrobe on her side of the room and opened the drawers, breathing a sigh of relief when she found a small pile of white sheets and a blue quilt. They would do for the time being, although she was desperately wishing for the down quilt from her bed in Watoria.

After making her bed, Freya eyed her bag of belongings before looking back at the soft mattress. Seeing no choice between unpacking or sleeping, she kicked off her boots and flopped down on the bed, burying her face in the pillow.

"Do you think we should wake her?"

"I don't know!"

"Well, I wouldn't!"

"I don't think Valkyrie take kindly to being woken by strangers."

"They don't," Freya mumbled into her pillow. "And you've already done it so you might as well stop hissing over there." Rolling onto her back, she rubbed her eyes, then sat up, frowning as her mind tried to adjust to the dim light coming through the windows. It seemed she'd slept longer than she intended.

Running a hand through her hair and frowning when her fingers snagged in the tangled brown locks, she looked at the three people standing across the room. A dark-skinned, waifish female with wide, bright blue eyes—Grevillea, she assumed—stood between two males, biting her lip. She had curly, black-brown hair tied up in a chignon and wore a flowing blouse and pants set in pale blue and beige. The male to the girl's right had similar coloring and striking green eyes, with short black hair cut close to his scalp.

The second male, the one who stood to her left, had hair that was a vibrant shade of red, with pale skin and a smattering of freckles across a perfectly straight nose.

Freya inhaled a bit, taking in their scents. The female carried the sweet scent of a witch, but the two males smelled heavily of wolf.

"A witch and two wolves." She stood and gave them all an appraising look. "I'll assume you're Gr—"

"For the love of all that's holy, please do *not* finish that sentence," the girl said, holding up a hand and closing her eyes. "Call me Lea. My proper name was a cruel, drunken trick on my parents' part that I have yet to forgive them for. And yes, I'm a witch."

Freya's lips quirked up in a smile. "Lea it is, then." Angling her head, she addressed the two males. "I don't know who you are, though."

The one on Lea's right lifted a hand in greeting, his green eyes brightening as he smiled. "I'm Lazarus Cailen, Lea's cousin. You can call me Laz."

"Cailen, as in Governor Cailen of Caelora?" Freya asked.

"The very same," Laz confirmed. "Rischa Cailen is my father."

"And King Salazar's cousin, making you one of Aerelius' cousins, too." She arched a brow at the other male. "And you? Are you a governor's son and cousin to the prince, as well?"

"Nephew, actually, and no, there's no relation. I'm Collin Maddix. My uncle is Gunnar Maddix of Allanor," the auburn-haired male said.

"Ah!" Freya smiled. "Yes, I believe my grandfather named your uncle as his successor. I've only met him once, but Governor Maddix seems to be a good man. He's done well by Allanor since he was appointed." As was tradition in Lindoroth, each governor chose their own successor prior to retirement. Freya's grandfather, Governor Jora Enrieth, had retired fifteen years past, naming in his place Lord Gunnar Maddix to succeed him.

"Yes, he always spoke highly of Governor Enrieth and was quite saddened by his passing," Collin told her, tilting his head to the side and running those stunning blue eyes over her. "Don't mind me saying this, but you look different than I expected. More... plain."

Lea smacked his chest. "She doesn't look *plain*, you buffoon."

Collin's eyes widened. "No, I only meant—"

She gave Freya a smile, then stepped forward and held out her hand. "Ignore him, please. He doesn't get out much. They live in the dorm just next door," she said, gesturing toward the window where their building could be seen about twenty yards off.

Freya shook the outstretched hand as she eyed them all suspiciously. "Are you all to be my watchdogs, then?"

Lazarus and Collin exchanged a confused look.

Lea's eyes widened in surprise. "Heavens, no!" She clicked her tongue then made a sound of disgust. "Is that what Balthana told you? Oh, I'm going to wring his—" Cutting herself off, she took a deep breath. "No, Freya, none of us are going to be your 'watchdogs.' Commander Balthana simply wanted to ensure you roomed with someone well-suited to helping you reacclimate to life in the capital. As Aer's cousin, I am just that. These two just like to follow me around," she added, jerking her thumb over her shoulder. "They're easy enough to ignore, though."

Freya bit back a smirk. "Alright, then. I'll hold you to that." At that, her stomach rumbled, reminding her that all she'd had to eat was the sandwich the commander had given her hours earlier. "Well, now that we're such good friends and all, care to tell me where I can get something to eat?"

"The dining hall is open for a few more hours, and we were just about to head over for dinner," Lea said. "We were hoping you'd join us."

"That sounds great," Freya said, surprised at how easy her answering smile came.

"Alright, then!" Lea beamed at her. "Let's go!"

"So, Freya, the most important thing to remember here is that Aldridge is full of cliques," Lea said quietly as the four traversed the grassy expanse of Aldridge's grounds toward the brightly lit stone building that housed dining hall. "Some are better than others, but it'd be in your best interest to cement your status as quickly as possible to avoid the wrong types trying to sink their claws in."

"The wrong types?" Freya eyed her dubiously, hoping her initial opinion of females in the capital wasn't about to be confirmed. "What does that mean?"

"Oh!" Lea covered her mouth with her hand when she realized how her words had been construed. "I don't mean—no, it's just that opportunism is rampant here. There are certain groups who are, to put it simply, cruel. Females, mainly, hoping to detract attention from others in the hopes of finding a mate." She rolled her eyes. "It will be especially awful this year, what with my cousin attending and all."

Freya sighed. "Well, I'm not here to find a mate, so they're in luck."

"They don't know that, though," Collin replied from beside her. "You're quite pretty, and considering your background and the fact that you're a half-blood..."

Lazarus snorted. "What my darling Collin is trying to say is, you will be, without question, competition. Or perceived competition. You won't be given time to prove otherwise before some of the more rabid females here make that determination."

Once again, Freya became suspicious. "How do I know you three aren't simply saying this to keep me close-by?"

Lea looped her arm through Freya's as they approached the outside stone patio of the dining hall, where the scent of deliciously cooking food from inside was wafting toward them. A dozen or so tables were scattered about, some crammed with students, others sitting empty.

"Again, you don't," Lea told her. "And nothing any of us say will convince you otherwise."

Freya looked at her, surprised. "So why should I trust your intentions?"

"Do you trust Commander Balthana?" Lea asked, arching a brow. "Do you trust his judgement?"

"Now and then."

"Then that's all you need for now." Lea paused as Lazarus opened the door for them. "The rest will come in time, Freya, but I do hope we can be friends."

Smiling, Freya followed the three of them into the dining hall, quietly and surprisingly finding herself hoping for the same thing.

Echoing voices buzzed throughout the large hall, far more than Freya had expected, despite the busy nature of campus earlier. Students sat at round tables, some perched on top, others in the benches around them, talking, laughing, and eating. There was a carefree air about the room, the sincerity of which Freya immediately questioned.

Lea tugged on Freya's arm and waved off the males. "Come, let's take a table while Laz and Collin get us some dinner."

Collin looked at Freya in question. "They've got most everything here, so is there anything you don't like?"

"Not in the least," Freya told him. "Feel free to surprise me."

As Lea led her toward the back of the room, Freya noticed two black-uniformed guards standing sentry along the wall. Her eyes were immediately drawn toward the table they were watching over, already knowing what, or who, she'd find there. There, holding court with a number of male and females, was Freya's old friend, the dark-haired Prince Aerelius of House Harridan. A striking female, blond with all the signs of a would-be royal, sat at his side, laughing with the small group that surrounded him. She looked the type to set her goal for a mate high.

There was no question who the female had set her sights on.

Despite not having seen Aerelius for six years, she immediately noticed the muted look of vexation on his face, one he wore when he was annoyed and trying not to show it.

Before Freya could glance away, Aerelius' dark eyes lifted and he sent a look of pure exasperation at Lea before his gaze slid to meet Freya's. His face took on a confused expression, then his lips tilted in a smirk, the same infuriating one she remembered from their youth. The one that somehow made his handsome face even more so.

"He's only here for dinner because the meeting with the head-mistress ran so long," Lea whispered, ignoring him and dragging

Freya's attention away from the prince's table. "I told the boys we wouldn't be sitting with him if the social leeches had descended before we got here, if that's what's got that look on your face. Unless you want to…"

"No, it's fine." Freya forced herself to focus on her roommate. "I'd rather get to know you three, if that's alright."

"Oh, I completely understand, trust me. And to be fair to my cousin, he can't stand the lot of them. He's just got to be polite, you know." They came to a stop at an empty table in front of a picture window that looked out over a large pond. "Maybe now that we have a Valkyrie witch to scare them all off, he won't have to worry about being bothered anymore."

Freya replied with a noncommittal hum as she took a seat across from Lea.

"Well, what can you tell me about this place I'll now call home?" she asked.

Lea puffed out a breath of air, blowing a few stray curls from her forehead. "Goodness, where to begin? Let's see… have you gotten your schedule yet?"

"No, I'm to meet with the headmistress tomorrow."

Lea nodded, narrowing her eyes as she bit her lip. "Well, there's only so much I can say without knowing who your professors will be, although those I've met already seem to be quite fair. As for the student body… I would keep to yourself for the most part, observe more than you interact for the first few days or even the week, otherwise you won't get a proper feel for the place."

"But above all, make sure you mark your place here," Lazarus said, setting two trays down and taking a seat beside her.

"Ideally in Combat," Collin said, putting a tray with a small bowl of soup, a piece of seeded bread, and a plate of fruit in front of Lea while setting another tray loaded with food down at his own place. "Otherwise, females like Myria—the shameless blonde fawning over the prince—will challenge you at the first opportunity they see."

"Yes, make it clear that you are *not* to be fucked with," Lea added sagely.

Freya nearly laughed at the way the curse sounded coming from the pretty girl's lips.

"But you just told me to observe more than interact," she pointed out, picking up her silverware and cutting into the roasted chicken Laz had just given her.

"Socially and in classes," Lea clarified. "I don't quite know what your social skills are like—"

"Lea!" Lazarus hissed.

"Well I don't!" Rolling her eyes, Lea looked at Freya. "You lived in the capital each summer, correct?"

Freya nodded. "Until I was thirteen, yes. Winter Solstice, too."

"Considering your parentage and the length of time you lived in the capital as a child," Lea continued, "I would assume you have some fairly-honed social graces and are highly intelligent. Therefore, you'll have a fair number of males attempting to court you."

All true, Freya thought, but her "fairly-honed social graces" told her not to confirm that.

"Well, I suppose we'll see how things go," Freya said. "I'm certainly not here to be courted."

Collin nodded slowly. "I'd suggest getting that information out there as soon as possible."

"Somehow I don't think that will be an issue," she muttered.

5

Freya woke with the sun the following morning. Her belongings had been waiting in her room when they returned the night before, so she pulled on sturdy black leggings, a pale blue, long-sleeved shirt, and her black ankle boots before slipping out of her dormitory and onto the quiet campus. She inhaled deeply when she stepped outside, savoring the scent of dawn —the sugary dew that sweetened the grass currently being devoured by small, winged sprites, the morning glory that climbed the front walls of her dorm taking root in the space between stones, and, if she wasn't mistaken, the not unpleasant earthy smell of a pond.

Turning in the direction where the scent of water was strongest, she found a narrow, overgrown path leading into the still-darkened woods, untouched by the morning sun. Water dripped from leaves in the tall oaks, the remnants of last night's rain.

Keeping to the center of the path to avoid slipping into any quag-mire that might hide beneath the underbrush, Freya followed the packed earth for several minutes before the path widened, opening onto a beige, sandy beach on the edge of a quiet lake. Crystal water lapped at the shore, with a sharp drop-off visible about ten feet out. Beyond that, Freya could just make out the mouths of dawnfish peeking through the surface, occasionally nabbing skitterbugs that dashed across the water. To either side, starting where the beach met the tangled brush along the bank, were lily pads the size of wagon wheels. Here and there, a bellowing toad occupied one, while small birds took advantage of the quiet morning to suck nectar from the large blooms that floated about.

It had only been a few moments, but Freya already knew this would be her favorite place on campus.

On a sigh, Freya took a seat on the sand, which was still cool from the night air. The campus was hardly a few hundred yards away, but the silence permeating the air around her made her feel as though she'd just stepped into her own bubble of solitude.

Leaning back on her hands and ignoring the chill that seeped through her pants, she looked out across the lake, watching as the sky grew brighter, shifting from lavender to rose, then to blue.

She'd just contemplated letting her wings out to warm in the morning sun when she heard a rustling behind her. Turning, she smiled when she saw Laz walking toward her.

"You found my spot!" she called. "That's unfair!"

He grinned and shook his head. "I'm sorry, Freya, but Collin and I claimed this the day we arrived."

Freya gave him a considering look. "We could duel for it. What do you say?"

Laz sat down next to her, legs bent, resting his forearms on his knees.

"I'd say you'd defeat me in all of thirty seconds, so perhaps we can settle on sharing time?"

Freya pretended to wrestle with the idea for a moment, then nodded. "I suppose that's acceptable. Where is Collin, anyway?"

"He'll be along shortly," Laz said, stretching out his legs and leaning back on his hands. "Had I known you'd be here, I would've had him bring some tea for you."

She smiled, amused. "You take tea on the shore of a hidden lake often?"

He grinned and wiggled his eyebrows. "Every morning."

"And Lea?"

"Hardly an early riser," he said, turning at the sound of footsteps. "Collin! Look who's found us out!"

Collin handed a steaming cup of tea to Laz before taking a sip of his own and sitting down beside him. "I apologize, Freya—"

"Not to worry," she said, smiling as she stood. "I've got to get ready for my visit with the headmistress."

"I can take you over if you need a guide," Lazarus offered. "When do you have to be there?"

Gauging the placement of the sun, Freya frowned. "About two hours."

"I'll meet you in front of your building in an hour," he told her. "I need to speak with her about my schedule as well, but I can show you around a bit first, if you'd like."

"That sounds great, Laz, thank you," Freya said. With a final wave to Collin, she headed back down the path through the woods.

EXACTLY ONE HOUR LATER, Freya stepped out of her dormitory. She'd taken the time to make herself fully presentable, bathing and then brushing her long hair until it shone before pinning it back at her temples. The tunic she'd donned earlier was tucked into the waist-band of her fitted leather pants, accentuating the slight curve of her hips.

"You clean up quite nicely, Freya," Lazarus said as he walked toward her. He chuckled when she frowned. "You looked more than a little road-weary last night. I'm surprised Balthana didn't tell you."

Freya's lip curled in annoyance. "I'm not. He's a menace, I swear."

He laughed. "Don't let him hear you say that." He inclined his head toward the path that led away from the housing area. "Shall we?"

She nodded. "Lead the way, sir."

As they walked, Lazarus pointed out the different areas of campus, giving her a somewhat abbreviated tour. Aside from the dining hall and main building that housed all classrooms, there were training and archery yards used for combat class, a library, and no less than a dozen flowering courtyards that Freya imagined made wonderful places to enjoy Iladel's warmer weather.

The headmistress' office was inside the academy's main building, a stone structure that stood five-stories tall with a clock tower jutting another three beyond that. It looked like a smaller, less opulent version of the royal palace.

"It's beautiful," Freya observed as they walked up the stairs that encircled a raised rose garden.

"Wait until you see the interior," Lazarus said, grinning down at her. He pulled open the door, carved with ancient runes of welcome and protection, and stepped aside, gesturing for Freya to pass.

When she entered the cavernous entry hall, she barely restrained her gasp of delight.

Stained glass windows of vines and flowers in reds and golds cast warm light over the entire space, softening its imposing feel. High, arched halls extended off the lobby on either side, and from her spot, Freya could just make out the spindles of railings along the second-floor walkways.

Columns wide as door frames rose to an arched ceiling painted with detailed frescoes of old Lindish tales, forming a rotunda around a giant central fountain. The stories of her kind—shifters, witches, and warlocks from eons past—were detailed in sharp relief, the carved wood painted in vibrant colors. It began in the center with the fiery burst of color depicting the Great Beginning, when the Mother Goddess and Freya's namesake had created their world. In the next section, the Mother's fire, according to their lore, spread across the heavens creating land and life in its wake. From there, the sculpted squares continued to spiral outward, showing the rise and fall of their people, from the time when the Linds and the Jotnar lived as one to the arrival of the humans on their shores. The kings and queens who'd reigned in the time prior to the ceiling's creation were interspersed among the other images, the depiction of some showing more reverence than others.

The final section showed Linds of all shapes and sizes marching through the doors to the halls of the gods, an afterworld of peace and contentment that all creatures hoped to achieve in death.

The wonder of it was like nothing she'd ever experienced. The thought of the amount of life and quite possibly death that had gone into its creation had Freya's head swimming. Beauty and sacrifice— that was what she saw there.

"There's your tale, just over there," Laz said, pointing.

Shifting her eyes to where he was pointing, Freya saw two squares —one showing the creation of the first shifters and witches, and the next showing the birth of the Valkyrie, female warriors who were vicious when set loose on a battlefield. The lines of both species had been watered down over the millennia as both races began to inter- mix. Magic, fluid as it was, shifted and evolved over time as shifter and magic-wielder mixed their blood. While true half-bloods— wielders of full powers from both races—were rare, all Linds possessed magic. Even shifters held a small spark that they were able to wield if necessary, although it paled in comparison to that of a true witch or warlock.

Dragging her eyes downward, she spied a small flock of golden doves hovering halfway between the ceiling and the glassy surface of a fountain, held in mid-air by some sort of earth magic.

"It's something, isn't it?" Laz whispered.

Freya nodded, still awestruck by the beauty that had been hidden just out of view from the outside. "That's certainly a word for it."

He inclined his head toward a set of double-doors to their right. "The Headmistress' office is just through there. I told Collin we'd meet him for lunch," he said as they walked the short distance through the doors and into the outer office. "He's going to grab Lea. Is that alright?"

Freya tapped her finger on her lips and frowned. "Hmm. That depends. Do you think they'll have that carrot soup again?"

He grinned. "Heavenly, isn't it? You'll have to ask Cook. She's a magician, for certain, but each day's menu depends wholly on her whims."

"I may have to get to know this Cook, weasel some recipes from her."

He barked out a laugh. "Good luck with that!"

Freya followed him into the headmistress' outer office, where a pale-featured statuesque female sat behind a desk writing rapidly in some sort of ledger. Stacks of papers sat precariously on the edge beside a handful of pots holding various colors of ink. She continued to scrawl in her ledger for a few seconds before she realized they were there, then lifted her thick, brown eyebrows in greeting.

"May I help you?"

"I'm here to see the Headmistress. I'm—"

Before she could finish, the door behind her opened and a short witch with blue-flecked brown hair and kind eyes stepped out.

"Ah, our missing student! Yes, I've been awaiting your arrival." She nodded at Laz. "Lord Cailen, I'll be with you shortly."

"Of course, ma'am," he replied somewhat bashfully. He squeezed Freya's shoulder and whispered "Good luck" before taking a seat on a long bench beneath the window across the hall.

Headmistress Dyren ushered Freya into her office, closing the heavy door behind them once inside.

"So, how are things so far?" the headmistress began once she'd seated herself behind a large, L-shaped desk that was nearly as cluttered as her assistant's. "Do you like your room?"

"It's quite lovely," Freya replied carefully as she took a seat across from her. "Not home, but I think I'll get used to it."

"That's quite wonderful to hear." Dyren smiled, then slid a piece of parchment across the desk. "Now, here's your schedule, dear. I wanted to go over it with you before classes begin tomorrow."

Freya picked up the thick parchment and scanned the list of courses. History, Civics, Toxins, Literature, and Combat. Freya's mind began to whirl at the last one, eager to begin working with trainers who weren't her father, her aunt, or the marshals.

"Do you have any questions? Concerns? I've looked over your records from secondary school, and your marks were all quite impressive. We've given you a regular first-year schedule, but that can be adjusted if need be."

"I'm sure it will be fine," Freya told her.

Pursing her lips, Dyren drummed her fingers on the blotter that took up a large chunk of her desk. "I have to ask, are you planning on telling others who you are right away?"

Freya sat back in the chair and frowned. "I'd hoped to hold onto my anonymity for a few days, just until I get a stronger feel for this place. I don't plan to wait long, though, nor do I think I'll be able to."

"Everyone in your hometown knew, then?"

"A few of the marshals knew whose daughter I was, but to other locals, I was just another Valkyrie. Outsiders didn't know, though." Freya eyed her curiously. "Why do you ask? I know being a half-blood might make people respond to me differently—"

She grimaced. "It's not so much your species that would concern me; it's your heritage. Parentage like yours carries a good deal of weight when it comes to mating and career prospects. Considering the heavy focus many females here tend to have on finding a mate when they arrive, that could cause some issues socially."

"Headmistress, I know my parents—"

"Your father was the leader of the Allanorian Army for nearly a century and had more victories than any soldier to come before him. The logical assumption is that his daughter would've inherited the same skills that allowed him to achieve his successes. One would also assume that he trained you as well." Dyren paused, a bit breathless. "And your mother—well, the Cantor line is an envied one."

"She was a witch who passed me her power, pure and simple." Freya shook her head. "I haven't come here to find a mate. I've come to hone my skills and because my mother and father insisted on it the day I received my invitation from the king." She sat back in her seat, more than a little annoyed. "I can't help it if the other females crumble under the weight of their own insecurities."

"It is an unfortunate fact of life here," the headmistress said with a sigh. "The idea of landing a half-blood with your lineage as a mate would be most appealing, considering you could pass on either half of your talents to offspring. I think you're smart to withhold information at first. You'll know when the time is right to reveal yourself." She pursed her lips before continuing. "I've known your father for some time, Freya. He's told me a good deal about you."

Freya arched a brow. "And?"

"Things are going to be different for you here," Dyren replied, her tone shifting toward stern. "Far from how they were in Watoria. You had a lot of freedom there, the ability to come and go as you pleased. That won't be the case here. You also won't be flitting about Iladel hunting creatures of the night with the marshals."

"Are you telling me I can't leave campus?" Freya asked incredulously.

"I'm telling you that when you do, you will be accompanied by at least one guard."

"Is this my father's doing?" Freya demanded. "I can assure you, Headmistress, I have no need for a bodyguard."

"As confident as he and I are in your skills, we are in agreement on this."

Freya rested her elbow on the arm of her chair and rubbed her hand across her forehead. She was quiet for a few moments as she took in the Headmistress' words. Finally, she let her hand drop and she sent the Dyren a steady look.

"Might I ask how you plan to enforce this? I have *wings*, Headmistress. Can your guards say the same?"

A satisfied smile played on the Headmistress' lips. "I plan to enforce it by appealing to your sense of self-preservation. Abiding by these rules will save you the frustration of dealing with those above me who've made or support this decision."

Freya huffed out an annoyed breath. She knew it was unlikely this had been the headmistress' idea and that it would be unfair to take out her frustrations on her, but as she was the only one here, Freya struggled to keep her annoyance contained.

"Alright," she said, choosing her words carefully, "I won't argue when your guard accompanies me off campus."

The headmistress gave an appreciative nod. "That's all I ask. Now, do you have any questions for me?"

Freya shook her head. "No, I think I'm alright."

"Lovely. Please let me know if there's anything else you'll need while you're here." Dyren rose from her desk to show Freya out. "And of course I'm always here if you need to chat. Do you need directions anywhere?"

"No, I'll just wait for Lazarus to finish up," Freya replied, standing and slipping her bag over her shoulder.

"Ah." Dyren gave knowing smile. "Yes, if you've fallen in with that group, you're in quite good hands, I can assure you. Lazarus and Collin have their hands in almost every social circle there is, and Grevillea is, well..." Smiling, she clicked her tongue and shook her head. "She's Lea."

"Well, they all seem quite nice."

"It sounds like you're well on your way to finding a home here," the Headmistress replied as she stepped from behind the desk to see Freya out. When they reached the door, she held out her hand. "It's good to meet you, Freya, truly."

With a small nod, Freya shook her hand.

6

Freya waited, ignoring the looks the female behind the desk kept indiscreetly sending her way while Lazarus had his appointment with Dyren. Her stares only served to reinforce Freya's choice to keep to herself for the time being, avoiding the shadow of her mother's magic and her father's military achievements.

Focusing her attention away from the bug-eyed secretary and through the leaded glass windows to the campus grounds outside, she began to take note of her fellow students and surroundings, happy for the opportunity to do so in a way that kept her own stares concealed. Leaning closer to the open window beside her, she inhaled, attempting to determine the species of Lind that roamed about outside. The prevalence of the fiercer beasts of the feline and canine variety told her that most of the shifters here had strong bloodlines. The sweet and spicy scents of witches and warlocks floated toward her, although they seemed to be far fewer in number than the shifters, at least from this narrow vantage point.

"Freya?"

Tearing her eyes from the busy campus, Freya smiled up at Lazarus. "All done?"

"All done," he confirmed. "Let's head over to the dining hall. I'm sure Lea and Collin will be waiting for us by now."

"Food sounds fantastic," she said with a grin, linking her arm through the one he offered.

"Then I shall escort you." Lowering his voice to a whisper as they began to walk down the hall, he added, "If we're sneaky, we might be able to slip into the kitchens and nab some of the leftover dessert from last night."

"I don't know..." Freya chewed her lip thoughtfully. "From what you've told me, Cook might carve us up for a feast tonight if we're caught."

He wiggled his eyebrows and grinned. "Which is why, dear Freya, we won't get caught."

She laughed. "Next time, maybe. I'd like to at least try to make a good name for myself before being banished by the kitchen staff."

After making their way through the food line and filling their trays, they found Lea and Collin seated at the same table as the previous night. Lea bounced a bit in her seat as Freya approached, then held out her hand and snapped her fingers.

"Let's see it," she demanded.

Setting down her tray, Freya handed Lea her schedule to look over while Lazarus took a seat beside Collin. After a few seconds, Lea let out an excited squeal.

"Ooo, we all have History together!" She let the paper fall to the table and clapped her hands excitedly. "It's going to be so fun!"

"Is that the only one?" Collin asked curiously. Reaching across the table, he took the paper and scanned it. Lazarus leaned over, resting his chin on Collin's shoulder as he read.

"And combat," Collin said, pointing.

"At least we've got the afternoon slot and not the morning one," Lazarus grumbled, slumping back in his chair. "Aerelius, too."

Freya gave him a curious look. "That bothers you?"

"No, no, Aer is like a brother to me," Lazarus replied. "His syco-phants, on the other hand..."

"Reprehensible," Lea told her.

"Shameless and opportunistic," Collin added.

Freya wrinkled her nose at that. "How unfortunate for them."

Collin handed Freya her schedule back. "You've also got Literature with me and Civics with Lazarus."

"And Toxins with me," Lea told her. "So you won't be on your own for any classes."

"That's good, I suppose," Freya murmured, looking over her course list again. Having always had an interest in toxicology, Toxins was the course she was most eager for, followed by Combat. The others, while she knew were necessary for her lot in life, did little to hold her interest.

"Do any of you know who our professors are?" she asked, picking up a piece of crusty bread and dipping it into her tomato bisque. "The commander didn't give me a great deal of information before he left."

"We met a few." Lea chewed on a carrot stick contemplatively. "Oh! Our Toxins professor, Doctor Florian, is a former assassin." She grinned at Freya's look of surprise. "He's served the Harridan line for nearly seven centuries, although I'm not sure what he did before that because no one really knows how old he is. He retired when King Salazar took the crown."

"But," Laz held up a finger, "it's never actually been *confirmed* that was his job."

"Or that he actually retired, come to think of it," Collin added.

"Officially, he was an officer of the court," Lea added. "A judge. It's quite common knowledge that was only a cover, though."

Freya gave her a dubious look as her excitement began to fade. "How has it become common knowledge?"

"My mother is good friends with King Salazar's first cousin, once removed—"

"Twice removed," Laz corrected.

"—who is a horrendous gossip." Abandoning her carrots, Lea took a large bite of a crisp green apple. "She told my mother of Florian's profession and was overheard by a maid, and well, I'm sure you can figure it out from there." She shrugged and wiped a bit of juice from her chin with the back of her hand. "Sometimes new kings will execute the prior king's hired assassin, but Uncle Salazar considered it a 'waste of a good mind' to have him killed. So when Florian voluntarily retired—I think he said the work had become 'boring'—Uncle Sal decided to put his expertise to use here."

Freya laughed. "I think I like King Salazar even more now."

"I'm certain he'll be *so* pleased to hear that," a reedy female voice said from behind her.

Freya's hand froze, her spoon poised halfway to her mouth. Glancing at the others, who were harboring varying degrees of annoyance, Freya set her spoon down and turned in her seat, then looked into the green eyes of the blonde female she'd seen at Prince Aerelius' side the night before.

Freya flicked a cursory glance up and down the girl's body. She was tall and thin, with just enough curve to avoid being considered lanky. She had a pretty face—high cheekbones, long, straight nose, and bow-shaped lips—and her wavy hair was long and honey-colored, streaked with shades of light brown here and there. Green eyes, vivid and sharp, glared down at Freya.

With a sigh, Freya lifted a brow in question. "And you are...?"

The girl's mouth dropped open in offense and the two females who stood beside her tittered in amusement.

"*I*," the girl began, "am Lady Myria Bryton of Saith, daughter of Governor Emric Bryton."

Freya leaned over and picked up a piece of bread, then winked at Lea, who appeared on the verge of laughter. She looked back at Myria, holding her stare in mock confusion for a few more seconds as she broke off a small piece of her roll and put it in her mouth. "I apologize for my ignorance, Lady, but for some reason I thought the governor had a son." She swallowed her bite of bread and smiled apologetically. "I can't say I've ever heard of you."

"As a recipient of the crown's charity, it's not surprising you've been raised outside the social loop," Myria said airily, brushing her hair from her shoulder. "It will mean something soon enough." She eyed Freya scornfully. "I saw the way you looked at the prince last night. Would you like a bit of friendly advice?"

"No, but thank you." Freya smiled.

One of the girls behind her—a brunette who might have been pretty if not for her sour expression—gave Freya a wide-eyed look of disdain.

"Well, take it as a gift, then," Myria snapped. "Whatever dreams you have in that tiny head of yours—you might as well give up on them now."

Freya eyed Myria curiously, then leaned toward her and sniffed. Angling her head to the side and biting back her glee at the girl's horrified expression, she narrowed her eyes. "Your shifted form is a cat, correct?"

Myria smirked. "It is. And based on the stench coming from you, I'd guess you're some type of bird." Leaning down so her face was inches from Freya's, she bared her teeth. "Do you know what big cats do to little birds?"

"I believe they eat them raw, although considering your ability to use cookware, I can't imagine why you would. All those feathers..." Freya shuddered.

Lazarus let out a loud snort.

"Oh, move along, Myria," Lea finally said through peals of laughter, waving her hand dismissively. "Go spew your venom elsewhere."

Myria's cheeks flamed as she ignored Lea and gripped Freya's chin. "I hope you realize what you've gotten into," she sneered. "I am not the kind of person you want to cross."

One corner of Freya's mouth curved up in a mocking smile. Letting her fingernails shift into talons, she wrapped her hand around Myria's wrist and squeezed, digging the sharpened points into the girl's skin and eliciting a sharp yelp of pain. "Keep. Your claws. To yourself." She released the girl's hand and shoved her back a step, sending her stumbling into her friends. One cared enough to grab Myria's arm to steady her, but the brunette leapt out of the way to avoid the blood that dripped from Myria's wrist.

Lips trembling and eyes wide with shock, Myria stared down at her hand, hissing at the thin streaks of blood that now coated it. Tear-filled eyes met Freya's, her voice quavering as she spoke.

"You are *finished* here." Then, cradling her scratched hand, she turned and sped from the hall.

Freya watched as Myria left, her two followers on her heels, one casting furtive glances over her shoulder as though fearful Freya might follow them.

Shaking her head, Freya turned back to her food.

"How long will that take to heal?" Collin asked, tilting his head in the direction Myria had just run.

Freya shrugged and picked up her fork and speared a piece of ham that dripped with some type of honeyed glaze. "My talons are only venomous if I want them to be, so she'll be fine in a few minutes." Closing her eyes, she savored the ham's sugary taste, Myria's threats instantly forgotten. "This is divine."

"There *have* been rumors that Cook was sent directly from the heavens," Lea said.

Freya frowned across the table when she saw Collin staring at her appraisingly. Lazarus seemed to notice at the same time, because he smacked Collin's chest lightly with the back of his hand.

"Stop, Collin," he admonished.

Freya gave Collin a curious look.

"Collin's goal is to become a scientist," Lea explained, rolling her eyes. "He's got a particular interest in venoms, so try not to be offended when he asks for a bit of yours. He's not intentionally trying to scare you off." She shot him a pointed look and tossed a raspberry in his direction.

Deflecting the projectile, Collin smiled sheepishly. "Not to worry, Freya. I'll wait until we get to know each other a bit better first."

"If you play your cards right, I might give you an entire feather," Freya teased, then laughed at his shocked expression.

"Now you've done it," Laz muttered.

Collin gave him a warning look. "It would do you a fair bit of good to take a deeper interest in your studies, too, you know."

"What do you plan on pursuing?" Freya asked Lazarus, taking another bite of ham.

He shrugged uncomfortably. "I haven't quite decided yet. Science is Collin's forte. I tend to lean more toward liberal arts."

"My cousin is a bit of a history buff," Lea explained.

"He's quite into politics, as well," Collin added, stretching his arm across the back of Laz's chair and smiling softly. He nodded toward Lea. "We've been trying to talk him into pursuing a career in that arena."

"And I've told *them* I don't have the stomach for scheming and betrayals, which is all politics is," Laz told Freya.

She nodded. "I couldn't agree more."

He elbowed Collin in the side. "See? I'm not crazy."

"I never said—" Collin rolled his eyes. "I merely suggested you put your skills to use in a more public forum than working with historical artifacts, that's all."

"Both are important to the furthering of our society," Lea interjected, pointing her fork at Collin. "Both are necessary to preserve the things we accomplish, so let's leave him be."

Freya sent Lazarus a sympathetic smile. "Try not to worry. The entire point of the first year is to find a concentration. You may find an interest in something entirely unexpected."

Laz's shoulders seemed to relax a bit at her words. "Thank you, Freya."

"What about you?" Freya asked Lea.

She shrugged. "Teaching, maybe. It's always been an interest of mine."

Freya grinned. "I could see that. You have that no-nonsense way about you that good teachers need."

"Do you have a concentration you'd like to focus on while you're here?" Collin asked.

Freya huffed out a sigh. "Politics, civics." She gave him a wry smile. "It's the family business, after all."

He laughed. "I certainly understand that."

Lea gave her a small smile. "It's not the worst thing in the world, you know, having to stay at court. The royal family is quite lovely."

"Oh, I know. Ordona... she loved to dote on me when I would stay here during the holidays," Freya said, "and Aer and I always got along very well, although I'm sure he's changed just as much as I have. I know nothing of the other court members, though, so I'll have to trust you three to fill me in."

"Don't worry," Laz said, tossing a bit of bread into his mouth. "Barely half are like our dear Myria over there."

Lea groaned and Freya dropped her head to her hands.

———————

7

The rest of the day was spent at the stores in Iladel acquiring texts and other supplies they would need for the first term, along with enough capital-appropriate clothes to last Freya for a year. They returned to campus later than planned. Lazarus and Collin had managed to secret away a good deal of food from the kitchen while the staff were occupied, resulting in a quick dinner by the lake. By the time darkness fell over the campus, Freya was more than ready to get a solid night of sleep before starting her courses.

When she rose at dawn for the second day in a row, she contemplated taking a walk to the lake but decided to let Collin and Lazarus have a bit of time to themselves before the day began. Instead, she opted for strolling the grounds, getting a better feel for her new home on her own before the rest of the residents woke for the day.

She dressed in a pair of slim-fitting gray pants and a sleeveless red blouse made of soft muslin trimmed in bits of silver. Topping her outfit with a leather jacket to combat the early-morning chill, she tugged on a pair of black leather boots that laced to her knees and made her way quietly from her dorm.

As she wandered the stone paths that criss-crossed the grounds and wound around the many buildings on campus, she found herself comparing her newer, quieter surroundings to her home in Watoria. Though small compared to Iladel, her home city was bustling, filled with the sounds of its citizens, the rattling wheels of carriages on the busy streets, and the sounds and smells of commerce. Woodsmoke from smiths and carpentry stalls and the perfumes and incense of the market district always filled the air, giving Watoria a smell that Freya thought of as distinctly *home*. While many of those things could be found in the busiest sections of Iladel, here on the outer edge of the city, the only sounds were buzzing insects, the whispered chatter of wood sprites, the quiet flap of pixie wings, and the twitter of birds. The forest surrounding campus seemed alive, breathing in the mountain air and exhaling the sweet scent of foliage, flowers, and the earthy scent of loam. It enveloped her in a way the air in Watoria hadn't, and as she walked, she struggled to decide whether that was a good thing or not.

That was until she saw the cinnabar-streaked hair and broad-shouldered form of Commander Balthana at the end of the path, waiting on the steps of the academy's administration building. As she approached, he gave her a nod in greeting.

"Settling in well enough?" he asked.

"Well enough," she replied. "Lea and the others seem nice. Is something wrong?"

"Aside from you assaulting a lady of Saith?" He shook his head. "Lady Bryton was quite upset yesterday, or so I've heard. As her father will be, when word gets back."

"You're here to scold me?" Freya held out her hands, palms up. "Go on, then, get the rod. But for the record, she deserved it."

Balthana stared down at her, stone-faced for several seconds, then shook his head. "Be that as it may, you've got a legacy and a future to uphold. You'd do well to remember that."

Before she could respond, he pulled a folded piece of parchment from the inside pocket of his uniform jacket and handed it to her. "As promised, your social schedule for the upcoming months, directly from the queen. If you've got any questions, Lea should be able to help."

Taking the paper, she unfolded it and scanned the list.

"Do each of these require special attire?" she asked, glancing up at him, tamping down the slight flare of panic that flickered in her chest. It had been ages since she'd had to dress for court functions, especially any so fancy as a ball. The last had been the Summer Solstice celebration her final summer in Iladel, but as that had been in the dead of summer, heavy ballgowns weren't required.

"It's uncommon to be seen at court functions in the same costume twice, so, yes, I would recommend purchasing something different for each." He nodded toward the schedule. "A few have a recommended color palette that will complement the theme of the night."

With a sigh, Freya looked back down at the list. The annual Commencement Ball for Aldridge in two weeks had a warm color scheme; purples, reds, and oranges that represented the sunsets that Saith, the king's ancestral homeland, were famed for. The queen's Nameday celebration seemed based on her native home in the southern realm of Edhil, with a theme of diamonds and sapphires—the two main jewel exports of the southernmost court. Scanning the rest of the list, she saw the other events—several dinners and a few formal gatherings—had similar specific themes guests were expected to adhere to.

Freya let her arms fall to her sides as she met the commander's eyes. He looked amused, which to Freya's recollection was never a good thing.

"Alright. Lea and I have already planned a trip into the city." Folding the parchment in half, she pointed it at him. "I'll warn you now, though... I will *not* hold back once I'm let loose in Iladel's boutiques. If the theme of the night is gemstones, expect my gown and hair to be dripping with them."

"Noted." At the sound of a door opening behind them, the commander flicked a glance over her shoulder. "Speak with Lea," he said. "Go shopping. Enjoy yourself. And try not to injure any more of your classmates, please."

She flashed him a grin and slid her schedule into her back pocket. "You've got nothing to worry about, Commander."

Lea insisted on arriving to their first class, Toxins, ten minutes early to ensure they were able to get good seats. Upon arrival, though, it became clear that their definitions of same varied a bit.

"We need to sit up front," Lea hissed from where she and Freya stood just inside the classroom door. "This way the professor will notice us, and we'll be far less likely to get distracted."

"No, seats toward the back are best," Freya replied, shaking her head and gesturing toward the center rows of the room's stadium-style seating. "You can hear better and keep an eye on the other students."

"You mean get distracted by the other students!"

Freya lifted her brows. "I won't get distracted."

"Well, I will!" Lea exclaimed. "And I'd bet ten sils you will, too."

Freya smirked and held out her hand. "I'll take that bet."

Scowling, Lea shook her hand determinedly. "Deal."

Biting her cheeks to hold in her laughter, Freya led the way toward the fifth row, three from the back.

Once they were seated, desks folded down over their laps, Lea smiled and looked around. Then slowly, the smile slipped from her face and her eyes narrowed.

"Well played, my lady," she grumbled.

Freya grinned. "I almost feel bad for tricking you."

Lea eyed her dubiously. "Almost?"

Freya pursed her lips in consideration, holding the girl's stare. "Alright. I'll bet you another ten sils that you'll end up preferring these seats to those down below before the end of the day."

"Deal."

Both turned to face the front, then Lea let out a muttered curse when she saw Myria, who'd just taken a seat in the center of the first row. "You knew she was there, didn't you?"

Freya shrugged innocently. "Perhaps it's just dumb luck?"

"Dumb luck," Lea scoffed. "Under any other circumstances, I'd be impressed with your conniving tricks."

Freya flashed her a smile, then looked around the room, curious to see what the workspace of someone with Florian's reputation held. There was a long table at the front, undoubtedly used for experiments, that the eight rows of seats were centered around. Shelves lined the walls, all full of books and vials, powders, glass containers, and an uncomfortable number of wet specimens. At a quick glance, Freya counted at least fifty creatures floating in clear liquid, their eyes cloudy with death. Shadowboxes with various instruments and others with small skeletons hung on the walls beside framed anatomical sketches.

"What are they doing?" Lea asked, frowning toward where a number of students—roughly half of the class—were congregating around the large table at the front of the room.

"I'm not sure," Freya murmured, watching as a few students walked away from the table holding small bowls and took their seats. "It looks like there is a... is that a spread of food?" She narrowed her eyes. "Should we—"

"No," Lea replied, putting a hand on Freya's arm. "Stay here."

"Why?"

"Professors... they do things *differently* here, at least that's what I've heard. We should wait."

Just then, Doctor Florian, a wiry, dark-skinned male with a shock of white hair and a long, thin nose stepped into the room. He wore sleek black pants and a forest green shirt woven through with glittering onyx beads and gold thread, the richness of which assured Freya that, despite his current position as a professor, Florian had maintained his wealthy status after leaving his royal post. As she took in his face a bit more closely, she saw lines of age creasing the skin around his eyes and jaw. Linds, both shifter and magic-wielder, could and did live for thousands of years, reaching adulthood around the age of twenty before the aging process slowed to a glacial pace. The signs of age Florian showed... Freya let out a quiet breath. He could easily be one thousand years old.

The room went silent as he walked swiftly toward the wide table that currently held the food, his sharp-toed black shoes clicking loudly against the wood floor. Pausing, he looked at the fruits and cheeses that had been left on the table, smiling softly at the absence of nearly half the original volume.

"Ah, I see many of you have partaken in my generosity," he said, turning his smile on the class. His voice was smooth and carried a tone that demanded attention in an unnerving way. "I always find a full belly helps students concentrate better, absorb more information than they would have otherwise." His eyes, flat and black, traveled over the rows of desks, seeming to touch on each student in turn. Freya didn't miss the slight lift in his brow when his gaze landed on her before skipping to Lea.

With a clap of his hands, the food disappeared. "Well, then, let's get started." He pointed a long finger toward a small male in the second row, then clasped his hands behind his back. "What would you say one of the most important lessons you could take from this class might be?"

Paling under Florian's gaze, the male shrank into his seat a bit. "I —I suppose one lesson might be how to discern between one toxin and another?"

Florian nodded and began to pace slowly. "Yes, of course. Another?"

The brown-haired girl Freya had seen with Myria at lunch the day before raised her hand. "The effects of toxins and their antidotes?"

"Very good, Lady Leston. Lady Calliwell, another?"

Lea narrowed her eyes, then tilted her head and smiled. "How to determine whether your food has been poisoned?"

"Certainly." Pausing, he studied the class once again before speaking before his sharp eyes landed on Myria. "Tell me, what is the side effect of consuming pure lindberry root?"

Myria sat up a bit straighter in her seat. "Severe stomach pain in mild cases, death in the most severe."

"Dependent on... what, Lord Raster?" Florian shifted his gaze to a pale-skinned male with bark-brown hair three seats down.

"The severity depends on the amount ingested and the method of delivery," Raster replied immediately.

Freya rested her elbow on her desk, covering her mouth with her hand to conceal her horrified amusement as realization sunk in. "Brilliant," she murmured.

Lea murmured a hum of agreement.

Florian shifted his gaze to Freya, and something in the way her looked at her had her hand standing on end. "Ah. What would be the most efficient method of delivery for lindberry root?"

Freya did her best to ignore the muffled snicker that slipped through Lea's lips.

"The most efficient way of delivering lindberry root poison is through sweet food." She bit her lip, then continued. "It's got a high concentration of natural sugar, so fruits that are also high in sugar generally work best to conceal the taste."

The corner of his mouth quirked up, then his eyes slid to Lea. "Lady Calliwell, what types of fruit would you say are the sweetest?"

Tears of laughter had formed in Lea's eyes. Taking a deep breath, she cleared her throat. "Well, Professor, I would say lindberries, themselves, can easily conceal the flavor of their root extract." Her lips twitched. "Jewel fruit—red, not green—would also be a good choice."

Freya's teeth clamped down on the inside of her cheek as Myria's hand froze over the bowl of fruit she'd been about to start eating.

An easy smile spread across Florian's pale face. "Correct. Grapes, sun fruit, and summer apples are also good choices."

Awareness fell across the room as the students who'd all been devouring those four things set their snacks down. Silence hung as Florian stared at each student in turn, his quiet demeanor slipping into something more sinister.

"There's one lesson I'm surprised none of you have mentioned. Would anyone care to take a guess as to what it might be?"

Freya slowly raised her hand. He gave her a slight nod.

"Take care in consuming anything of unknown origins?"

"Precisely." Florian grinned, wide and wicked, at the male in the front row who'd been the first to answer one of his questions suddenly began to wretch. "If you don't know where a spread of food came from—" he raised his voice as three other students began to heave and a fourth vomited on the floor "— then it's best you don't consume it." Mock sympathy filled his features as Myria's friend clutched her stomach and began to sob in pain. "Now... who would like to inform our victims of the antidote?"

Raster raised his hand, staring wide-eyed down at his writhing classmates. "Time."

Florian nodded sagely. "Time. Those of you who consumed fruit will spend the remainder of the day in the infirmary. Any work you miss in other courses will be your responsibility to make up. That goes for this course, as well." He snapped his fingers and the poisoned students disappeared. "The rest of you, open your books."

8

The rest of their first Toxins session was relatively tame compared to those first few minutes. The bulk of the remaining two hours consisted of a review of basic poison-handling skills, along with a less-than-subtle threat from Florian that today's experiment wouldn't be the last of its kind. While most students seemed terrified to speak up, a small handful were clearly eager to dive in, despite the fact that their professor seemed more than inclined to poison anyone who answered incorrectly. Not wanting to fall victim to her mercurial professor next, Freya made sure to keep Toxins at the top of her list of class priorities.

After sitting through a Civics course with Lazarus that promised to be mildly interesting, he and Freya made their way to the dining hall for lunch with Lea and Collin. The hall buzzed a bit louder than the previous two days as students congregated, excited to share bits of their first day with one another. There was a more hurried feel as they squeezed their conversations and lunches in during the limited time between morning and afternoon courses.

Once they'd eaten their fill, the four returned to their rooms to change into proper sparring clothes for Combat, which would encompass the entire afternoon.

Freya smiled as she slid into her soft leather pants and a fitted white shirt, happy to have them on once again. As she stepped into her dirty, scuffed boots and began to lace them up, she couldn't help but wrinkle her nose. A new pair would definitely be in order when she and Lea made their next trip to Iladel.

"I adore your pants, Freya," Lea commented as she dressed. "Are they custom made?"

"They are," Freya replied, brushing a hand along the soft, spelled material that covered her thighs. "The leatherworkers in Allanor are incredibly skilled." The spellwork that strengthened the material was one of Freya's more closely-guarded secrets when it came to her protective attire. The protections she'd woven in had saved her skin from being sliced and burned on more than one occasion.

Inadvertently, she glanced at Lea's thick, black pants and gray muslin shirt. A pair of flexible leather slippers, seemingly never worn, sat on the floor beside her bed. Lea followed her gaze and flushed.

"I told my mother I needed proper boots for this, but she insisted on flexibility, as though I'm going to be dancing or some nonsense." Dropping onto the edge of the bed in frustration, she tugged on the shoes. "I know I'm just asking to get my toes broken in these."

"Could you heal yourself if you did?" Freya asked.

Lea shook her head reluctantly. "My magic is purely elemental, so at best I'd be able to treat the pain with some earth magic, but I wouldn't be able to heal it."

"Well, not to worry." Freya flashed her a smile, then leaned into her wardrobe and pulled out a pair of black boots that laced up the calf. "You look to be about my size," she said, tossing the boots toward Lea. "The toe is reinforced with Caelorian steel, so take care if you start throwing kicks about. I'll be needing a new pair, myself, so we should take a trip to the leatherworker on our shopping trip."

Lea toed off the slippers, then took the boots with a relieved sigh and pulled them on. Once they were laced up, she wiggled her toes and smiled. "I expected them to be heavier, but they fit like a second skin. Thank you, Freya. The bulk of my physical training was with instructors who were too afraid to hurt me, so those silly things were more than adequate," she said as she kicked her discarded pair toward her armoire. "I appreciate the help."

"Of course." Freya bit her bottom lip. "And I suppose we should decide when we're going shopping."

Lea squealed, then clapped her hands in excitement. "Ooo yes!" She beamed and bounced on her toes. "We've got *so* many events in the coming months. Oh, this is going to be so exciting!"

Freya laughed. "I didn't expect quite so much enthusiasm, but I suppose it's appreciated."

"Oh, shush!" Lea huffed, exasperated. "I see right through your ruse, Freya. You're no stranger to formalwear, and I would even go so far as to say you enjoy putting on some finery now and then."

Freya sneered, but chose not to confirm Lea's very true assessment. Iladel was home to some of the five realms' finest wares, from gemstones and silks to culinary delicacies. Only a fool wouldn't be eager to explore and sample them all, especially when, according to the commander, her expenses were covered.

If there was one thing Freya wasn't, it was a fool.

"Friday, then?" Freya asked.

Lea nodded as she twisted her curly hair back into a tight plait. "Yes, that should give us enough time to go over what we'll need."

"So, will the boys be attending the same events?" Freya asked as they made their way outside and toward the training yard.

"Of course!" Lea said, laughing. "Lazarus is part of the royal family, just like me, and he and Collin are hardly ever separated. Besides," she added, "it's only fair they be forced to submit to the court's whims now and then."

Freya laughed. "They've been together a while?"

Lea rolled her eyes. "They met when they were children, back when their families would summer in Edhil. If you ask Laz, he'd say he laid claim when they were twelve. If you speak to his more sensible other half, you'd know they started seeing each other when they were sixteen."

"Laz does seem to be the dreamer of the two, doesn't he?"

Lea snorted. "At times, although he's much smarter than he lets on."

The yard was more crowded than Freya expected when they arrived, and as they got closer, she saw the cause. Two of the prince's black-uniformed guards stood sentry along the outer walls, blocking the entrance as a gaggle of females hovered nearby.

"Ugh, lovely," Lea groaned. "I do hope this passes soon. Although, considering my cousin's tendency to attract attention..."

"We'll be subject to an audience every day?" Freya finished, eyeing the crowd with annoyance.

Lea halted in her tracks, touching a hand to Freya's arm to stop her. "Freya, while I adore you and am quite certain we're going to be great friends, I have to ask that you consider carefully how you handle my cousin when you're instructed to spar with him."

"When? Not 'if'?" Freya asked, casting a wary look toward the yard.

"We'll all be required to spar with each other, and, knowing him, he'll request to spar with you immediately. He's just that cocksure, as I'm sure you recall, and he'll want to feel you out a bit, see how you've changed over the last few years." Lea sighed and put her hands on her hips. "And while I would kindly request that you spare *me* from your years of experience and expertise, I would also advise you against embarrassing Aerelius in front of the entire school."

"Tell me what kind of warlock he is and I'll gladly promise not to sully his reputation," Freya said, sending Lea a sly look. One of her biggest annoyances since she'd last seen the prince was that her father wouldn't tell her what powers the prince possessed. As hybrid of a shifter and a witch, Freya's power had emerged when she was a small child. Linds who were pure warlocks, like Aerelius, didn't reach their emergence until around the age of fourteen. As magic could fall into any of the five categories—earth, air, fire, water, and spirit—it was anyone's guess what he could do. All Freya knew was that Aerelius' had manifested not long after her last visit, and, as a royal, it would be stronger than that of the commoners she'd faced in Watoria. If she knew her old friend, he'd been honing his magic ever since.

"I can't tell you that, although you'll find out soon enough. Everyone will."

"Can't or won't?"

"*Both.* I can't because I promised my aunt and uncle I'd let Aer show his power on his own terms, and I *won't* because he's my cousin and, despite his narcissistic tendencies, I love him and will honor that promise."

Narrowing her eyes, Freya looked over the small crowd that had gathered outside. Smiling at Lea, she nodded. "Alright, Lea. I'll be sure not to embarrass his highness in front of the entire school."

Lea eyed Freya suspiciously. "Why do I feel as though you're pulling another one over on me?"

Freya gave her a shocked look. "You know, Lady Calliwell, if we're to be friends, you should really try to sort out your trust issues." Patting her friend on the shoulder, she started walking toward the entrance, slipping her course schedule from her pocket. When they reached the line of guards, she held it up.

"I'm scheduled to be here," she told the one before her, a tall, ruddy male with a stony expression. "I'd like to pass, please."

Recognizing them both, the guard nodded gruffly and motioned for them to enter.

Once through, Freya took a long look around the yard, taking in the space and those who occupied it. The main feature was a wide, round sparring ring encircled by a wooden rail. There was an area at the far end with targets set for knife throwing and heavily-padded wooden practice mannequins. A door just beyond led to what Freya guessed was the archery field.

Freya let out a quiet groan as she looked around, taking in the faces of her classmates—roughly twenty, if her estimate was accurate, including a handful of onlookers that had come in before the guards and prince had arrived—and finally, the commander, who stood speaking to one of his officers and Prince Aerelius near the knife-throwing targets. Averting her eyes before any of them saw her, she pointed toward a low bench against the wall on the other side of the dirt yard.

"Laz and Collin are over there," she told Lea. Without waiting for a response, she made her way over toward where Lazarus and Collin had begun their warmup stretches, ignoring the slight pang of nerves that struck. She had the utmost confidence in her skills, but it had been quite some time since she'd had to demonstrate her abilities to others.

"This won't be so bad," Lea commented as she dropped down on the bench beside where her cousin stood. "Aer's guards seem to be doing a fine job keeping the vultures out."

"A few made their way in," Laz muttered, bending at the waist to stretch his back. "A handful of Myria's followers managed to sneak in before Balthana ordered the guards to block the entrance. I spoke with Aer and he doesn't seem terribly thrilled about it."

"Oh, I'm sure he isn't," Lea murmured. "The girl is vile. Although I don't know what he expected when he decided to enroll."

"Is he our trainer?" Freya asked, turning her attention toward the officer standing beside Balthana. He was tall, square-jawed and bronze-complected, with pitch-colored hair. His build was broad for a Lind, but even standing still he carried an edge of grace.

Lazarus nodded. "Officer Zane Ristheld. He worked under your father for quite some time in Allanor and retired from field work several years ago."

Freya eyed the male in consideration. "Is he good?"

"Quite," Collin replied. "If not a bit intimidating to some. He's vicious in his shifted form."

Freya gave a quick sniff, drawing in his scent as best she could from her distance. "Hawk?"

Lea nodded. "He's all predator."

As if on cue, Zane clapped the commander on the shoulder and stepped away to address the students.

"Eyes on me, all of you!" he hollered. The tenor of his voice seemed to match his harsh, imposing appearance, instantly demanding the full attention of those around him.

As Freya's classmates faced forward, she made sure to fall into line toward the back where she could observe those around her a bit better. The commander didn't miss her placement, though, and sent her a pointed look when he saw her.

Ignoring his stare, she focused her attention on her instructor.

"For those of you who've not met me, I am Officer Zane Ristheld," he began once the din had settled. "You may address me as Officer Ristheld. For your first term at Aldridge, we'll be covering the basics of combat. I am aware that some of you have come to me with a good deal of training under your belt, while others have not, so today, I will be assessing each of you and will sort you all into groupings based on skill level. Today you'll be sparring with one another in basic physical combat—no weapons other than those you were blessed with at birth. If you're a shifter, that means you can fight in your shifted form. If you're a magic-wielder, feel free to throw some spells about."

Freya stilled and looked around the yard, watching as her fellow classmates did the same. Flaring her nostrils, she inhaled the scents of those around her. In addition to Ristheld's avian scent, she caught whiffs of feline, vulpine, and canine, along with a few magic-wielders —one witch and two warlocks, if she wasn't mistaken—and something else she couldn't quite place. It was a softer, more appealing magic, carrying the light scent of something sweet.

Someone was cloaking and doing a damn good job of it.

She smiled to herself, already accepting the unspoken challenge. That unknown... if she wanted to cement her place here, that would be her opportunity.

Ristheld began dividing them up into pairs, and she heaved a sigh when he directed her toward the end of the ring to spar with the pretty blonde Lady of Saith.

Freya returned Myria's cocksure look with an appraising glance. She'd scented feline on Myria the day before, and as a highborn lady, she was likely one of the more ferocious cats—a lioness, most likely.

"Is this the part when you ask if we can start over?" Myria asked, putting her hands on her hips as Freya approached. "Begin with a clean slate?"

Freya snorted. "If I thought it worth asking? Perhaps. I'm certain that would be out of the question, though, and I'd think far less of you if you allowed it." She glanced around the yard, taking in the space now that the other students were taking their places. It was large, enough that the ten pairs of students who were getting ready to square off had easily twenty- feet on either side to fight. Looking back at Myria, Freya wondered if that would be enough.

"So, little birdie," Myria said, her tone smug. "Should I fear for my life, or will you promise not to peck my eyes out?"

Freya cracked her neck and shook out her arms. "I suppose we'll find out."

Myria huffed and shook her head, then dropped into a fighting stance.

"Begin!"

Faster than Freya expected, Myria spun, then kicked out, her booted foot stopped by Freya's hands just as it would've connected with her ribs. Freya shoved hard, swiftly flipping Myria to the ground. Myria leapt to her feet, a low growl emanating from her throat. The two squared off once again, reassessing one another now that a mild indicator of skill had been given.

"Halt!"

She and Myria, along with the rest of the students, froze at the sound of Balthana's bellow, standing straight as he made his way across the floor. He'd been silent thus far, slowly circling the yard, watching the other students, going unnoticed despite the vibrant hair that stuck out like a beacon.

He came to a stop less than a foot away from Freya, standing so close she could smell the mix of sweat and shifter that emanated from him. Clasping his hands behind his back, he looked first at Myria before setting his steely gray gaze on Freya.

"What do you think you're doing?" he demanded.

She tilted her chin up a fraction. "Sparring. You?"

He heaved out a sigh and raised his eyes to the heavens. "Enough of this nonsense, Freya. We had an agreement. Lift the glamour and be done with it already."

Her cheeks flamed but she refused to break his gaze. "No."

Not here not here not here.

The yard was silent as death, assuring her that no one would miss this exchange.

"Now."

"No," she growled. "You're the one who sent me—"

"I *allowed* you to live in anonymity for six years."

When she didn't respond, he arched a brow. "Shall I do it for you?"

She stiffened. "You're threatening me now?"

He leveled a glare at her. "No. I'm ordering you to stop being insufferable and do as you're told."

"Ordering me?" She snorted. "I'm not one of your soldiers."

Myria sucked in a gasp and there was a flurry of hushed whispering to her right.

Balthana's lips curved up into a smile that was part cruel, part warning. It was one Freya knew all too well.

Taking a hurried step back, she held up a hand and drew her magic forward, preparing herself for defense. "Don't you—"

Freya froze just as she would've thrown her power at him, immobilized as the magic that had been concealing her appearance for nearly six years slipped away. Her brown eyes melted into a deep, steely gray, while the sharper lines of her jaw softened. The willowy frame she wore shifted slightly, revealing sleek, defined muscles, clearly visible through the leather sheathing her legs. She let out a muttered curse as magic prickled along her scalp, transforming her long auburn hair to a deep chestnut and revealing the rose-pink streaks that wound through it.

When her father gave a small wave of his hand, she let out a yelp as her wings, now dusted with the same shades of pink as her hair, burst from her back.

She glared up at him, her feet silently slipping into a defensive stance and pearlescent wisps of magic swirling around her fingers as hushed whispers tore through the yard.

"Did you see that?"

"Is that his *daughter?*"

"She's supposed to be in Iston!"

"Has she been here this whole time?"

"Do you see her *wingspan?*"

She'd hoped to remain inconspicuous for a week, continuing to ride the rumor that Byrric and Cina Balthana's daughter was well-established in Iston, living among the other Valkyrie before she lifted the glamour that he'd allowed her to wear outside the capital. Now, thanks to her insufferable father's need to let everyone know she'd returned, she'd barely made it two days.

Sneering, Freya gave her wings a heavy flap, flaring them wide in a clear challenge to the dove gray pair that were projecting from the commander's own back.

"Do you know, Commander, that you're a real pain in my ass?"

Byrric Balthana shrugged, then shifted his flat stare to Myria, who was standing gawping beside Freya. "Close your mouth, Lady Bryton, before you catch a fly."

"Y-yes, sir," Myria replied, her cocky tone long gone as her eyes darted between Byrric and Freya.

Chuckling darkly, he shook his head, then waved a hand, indicating to all the onlookers. "Everyone knows who and what you are now, Freya. Do you know what that means?" He lifted his brow in question.

"You're shit at surprises?" Freya asked sweetly. A small choking sound slipped from Myria's throat.

He pointed a finger at her in warning. "No. More. Glamours. I allowed it for long enough. Your fun is over. Are we clear?"

She ground her teeth together. "Crystal."

With a nod, Byrric moved to walk past her. As he did, he patted her on the shoulder.

"It's good to have you here, Freya."

She grunted in response. Her lip curled up in annoyance when she saw the stares that lingered in her direction as her classmates sized up a new opponent. A moment later, the commander barked an order for them to get back to work.

All but one complied immediately, and Freya could practically feel his gaze burning straight through her.

Her jaw tensed in annoyance when she looked over Myria's shoulder to where the dark-haired prince leaned against the wall, arms folded as his partner rubbed at his own wrist, wincing in pain.

When he gave her a slow smile, the warning was clear.

"So... I was thinking..." Myria eyed Freya's wings warily. "Maybe we could revisit the idea of starting over?"

Freya laughed and shook her head. "Not a chance."

9

When Ristheld called for students to switch partners a short while later, Freya was thankful that Myria had given her a solid run for her money. When she'd shifted into her sleek, rust-colored lioness form, Freya had been certain she'd be easy to take down because Myria didn't seem the type to have mastered any true defensive maneuvers. If anything, Myria had been a solid reminder not to make assumptions about one's opponent. By the time they were through, both were sweating, a bit bloody, and out of breath. Between Myria's speed as a cat and ability to alternate between full and partial shifts in mid-action, she'd given Freya one of the best workouts she'd had in months.

"Thanks," Freya told her, retrieving a skin of water that was hanging from the nearby rail. "I needed that."

Myria wiped sweat from her forehead and narrowed her eyes. "You ripped my pants and it's going to take me a full day to heal from the sand burn you gave me."

Freya sent her a dry look, then assessed the damaged material. She flicked her wrist, taking a small pleasure when Myria's face paled as Freya's magic stitched the fabric of her canvas pants back together.

"Better?"

Recovering herself, Myria took a large gulp from her own canteen, then slammed the cap back on.

"So you've got a bit of magic," she growled. "Being a half-blood still won't get you more than—" She froze and her glare slipped into a sweet smile as she looked behind Freya, where heavy footsteps were approaching.

"Aer! Here to spar with me?" Myria purred. Her smile faltered when the prince draped an arm around Freya's shoulders.

"Not today, Lady Bryton." Aerelius grinned down at Freya, who smirked up at him. "Officer Ristheld?" he called.

"Yes, Your Highness?"

A sly smiled tugged his lips. "I'd like to take on my old Valkyrie friend."

"I think that sounds like a wonderful idea," she called back. "I've been so eager to learn the prince's secrets." She gave Aerelius a sweet smile. "Hopefully he won't go too hard on me."

"Of course not, Lady Balthana," Aerelius replied with a mocking grin. "Or is it Enrieth? I can never recall which parent's surname you use."

Ristheld nodded. "I'll allow it."

Arching a brow at Myria, who'd gone from fawning to fuming, Freya gave her a questioning look. "Shouldn't you be finding a new partner, Lady Bryton?"

Myria opened and closed her mouth before looking desperately at Aerelius, who'd taken a sudden interest in his fingernails, then toward Ristheld, who was making his way toward them.

"Lady Bryton! You'll take on Lady Calliwell."

With one last stormy look in Freya's direction, Myria strode off toward where Lea was waiting, hands on her hips. When Lea met Freya's eyes, she gave her a look of warning, reminding Freya of her promise not to embarrass Aerelius in front of the entire school.

"I'm curious..."

Freya sighed when the prince spoke, then turned to face him. "Curious about what, highness?"

He tapped a finger on the ridge of her wing—a daring feat,

considering touching a Valkyrie's wing was often cause for losing a hand, not to mention extremely intimate. "Are those wings still as cumbersome now as they were when we were children?" Folding his arms, he leaned casually against the railing. "You could hardly hold them off the ground back then. Always tripping over them, dragging them on the palace floors."

"Not nearly as cumbersome as that ego of yours," she quipped.

Officer Ristheld shouted for them all to begin.

"Are we restricting usage of power?" Aerelius asked her.

Angling her head to the side, she appraised him, realizing his magic was the scent she'd been so eager to take on earlier.

"No restrictions," she said, although something in her mind screamed at her to recant. "Do your worst."

Aerelius pushed himself off the fence, then crooked his fingers, and she felt a gentle tug low in her belly in response. His eyes, a mesmerizing shade of brown, held hers, beckoning her toward him.

The edges of her vision began to darken as her eyes homed in on his, which were soft and gentle, the color of chocolate fading into a vibrant green along the outer edges. It had been nearly six years since she'd seen him last, but surely she would've noticed such a lovely color before now, right? And the hard lines of his jaw... she could almost feel his smooth, golden skin beneath her fingers, the dusting of stubble on his chin, the high cheekbones that accentuated his ethereal beauty... the memory of a kiss in the palace gardens flashed through her mind, a hand on her cheek...

Frowning, she took several slow steps toward him, then froze as unease struck. She rolled her shoulders in an attempt to shake off the odd feeling that was coursing through her, yet it persisted. She struggled to place it, but her mind felt... addled. Heat pulsed through her, causing her cheeks to burn, and there was a strange fluttering deep inside her torso.

She sniffed the air, trying to ignore the growing intensity of the feeling along her skin. Soft, like fingers dancing along her arms, her legs, down her back—

Freya let out a low growl as she was hit with the scent of a spirit-user, a warlock gifted at influencing all manner of emotions. Based on the fluttering in her stomach, the prince's gifts lie in manipulating positive emotions—things like happiness and lust.

She took a heavy step back. Somehow, he'd been masking his scent, one she would've known instantly otherwise. It nearly pained her to move away from him, as the need to touch him had become almost unbearable.

His infuriatingly handsome smile did little to diminish that need. The feeling of lust pressing in around Freya was becoming increasingly more bothersome.

The prince's eyebrows lifted slightly, beckoning once again, but he didn't make any further move toward her. "Miss me, Valkyrie?" His voice was as smooth as silk when he spoke. "You seem a bit flushed."

Yes.

Clenching her teeth, Freya shook off the thought and took a deep breath.

Two could play this game.

She deftly plucked a non-venomous feather from the lower edge of her wing, keeping her eyes locked on Aerelius, then pricked the back of her hand with the metallic tip of the shaft. The pain, the quick scent of blood, snapped her back to where she needed to be—clearheaded, ready to fight, and unwilling to fail.

Twirling the long plume between her fingers, she lowered to a crouch, her wings flaring out behind her. Then she smiled at the prince.

His eyes widened almost imperceptibly, and she realized, once again, that the yard had gone quiet.

The pheromones that Freya's blood was giving off—thanks to his magic—were incredibly potent in the air, allowing her to effectively turn his own power against him. And, based on the grumbles from the shifters around them, it was having quite an effect on the other students as well.

"What's wrong, highness?" She cocked a brow when his jaw clenched. Even a warlock wasn't immune to a scent that strong.

"Haven't you fought someone who knows how your kind works before?"

"You've grown cunning," he commented, giving her a lopsided grin. "A wonderful quality for a —"

Freya launched herself forward, grabbing him by the arm and spinning him around in one quick motion. Before he had the chance to struggle, she yanked him back against her chest and pressed the tip of the feather to his throat.

She put her lips to his ear, then grinned when she saw Lea's exasperated glare. "Now that we've established I can handle your magic, care to take me on in a real fight?"

He chuckled. "I was *so* hoping you'd ask."

With a growl, he latched onto one of her wings and flipped her onto her back, slamming her to the ground and pinning her torso between his muscular thighs. One hand held a wing down; the other pinned both of her wrists to her chest. His power washed over her in waves, causing her to squeeze the still-healing wound on her hand to keep her centered.

Someone—Myria, Freya realized with annoyance—let out a whooping cackle, and a few other snickers rose around her.

Steeling herself, she let her magic surge forward, forming a protective barrier against his, then she pretended to falter as he hit her with another dose of his power. Dragging her lower lip through her teeth, she arched her back as though struggling through the lust he was forcing on her. Which, if she was being honest, was a bit hard, even with her magic shielding her. He was far more powerful than the spirit users she'd faced in the past.

He nearly faltered as she pressed against him, but set his jaw and tightened his grip on her wrists. "What were you saying about—"

Before he could finish, Freya snapped her wings upward, using all her strength to hit him square on the chin with the hard ridge of one and taking him off balance when he lost his grip on the other. She threw her fists up, cracking them against his jaw and shattering his hold on her. Grabbing his shoulder, she gave her wings another heavy flap and flipped him over, reversing their positions. Using her thighs and just a touch of magic to pin his arms to his sides, she touched the tip of her feather to his cheek, dragging it lightly across the smooth skin until it was pressed to the underside of his chin. His entire body stilled as annoyance flashed through his eyes.

"I was *saying* that you seem to rely too much on your power and not enough on your strength." She wrapped her magic gently around his throat and pressed lightly, relishing the wide-eyed unease that had replaced the smug attitude of moments before. "Have you forgotten I have six limbs and a boatload of magic to contend with?"

A slow smile curved his lips, but before she could react, a fresh wave of heat shot through her, nearly obliterating the shell of magic she'd put up around herself. She was slammed with the sensation of hands gliding across her body, teeth running along her neck, fingers sliding—

Freya pressed her magic harder against his throat. "Nice. Try." With a huff, she pushed herself off him and stood, then cracked her neck to try to get rid of the residual lusty feelings he'd planted in her mind.

Aerelius stood and dusted off his pants, then gave her a crooked smile. "You could have at least helped me up, my lady."

"So you could pull me back to the dirt again?" she scoffed. "I wouldn't have fallen for that trick when we were children, and I'm certainly not going to now."

Shooting a glare at her father who was watching their exchange in amusement, she strode past the prince and hopped up onto the wood rail that surrounded the training floor, studiously ignoring the stares of the students who were slowly returning to their sparring.

Aerelius walked toward her, stopping a few inches from where she sat. Plucking the canteen from the post she'd hung it from, he handed it to her, then leaned down and put his lips to her ear. "That was a good fight, Valkyrie. We'll have to do it again sometime."

Unable to suppress her grin, she pressed a hand to his chest and gently shoved him back. "Anytime, highness. Just be forewarned, I won't go so easy on you next time."

He tapped her nose and gave her a sly grin. "I'd expect nothing less."

She frowned curiously. "How did you mask your scent, anyway?"

His lips tilted up. "My mother taught me. I'm sure you've done it a time or two."

She took a swallow of water and handed him the canteen. "Yes, but I'm a full half-blood. Your power is too... specific for something like that."

With a shrug, he drank, then twisted the cap back in place and gave it back to her. "My power lets me fog minds. Masking my own scent to allow for the element of surprise is a facet of that."

"Switch out!" Officer Ristheld called.

With a huff, she shook her head and grinned. "I'll get you back for this, Aerelius Harridan, mark my words."

"I look forward to it," he said, before turning to walk toward Lazarus, who stood on the other side of the floor.

And despite her annoyance, she couldn't help but smile a little at the retreating back of her old friend.

Her smile broadened when she saw Collin approach, his red hair slicked back with sweat and his cheeks pink from exertion.

"You look like you need to work off some steam," he commented.

Freya snorted. "You can say that again."

He grinned when he looked over at where Aerelius and Laz were squaring off. "Laz and I had Aerlius use his power on us once, just to see what it felt like. I've always heard you don't know what spirit users feels like until it's too late, and I wanted to know what to expect." He leaned against the fence beside her and folded his arms. "So, I understand. You feel... twitchy, right?"

"That would be one word for it," she muttered. *Deprived* might be another.

"You need to burn it off, then," he told her. Holding out a hand, he tugged her down from the fence, blue eyes twinkling. "And considering your father just revealed you to everyone without your permission, I'll even let you get a few good hits in."

"Let me?" Annoyance with the prince suddenly gone, Freya

narrowed her eyes at Collin. "I just beat Myria and the prince fairly well." She put her hands on her hips and tilted her chin up a fraction. "Why are you so confident?"

"Despite her demeanor, Myria doesn't know how to fight dirty, and Aer relies far too much on his ability to emotionally manipulate his opponent." He flashed his teeth in a smile that was both amused and wicked; surprising, considering his relatively subdued nature. "I can't do the latter, but I'm quite skilled at the former."

"So says you," she countered. "But I'd like to see what you've got." Stepping back, she flared out her wings and lowered into a crouch.

Collin laughed. "Well, then, come on, my lady. Let's see if you can get the drop on me."

fter handing a thorough beating to Collin fueled largely by her annoyance with the prince, Freya sparred with a handful of other students before her first Combat class at Aldridge finished. By the time Ristheld dismissed them, she felt as though she'd gotten a good feel for the skills and weaknesses of her fellow classmates. Of the ten she faced off with, seven—including Collin, Myria, and Aerelius— all seemed to have fairly honed physical combat skills, telling her she'd likely end up grouped with them once Ristheld split them up. She was all but certain the other three had let her win.

Once they were released from the yard, Freya didn't hesitate in taking to the sky and flying off. She didn't care who saw or what their reactions might be; she just wanted to be alone, away from her friends and, even more so, her father.

As she glided high over campus, taking in the breathtaking landscape that surrounded it, she questioned whether her annoyance with him was truly justified. When King Salazar, a longtime friend of Byrric's, requested he retire from the Allanorian Army eighteen years ago to take on the task of commanding Lindoroth's Royal Army, he'd leapt at the opportunity, citing the social and financial benefits for his family as his reasoning. Cina had always supported him, despite Freya's frequent protests at her father's absences. Her mother took her to Iladel each summer to spend the season with Byrric and the royal family, but he rarely returned to Allanor for more than a few days at a time.

After Cina died, just before Freya's thirteenth birthday, Freya had hoped it would bring her father home or, at the very least, encourage him to bring her to live with him at Court, but neither of those things happened. He'd hesitated when she expressed interest in working with the marshals, but relented, with the stipulation that her time with them would end once she graduated. He'd balked slightly when she insisted on glamouring her appearance after they moved to Watoria, but she'd made it clear that wasn't a battle he would find worth fighting. With Byrric gone, she was guaranteed to receive unwanted attention from others, but all she wanted to do was learn and work.

She huffed out an annoyed breath as her feet touched on the warm sand at the lake, then sat down and spread her wings so she could soak in some of the late afternoon sun. As far as anyone else knew, her father had sent Freya to live in Iston, a small region that straddled the border between Allanor and Caelora where there was a high population of Valkyrie. For her own security, the general field marshal of Watoria and a select few of his subordinates were aware of her true identity, and as Freya wasn't an uncommon name in the Western regions, she'd been able to remain fairly hidden in plain sight.

Several minutes went past as she sat in silence staring out at the water, watching as the sun glinted off the rippling surface, reflecting off the scales of a school of fish zig-zagging just beneath. A large seahawk swooped down and dipped its feet in the water, then flew off, clutching its dinner in its sharp talons. She smiled at the beauty of it, the deftness with which the raptor swiped and pivoted before any of the cinderfish—small black creatures with a bite so painful it seared its victim's insides—could latch onto its feet.

There was a heavy thump beside her. She let out a quiet breath as she registered her father's scent.

"Your mother and I used to come here."

"I told you I was going to drop the glamour in my own time," Freya snapped, ignoring his attempts at small talk.

He sighed and sat down, then leaned back on his hands. "And I was tired of waiting. You're my daughter, Freya, and you're incredibly powerful. Those aren't things that should be kept hidden."

Freya picked up a small twig from the sand in front of her and began to twirl it between her palms. "All I asked for were a few days. Just a few *days* to establish myself here as Freya, not your daughter, not a Valkyrie half-blood." She tossed the stick away and rested her arms on her knees. "I suppose that was a fool's dream."

"You have a future, Freya, and it's not something you can escape. Hiding beneath magic won't change that."

"I'm not trying to escape anything. I'd just hoped to avoid it a bit longer."

"You think the friends you've made—"

"You mean the ones you provided me?"

"Are you saying Lazarus, Collin, and Lea aren't your friends? That Aerelius isn't *still* your friend?"

"No, I'm not," she admitted sullenly. "I think Lea, Lazarus, and Collin are quite wonderful, to be honest. As for Aer... I suppose we'll see." The uncertainty of that statement made her heart clench a little. She certainly hoped they would fall back into some semblance of their old friendship, but it was hard not to wrestle with the question of whether or not they'd both changed too much to find it.

With a huff, she leaned back on her hands, mirroring his position. Glancing up at him, it was easy to see that they were related, even despite the hair and wings. The shape of her eyes and mouth, and even the way she carried herself, were inherited directly from him. While there was an unmistakable resemblance to her mother, it would be clear to anyone with eyes that he was her father.

The two were silent, sitting almost companionably as the sky began to shift toward sunset. She didn't dislike Byrric or his company, necessarily, but he tended to be more of a political pragmatist than a father, something she still struggled with. Although she wasn't terribly vocal about it, she rarely disagreed with the decisions he made, including those that involved her. He raised her to ask questions, to push back, even with him, something she was sure he regretted once she came into her ability to reason.

"You did well today," Byrric said after a moment. "Officer Ristheld was quite impressed."

"I suppose when your father puts a sword in your hand at age five, impressive skills are inevitable."

He gave her a disparaging look. "Please, Freya. It was a dagger."

"Maybe to a grown male," she said with a laugh. "I was hardly three feet tall!"

"And you wielded it proudly," he replied. "Those skills have gotten you far in this life."

"I know." She turned her head to face him. "And despite what I might say, I'm appreciative of that."

"That's good to hear," Byrric said. He stood, then held out a hand to help her up. "I acknowledge that our relationship is not so typical, but please trust that I have always had your best interest at heart."

Freya dusted the sand from her pants and hands before responding. "I know you did—do. I've never questioned that, only your methods."

"You needed to stay in Watoria to grow," Byrric told her. "I do not regret leaving you there. After Cina died, your aunt did far more for you there than I could have here."

"Would life in Iladel have been so bad?" she asked. For a moment, she almost felt like a small girl again, saddened to watch her father leave, knowing she'd only see him a few months out of the year.

"They're a different sort here, Freya. You would not have grown into who you are had you been raised in this world. Your mother chose right when she decided you would stay in Allanor after I took my post here. There, you had family, friends, the ability to pursue your own interests. Here, you would've had governesses and a father who was routinely away from home."

Freya thought back to her lengthy visits to the capital. For those few months of each year, she'd been subjected to formal dinners in fancy dresses with the royal family, throwing knives and swords with the prince and pages in the palace training yard during the day, along with the occasional magic lesson from the queen, who was gifted with earth magic. She'd always loved the way Queen Ordona would dote on her, sneaking Freya and Aerelius cookies and milk late at night to eat on the palace steps, long before the sardonic smirk and matching demeanor had become a permanent fixture on his face.

But there had also been times where the lovely queen's features and words had turned cold, projecting an air of unrelenting authority. There were times the king had chastised Aerelius for not exuding behavior befitting his station, when her own father had instructed her on how to perfect being seen and not heard. Freya and Aerelius were frequently left to play on their own, their shared love of mischief often landing them in trouble with one of their parents or another. They'd become friends, and good ones at that, although her six-year-long absence had likely damaged that friendship a good deal.

"Aer didn't turn out so badly, did he?" she asked, unable to help smiling at the memory of their younger years. "Prickishness aside, of course."

Byrric ran a hand over his face and groaned. "Freya, I know you were close with the prince when you were children, but please take some time to get to know him again before assuming anything about his... demeanor."

"I think his prickishness was demonstrated quite fully today."

"That was a person feeling out their opponent, and you damn well know it," he replied, his tone a warning. "Before you make rash judgments about anyone here, watch for a bit. Get to know the school, the city, the students."

"Despite our lacking relationship, I *am* still your daughter," Freya said tiredly. "Assessing my surroundings was one of the first lessons you and Mother taught me. Although that might be a bit difficult, now that you've shined a damn beacon on me." Freya bit her lip and averted her eyes, staring out across the water as she wrestled with the question she had hoped to avoid asking. Resigned, she looked back at Byrric "And the other students?" She shook her head and groaned. "I know I shouldn't care what they think..."

"There were a few who made comments regarding the benefits of befriending a Valkyrie, especially a half-blood who has me for a father," he said without a hint of arrogance. "By and large, they were impressed, perhaps a bit intimidated, and more than a little intrigued."

"About?"

"What you can do," Byrric replied. "There are very few Valkyrie who venture this far from Iston."

She huffed out a laugh. "So I'm a shiny new toy, then?"

"Look at it this way." He picked up a rock and sent it skipping along the rippling surface of the lake. "You know the espionage skills you and Aerelius tried to perfect as children?"

"Yes, of course," Freya replied, smiling. One of her fondest memories of her summers in Iladel was when Aerelius had snuck her into the palace's labyrinth of secret passageways. The spy holes and secret chambers had fascinated them both, and they often stole away after their parents tucked them in at night to slip through the castle unseen and pilfer treats from the kitchen or play tricks on the palace guards.

"Well, view your popularity as a means of honing those skills by infiltrating the myriad social groups that exist here at Aldridge," Byrric continued. "Watoria is behind you now. Start to form new connections, get to know the students, their families, their goals. You'd be surprised at how useful that information might be in the future."

"Alright, Commander, I will make the best of this situation you've helped put me in," she resolved with a smile. "Maybe I'll even make a friend or two that you haven't lined up for me."

"With your charms?" He laughed and shook his head. "I have no doubt."

11

Freya was pleasantly surprised to find that Lazarus and Collin had pilfered another meal from the dining hall while she'd been off with her father. When she walked into her room, they and Lea were all sitting on the floor with a spread so large it might've made a Solstice celebration seem meager.

"No dining hall tonight?" Freya asked lightly, kicking off her muddied boots and sitting down beside Laz. He handed her a seeded breadstick and slid a plate of hard cheese and fig jam toward her, which she gratefully started nibbling.

"As your roommate," Lea said slowly, "I chose not to subject myself to the incessant curiosity of the masses."

Freya spread a bit more jam on her cheese. "Meaning?"

"*Meaning*, word of your father's stunt in Combat quickly made the rounds, and now everyone knows who and what you are." She clicked her tongue and shook her head. "Others began asking *me* questions, which I didn't particularly care to deal with."

Freya winced. "I'm sorry, Lea. He's insufferable."

Lea narrowed her eyes. "Aerelius wanted to come over, but I told him to give you a bit of space after his little display. Was that the right thing to do?"

"It was," Freya said, relieved at her friend's forethought. "I just came from talking with my father, and I don't really care to hash anything more out tonight."

"Do you truly feel your father was wrong?" Collin asked. "In wanting everyone to know who you are?"

Freya shifted uncomfortably. "No. It's honestly quite rare I disagree with his choices, even when they involve me."

Lea smirked. "Is that so?"

Collin sent her a silencing look before asking, "Then why do you seem so unhappy?"

"It's his methods that infuriate me. I thought we had an agreement that I could take my time settling in, but he clearly felt otherwise." Freya pouted a bit as she examined her fingernails. "And it hurts when your wings are forced to extend like that."

"What's done is done, though," Collin said with a shrug. "Now you simply need to figure out how to deal with it."

"And we're happy to provide some insight on those worth allowing into your social circle," Lea told her. "I wasn't wrong when I said you're best avoiding falling in with the wrong types."

"Such as...?"

"Social vultures," Laz said. "Myria and her ilk."

"Yes, don't be surprised if she attempts to befriend you now that she knows who your father is," Lea added.

"Myria is part of a governing house, though, so don't turn her away on instinct," Collin cautioned. "Having a good relationship with her could be beneficial."

"True," Lea allowed. "Your species likely doesn't matter to her, but Byrric has significant political power, not to mention the king's ear."

"Which was exactly why I didn't want to be outed as his daughter so soon," Freya groaned. "I spent my childhood being paraded around the royal court. As much as I hated being away from my father, living in Watoria was quite freeing."

"Because you glamoured yourself?" Lea asked quietly. "I have to admit, we *were* a bit surprised when you showed up looking a bit... unlike your description."

"Partly. Very few who lived there knew who I was, and those who did just didn't care as much. The marshals saw me as an asset because my parents trained me, but they let me work with them because of my skill. No one was trying to get Byrric's ear or hoping I could use my familiarity with the royal family to land an audience. I was just... me." Freya tugged on her hair. "I glamoured myself so that this blasted hair didn't stick out like a beacon and blow my cover, so to speak."

"It *is* quite unique," Collin admitted, his blue eyes dancing with interest as he scanned her newly-revealed features.

"Thank Byrric for that," Freya grumbled. "Apparently, male Valkyrie aren't unlike peacocks when it comes to their appearances."

"It's lovely, though," Lea commented, lifting the end of Freya's braid from her shoulder. Wrinkling her nose, she pulled at her own dark curls that now tumbled over her narrow shoulders. "I'd love a bit of pink in my hair, to be honest. It would make my eyes stand out, don't you agree?"

"You never know, Freya," Laz said with a laugh. "You may start a trend."

Freya gave them a half-smile. "Maybe. It's just so frustrating that my reputation is tied to his."

"Irrevocably so, unfortunately," Collin agreed. "Although you knew that before you got here."

"Well I think you're both wrong." Lazarus gave Freya an encouraging smile. "You'll forge your own reputation sooner than you think. And look at the bright side," he added. "That whole 'receiver of the crown's charity' spiel Myria was spouting just got put to rest quite cleanly."

Freya couldn't help but smile at that.

FREYA WAS thankful that her first class the following day was History, the only other course she had with Lea, Lazarus, and Collin. As with Toxins, Lea insisted on arriving early to ensure they got the best seats.

Pursing her lips, she looked around the room, taking in the number of students who seemed to share the idea of arriving early.

"The back is still mostly empty," Freya said.

Lea sent her an annoyed look but relented when Collin began to lead the way toward the back of the room.

"I prefer it, too," he told Freya, who was trying hard to shut out the whispers about "the commander's daughter" and "the Valkyrie who'd flattened the prince," that followed. "It's more comfortable when you can see everyone else, don't you think?"

She shot an I-told-you-so look at Lea. "Exactly."

Freya looped the canvas satchel containing her texts around the back of her chair and took a seat beside Lea, while Lazarus and Collin sat behind them in the back row. Slowly, the room continued to fill, and more than a few furtive glances were sent in her direction as they waited for their professor to arrive. Her instinct was to look away when she caught the eyes of others, but she forced herself to meet their gazes, holding them until they looked away.

The seats immediately surrounding them remained mostly empty.

"Speaking of seats," Freya said, nudging Lea as she recalled their previous conversation. "I believe you owe me twenty sils."

Lea sent her a scathing look. "I'll buy your outfit for dinner this weekend. How does that sound?"

"Dinner?" Freya arched a brow. "What dinner?"

Lea gave her a curious look. "Byrric hasn't told you? We're doing a family dinner at the palace."

"But we're not family."

"You're as good as," Lazarus said. "And if Collin has to be subjected, it's only fair that you do, too."

Collin's answering smile more closely resembled a grimace. "Yes, please, Freya. Don't leave me alone with that clan."

"It doesn't sound as though I have much of a choice," she murmured.

"So we'll still plan to go shopping later this week?" Lea said, clasping her hands hopefully in front of her chest. "We can get fitted for dresses for the Commencement Ball, too!"

"Formalwear, hmm? I suppose spending a bit of Byrric's money would be a good way to get back at him for yesterday." She wiggled her eyebrows. "I think Edhilian gemstone barrettes to set off my hair might be nice."

"Heavens, no!" Lea pressed a hand to her chest. "Opal is far more appropriate for a casual palace dinner. Save the gems for the ball."

Freya tapped a finger to her lips. "Yes, green opal. The shade is one of my best colors, actually."

"There's a lovely jeweler in Iladel who I've used on several occasions. Here name is Rosina, and she does wonderful work." Lea squealed and clapped excitedly, then turned to Laz and Collin. "Oh, this will be so fun! Do you two want to come?"

Lazarus laughed as Collin gave her a dubious look. "Not on your life, dear cousin."

"Oh, why not?" Lea whined. "You'll need something new, too!"

"Which is exactly why Collin and I employ personal shoppers," he said with a grin. "And it's quite impossible for you to make a quick decision when it comes to fashion."

"He's not wrong," Collin whispered to Freya.

"It's fine, Lea," Freya said, laughing. "A bit of girl time would be nice."

"I suppose," Lea said with a sigh. "It *has* been awhile since I've had female company."

"So... how long do you think this will go on?" she asked Lea, letting her eyes drift across the room.

"The whispers will stop soon enough," Lea replied. "Once the sucking up begins."

"You know, they'd have far more luck sucking up to the prince," Freya commented.

Lea laughed. "It's been some time since you've been around my cousin, hasn't it? He is the epitome of unapproachable."

Freya inclined her head toward Myria, who sat in the front row. "She seems to have made her way in."

Lea waved off her comment. "He tolerates her for his mother's sake. Myria's parents and the queen are friends. Lucia Bryton has high hopes of her daughter gaining upward mobility, although I don't think she ever truly believed Myria would land Prince Aerelius."

"They do nothing to discourage it?" Freya frowned. "That's a bit cruel."

"Oh, Aer discourages it, often and loudly," Lea said. "Myria simply doesn't listen. By the way." She leaned toward Freya, eyes gleaming. "Aer is in this class, too."

Before Freya could respond, two black-uniformed officers entered the room, each taking up flanking positions beside the door. The prince strode in a moment later, and the room went silent. He was dressed in a cobalt suede tunic, belted at the waist over fitted black pants tucked into gleaming, knee-high boots.

Movement at the front drew Freya's attention to where Myria half-rose from her seat, a hand in the air in greeting.

Aerelius let his dark eyes roam over the room, taking in the students, the empty seats, before landing on Freya and the others. Mirth shifted into his dark eyes, and a smirk twitched the corners of his mouth.

Laz snickered from the other side of Lea as he waved Aerelius over. "Freya, we probably should've mentioned... putting the prince on his ass on the first day of Combat will draw just as much attention to you as who your sires are."

"Attention based on skill is *never* unwelcome," she told him haughtily.

There was a loud *thud* as Aerelius dropped his textbook on the desk next to Freya.

She smiled sweetly. "Good morning, Highness. Sleep well?"

"Funny thing," he said, rubbing his jaw as he sat down and brushing lightly over the scruff. "I had this horrendous bruise on my chin that took several hours to heal before I could doze off."

Freya stuck out her lower lip in a mock show of sympathy. "You should really take better care who you challenge in a fight, then. Don't you think, Lea?"

Lea nodded sagely. "Without question. Our Lady Valkyrie here has quite the upper hook, from what I hear. Isn't that correct, Myria?" she called.

Turning, Freya saw that Myria was staring unabashed at the five of them, her green eyes blazing. At Lea's call, her face went crimson.

"A few lucky shots do not make a good fighter," the blonde shot back. Clenching her jaw, she sent an annoyed look at Freya, then turned and faced forward.

"You shouldn't goad her," Aerelius commented as he flipped idly through his text book. "Myria can be quite vicious when she's angry."

"Oh?" Lea lifted her brow innocently. "What would you know about it?"

Aerelius angled his head to the side and gave his cousin an amused look, then shifted his eyes to Freya. "So, Valkyrie, I hear you'll be gracing us with your presence at dinner this weekend."

"I've heard that rumor, as well," she replied. "Although, funny enough, no one has yet told me that I'm to attend."

"I do hope you've managed to acquire appropriate attire," he continued. "I hear Allanor's capital is a bit lacking when it comes to fashion."

"It might surprise his Highness that I *do* recall what it means to attend a royal dinner. You act as though I was raised in the slums of Jotunheim."

"And even if she *were* raised in that wretched empire," Lea interjected, sending Freya a sharp look, "that's what she has me for." She gave the prince a brilliant smile.

"Yes, I can only imagine what the two of you will come up with when left to your own devices," he muttered.

"I was thinking chartreuse, personally," Lea began, tapping a finger thoughtfully against her chin.

"Oh, certainly," Freya added, grinning. "Thigh-length, perhaps with some contrasting beadwork in a scandalous design. I saw one once in the shape of a man's—"

"I see your sense of humor has improved with age," Aerelius said, shaking his head. "Although I think you've sufficiently scandalized poor Professor Livurnia," he added, nodding toward the front of the class.

Freya turned and immediately cursed the flush on her cheeks when she saw the small, bird-like female who'd just walked in.

"You could have warned me," she hissed at Lea.

"Then how would I be able to call payback?"

12

The rest of Freya's first week at Aldridge went by uneventfully. She still received stares and was subjected to whispers and hushed conversations that seemed to follow her wherever she went, but those things had begun to die down by the third day.

By the time she finished Combat class on Friday, where, quite notably, the prince had avoided her entirely, she had begun to break through the whispers to get to know some of her fellow students, many of whom were interested in seeing her technique firsthand. Most were the lords and ladies of Iladel and the various eastern regions within the five realms, as well as the children of the realms' governing houses, which was perfectly typical of the wealthier regions of Lindoroth. There were a few—hardly a handful, so far as she could tell—who'd been offered places at Aldridge based solely on skill and merit. They were more reminiscent of what Freya remembered from Watoria, where the wealthiest residents more closely resembled the middle-class citizens of Iladel. They were the children of the most skilled smiths, business owners, teachers, and servants who'd shown promise in some way or another. They would be scrappy, Freya thought, willing to work and fight twice as hard as the more privileged students to prove their worth.

Most students sought to become educators, historians, archivists, scientists, or physicians. The jobs were plentiful in each of those fields, and while some positions would be more competitive than others, very few students of any background would have trouble finding work upon graduation in those areas.

The rest—those who sought power and influence in a world ruled by such things—would be ruthless. They were the children of politicians who hoped to continue their parents' legacies, the children of wealthy lords and ladies who would come into their own power someday, and those of the lower classes who had the skill and drive to climb the social ladders and had no qualms stepping on others in order to gain the fame and notoriety they sought. Those were the ones who wanted to change and shape history, but not always for the better.

Once Combat let out for the day on Friday, Freya was eager to leave school grounds with Lea for their shopping trip. Her excitement waned, however, when she was stopped in front of the academic building on her way back to her room by one of Byrric's underlings.

"Lady Balthana," he said as he descended the steps toward her. "Commander Balthana requests your presence." He held out a hand toward the building's main office. "He's just inside."

Resigned, Freya turned to enter the building. When she stepped inside, she found Byrric and the headmistress' assistant laughing and couldn't help the slight curling of her lip. Despite her mother's death being so long past, she couldn't help the twinge of annoyance she felt when she saw her father laughing so freely with another female.

"You needed to see me?" she asked by way of greeting.

"Ah, Freya!" Byrric flashed her a smile. With a quick farewell to the assistant, he led Freya back outside and through the outer doors onto the building's patio.

"I hear I'm to dine with the royal family," she said dryly.

"Yes, that's what I'm here to speak to you about. You'll be

presenting yourself to Salazar and Ordona, so make sure you're dressed appropriately," he told her.

She arched a brow. "Why is it no one seems to have faith in my ability to dress myself? First Aerelius, now you. I *have* been to royal parties before."

"Well, it's been some time," Byrric replied. "And this is the first time you'll be seeing the king and queen in six years, so I felt a reminder to bring Lea with you to choose your attire was in order."

"And here I was under the impression the king and queen adored me, no matter what," she said with a smirk.

"That is beside the point, Freya."

"Oh, fine. I'm headed back to the dormitories to meet Lea now, so you can stop fretting." She took in the position of the sun before continuing. "Speaking of which, I've got to go. I promise I will be perfectly proper tomorrow," she added when she saw his look of warning.

He patted her shoulder. "I know you will." Then, without a word of farewell, he spread his wings wide and flew off.

"Goodbye to you, too," she muttered.

ONCE THEY'D both bathed and changed, Freya and Lea made their way to the front gates where Lea said a carriage would be waiting to take them into Iladel for a few hours of shopping and dinner. As they traversed the grassy lawn toward Aldridge's entrance, she walked with bated breath, hoping the Headmistress and her blasted father had forgotten their decision to attach guards to her when she left the university's grounds.

When they arrived at the gates, her fears were realized. There, next to the carriage, were two officers, clad in their spotless, navy blue uniforms.

"Oh, just ignore them," Lea told her. "That's what I always do."

"Is one yours, then?" Freya asked, narrowing her eyes at the motionless guards.

"Iska, there on the right. He's been my shadow for, what's it been, fifteen years, Iska?"

The tall, brown-haired guard gave a small nod. "Give or take, Lady Calliwell."

Lea sighed and shook her head, then looked back at Freya. "The fool refuses to address me by my given name, no matter how many times I order it."

As Lea and Freya approached the carriage, the second guard stepped forward, an amber-skinned male with black hair that fell in waves to his shoulders.

"Lady Balthana, my name is Rissen." He gave a small bow. "I've been assigned by the commander as your personal guard."

"Hello, Rissen." Freya gave him a tight smile. "I don't suppose I could offer you a few hundred of the commander's sils to busy yourself elsewhere, could I?"

Lea snorted as Rissen gave her an apologetic look.

"I apologize, Lady, but that would be highly improper."

"Yes, I suppose it would." Freya narrowed her eyes. "You can't fly, can you? All I smell on you is wolf."

He smiled easily. "I've been given explicit instructions not to answer that question."

Mentally, she cursed her father. "Alright, then. Let's get to it."

After boarding the carriage, their guards situated on the rear rumble-seat, Lea immediately began listing the places they were going to visit.

"First, the dressmaker. You'll need to be measured for a gown for the Commencement Ball next week, and Kallan will need at least half that time to design and make it for you. He'll help us acquire accessories and shoes to complement it, of course. He'll also be able to provide something perfect for dinner tomorrow. Even though it's somewhat casual, we'll still go with dresses. Lighter, maybe something a bit floral? Then afterward, there's a lovely jewelry shop I always love to visit."

Freya made a face. "I've never been too big on florals, to be quite honest. Between the pattern and my hair, my appearance tends to lean toward garish."

"Oh, that's highly unlikely. Regardless, something that's reminiscent of the king's Saithian heritage will be most appropriate." She eyed Freya's hair curiously. "Since you were able to glamour your hair to appear brown, would you consider changing the color to match an outfit?"

"I think I've had about enough of glamours for the time being, honestly, and Byrric would give me more grief for it than it's worth."

Lea nodded. "Alright, then we'll make sure to find something to complement your natural color."

"So, where will we eat?" Freya asked, shifting so she was facing Lea a bit better. "I was far pickier the last time I dined in the capital, so I'm eager to see what's available."

"There's a small restaurant that features cuisine from each of the realms," Lea said. "I dine there at least once any time my family would come for a visit. I'd love to show it to you."

Freya grinned as her stomach rumbled. "That sounds perfect."

"OH, Lea, that looks fabulous on you!" Freya gushed as she watched her friend get fitted for a flowing, turquoise gown. Kallan, a flame-haired warlock who hardly came to Freya's shoulder, had been fussing over her for the past hour, using his sorcery to design patterns and beadwork that perfectly accented Lea's body shape and coloring.

"Lady Calliwell has always been one of my easiest customers," the small male said as he twisted a bit of gossamer fabric around Lea's hips.

"Oh, you shush!" Lea said, laughing. "Wait until you get Lady Balthana up here."

Kallan sniffed. "Lady Calliwell, your level of modesty is unbecoming. Embrace your beauty, my dear." He brushed a hand down her side, over the dip of her waist, then stepped back, watching with a small smile as a glimmering sunburst of color appeared, a cluster of yellow beads fanning across her torso, shifting seamlessly to shades of green, then blue.

"There," he said, clasping his hands in front of his chin and nodding in satisfaction. "Yes, I think that will do quite nicely for the Commencement Ball. The green and blue will be mixed with Edhilian emeralds and sapphires, of course, and their canary sunstones have been all the rage this season." He looked up at Lea, an eager expression on his face. "Well?"

Lea bit her lip as she stared at herself in the mirror. She brushed a hand over her hip, gently touching the illusion of beadwork that highlighted her hourglass figure. "It's quite lovely, Kallan. I dare say you've outdone yourself."

"I think it's perfect," Freya agreed. "The colors look beautiful on you."

Lea narrowed her eyes at her reflection. "Yes, this will work perfectly."

Kallan laughed. "Indeed." He gestured for her to step down. The dress faded away as she took a step off the pedestal, leaving her in just her undergarments as the design transferred onto a plain piece of parchment that sat on a small table. "Go on, get dressed. Lady Balthana?" He smiled at Freya as Lea disappeared behind a curtain to redress. "Up you go."

Freya slipped out of the thin robe she'd donned when they arrived, then allowed Kallan to help her onto the pedestal.

"It's been nearly six years since I've had to acquire this type of finery," she told Kallan. "And fashion in Watoria... I'm not quite sure what I should be looking for."

"Yes, they go for function over form, from what I hear," Kallan finished, nodding. "Not to worry, my dear. You're in good hands." Stepping back, he tapped a finger against his chin thoughtfully. "That hair does limit us a bit, especially if we're attempting to emulate the realm of Saith..." He pursed his lips as he scanned her, head to toe. "Something to add the illusion of curves, certainly."

Freya arched a brow at his bluntness. She'd never been opposed to her narrow hips and average chest—it was far easier to find ready-made leathers that fit with a figure like hers—but it surprised her a bit to hear someone else say it so blithely.

"What about something with a bit of cinching at the waist?" she suggested.

Frowning in thought, he nodded. "Yes, with heavy beading on top to draw the eye. Now for color..."

Freya glanced over at Lea, who'd just stepped out of the dressing room.

"Any luck?" Lea asked.

"I'm in need of some curves, according to Kallan," Freya said dryly.

"Oh, please! Kallan, let's not discourage the girl so soon!"

"Well, I won't design my dresses for features that don't exist," he replied, clearly exasperated. "Now shush, both of you, and let me think." He circled Freya, taking in each aspect of her figure. "Alright, I've got something." With a wave of his hand, magic washed over her, prickling her exposed skin as a strapless peach gown began to form, fitting tight around her chest and ribs before flowing out into layers of gossamer that fell to her calves. He spent several minutes tapping her waist, where wisps of pink, the same color as her hair, appeared to weave themselves into the layers of her skirt, shifting in depth as she turned this way and that. After a moment, he made a small "hmm" noise and a burst of rosestones mixed with emeralds swirled across the upper part of the bodice. A dusting of diamond crystals began to glitter throughout the skirt.

When the dress finished materializing, Kallan stepped back and nodded. "Yes, that will do nicely, don't you think?"

Freya twisted her hips back and forth, smiling softly as the shades of peach and pink shifted with her movements. The beadwork glittered, highlighting the streaks of pink in her chestnut hair without making them seem garish.

"I think it's perfect," she said, grinning. She sent an expectant look at Lea. "Now, let's see about some shoes, shall we?"

"A bit overdone for a simple dinner, if you ask me."

Freya spun toward the door, then bit back a curse when she saw

Aerelius standing in the archway, hip resting against the frame, a crooked smile on his lips.

"Oh, look, it's my cousin," Lea sighed. "Fancy meeting you here."

He gave her a nod of greeting as Kallan gave the prince a low bow. "Your Highness. If you're in need of a fitting, I'm just about finished with Lady Balthana."

"Not to worry, Kallan. Since tomorrow will be Lady Balthana's first dinner with our monarchs in quite some time, I thought I might come offer my expertise in the area."

Freya's lips quirked in amusement. "You're an expert in women's fashion now, Highness? Things *have* changed in my absence, haven't they?"

Lea snorted out a quiet laugh. "You'd be surprised at what an eye for fashion my cousin has, Freya. Come, Kallan, take me to the shoe section."

The dressmaker hesitated for a moment, his eyes darting between Freya and the prince before nodding at Lea. "Of course, Lady Calliwell. I've got a lovely pair in mind."

When they were gone, Freya gave Aer an exasperated look. "This is for the ball," she said, gesturing needlessly toward the dress. "We haven't gotten to dinner attire yet."

Aer nodded thoughtfully. "I assumed as much. This looks lovely on you, though. I can't quite make out the beadwork," he said with a sly grin. "Would you mind coming closer?"

Freya rolled her eyes. "The moment I step off this pedestal, Kallan's magic fades and I'll be left in my undergarments. A noble effort, however, if not a bit childish."

Sliding his hands in the pocket of his gray pants, he sauntered toward her, his eyes teasing. "I don't suppose you'll save me a dance?"

She huffed out a small breath. "Have you only come to offer your judgement? I'd like to get Kallan back in so he can finish up."

"In a moment." He twirled his finger. "Turn around, please. Face the mirror."

"Why?"

He frowned. "Because I'm your prince and I asked you to?"

She gave him a withering look. "*Why?*"

He stepped up on the pedestal, putting himself within inches of her. "Lady Balthana, will you *please* turn around?"

Freya had to crane her neck to look up at him, as he stood nearly a head taller. She held his eyes for a moment, caught off guard by his sudden proximity. His eyes didn't flicker with mischief like they had in training yard; instead, they seemed to reflect the uncertainty she felt inside, questioning whether it was alright to come into her space.

"How do you plan to wear your hair?" he asked, twirling a strand around his finger before letting it fall to her shoulder.

Freya swallowed hard, then turned to face the mirror. "I haven't decided yet."

He made a small hum in the back of his throat. "Up off your neck will show off the beadwork nicely." Then, grinning, he rested his cheek against hers and met her eyes in the mirror. "Do you recall that summer when you taught me how to put twists in your hair?"

"If you're referring to the time you braided a dead garter snake through my hair, yes, I remember that quite clearly," she said dryly.

He chuckled, then gave a lock of her hair a gentle flick, to which she sent an elbow into his stomach that he deftly dodged. "After your show in Combat, I'd say you've gotten your retribution."

"Hardly. You pulled just as many tricks as me." She spun and jabbed a finger into his chest and glared up at him. "We were sparring! I should've known about your powers beforehand!"

He grabbed her hand, immobilizing it before she could poke him again. "Now you know."

She pulled her hand away. "Why are you really here, Aer? Do you find me incapable of presenting myself to the king and queen in a manner suiting my station?"

"You *were* quite the barbarian in Combat," he mused. "You tell me." He stepped off the pedestal and walked toward one of the clothing racks that Kallan had filled to bursting, then ran his hand along the fabrics. Idly, he began to sift through the rack in front of him.

"Perhaps someone should have ordered my father not to train me so well, then," Freya suggested, smoothing a hand over the bodice of her dress, admiring the beadwork in the mirror.

Aerelius stopped and looked at her as though the mere thought was insane. Which, she supposed, was fair. No child of Cina Enrieth and Byrric Balthana would have gone untrained, even if she ended up going her entire life untested.

Freya watched the prince with mild interest as he began to pull items from the rack.

"Are you looking for something in particular?" she asked.

"Perhaps." He handed her two hangers. "Here. These should work."

With a frown, she took the garments and looked them over. He'd chosen a short sleeveless dress in silk the color of seafoam embroidered with thin gold thread. Golden vines snaked up the sides that matched the shimmering leggings he'd handed her perfectly. She nearly growled when she realized they were the exact items she'd been eyeing not an hour earlier.

"You've got quite the eye," she said quietly, turning the dress around to examine its design more closely.

"What are friends for, if not to help with fashion choices?"

"Are we all decent in here?" Lea called from just outside the door.

"Not remotely!" Aer called back, laughing when Freya threw the gold leggings at him.

"Bastard," she muttered.

"I could have you tossed in the dungeon for such disrespect," he said, his voice still tinged with laughter.

"I'd love to see you try, cousin," Lea said airily as she walked in. "Our Lady Freya would be in the skies before you got hands on her. And that's not even considering what *I* might do."

Freya gave him a small shrug. "She isn't wrong."

Kallan cleared his throat, reminding them all of his presence.

"Lady Balthana, have you chosen something for dinner?" He gestured toward the dress that was still in her hand.

"I did. If you wouldn't mind getting me out of this dress, I'll try them on." She sent a pointed look at Aerelius. "If you'll excuse us?"

"You'd ask me to leave after I just chose such a lovely ensemble?" Aerelius put a hand over his heart in feigned insult. "You wound me."

"Out!" Lea yelled, tossing a slipper at him, which he narrowly ducked. "Before I sic Freya on you!"

"Will you two *please* stop throwing things at me?" he exclaimed.

Freya gave Aerelius a bright smile. "I'll see you tomorrow, Aer."

He scowled at her. "And I think *I'll* see about finding you a new roommate, Valkyrie. *Grevillea* is clearly a terrible influence."

Kallan, who was becoming noticeably uncomfortable, cleared his throat again, this time a bit louder. "If Your Highness wouldn't mind... it might be easier to arrange the ladies' outfits without any distractions."

"I suppose I see the sense in that," Aerelius replied. "Ladies, until tomorrow."

"Oh, Aer?" Freya called, just as she was about to step down from the pedestal. She crooked a finger toward him.

Smiling, he walked toward her, stopping just inches from where she stood. "Yes?"

She let her eyes run over his face, cataloging his features for a moment, then wrapped her fingers in the collar of his shirt and tugged his face toward hers. "If you try to take Lea away from me," she whispered, "I'll make sure the next feather I aim at your throat is filled with venom."

Gently, he disentangled her fingers from his shirt, then kissed the back of her hand and sighed. "Oh, Freya. How I've missed you."

13

The better part of the following day was spent preparing for dinner at the palace. Lea and Freya's purchases had been delivered that morning, altered by Kallan to their exact measurements. Lea had called for two of the palace's pixies, Rini and Tyna, to come assist with their hair and makeup, insisting there were no finer hands to entrust themselves to.

"Their level of detail is beyond comparison," she explained when Freya questioned her. She wiggled her fingers. "It's those tiny hands. You'll see."

Knowing better than to challenge Lea's decision, Freya simply nodded and went along. The final fitting of her outfit didn't take long, and once Kallan had ensured their clothing fit as intended, he presented them each with the accessories he'd chosen.

He handed Freya a square black box. "You won't need much with all of the gold in the outfit his highness chose, but I thought some additional shimmer would finish it off nicely."

Freya opened the box, then squealed in delight when she saw the jewelry inside.

"Oh, it's lovely!" She touched the delicate gold strands that were nestled in the bed of black velvet and smiled. Small leaves and flowers crafted with such clarity they appeared as dipped versions of the real thing adorned the chains. As Freya ran her fingers over them, she saw they were nearly translucent.

She touched a hand to her throat, realizing in dismay that the high cut of her dress would make a necklace an impossible accessory. Before she could voice her concerns, Kallan had nodded toward Rini and Tyna, who were fluttering in midair just beside the door.

The two tiny females, small enough to perch on Freya's shoulder, had a typical pixie appearance, making it difficult for Freya to tell them apart at first. Both had hair the color of polished silver, with glass-like eyes and ghost-white skin. Their wings, fluttering rapidly behind them, were nearly translucent, but when the sunlight hit them, they glittered in shades of purple and blue.

"They'll work the strands into your hair," Kallan explained. "When open, the clasp doubles as a pair of clips. The reflective nature of the leaves will pick up the color of your hair nicely."

Freya beamed at him. "It's perfect, Kallan, thank you."

"And what have you got for me, kind sir?" Lea asked primly.

"Silver, my dear," he told her, handing her a box identical to the one he'd given Freya.

Lea eagerly tilted the lid up, then sighed with delight when she saw the wispy silver necklace and matching ear cuff within. Like Freya's, the strands were thin, but instead of foliage, Lea's necklace had tiny charms depicting the moon in its various stages.

"When I was born," she explained to Freya as she brushed her fingers across the charms, "the moon was the brightest it had been in decades. It's become a bit of a good luck charm for me."

"They're beautiful," Freya said.

"I'll pass on your thanks to the jewelry maker," Kallan said. "If you ever need pieces made, Rosina is the best you'll find, as I'm sure Lady Calliwell will attest."

"I have no doubt," Freya murmured, still a bit awestruck by how perfect her necklace was. "I can assure you she'll be getting my business in the future."

"I've already commissioned her for the ball next week," he told her.

"Smart thinking," Lea said.

Kallan gave her a small smile and a nod in thanks. "I'll let you both finish preparations. Please call on me if there's anything you need. I'll return in a week with your gowns."

Once he'd left, the pixies swooped in to begin their work. When they spoke, their voices were high and melodic.

"Makeup first," the one on Freya's left sang. "Rini, you take the Valkyrie."

Rini smiled brightly at Freya, then fluttered over and came to a stop by her shoulder. "I'm going to make you look like a goddess, darling."

Freya exchanged an excited smile with Lea, then nodded at Rini.

"That sounds perfect."

IT TOOK NEARLY two hours for Rini and Tyna to finish their work, but when they were done, Freya couldn't stop staring at the results.

Her hair fell in a sleek curtain to her waist, the golden strands of her necklace pinned at her temples and looping around the back. The chains were so fine they were nearly invisible, lost in her pink and brown locks, but the leaves and flowers gleamed throughout, subtly reflecting the afternoon sun that streamed through the window. A light dusting of gold on her cheeks had left her skin glowing and ethereal.

When she turned and looked at Lea, her eyes widened, her own appearance forgotten.

"Lea, you look gorgeous!"

Lea flipped her dark curls over her shoulder and frowned at her reflection. "I do, don't I?" she said playfully.

Tyna had given her friend a slightly silver glow and smoothed her hair into dark ringlets that hung to the center of her back. A few locks were twisted away from her face, revealing the delicate silver cuff that adorned one ear. The natural brown tones of her skin gleamed against the deep ruby color of her dress.

"If they do this well for a simple royal dinner," Lea said, "can you just imagine how we'll look for the Commencement Ball?"

Freya bit her lip and shook her head, then looked at herself in the mirror, where her reflection stared back, wide-eyed. Meeting Rini's eyes, she grinned. "Thank you, Rini."

The small pixie gave her a satisfied smile and a small nod. "It was my pleasure, Lady Balthana."

"Ah!" Lea exclaimed when there was a knock at the door. "That must be the boys."

After a nod from Lea, Tyna snapped her fingers and the door swung open, revealing Lazarus and Collin waiting on the other side. Lazarus wore a cerulean doublet fastened at the neck with onyx buckles and black pants tucked into high black boots. Collin appeared to have taken care to match, wearing a white tunic with a black vest and cravat in the same shade as Lazarus' jacket.

Laz let out a low whistle. "Well, don't you ladies look lovely."

Lea gave a low curtsy and preened. "Likewise."

"Shall we go?" Collin asked. "Our carriage awaits."

"Lead the way, sirs," Lea said, waving them toward the door. "Rini, Tyna, thank you both for all of your help."

"It was our pleasure, dear," Tyna said with a smile. "We'll return the morning of the ball to assist you again."

"Have fun, children!" Rini sang after them.

Freya tossed her a quick wink, then followed the others out of the room.

THE TRIP from Aldridge to the palace was about two hours up a wide road that wound through the foothills and into the forest of the mountain. The trees were so dense, interspersed only by hard, granite ridges and boulders, that Freya almost found it hard to believe that there was a palace nestled deep inside. She itched to let out her wings and fly there as she would've done as a girl, but she couldn't bring herself to risk marring the pixies' hard work.

When they finally emerged from the dark forest that opened onto the palace lawn, Freya was struck, as she had been when she was a girl, at its sheer size and grandeur. The castle had been built of pale gray limestone that had been mined from the northern quarries of Caelora and carried south to the capital by the first king's slaves nearly five millennia ago. Bastions cut with hundreds of arrow slits rose high above the ramparts that surround the castle, and leading up to the mammoth front gate was a giant, creaking drawbridge that spanned the distance across a moat, from the lawn to the gatehouse where the iron portcullis was slowly rising to allow them passage.

"It's lovely, isn't it?" Lea whispered. "I've visited a number of times over the years, but I'll never quite get used to its beauty."

Freya smiled wistfully as she watched the palace loom closer and a spark of excitement lit in her chest. "It's more beautiful than I remember." Her smile turned to a grin as their carriage rattled across the wooden drawbridge. "Aer and I used to dare each other to climb under the drawbridge." She rolled her eyes. "Once I finally got up the nerve, I was halfway there when he told me there was a troll living beneath it."

Lazarus laughed. "That sounds like Aer. What did you do?"

"I kept climbing," Freya replied, sticking her hand out the window and letting the soft breeze bush over her fingers. "I hadn't quite gotten the hang of my wings yet, otherwise I would've flown up and popped him a good one right then. There was no troll, but I did find a door. Small, too, nearly impossible to find unless you're a misbehaving seven-year-old girl willing to face a bridge troll. Aer was quite furious I found it before he did. I wasn't able to open it, though, and I have no idea what its purpose was."

"Perhaps a simple way of tossing people into the moat?" Laz suggested. He shrugged at Lea's wide-eyed look. "What? It could be!"

"I've heard of those," Collin said with a nod. "The palace had a number of secret entrances built into it back when King Eroan resided here. A means of execution is its most likely purpose."

"He was a paranoid old bat, that one," Laz said. "My grandfather —King Salazar's uncle—used to tell us stories of how King Eroan killed all of the slaves who built the castle, along with the architect, so no one would ever know the secrets of its construction."

"Laz's grandfather was good friends with mine," Lea explained. "The two of them loved to gather by the fire and terrify us children with stories of dead bodies and ghosts in secret passageways."

Freya laughed. "It's been quite some time, but I don't recall seeing either of those things on my explorations."

Lea's eyes grew round with excitement. "Yes, Aer told me you two used to go exploring. Oh, is it wrong that I so desperately want to beg you to take me through the passages? My mother always forbade it."

"For good reason," Collin said with quirk of his lips. "Your sense of direction is horrifying."

"But," Freya said, holding up a finger, "a Valkyrie's sense of direction is unmatched."

"See, Collin? Problem solved." Lea grinned. "As long as Freya is with me, I'll be perfectly safe."

The carriage rolled to a stop just inside the gatehouse, and a few seconds later, Iska and Rissen pulled open the carriage doors to help them out. The guards that Lazarus' parents—Governor and Lady Cailen of Caelora—had assigned to shadow him and Collin were dismounting from their horses, having ridden about a half-mile ahead to watch for any potential dangers on the road.

Two servants waited for the group at the top of the sweeping staircase that led up to the palace's main door.

"My lords, and ladies," a fairly squat male said in greeting. "If you'll follow us, we will escort you to their majesties."

The two servants led them through the entryway and into the main hall where Freya's father was awaiting their arrival. He had divested himself of his uniform for once, opting instead for charcoal gray dinner attire.

"Don't you look dashing, Commander," Lea said, smiling cheekily. "Isn't it nice to be out of that stodgy old uniform for once?"

He arched a brow. "Why yes, Grevillea, it is."

Lazarus choked back a laugh, then nodded at Byrric in greeting. "Good evening, Commander Balthana."

"Lord Cailen," Byrric replied. "Lord Maddix, I hope you've come to keep these three in line," he said to Collin with a smile.

Collin sighed. "That does seem to be my lot in life."

Byrric patted him on the shoulder, then held out his arm to Freya. "Come, the king and queen await."

Gently, Freya laid her hand on her father's arm, surprised when she felt a flutter of nerves in her belly. The king, while gruff at times, had always been kind when she was a girl, and the queen had often been like a doting aunt. Freya's mother had told her once not long before she was killed that Ordona had always wanted a daughter and that Freya had helped fill that void, at least during her summer visits.

But Freya hadn't seen them in years. She'd been a different person then, although she'd changed in what she thought were good ways. Despite the infrequency of his visits, when Byrric had been present he'd drilled into her the importance of taking pride in one's accomplishments and not diminishing her skills to put others at ease. He'd taught her how to dance the fine line between arrogance and confidence, one she teetered on for quite some time before learning to let her actions speak for themselves.

She wondered how much Byrric had kept Salazar and Ordona abreast of her progress over the years.

"I see Kallan got his hands on you," Byrric said as they made their way down a long, arched hall toward the dining room. A small muscle twitched in his jaw when he saw the golden threads Rini had woven through the small braids that twisted away from Freya's temples. "Dare I ask how much of my money you spent?"

Freya shrugged, thankful for the distraction from her thoughts. "I'm not sure. There weren't any price tags on the pieces, and since Aer chose the outfit, I couldn't very well disobey him, could I?"

Byrric sighed. "I suppose I should talk with his highness about how best to spend my money."

Freya laughed. "You think too highly of your influence on him."

He gave her a pointed look. "Do I?"

"In some ways," she amended, then gave him a sly smile. "Although, I may consider making him a frequent shopping partner."

"Gods, help me," Byrric muttered.

They came to a stop outside the doors to the dining room, and Freya's nerves did another quick flutter.

Seeming to sense her unease, Byrric patted her hand. "They're eager to see you," he said quietly before pulling open the door. "There's no need to worry."

Freya hoped he was right.

14

Despite her nerves, Freya couldn't help but smile as she stepped into the dining hall and saw the opulence she'd look upon in wonder as a girl. Similar to the main academy building, stories of gods and Linds were carved into the high, coffered ceiling, the beams between sections gilded in gold. Only, these focused solely on the Harridan family line. Fierce dragons, kings and queens, royal crests, battles, and old runes were cast in sharp relief in the flickering candlelight from the gas-fueled chandeliers, shifting the shadows of the carvings, often giving the appearance of movement. Pale gold drapes were thrown open, giving the room a view of the setting sun. The dining table in the center, large enough for forty, was set with porcelain and crystal settings. Candelabras were set at the center and either end of the table, the golden candles shimmering under their flickering flames.

"In case you were unaware," Lea whispered, leaning in, "my family is quite fond of gold." She nudged Freya with her elbow. "But at least your outfit matches."

Freya smiled, then schooled her features entirely when her father gave them a chastising look.

Four people approached, Lea and Lazarus' parents, Freya

assumed. A dark-featured male with a complexion that matched Lea's and a female with honey-gold skin took Lea's hands, a soft smile on her pretty face. Lea's mother had the same dark hair and soft expression as Queen Ordona, her older sister by several decades, but it was clear Lea had gotten most of her looks from her father.

"Mother," Lea said with a smile. She shifted her eyes to the male at her mother's side. "Father, I'd like you both to meet Freya Balthana."

Freya smiled. "Governor and Lady Calliwell, it's lovely to meet you."

"Orin, please." Two dimples flashed in the governor's cheeks when he smiled at her. "Byrric has told us so much about you."

Lady Calliwell took Freya's hands and squeezed. "It's wonderful to meet you, dear. Please, call me Perida."

"And these are Governor and Lady Cailen," Byrric said, holding a hand toward Lazarus' parents. His father, King Salazar's cousin, had the typical Harridan dark hair and dark eyes, with a jaw that looked to be carved in stone. His stature resembled that of Salazar—tall, lean, nearly catlike in the way he moved. His mother had the deep umber skin so common in the southern regions of Edhil, her ancestral homeland.

Governor Cailen gave Freya a terse nod. "Lady Balthana, a pleasure."

"Likewise," Freya said, noting the severe lack of warmth compared to Lea's parents. She smiled at Lady Cailen. "My lady."

Lazarus' mother smiled demurely. "It's wonderful to *finally* meet the Commander's daughter in the flesh." She shot Byrric a chastising look.

"Now, Alyndra, let's not start guilt-tripping the poor girl so soon," a soft voice spoke from behind.

Lady Cailen flinched, then turned to face the queen. "No one is guilt-tripping anyone, Ordona. I was simply stating a fact. Byrric has kept her sequestered for too long now."

Freya watched as the queen silenced her with a single look, then turned her gaze to Freya. Immediately, her face brightened and a smile curved her red lips.

"Freya," she said quietly, then opened her arms. "Come here, dear."

Grinning, Freya stepped into Ordona's embrace, eagerly accepting her warm hug. The familiar scent of roses and vanilla greeted her. She inhaled, then tightened her grip.

"My Queen," she said quietly, surprised when tears thickened her voice. When Ordona leaned back, leaving just her hands on Freya's shoulders, Freya saw her eyes were a bit red as well.

Ordona cupped Freya's cheek in her hand. "It's so very wonderful to have you back," she said. "Oh, it seems like just yesterday I was taking you children on walks through the gardens." She took Freya's hands and stepped back, taking her in. "You've managed to get the best of Byrric and Cina, haven't you?"

"I like to think so," Freya said as the queen released her hands.

Ordona dabbed her eyes with the back of her hand, then smiled at Lea, Laz, and Collin. "And you three... I hear you've been doing well helping Freya reacclimate to life here in Iladel."

"She's quite the shopping partner, as I'm sure your son has told you," Lea said.

Ordona arched a thin, dark brow as she took in Freya's outfit, made that much more opulent now that it was in a setting that complemented it so well. "Yes, Aerelius said he enjoyed helping you spend your father's money," she said with a wry smile.

"The boy's got good taste, at least," Byrric muttered.

"Indeed," Ordona said. "Come, Salazar is waiting in the library." She looped her arm through Freya's and patted her hand. "It really is lovely to have you back, darling."

Freya smiled up at her. "It's good to be back, Your Majesty."

When they entered the palace's library with its endless walls of tomes, thick drapes, and leather-and-velvet furniture, they found King Salazar standing by a window, a cigar in his hand, the golden ring he wore on his thumb gleaming in the sunlight. A tall, lithesome male, he had wavy dark hair that just brushed the shoulders of his gold-trimmed burgundy coat. He was a cat shifter—lynx, to be exact—and even in his non-shifted form, he moved with a silent, predatory grace that often set others at unease. Freya was surprised, as she took him in for the first time in six years, to see that the resemblance to his son had become more striking in her absence.

"Freya!" he boomed, stabbing out his cigar in a glass dish. He strode toward them, his shiny black boots silent on the marble floor. "The rogue student has finally arrived!"

"Oh, Salazar, let the girl be," Perida said, picking up a glass of wine that had been sitting on a small table. "She's here, isn't she?"

King Salazar gave his sister-in-law a flat look. "More than a week late."

Freya exchanged a glance with Byrric, who was sending her a look that simply said, "I told you so." She should've known not to expect him to come to her defense.

Freya felt her face flush, so she ducked her head as she curtsied for him. "Your Majesty, it's wonderful to see you. I apologize for my delayed arrival."

Salazar pointed a slender finger at Byrric. "If she were anyone but your daughter, I'd have her flogged in the city square for her disobedience."

"Now, Father, after the commander's display during Combat, I think she's been sufficiently chastised." Aerelius appeared at his father's side, a glass tumbler of amber liquor in his hand. He looked to be on the verge of laughter as he greeted her. "Lady Balthana."

Freya gave the prince a small nod. "Your Highness."

"So, who's hungry?" Lazarus said, dispelling the awkward silence that hung in the air. "I think we should eat."

"Excellent idea," Orin Calliwell replied, rubbing his hands together. "I'm quite famished, myself."

THE AMOUNT of food the palace's kitchen had provided would have fed half of Watoria, Freya thought, as servants brought out dish after fragrant dish. The dining table that had looked so vast when she arrived now seemed to buckle under the weight of the dishes laden with food from all over Lindoroth.

As much as Freya wanted to restrict herself to one plate, she allowed Lea to talk her into trying a bit of everything.

"Trust me, it will be worth the bellyache later," she whispered. "Kallan was quite smart when he made these outfits so flexible."

Freya smiled and put a hand on her stomach, suddenly thankful for the loose, flowing fabric of her dress.

"Are you enjoying the food, Freya?" Perida asked from Lea's other side.

"Oh, it's fantastic," Freya gushed. "It's been a long time since I've had a meal like this." She looked down the table to Ordona, who sat at the end opposite her husband. "Do you still employ the same kitchen staff?"

Ordona smiled knowingly. "We do, so if you're planning on sneaking to the kitchens for treats, you'll find yourself in luck. Maghda has already been informed of your return."

Freya laughed at the mention of the cantankerous witch who'd been ruling the kitchens on the lower level of the palace for more than a century. "I couldn't possibly fit any more." She set her napkin beside her plate and glanced at the clock above the mantel, hoping the king and queen would dismiss them so she could get up and walk off some of what she'd eaten.

"Now, Salazar, did I hear correctly that a Jotunn was spotted in Iladel last week?" Rischa Cailen asked, dashing her hopes.

Freya didn't miss the odd look the queen gave her husband.

"Yes, an emissary for Empress Lessia paid a visit to discuss a potential trade agreement," Salazar replied, stuffing a bit of bread in his mouth. He chewed and swallowed, then continued. "He'll be returning in two weeks for further discussion."

"How are relations with Jotunheim?" Orin asked. "One of my border scouts has reported a bit of skirmishing in the northwestern region of Caelora. Lessia up to her old tricks again?"

"The lower creatures of Jotunheim continue to test our patience in some areas due to their own internal squabbles that tend to spill into our lands," Salazar said. He dabbed at his chin with a white napkin and looked at Freya. "Draugs and the like. Freya here has had to take down more than one of them, hasn't she?"

"I have," she said with a nod. "They like to slip in through the waterways."

"*That's* what they had you doing in Watoria?" Alyndra stared at her, aghast. "Salazar, *really.*"

Freya exchanged a look with Aer, who appeared to be holding back a grin.

"Waste of good talent not to use her, isn't it?" Orin said. "If Lessia insists on allowing them through, using our best assets to dispatch them should be a given."

"Precisely," Salazar said, sending Alyndra a sharp look. "Byrric and Cina didn't train her up to sit around and do nothing, after all."

"I'm certain the marshals were quite fortunate to have her," Rischa Cailen said.

"And she, them," Byrric added, spearing another slice of roasted beef.

I'm right here, she wanted to say.

"Indeed," Salazar murmured before turning back to the governor. "Despite that, Caelora, as always, has done well maintaining the security of our lands."

Laz's father gave a small nod. "Your confidence in my border security means more than you know."

"Is there anything you have need of from us?" Ordona asked.

"No, Your Majesty, although the offer is much appreciated."

"Why the sudden interest in trade, anyway?" Orin asked.

"There's always been interest," Salazar replied. "Every now and then, Lessia pushes a bit harder, tries to approach from a different angle, but until she manages to control the dregs of her lands, they'll have to make do with the agreements already in place."

"You don't want to increase trade with them?" Freya asked curiously. Jotunheim was well-known for their stone and metalwork, and their leather was second only to that of Allanor.

"They're hoping to use us to further their trade relations with the humans," Rischa explained as he dished up a second helping of steamed carrots. "Now that new rulers have arisen in Dystone, Empress Lessia hopes to get her claws in."

"Perhaps becoming less of a tyrant would make other nations more open to working with her, as well," Orin muttered, taking a swig of wine. "She treats her citizens like chattel. It's no wonder—"

"I think it's time for a subject change," the queen cut in. "Freya, dear, how do you like Aldridge so far?" Leaning forward a bit in her seat, she smiled at Lea, Aerelius, Laz, and Collin. "I'm quite thrilled you all have become such good friends."

Freya smiled and set down her fork. "It's wonderful. I can't thank you and King Salazar enough for allowing me to attend."

Salazar laughed, seamlessly shifting with the change in conversation. "Your kind of skills should be honed, not wasted!"

"Oh, you should have seen her in Combat on our first day," Aerelius said, taking a small sip of mead, his eyes dancing as he caught her gaze over the rim of the glass. "She was quite vicious."

Freya sent him a sweet smile. "I was simply doing as Officer Ristheld instructed."

Salazar let out a hum of amusement. "Indeed. Byrric told me you two put on quite a show. I suppose that will teach you not to underestimate your opponents, Aerelius."

"And, if I'm not mistaken, you were the one who wanted to use our full powers," Freya said, sending the prince a bright smile. "Now next time you challenge me, you won't be caught off guard."

"By things like venomous feathers at my throat?" Aer said dryly. "You could've killed me, you know."

"It wasn't a venomous feather. I'm not a complete fool." Freya dared a look at the monarchs to see how they were reacting. Ordona appeared curious, where Salazar appeared amused.

Byrric cleared his throat and sent her a sharp look.

"Oh, did Freya tell you we both found dresses for the ball?" Lea exclaimed. "We're going to look *so* lovely!"

Bless her, Freya thought. Lea's ability to divert a conversation on the spot was coming in quite handy.

"That's wonderful, girls!" Lady Calliwell said.

Lazarus groaned. "Gods above, if I have to hear about these dresses one more time..."

"And you two?" Lady Cailen asked, shifting her attention to Lazarus and Collin.

"Lazarus and I both had fittings with our shoppers last week," Collin assured her with a smile. "You've got nothing to worry about, my lady."

Lazarus' mother gave him a grateful smile. "I don't know what we'd do without you, Collin."

"Perhaps teach our son to keep himself in line instead of relying on others?" Lazarus' father grumbled.

"Shush, Rischa," Lady Cailen hissed.

Queen Ordona looked at them all fondly. "Well I think it's wonderful that the children have all grown so fond of one another. Now, let's say we have some dessert?"

15

After a dessert of chocolate mousse topped with fresh lindberries and cream, Queen Ordona insisted Freya, Lea, Lazarus, Collin, and Aerelius spend some quality time together while their parents retired to the drawing room.

"They always do this," Collin said as they made their way down the hall toward the gardens. "Shuffle us off so they can drink the night away without 'setting a bad example for *the children*.'"

"I'm sure one of these days our parents will realize we're not actually children anymore," Lea replied. She elbowed Aerelius, who was walking beside her. "Except Aer, of course. He'll never grow up."

"I believe you're referring to your other, far less handsome cousin," he said with a smirk.

Freya laughed. "Does that mean you're *not* still braiding dead snakes into girls' hair?"

Lea looked up at him in horror. "You didn't!"

Aer shrugged. "We were barely seven. And while tempting, I set that pastime aside long ago."

"Was this in your 'boys tease girls because they like them' phase?" Lazarus asked. He took a swig from the bottle of mead he'd swiped from the dinner table before they left. "That lasted quite some time, if I recall."

Aer danced his fingers along Freya's shoulder. "Who says it ended?"

Freya rolled her eyes and swatted his hand away. "Idiot," she muttered.

The five of them came to a wide stone archway that opened onto a path that wound through the largest of the castle's gardens. The area was carpeted with soft grass and stone beds bursting with flowers, with lush greenery dotted all around. Night-blooming varieties had opened their petals wide, soaking in the moonlight as pixies fluttered about sucking nectar from the sweeter blooms.

"Oh, it looks just as I remember!" Freya exclaimed, smiling at Lea. "There's a fountain just beyond those hedges, correct? Down the path?"

Lea tucked her arm through Freya's. "Yes, let's go see if the cinderfish have started nipping at the pixies yet."

The two of them led the group past a tall row of hedges and down a path that cut through a small grove of red-leafed jewel fruit trees before coming upon the fountain that Freya had loved to play around as a girl. Great care had been taken to carve fish, aquatic plants, ships, and merfolk into the stone. Pixies lounged about on the green lily pads that floated on the surface of the mirror-like water, their voices quiet and melodic as they conversed with one another. Every now and then a wide-mouthed cinderfish would poke its head above water, only to be slapped down by one of its would-be prey.

"You'd think they'd find a better place to congregate," Collin muttered as they made their way toward a covered pergola outfitted with wrought iron furniture with cushions the color of spring leaves. He took a seat on a wide, coral-hued couch. "Eventually one is bound to get caught."

Lazarus sat down, stretching his legs along the length of the couch and leaning back against Collin, resting his head on his shoulder. Lea sat down in a wide chair beside them, leaving Freya and the prince to claim the remaining sofa.

"They do," Aerelius replied, taking a pull from his own bottle. "At least twice a week, we find a dead fish or two out here." He offered the bottle to Freya, who took it.

Freya took a long sip of mead, considering. "Why not just find new fish? I hear pixies get along famously with dawnfish."

Aerelius gestured toward the end of the pool where gentle streams of water flowed from the hands of three stone mermaids. "There's a small channel that flows from this pool into the next, and that one is connected to the lake. The cinderfish come in through there."

Freya smiled at the gently rippling water and took another sip of mead before handing the bottle back to the prince. "Everyone gets their secret passages then, don't they?"

"Speaking of..." Lea turned in her seat, her face eager as she looked at Freya. "I still want to see the tunnel system in the palace."

"Why am I not the one you're asking?" Aerelius said. "I do live here, after all."

"Yes, but I trust Freya not to scare me into a heart attack while we're in there." Lea arched a pointed brow at her cousin. "You wouldn't last five minutes."

"She's not wrong," Lazarus said, sending Aerelius an apologetic look.

The prince huffed in annoyance. "Freya doesn't know all of the passageways."

"I don't?" Freya sent him a questioning look.

"In your absence, Lady Balthana, I continued our exciting pastime and found a number of other passageways and chambers." He sipped, smiling smugly. "So, no, you don't."

Freya clenched her teeth at his tone, a bit annoyed at the hurt she felt at his words. Yes, hunting for new passageways had been *their* thing. Freya and Aerelius had been left to their own devices quite often as children, and as their friendship grew, so did their determination to find all of the castle's secrets, knowing how valuable they could be. For the last two summers Freya spent in Iladel, they walked the halls and grounds on the hunt for concealed openings and hidden staircases, some days finding as many as three or four passages or chambers they hadn't known existed, other times, finding none for days on end.

"Well, it's a shame my father insisted I remain in Watoria all this time," she said, accepting the bottle back from Aer.

"Insisted?" Aerelius laughed. "From what I hear, you quite enjoyed your life there. Working for the marshals, correct?" He shook his head. "That's a bit beneath your station, don't you think?"

Lea threw the cork from her bottle at him. "You shut your mouth Aerelius Harridan! That's noble work and you know it!"

Freya sent him a challenging look. "Why, pray tell, would helping keep my city safe be considered beneath me?"

Aerelius held her stare for several tense moments. "Considering your obligations here in Iladel, I would have expected a less hazardous occupation."

Lazarus scoffed. "That sounds to me like you're questioning the commander's judgement, cousin. He's the one who allowed her to do it, after all."

"With the king's permission, I might add," Freya said.

Aerelius sent Laz a sharp look. "The king offered her an invitation to Aldridge when she was just a child and agreements were made to send her. Living anywhere but Iladel was a foolish choice."

"I'll be sure to let my father know how highly you think of his decision-making skills," Freya said dryly. "And please stop talking about me as though I'm not right beside you."

"Children, let's not fight," Collin murmured. He'd leaned his head back against the couch and was staring up at the night sky. "It's such a lovely evening."

"Agreed," Lea said with a nod. "We're all here now, so we should focus on moving forward. And besides, it's not like any of us were raised here," she added. "Lazarus, Collin, and I weren't required to move when we received our invitations, and we were just a few years older than Freya was when we got them."

"Your circumstances were a bit different, wouldn't you agree?" Aerelius replied.

"There's nothing to be done for it now, anyway," Freya told him, turning to avoid the stare that felt like it was singeing her skin. "So please, just drop it."

She didn't like to admit that, despite her father allowing her to grow on her own and become her own person before shuffling her back to the capital, she *did* feel a bit lost at times. The students at Aldridge were what she expected, but also different. Even though she'd never been terribly close with her fellow students in Watoria, she'd grown used to the supportiveness of those who she'd gone through primary and secondary school with. The same comfort from that supportiveness seemed to be lacking in large quantities here. Lea, Lazarus, and Collin were proving to be wonderful friends, and she knew she and Aerelius would get back to where they'd been sooner or later. Yet the sense of camaraderie she'd been hoping to find among the rest of the student body simply didn't exist.

She slid a glance at her old friend, trying not to make it obvious that she shared a bit of the hurt he was feeling. With as close as they'd been and as much as they'd shared, being separated from him had been difficult, despite the friendships she, and she assumed he as well, had formed in the interim. Each summer and at every winter solstice, they'd been inseparable, a fact both of their parents were both thankful for and wary of, considering their minds tended to travel along the same mischievous channels at times.

"Sil for your thoughts?" he said quietly when he noticed her staring.

She gave him a tight smile. "I'm just... happy to be back, is all."

His expression softened a little, leaving behind only a hint of his normal mirth. "Well, threats of physical harm aside, it's nice to have you back." He nudged her chin with his knuckle, then held his hand out in question, forcing her lips to curve into a smile. "I've missed you, Valkyrie."

Something loosened in her chest at his words, a tightness she hadn't realized had been lingering there since she'd first arrived at Aldridge, making room for the warmth his words brought on. With a smile, she took his hand and let him lace their fingers together. "I suppose I've missed you too, highness."

16

The start of Freya's second week at Aldridge was wildly different than her first. Once the initial surprise of her identity had waned, students began to approach her more, initiating contact instead of whispering and staring from afar. Lords and Ladies from all over Lindoroth slowly began to warm up to her, some going so far as to invite her to join them for meals. Some appeared intent on befriending her due to her connections to the palace, but fortunately, those seemed to be fewer than Lea had first insinuated. While she hadn't accepted any of the invitations to join others for meals, she'd made it a point to ensure she sparred with others outside of her own group or make small talk with her fellow classmates in class.

"Lady Balthana!"

Freya spun at the sound of a male voice calling to her from down the hall. She'd just left Civics and had split off from Laz moments ago for her literature course. Frowning, she stopped and waited for the owner of the voice to appear, then smiled when she saw Lord Jarrison, one of Florian's unsuspecting victims from her first day.

"Lord Jarrison! How are you?"

"Gareth, please," he said with a quick grin. "Lord Jarrison is my father. May I walk you to your next class?"

"Oh!" She glanced around the crowded hall, then nodded. "Of course. I'm heading to Literature next. You?"

"History, but it's along the way." He held out a hand for her to proceed. "So, tell me. How are you enjoying Aldridge? It must be a change from Watoria, no?"

"Quite," Freya said. "It's certainly different than what I'm used to, but I'm enjoying myself so far. You?"

"I miss my home in Caelora, of course, but the warmer weather of the capital certainly agrees with me," he said with a laugh. "It's much quieter here than what I'm accustomed to."

Freya grinned. "The silence has been quite a change, I'll agree. Did you live in Caelora's capital?"

"No, Kildin was about two days' ride from my home. My family is from Greyonne, a mining town toward the north."

"Your family were miners, then?"

"My family owns a steel mill there." His smile was proud, but not arrogant. "We produce nearly half of the steel in Caelora."

Grinning, she gestured toward her steel-tipped leather boots. "I suppose I have your family to thank for my boots, then?"

He laughed. "Yes, we've got partnerships with some of the best leatherworkers in Allanor. My uncle married a leatherworker from Watoria and..." he pointed toward her ankle. "I believe that's her maker's mark just there by the heel."

"Well, please tell your uncle and his wife that these boots have gotten me out of more than one bad predicament in recent months."

He grinned. "I'll do that, my lady."

"So, have you given any thought to what you might focus your studies on next year?" she asked as they turned down the hall toward her literature class.

He shrugged. "Economics, most likely. Family expectations and all that." He smiled at her. "I'm sure you can understand what that's like."

She laughed. "More than you know."

They exchanged small talk for the rest of the short walk to Freya's literature class, then paused outside. Freya cocked a brow when Gareth's face flushed a bit.

"I was wondering... will you be attending the ball this weekend?" he asked.

Her heart clenched a bit at his question. "I am. You?"

"Yes, with a few friends." He scratched his head nervously. "I'm assuming you'll be going with Lea, Lazarus, and Collin, but the rest of us have planned a small gathering for when we return. Would you—"

"Ah, my lady Valkyrie!"

Freya closed her eyes and huffed in annoyance at the sound of Aerelius' voice.

"I'm so sorry about this, Gareth." Pasting on a smile, she turned to face the prince, who was being shadowed closely by his two hulking guards. "Yes?"

"I seem to have lost my way," Aerelius said with feigned confusion. "Would you mind showing me how to get to my Toxins class?"

"We can speak later," Gareth murmured, touching Freya on her arm. He gave Aerelius a nod. "Your Highness."

She sent him a wave, then faced the prince. "Really, Aer? You've gotten lost?"

Aerelius shrugged, then rested his shoulder against the wall and gave her an easy grin. "I saved you from a great deal of annoyance." He lifted a brow. "So, will you be walking me to class, or will I be left to fend for myself in these wretched halls?"

Freya laughed and patted his cheek. "No, my prince, I will not."

Without another word, she brushed past him and into her classroom, where Collin was waiting in the back row. When she approached, he grinned.

"Fighting off the males already, Freya?"

Freya rolled her eyes and sat down, dropping her bag to the floor beside her. "I wouldn't go that far."

He laughed. "I'd expect a few more of the likes of Gareth Jarrison to come sniffing about now that you've been deemed approachable."

"Deemed approachable? You make it sound as though I'm some enigma. I'm no different than the rest of you."

"That's not true, and you know it." Collin lowered his voice as Professor Viridian walked in. "You're rare, you're beautiful, and you smell good. That kind of thing—" he inclined his head toward the door "—is going to keep happening, Freya."

Jaw clenched, Freya faced the front, her expression stony. "I'm just here to learn, Collin. To get to know people," she murmured, then forced a smile. "Thank you, though, for the compliments. It's nice hearing that from someone who isn't trying to stake some sort of claim." She frowned. "Although it is a bit odd to hear you say I smell good."

He grinned and tapped his nose. "Wolf, remember? And I wouldn't say any of it if it weren't true. Just make sure you let them down easy, otherwise you'll end up with a load of aggravation."

"Entitled fools," she muttered, although, even as she said it, she realized she didn't think it was true of Gareth. "It makes you wonder if some of them have ever been told no in their lives."

"Unlikely," Collin agreed as he looked around the room at their classmates. "A fair few assume their name alone will open every door for them, and rightly so, in some cases." He nodded toward a small group at the front of the room, where two high-born females were chatting with two working-class males. Freya recognized the females as Myria's followers from their encounter at lunch. "There, for example. Ladies Leston and Morcin. I went to school with them in Caelora, and they are the epitome of entitled. In exchange for completing assignments and running their errands, they both allowed members of the lower strata to associate with them." He gave Freya a flat look. "They use those students they deem beneath them to do any kind of work that requires the least bit of effort, all so they can focus their attention on socializing, climbing the right ladders. When they're told no, they do all they can to ensure that person is ostracized so badly they'll never recover."

"And the students they use? Do they simply discard them?"

He nodded. "Once they're no longer of use, they're cast to the side, social pariahs."

"I just can't fathom being so vicious," Freya said quietly. "The students I went to school with in Watoria were always so supportive. There was never so much competition for the opposite sex or anything, really. I just assumed it was normal."

"It's a different world out here," Collin replied. "It can be hard to get used to. But your ignorance is your own sort of privilege, Freya, in both good ways and bad."

She eyed him curiously. "How so?"

"You haven't had the chance to view much of the world outside of your place in Watoria," he explained. "Here, you'll be forced to change the way you see things, but you'll be able to use your knowledge of the lower classes to better your position."

She sighed and stared down at her desk. "I suppose you're right. I hadn't really thought of it that way." She ran a hand through her hair in annoyance. "I wish my father hadn't sent me away."

"I wouldn't be too upset with him. Yes, you might've been a bit blinded when you arrived, but now that you know what you *don't* know, you'll be alright."

She frowned, not quite convinced.

"Really, Freya. Byrric knew better than to throw you to the wolves, and he wouldn't have sent you to live in Watoria without good reason. It gave you knowledge the rest of us simply don't have. It makes you better than those other girls without even trying, and not just because you can kick all their asses ten times over," he added with a grin. "Your future will be better for it, trust me."

Freya laughed and flushed at the compliment. "Thank you, Collin. That means a lot to me. Truly."

Smiling, he patted her on the shoulder. "Like I said, I wouldn't say it if it weren't true."

17

The following day was the Commencement Ball for the students of Aldridge, a much-anticipated event that was meant to help students kick off the new academic year on a high note. The annual tradition hosted by the palace provided a fun atmosphere for students to get to know one another outside of classes and away from the pressures of school. It was also the first official gathering of the year where many students, both male and female, would truly start sizing up any competition they might have when it came to finding a mate. Many of the females, Freya knew, would bat their eyes as males strutted around them like peacocks in a silly dance that said little about the individual and much about their aspirations.

Lea arranged for Kallan to come to her and Freya's dormitory for their final dress fitting after breakfast, so after they left the dining hall on Saturday morning, the two rushed back to their room, eager to see his final creations.

"It's funny, you know," Lea said as they hurried across campus. "When we met, you didn't strike me as the type to be excited about ball gowns. Quite the opposite, actually. I thought I might have to wrestle you into a gown, to be honest."

Freya sent her a shocked look. "Just because I enjoy the occasional messy slaughter doesn't make me an animal." She sent a wave toward the group of students who were congregated in the small common room before starting up the stairs, eager to see Kallan's final creation. "I also enjoy a custom ball gown just as much as you."

"Ah, at last!" Kallan exclaimed when they walked in. He spread out his arms, showing them the boutique he'd turned their room into. Freya grinned when she saw Rini and Tyna hovering in mid-air beside him.

Lea clapped her hands excitedly. "Oh, this is so exciting! I haven't been to a ball in so long!"

"Don't be so dramatic, Lea," Aer spoke from behind them as all three males appeared in the doorway. "You made it to my nameday celebration four months ago."

"Ugh!" Lea groaned. "Go away, all of you!"

Freya scowled at the prince. "You'll see our dresses tonight, highness."

Aerelius went inside and sat down on her bed, reclining back against the headboard and crossing his legs at the ankles. His eyes crinkled at her annoyance. "Laz and Collin informed me they were coming here, and as the crown prince, I thought my input might be worthwhile, as well."

"And we've heard enough about these dresses that we found it imperative we offer our opinions," Lazarus said, grinning cheekily at Freya.

"Apologies, Kallan," Collin said, sitting down on the floor against Lea's bed. "I tried to convince them otherwise."

The dressmaker let out a suffering sigh. "Very well." He held a hand toward Lea. "Lady Calliwell?"

"Isn't there a tradition against this?" Lea whined. "No one can see a lady's dress before the event?"

"That's in regards to weddings only," Aerelius said. "Noble effort, though."

She sent him a withering look. "Fine." She looked at Kallan. "Some privacy?"

Kallan sent an exasperated look at the three males, then waved his hand, creating a shimmering curtain that separated the dressing stand from the rest of the room. With one last haughty look toward her cousins and Collin, Lea stepped behind the curtain so she could undress.

"You three are insufferable," Freya grumbled.

"I thought you wanted our opinions?" Laz exclaimed.

"No, we merely suggested that, in your opinion, our gowns would be perfect."

"Semantics," he said with a wave of his hand. "And Aer has already seen yours, so it's only fair that those of us whom you actually like get to see, too."

"Freya likes me, don't you?" Aerelius said with a sly grin.

"That depends," she said airily, folding her arms as she waited for Lea to reappear.

"On?"

"Are you playing pranks or showing me the new secrets you've discovered in the castle?"

"I've long outgrown my prank-playing phase," he replied. "So I suppose the latter."

Freya pretended to ponder his response for a moment before replying. "Then I suppose I find you tolerable." She walked over to the bed and shoved his feet over the edge, nearly causing him to tumble to the floor. "As soon as you get your filthy boots off my quilt, that is."

Collin laughed and Laz snorted. "You two are a match made in the heavens, aren't you?" Laz said.

Aer laid a hand over his chest and smiled. "If only Freya would see it that way."

Freya rolled her eyes. "Lea, hurry up!"

"Coming!"

A moment later, Kallan appeared, then waved his hand to dissolve the curtain.

"Oh, Lea!" Freya sighed. "You look perfect!"

"So very lovely, my lady," Tyna gushed. Rini nodded in agreement.

Lea gave a small curtsy, setting the beads that were scattered across her dress dancing. Kallan had paired it with delicate beaded slippers that matched the beadwork on her bodice perfectly. "It *is* lovely, isn't it?"

"Come on, give us a spin," Collin said, making a twirling motion with his finger.

Lea obeyed, and Freya's grin mirrored hers as the layers of her turquoise skirts spun out around her.

"Lady Balthana?" Kallan said, stepping aside so Lea could step down. "Your turn."

With one last look at the three males, Freya stepped onto the dressing pedestal and waited as Kallan replaced the curtain. When he had, she stripped down to her undergarments.

"Now this should fit just about right," he told her, pulling her gauzy dress from its hanger. "I may need to adjust the length a bit, but we'll see. I allowed enough space in the back for your wings, should you need to let them out."

Freya braced a hand against the wall as she stepped gingerly into the dress, then held her arms above her head as Kallan hooked the buttons that ran from her tailbone to the bottom of her rib cage, just below where the base of her wings would be. Once they were fastened, she turned and faced the mirror he'd set beside the window. Grinning, she bounced a little on her toes.

"It's perfect," she whispered excitedly.

It was as though Kallan had spun a sunset from fabric and gems and fitted it perfectly to her body. Already, she could imagine herself dancing alongside her friends, her skirts fluttering out like petals, the gemstones sprinkling across the fabric shimmering in the castle lights.

The dressmaker spent the next few minutes adjusting the skirts, altering the lengths of the layers to give it a slightly fuller appearance, and her, a curvier silhouette. When he was done, he stepped back and gave her a once over, then nodded.

"Yes, that will do. Have you given any thought to how you might wear your hair?"

Freya shook her head, unable to pull her gaze away from the glittering gown. "I thought I would leave that to Rini's discretion."

"Wise choice," he agreed with a nod. He held up a pair of pale pink satin slippers. "I thought these would complement the warmer shades in your dress nicely, and they won't pinch."

Freya held out one foot, then the other as Kallan slipped them on.

"Freya!" Lazarus called. "Some of us would like to eat lunch sometime today!"

Kallan shook his head in amusement as he adjusted a few measurements. "Done!" He took a step back, then pulled aside the curtain.

"It's a bit loose," Aerelius said, narrowing his eyes when he saw her. He waved his hand over his chest. "I think it needs to be a bit tighter in this area."

Freya scowled at him. "You're a pig, Aer."

"I'm joking! You look beautiful, Freya," he said, his voice full of sincerity. "The emeralds truly bring out your eyes."

"Yes, Kallan has worked his magic well," Lazarus said. "You both look lovely."

Collin stood. "Let's let these two finish getting ready. We'll have someone bring you lunch shortly."

"Thank you," Freya said. "That's much appreciated."

"Now shoo!" Lea said, laughing. "All of you, go!"

"We're leaving!" Lazarus exclaimed. "We'll see you tonight."

After they left, Freya and Lea spent the next several hours getting fussed over by Rini and Tyna. Since Freya had chosen to ignore the prince's suggestion to wear her hair up, Rini spent nearly two hours setting gentle curls that flowed down her back, making sure each had a mix of pink and brown. When she was done, she spent another hour separating out a handful of the pink strands to create an elaborate fuchsia circlet atop her head that she wove through with strands of gold, dripping with emeralds and rose stones.

When the pixie fluttered back to examine the final product, she sighed and clasped her tiny hands in front of her. "Oh, my Lady, you look like a dream," she cooed. "And I'm not just saying that because of all the work I did."

Freya laughed, then leaned toward the mirror to get a closer look at the intricate braids and beadwork Rini had pulled off.

"Well, I think we look positively gorgeous," Lea said, smoothing a hand across the sleek twist that hung over her shoulder. She grinned at Freya. "I have a feeling we'll both be paired off by the end of the night. How about you?"

Freya laughed. "On the hunt for a mate already? The year's barely started!"

"It's never too early," Lea said. "Unlike those lucky ones who get betrothed when they're still toddling about, *some* of us have to find a mate the old-fashioned way."

"I believe betrothals *are* the old-fashioned way," Freya pointed out.

"True." Lea leaned forward and dabbed the corner of her mouth with the tip of her pinky, wiping away a small smudge of lip rouge. There was a sharp rap at the door.

"Oh, that must be transport!" Lea said as she began frantically looking around for her clutch. Picking up her own, Freya opened the door and revealed Rissen on the other side.

"My ladies," he said with a bow. "Your transport awaits."

Freya turned toward Rini and Tyna, who were hovering in the air beside the door.

"Thank you both," she said.

Rini smiled and gave a small nod. "It's our pleasure, my lady. If there's anything else you need, we'll be at the palace with our sisters."

In a quick flash of light, the two pixies vanished.

Lea smiled at Rissen. "Lead the way, sir."

18

The monarchs had chosen the palace's outdoor ballroom, a vast space on the roof of the main ballroom, for this year's gala. The tri-colored parquet floor was bordered with marble trellises dripping with lilac, their perfume floating pleasantly across the space. Softly glowing pixie lights dotted the air above the dance floor, and harpists were stationed at each corner, their lovely music wafting through the crowd. Long tables, set for fifty guests each, ran along the outside of the trellises, their gleaming gold settings shining in the last dregs of sunlight. A row of pale beige columns wrapped in deep green ivy separated the dining area from the dance floor. The evening air was balmy, the nighttime mountain chill no doubt held at bay by some spell.

Freya sighed in contentment as she and Lea stepped off the curved staircase that rose up from inside the palace to the roof.

"I don't remember it being so beautiful," she murmured. "Aer and I used to play up here as children, but it's so much more colorful, more... shiny than I remember. Have you noticed that everything here is shiny?"

"It's one of the prettiest places in all the land, especially when they do it up like they have." Lea smiled softly and looked around.

"Oh! There are Laz and Collin." She took Freya's hand and led her toward the table where the two males were talking with a few of their classmates. Freya recognized Gareth as one, but the other two were unfamiliar.

"Lady Balthana, Lady Calliwell!" Gareth and the others stood as they approached. "Will you be joining us this evening?"

"Of course they will!" Lazarus said, squeezing Lea's shoulder. "Freya, these are Lords Derron Wailend and Aldric Helburn, and I believe you know Gareth. The four of us grew up together in Caelora."

"It's lovely to meet you both," Freya said with a smile before turning her attention to Lazarus and Collin. As with dinner the week before, Lazarus and Collin had taken care to coordinate their outfits. Collin wore a thigh-length black brocade jacket over a cream-colored vest made of crushed velvet, and a gray tunic over slim-fitting black pants and soft leather boots. Laz wore a cravat and vest in a matching shade of gray, topped with a jacket made of unbleached silk. His pants were black, and the black boots he wore had about a dozen silver buckles each.

She beamed at them. "You two look even more dashing than you did last week! I'm quite impressed."

"Why, thank you, Freya," Collin said. "Likewise."

She was about to turn and make small talk with one of the males at Laz's side, but all three who were facing her stiffened at the sight of something over her shoulder. She'd hardly turned her head to see what had caused such a reaction when she heard her father's voice.

"Freya, Lea, Lazarus, Collin. You're to join me at the front."

Freya tensed at his commanding tone. "If it's all the same to you, Commander—"

"It's not," he said abruptly. "Come."

Freya exchanged a confused look with the others, then forced her shoulders back as they left Laz's friends behind and followed Byrric toward a small table at the front set for what Freya had always called "secondary royals." They were the ones who were related to the ruling monarchs, like Lea and Lazarus, or were closely associated, like herself, Byrric, and Collin.

Guards stationed near the royals' tables stepped forward at their approach and pulled out chairs for Freya and Lea. The table for the monarchs was still empty, awaiting the royal family that had yet to be announced.

"Let's hope they don't take too long," Lazarus grumbled. "I'm starving."

Collin sent him a silencing look and he mimed zipping his lips.

Her father remained standing, and Freya eyed him suspiciously. He had donned his dress uniform tonight, a far cry from his normal garb. The black material was smoother, less sturdy than what he'd wear in the field. The fastenings gleamed, the red epaulettes giving his broad shoulders an even stiffer appearance.

And his expression...

"Did the laundress starch your uniform too much, Commander?" she wondered aloud. "You're far more tightly wound than normal."

Ignoring her jab, he clasped his hands behind his back and inclined his head in the direction of the entrance. "Your monarchs approach."

Just then, the music stopped and one of the king's guard appeared at the top of the stairwell.

"Please stand for the royal family!" he called.

Everyone who'd been scattered about the ballroom obeyed, scurrying off the main floor and forming a line along either side of the room.

"Finally," Lea murmured when the prince appeared, Queen Ordona on his arm. All of the guests bowed or curtsied as they walked slowly toward the table at the front of the room. Both offered their guests small smiles as they walked, taking time to acknowledge those who were paying them deference. When the pair reached the ivory-and-gold-adorned table, Aerelius pulled out a chair for his mother in the center, then stood behind the seat beside her. A moment later, King Salazar appeared, his eyes locked forward, not sparing a glance for his guests as he strode toward the table. When he chose his spot beside Ordona, he faced the room and stood quietly for a few moments. Then, with a nod, he called "Rise!"

"Welcome, all, to our annual Commencement Ball," Ordona called, her smile soft and graceful. "We hope this night finds you well and that you are just as eager as we are to see where this first term brings you. Dinner will be served shortly, but until then, please, enjoy the company of your friends."

"Shall we dance?" Lea asked as the harpists resumed playing a song with an upbeat tempo that beckoned guests to the dance floor.

Freya smiled and took Lea's outstretched hand. "I'd love to work up an appetite." She quirked a brow at her father, already annoyed with his gruff attitude tonight. "Unless that's a problem, Commander?"

"Don't go far," he ordered, his eyes scanning over the crowd.

She narrowed her eyes. "Why?"

He gave her an exasperated look. "Because I said so."

She huffed. Grinning, she tugged Lea out onto the dance floor. For the next hour, the two danced with Lazarus, Collin, and several of their friends from school, Freya smiling so much she felt her cheeks might burst as she let Lazarus twirl her around the dance floor, showing off his flawless skills as she struggled to recall her own steps.

"It's been some time!" she said with a laugh. "My lessons stopped when I left the capital."

Laz laughed. "It's quite alright," he replied. He leaned in to whisper. "I see quite a few males eyeing us right now, so I suppose it's good I don't mind my toes getting trampled."

She bit her lip and tossed a glance over her shoulder, where Gareth and Derron were standing, whispering to one another. Looking back at Lazarus, she smiled.

"While they *are* quite handsome, I think you're quite right."

He grinned, then took her hand and twirled her so quickly she thought she felt her head spin. When he pulled her back toward him, he gave her an apologetic look.

"It appears I'll be handing you off, after all."

Before she could respond, she felt strong hands take her waist and turn her toward her new partner.

"You look lovely tonight, Valkyrie," Prince Aerelius murmured, giving her a crooked smile as he fit her hand in his. "Thank you for saving me a dance."

"I don't recall promising that, actually," she said, resting her hand gently on his shoulder, then sent a dubious look toward his outfit. His doublet was a dusty shade of peach, with gold embroidery wound throughout, the fastenings set with glittering emeralds.

She gave him an exasperated look. "That's quite an outfit, Highness."

"As your dance partner for the evening, I thought it prudent we complement one another," he said, his eyes dancing with mirth.

"For the evening?" Freya eyed him suspiciously. "What have you got up that sleeve of yours? Why do I feel you and Byrric are up to something?"

"Oh, come, Freya! Don't you recall our lessons? We made wonderful partners!"

"We were eight when our parents forced that wretched instructor on us, and if I recall, you delighted in stepping on my toes," Freya said. "I'm sure you've had far better partners since."

"Nonsense! Admit it," he whispered, leaning closer. "You missed dancing with me."

She sighed and looked around the room, then tried not to be annoyed as she saw some of the looks she and the prince were receiving from other partygoers. Disdain seemed to drip from the pores of females who quite likely wondered why Prince Aerelius would waste his time on a Valkyrie who would almost certainly be sent into the field with her father once her time at Aldridge was done.

A bunch of damned fools, all of them.

Smiling, Freya looked up at the prince. "I suppose there are worse dance partners to have."

He slid his hand further around Freya's waist, pulling her closer, smiling when she didn't try to stop him. "You suppose? I saw how you were floundering with my dear cousin. He's not half as good at leading as he'll have you believe."

"He seemed to hold his own quite well," she replied, watching as Lazarus and Collin began their own spin around the dance floor, their steps more sure than hers had been when she and Laz had danced. Nearby, Lea laughed with Derron and Gareth just off the dance floor near the tables.

"You really do look lovely tonight," Aerelius said quietly after they'd danced for a few moments in silence. "Rini did a wonderful job."

"Are you saying I need magical creatures to look lovely, Highness?" she asked teasingly.

"Only that they seemed to understand the importance of your appearance this evening," he replied. "Now, if you'll excuse me, I've got a quick announcement to make."

Frowning, Freya opened her mouth to ask what he meant, then closed it when he deposited her on the edge of the dance floor with Byrric. She hadn't realized he'd been directing her toward the edge until her father took her by the elbow to steady her.

"Aer—"

The prince gave her a wicked grin, then moved to stand in front of the monarchs' table. Freya took a step forward to find her friends but was stopped when Byrric put a strong hand on her arm.

Freya looked up at her father, wide-eyed. "What's—"

"Attention, everyone!" Aer called. He made a silencing gesture toward the harpists, who immediately ceased their playing.

"What is he doing?" Freya hissed, looking at her father.

Byrric merely shook his head and put a finger to his lips.

Her eyes darted around the room, watching as the partygoers stopped what they were doing and turned to face their prince. A hand touched her elbow, and she jumped, then let out a breath of relief when she saw Lea, whose expression appeared concerned.

"Are you alright?" she asked.

Freya nodded absently, then scanned the crowd, her eyes stopping when she saw Myria on the opposite side of the room, shoulders back, a smug smile on her face. Two of her friends were standing behind her, whispering fervently to one another.

"Would you look at her?" Lea whispered in disgust. "When will she get it through her head that the prince will never choose her?"

Freya stared at her, stricken. "*That's* his announcement?"

"He couldn't have waited until after dinner?" Lazarus sighed, sending Freya an apologetic look. He folded his arms and leaned back against a pillar as Aerelius began speaking a few words of welcome before diving into his speech.

"Long ago, my parents informed me of what my future held," Aerelius said. "A crown, of course, but also obligations that were hard to understand at the tender age of five. Responsibilities that far surpassed the mental capacity for a child who'd barely learned to read." He paused, letting the crowd laugh before he continued. "As you all know, the day that I must take on those responsibilities is rapidly approaching. In just one year, my father will pass his crown to me and I will become your new king." He slid a look toward Freya, one filled with the promise of pure trouble.

Freya gasped as the other guests applauded loudly. She stared up at Byrric, whose gaze was trained on the king and queen. His hand tightened on her elbow. Salazar oozed annoyance, while Ordona looked a bit like she wanted to throttle her son.

Aer cleared his throat, then ran his eyes over the room, taking in his future subjects. "As you all know," he continued, silencing them once more, "many Lindorothians enter into their first year at Aldridge attempting to, among other things, find a mate." The corner of his lips pulled up in a crooked smile when whispers began to flutter through the crowd. "However, that will not be the case for me, as mine was found long ago. I thought tonight would be a fitting time to introduce her to the world."

Myria smoothed a hand over her hair as Freya's blood began to boil.

"Chin up, darling," Lea murmured.

"Is he drunk?" Freya hissed.

"Oh, most assuredly," Laz replied. "There's nothing for it now, though."

"Lords and Ladies, I would like to introduce my betrothed, your future queen and, most importantly, my oldest friend." He held a hand out. "Lady Freya Balthana."

"I told you we'd be paired off by the end of the night," Lea whispered, laughing.

"Go, Freya," Byrric ordered when Freya froze, finally releasing her elbow. "Now."

"You bastard!" she hissed at her father. "We were supposed to wait—"

"Smile," he snapped. "You've had plenty of time to prepare for this, now *go*."

Murmurs of surprise rippled through the crowd, and she felt a sharp jab in her back.

"Go!" Collin whispered urgently. "Be angry with him later!"

Freya took a deep breath and put on her brightest smile, then stepped forward, sending a quick look toward the queen. Ordona gave her a small, encouraging nod.

Then, she stepped forward and took the hand of her fiancé.

19

Freya's mind whirled as the prince took her hand, then bowed slightly and laid a small kiss to the back of her palm as applause erupted once again. Months. This announcement was to be made months from now, not on this night, not when she was only just returning to her life at court. She should've known Aer wouldn't keep quiet about their betrothal for long, but she thought the nine months between now at his nameday celebration was a more than easy task.

Clearly, she was mistaken.

Her face frozen in a wide smile, she put a hand to his cheek, drawing him up. As she met his eyes, she was surprised to find softness mixed with a teasing gleam.

"I may murder you on our wedding night," she said through clenched teeth, knowing she'd never be heard over the calls of 'Congratulations!' that rang out. "If not before."

Smiling, he put a hand on her hip and kissed her cheek, then brought his lips to her ear. "I'll be sure to make you fall madly in love with me long before then."

"Highly unlikely, after this stunt." She feigned an embarrassed giggle.

"A dance!" someone called.

"Shall we?" Aerelius asked, giving her an expectant look.

"You haven't given me much of a choice, have you?"

With a sigh, Freya allowed him to lead her onto the floor, then let him draw her arms around his neck as the harpist began to play a traditional engagement waltz. When his hands settled on her waist and they began to move slowly around the floor, Freya let a small, feline smile creep across her lips.

"That smile is a bit unnerving, my love," he said. "What do you have cooking in that lovely mind of yours?"

She slid her hand down his shoulder, across his muscular chest, and laid it above his sternum, atop the emerald buttons that matched the ones in her hair so perfectly.

"You had this planned all along, didn't you?"

He made a hum of acknowledgement. "And if I'd told you, you would've feigned illness and refused to come."

"You think so little of me." She held his gaze as she drummed her fingers lightly over his chest, waiting until she felt his heart pick up a beat before speaking. "Aer... do you know what's right here?" She tapped the center of his chest.

He laid his hand over hers and smiled. "My heart?"

"And your lungs." She trailed one finger down his sternum, letting it come to rest at the end, doing her best to make it look like a caress that dripped with affection. "And right here is a tiny bone, a little protuberance, if you will."

His hand tightened on her waist as a slow smile quirked his lips. "I won't like the rest of this explanation, will I?"

She spread her fingers, laying her palm flat, the heel against the small bone at the end of his sternum, and pressed. "If I hit hard enough, it would snap. Do you know what happens when that bone snaps, Aer?"

"No, but I'm sure it's *quite* gory," he whispered, his breath warm against her neck.

Freya slid her hand back around his neck and smiled. "If done just right, it would puncture your heart... your lung, if done correctly. It hurts quite a lot, from what I've witnessed."

She felt his lips curve against her ear as he spoke. "My guards would be on you in a heartbeat."

"I'd take to the skies before you even hit the floor," she whispered back, trailing her fingers along the back of his neck and giving his dark hair a tug. "You'd be bleeding out internally and I'd be miles away. I'd like you to remember that if you ever think to put me in a position like you did tonight again."

Infuriatingly, he chuckled, his breath soft against her hair as he tightened his hands around her. "You know, I don't think our parents could have chosen a better pairing, do you?"

This time, her smile was genuine. "You've got quite a twisted mind. Do you suppose I should let you try to woo me?"

"I'd have you with one kiss. Shall I prove it?"

"Possibly," she said thoughtfully. "If I wanted our first kiss in six years to be in front of two hundred onlookers."

"Shall we make a wager, then?"

"Who informed you of my fondness for bets, Highness?"

"Are you telling me you've outgrown that penchant since you were a girl?" He tapped his chin then pointed at her. "I believe you still owe me two sils for that time I spent an hour alone in the dungeon."

She laughed. "Alright, what's your wager?"

"I'd wager," he said slowly, "that you'll break before me."

"How so?"

He turned his head slightly so that his lips brushed against her temple. "Before our wedding day, I'd bet that you'll admit your love for me."

She snorted out a laugh. "You mean before you admit yours for me? Not a chance."

"Is it a bet, then?"

She sighed. "Are we back to this now? Making wagers for every small thing?"

"I would think undying love would be quite a large thing, but I suppose I see your point." He grinned down at her, his expression pure trouble. "What do you say, Valkyrie?"

She narrowed her eyes up at him, staring into his infuriatingly handsome face. "What do I get when I win?"

"A lifetime of servitude from your devoted husband?"

"I'll already have that."

"The love of a lifetime?"

She arched a brow.

He frowned, considering. "Whoever wins gets to choose the name of our firstborn."

At that, Freya threw her head back and laughed. "I'll take that bet."

"It's nice to know some things haven't changed," he said wistfully.

"Some things do," she said. "I'm sure *we* both have."

"True enough." He leaned back and smiled at her. "Do you know what I was thinking about just the other day? That time in the gardens when you let me kiss you for the first time." He slid a hand down her arm and curled his fingers through hers, then brought their joined hands up to rest on his chest. "I think I held your hand just like this, didn't I?"

She tilted her chin indignantly. "Hardly a peck on the lips, and I believe you got a bit of drool right here," she said, tapping her cheek with her pinkie. "Hopefully your skill has improved since then."

"You remember things quite differently than I." His thumb began to trace small circles on her lower back, and his eyes turned serious. "Are you angry, Freya?"

She sighed, letting him set aside their banter, her hand relaxing on his shoulder. "No, Aer, I'm not angry."

"Are you happy, then?"

"I suppose I'm not...unhappy. I've had thirteen years to get used to the idea of becoming queen and I've become quite content with it. I truly believe I—no, *we*—can do a lot of good for Lindoroth. I'm not overly thrilled with *you* right now, though. We were supposed to announce at your nameday celebration, not now, not when I've barely gotten my footing here."

"Does that mean I won't be getting a kiss from my future mate tonight?"

Freya gave him a deadpan look. "You're surely joking."

He laughed, then pulled her close, resting his cheek against her hair. "In time, then, Freya. In good time."

THE REST of the night passed by in a blur of bows, curtsies, kissed hands, poisoned scowls from the slew of females who'd surely hoped Aerelius would cast his sights in their direction, and disappointed stares from the males who'd hoped to catch Freya's eye.

In a way, Freya felt bad for the females who wanted the prince. The hope that he would seek out a mate once he was surrounded by such an eligible pool of females was popular, but to the well-informed, unreasonable.

But there was always hope from the ladies of the five realms that the crown prince would choose one of them.

By the time the last guest departed for the evening, Freya collapsed in a chair in the now-empty ballroom at a table with Lea, Lazarus, Collin, and Aerelius.

"Well, cousin, I have to hand it to you," Lazarus said, shaking his head as he looked at Aer. "You're quite adept at making a splash."

Freya sent a disapproving look at her betrothed, who sat next to her, his arm stretched across the back of her chair. "That's certainly one way to describe it."

Aer smirked at her. "Try not to take it so hard. There were too many males gawking at you. I simply stopped their advances before they began."

"How noble," she said dryly.

"It's not entirely without merit," Collin said, then quickly backpedaled when Freya shot him a look. "Although, perhaps it could have been handled better."

"Nonsense," Aer said with a wave of his hand. "Our subjects

should always expect the unexpected from their monarchs. Isn't that right, Valkyrie?"

She sent him a withering look.

Lea snorted. "I'd say Aer was just as eager to get those rancid females off his scent sooner rather than later."

He shrugged. "True. I simply killed three birds with one stone." He gave Freya an easy smile. "Now we can move forward in peace."

"Peace," Freya scoffed. "*You* won't be returning to a dormitory full of females who were hoping to land themselves a princely husband."

"I can't help my irresistible nature, Freya, or your fantastic luck."

"Ugh." Lea shook her head. "Can we leave now? Or will you be forcing Freya to move into the palace immediately?"

Freya laughed. "As if that would happen."

"Technically—"

Freya froze, then pointed a finger at Aer. "If you have any hopes of wooing your future bride, Your Highness, I'd stop right there."

He held her gaze for a few seconds, and Freya could see the desire to argue in his eyes. But, wisely, he held up his hands. "Alright, fine. Considering your death threats earlier, I'll agree to table that idea for now."

"Death threats?" Collin's eyes widened. "Gods above, and you're to *marry*?"

Freya gave a small shrug. "I simply reminded my beloved prince that I'm quite skilled in certain methods of internal injury should he choose to anger me."

Aer scoffed. "Puncturing lungs wouldn't constitute an *injury*, my lady."

"Well, this will certainly be the *least* dysfunctional reign Lindoroth has seen in centuries," Lea said. "I can only imagine how the children will turn out."

"Vicious, I'm sure," Aer said with no small hint of pride.

Freya preened. "If I have anything to do with it, that is."

"At least you're in agreement on something," Laz muttered.

"Freya, dear?"

Freya's head snapped up at the sound of the queen's voice. "Your Majesty," she said, leaping from her seat.

Ordona smiled softly at the others before returning her gentle eyes to Freya. "I was hoping we might take a few minutes to talk, if that's alright."

"Of course," Freya replied.

"Mother..." Aerelius began.

Ordona gave him a look that withered the words at his lips. "After your stunt, Aerelius, you're lucky I don't have you tossed in the dungeons. I'll only borrow her for a few minutes, then you can have your betrothed back. Freya?"

Without another word, Ordona swept off, her heavy skirts swishing behind her, leaving Freya to scurry after. She followed the queen down the stairs and through the castle halls to her private chambers, separate from those she shared with the king. After they were both inside, she shut the door and faced Freya, a sympathetic smile on her face.

"I am *so* sorry, Freya," she said, drawing Freya into her arms. "My son takes after his father in his impetuousness, I'm afraid."

Freya smiled at Ordona as she stepped back. "It's not your fault, Your Majesty. I can't say it surprises me that he chose to reveal your plans in such a spontaneous way."

"Plans nearly twenty years in the making," Ordona said with an annoyed shake of her head. "We were discussing this before the two of you were even born, did you know?"

Freya shook her head, a bit surprised. "No, I wasn't aware. I assumed it came about when we were children."

"Confirmed, certainly, especially once we knew you were a true half-blood and we saw how well you two took to one another." She walked away from Freya and picked up a jug of mead, then poured them each a glass. "I do hope you'll be able to find that closeness again." After handing Freya hers, she held her own up. "Well, we've got to toast to something, wouldn't you say? What shall it be?"

Freya pondered for a moment, then grinned. "Infuriating males?"

Ordona let out a peal of laughter.

20

F reya and Ordona talked a while longer, the queen reassuring her that they'd speak again soon. When she stood to walk Freya out, however, they were stopped by King Salazar, who'd just arrived with Byrric and Aerelius in tow.

"Ah, Freya! I was hoping I'd find you here!" Salazar brushed past her into the queen's chambers, cigar in hand. "Stay, we've got a few things to discuss."

Freya sent her father, then Aerelius, a confused look, but neither appeared able or willing to offer any insight. Byrric studiously avoided her gaze, while Aer slid his hands in his pockets, appearing perfectly at ease.

Infuriating fool.

"Sal, is this really necessary?" Ordona asked. "It's late. Surely this can wait until tomorrow."

Salazar waved off her concern. "Aerelius has chosen to drag this into the open now, so now is when it shall be discussed."

Freya sent a "see what you did?" look toward her prince before smiling at the king.

"Was there something you wanted to discuss with me, Your Majesty?"

"With all of you," Salazar replied, sitting down in a chair beside the fireplace and crossing his ankle over his knee. He gestured toward the rest of the queen's sitting area. "Sit."

Freya sat down on a small velvet chaise, shifting slightly when Aerelius took a seat beside her.

Eyes narrowed to slits, Salazar stared between them for a moment. He puffed contemplatively on his cigar, then nodded. "You two are ideally suited for one another. Your children will be lovely, I'm sure."

Freya's brow lifted at the bold statement and cast a quick look at Aerelius. He leaned back in his seat and stretched his arm along the back of the chaise, a look of arrogant insult blooming on his face.

"We already knew that, Father."

Freya frowned at the king. "Has someone suggested otherwise?"

"Of *course* not, dear," Ordona replied, shaking her head in frustration. "Salazar—"

"There is already talk that, as somewhat of an outsider, you may be ill-suited to be queen, despite your lineage." Salazar took a sip of wine. "Some might find logic in that sentiment."

"Some would be fools," Byrric muttered.

"Agreed," the king said with a nod. "That said, to avoid any potential annoyances in the upcoming months, we need to begin working immediately to solidify Freya's place here at the palace."

"What would you suggest?" Aerelius asked.

"Set a date, for one. Our original plan was to announce the engagement at your nameday celebration in nine months, with the wedding just before the coronation a year from now. That's been shot to hell, so I think Winter Solstice would be an ideal time for a wedding, instead."

Freya's eyes widened as she looked up at her father. "So soon?"

"Oh, Sal! That's hardly time to plan!" Ordona groaned. "I will not rush the future king's wedding simply because of some arbitrary schedule you've concocted."

Freya opened her mouth, then closed it, dumbstruck and more than a little disappointed that her wedding was now hardly three months away. She was supposed to get a full year at Aldridge, or so her father and the king had promised, but now that her status had been announced to all, she'd be lucky if she was allowed to finish out her first term. She tried to take comfort in the fact that her betrothed was her friend, a male she cared for and not a complete stranger, but even with that consideration, the sudden change in circumstances was a bit dizzying.

Aerelius brushed a gentle finger along the back of her neck in a calming gesture. "Is there a reason for your haste?"

"Logic, Aerelius. We cannot announce a royal engagement and wait a year for the wedding. Had we done as we'd originally discussed, the wedding would have been at midsummer. *Your* haste has altered that plan."

Byrric cleared his throat and gave Aerelius a disparaging look. "Ordona has a point, Sal. Do you truly expect to plan a royal wedding in just a few months?"

Salazar dismissed the concern with a wave of his hand. "Find me a female in this palace who isn't chomping at the bit to plan a royal wedding and I'll eat my own shoe. Planning is a non-issue."

Ordona gave Freya an apologetic smile and a small shrug. "We'll get started right away, then."

Frowning, Freya looked at the king. "Your Majesty, you said there were other things we needed to discuss? Aside from the wedding?"

He nodded, then took a puff of his cigar and tapped it into the glass dish at his side. "Yes, we need to discuss your living arrangements now that your identity as the next queen has been revealed."

"What's wrong with my living arrangements?"

"They aren't here." He looked at Byrric. "She'll move to the palace immediately. Her chambers have already been secured, so it will be a simple matter of moving her belongings from Aldridge here."

"What—" Freya sent an alarmed look at Ordona before responding to the king. "Your Majesty, with all due respect—"

"Is this really necessary?" Aerelius asked. "Wouldn't it be better for her to remain in a position to get to know her future subjects? That was largely the purpose of our attendance there, after all."

"An excellent point," Ordona said with a firm nod. "Many of the students who attend Aldridge will hold highly influential positions upon graduation. Now would be the ideal time for her to get to know them on a more personal level."

"She is under no obligation to become friends with her subjects, Ordona!"

"It will make her a more favorable queen in the long run if she does, Salazar," Byrric replied. "A future queen who knows her people—"

"Puts herself at risk!" Salazar shouted. "It was one thing when no one knew who she was. The wolves will descend immediately, and you damn well know it!" He pointed a finger at the door. "Half the females who were in that ball are likely planning her demise as we speak."

Freya opened her mouth to argue, then thought better of it and flopped against the back of the sofa. She flinched when Aerelius danced his fingers along the back of her neck, then stilled, allowing him to offer her a small bit of comfort.

He leaned over and put his lips to her ear. "Just let him get it out of his system."

Freya clenched her jaw, then nodded. A battle of wits and wills would always rage between them, but even that stubbornness wouldn't stop Aer from standing by her in times of confrontation. The thought gave her little comfort at the moment, though, considering he wasn't yet in a position to overrule his father's decisions.

"You're being unreasonable, Salazar!" Byrric snapped. "Just because your impetuous son chose now as the time to announce their engagement does not mean my daughter needs to be uprooted from where she belongs!"

"She belongs here, not slumming with the lower classes!" Salazar roared.

"That's a lovely opinion you have of the people you've allowed to educate me," Aerelius said.

"I should bring you home, as well! I was a fool to think it was a good idea to let you go to that school!"

"You're a fool if you think it wise to abbreviate their education," Byrric growled, cutting off the argument between father and son. "The social aspects alone—"

"And you'd do well to remember who you're speaking to! She can still receive her education at Aldridge, but she will no longer live on campus."

Furious, Freya's frayed nerves finally snapped. "All of you, stop! *I* would like to speak, if that's quite alright."

Salazar's jaw tensed, but when Ordona laid a hand on his shoulder, he held back his response.

Freya nodded her thanks to the queen before addressing the king. "Your Majesty, I've lived among the 'lower classes' for most of my life. There is merit to the idea of letting my future subjects see me as more than just the prince's betrothed, more than just the future queen. I can get to know them, form potentially beneficial social relationships." She took a small breath before continuing. "I can only speak to the perception of the citizens of Allanor, but the idea of their monarchs existing in the same world as them was a difficult one to grasp because the royal court is so far removed from the outer regions. Subjects who know their queen, who know that she's been living and fighting right alongside them, will defend her should unrest arise. They will defend her king, her family. You may not see the benefit in that, but it's quite clear to me."

She paused to look at each of them in turn. "You three chose me as Aerelius' betrothed based on the commander's status in our world, my mother's power, and the skills you knew those things would give me as an adult. I've worked hard since then to hone those skills, to be the type of female worthy of the crown because I know the good we—" she glanced at Aer "—can do." Now, she directed her words at the king. "But Your Majesty, for all intents and purposes, I am one of those citizens you're casting such disdain toward. I might be a Lady of Allanor, but I'm no royal. Let me prove my worthiness to the people of Lindoroth before I take my crown. Let them see me for who I am, base their reverence for me on truth, not title."

She held Salazar's gaze steadily, refusing to blink as he appraised her through narrowed eyes.

"Sal..." Ordona murmured.

With a clenched jaw, the king nodded tersely. "Alright. I will allow you to live at Aldridge *for now*." He held up one finger. "But you will have two guards with you at all times." He inclined his head toward Aerelius. "Same as the prince. And once this term is over, you'll move in here."

She bit hard on the inside of her cheek, wanting desperately to argue her ability to defend herself. Aerelius' quick tug of her hair stopped her.

"I can accept that. But if you don't mind me asking, why not assign them to me when I arrived?"

"No one knew who you were when you arrived, and that would've raised too many questions. And that's another thing!" the king snapped, his face reddening with temper again. "Now that this is out, I will expect the two of you to behave as future mates when you're in public. Not tossing each other about in the combat ring!"

The room was silent for a moment, then Aer laughed as Freya shifted uncomfortably in her seat. "And how is that, Father? Hand-holding? A kiss between classes? Fornication on the campus lawn?"

Freya elbowed him as her cheeks flamed red.

"Be nice to one another," Byrric told them. "No snark, no sass."

"I won't have my future bride changing herself to suit some fabricated idea of propriety," Aerelius said, his voice turning serious. "I quite like her *sass*, as you call it."

"No one is asking her to change who she is," Ordona replied patiently. "But anyone who spends two minutes with the two of you know you'll take any opportunity to swipe at one another."

"In good fun!" Aerelius exclaimed.

"Aer," Freya murmured. Then she gave her father a tight smile. "As I said when I arrived in Iladel, I will be the picture of propriety." Sending a pointed look at Aerelius, she added, "As will he."

He smiled, then brushed a hand against her cheek before resting his arm along the back of the sofa. "Of course, my love."

"Well, I think we're done here," Ordona said. "Why don't you two take a walk? It might do you some good." She smiled at Freya. "We'll meet soon to begin planning."

Freya gave her a small nod as her mind continued to try and catch up to the sudden turn the night had taken.

"Thank you, Mother." Aerelius stood up and held out a hand to Freya. "Come, let's let these stodgy old fools continue their discussion without us. There's something I'd like to show you, anyway."

Freya slid a look at the others and could tell any further discussion was closed for the evening. With a small sigh, she let the prince help her to her feet and lead her from the room.

21

Freya and Aerelius walked in silence for a few minutes as he led her to the gardens they'd gone to the previous week. Now that they were away from the eyes of their parents and party-goers, the mood between them shifted, as though neither were quite sure how to proceed now that their betrothal was no longer a secret.

"Where are we going?" she asked after they'd been walking for a few minutes.

"You'll see," he told her, turning down a path that appeared far darker than the rest of the garden, despite the full moon overhead.

Freya bit her tongue a half dozen times before finally speaking again.

"Are you planning on murdering me?" she teased. "I can assure you, there are far better places than a darkened palace garden to do it."

"Ah, but those places wouldn't allow me the benefit of palace guards who will assist in covering up my crime." He stopped in front of a towering honeysuckle bush and slid a section of the sweet-smelling flowers out of the way. "Or secret passages."

Curious, Freya came to a stop beside him, then bit her lip and grinned when she saw the unassuming door that stood before them.

"Where does it go?" she whispered, her eyes widening in excitement.

Aerelius shrugged. "I only found it a few days ago. I thought I'd wait for you to find out."

Freya smiled, touched by his forethought, then frowned. "This is hardly well-hidden. All you had to do was push those branches aside."

"We scoured this garden top to bottom when we were children," he reminded her. "Or so we thought. I stopped searching here long ago, so it was easily missed."

"Hmm. As I recall, this bush was always full of bees, correct?" Freya asked, touching one of the pink blooms. Their excursions through the palace gardens had always been during the day, when pollinating insects were most abundant. A bush full of bees was as likely to draw them in as a pond full of snapping cinderfish.

"It was," Aer replied. "And pixies, although they stay to the more brightly-lit areas after sundown."

Freya cast her eyes up, then along the wall that the door was cut into. She couldn't tell from her position which portion of the castle it was attached to, but her fingers were itching to pull up the ancient latch and find out.

"Shall we?" the prince asked. "Or would you prefer we wait until we have to fight off legions of bees to satiate our curiosity?"

She smirked. "I'm sure if I shoved you in front of me as bait, the bees would leave me be."

Aerelius pulled open the door, the hinges protesting loudly as he did. "Are you saying I taste sweet, Lady Balthana?"

She stepped past him into the darkened tunnel, patting his cheek on the way. "Only that I'd put my own well-being above yours should we be attacked by a swarm of stinging bugs."

"I think my mother might protest that."

"Unlikely. Your mother adores me."

The prince chuckled quietly as he pulled the door shut behind them. Once they were in full darkness, Freya rubbed her fingers together and conjured a small, glowing orb of light, illuminating the space around them.

They were in a narrow stone tunnel, barely wide enough for the two to walk abreast without touching. The floors were covered in a fine layer of dust and the walls were spattered with green and white lichens. Freya raised the light a bit higher, but aside from a slight right curve in the tunnel, there was no indication where it led.

"Your lights have improved," Aerelius commented, tapping a finger lightly to the glowing orb.

"I did a lot of hunting in the dark in Allanor," she murmured, staring into the darkness. "Where do you think it goes?"

"Straight and to the right?" Aerelius replied.

She shoved him and rolled her eyes. "I can *see* that, you imbecile. I would imagine it goes a bit further beyond that, though."

He gave her a grin. "What do you say? Shall we go exploring tonight?"

Freya gnawed at her lip. She was dying to go into the recesses of the tunnel and find where it went, but it was getting late and she could practically hear her father chastising her for behaving improperly with the prince.

"You're adults now, Freya. You can't go galivanting off in the dark like children."

Freya sighed. "Another night, I promise. It's getting late and I've already suffered enough of my father's ire this week." She smirked up at him. "Besides, I don't know that I trust you not to abandon me if a rodent pops out and startles us."

He sent her a withering look. "That happened once, and a rat had no business in that passageway."

"It was a *rat,* not a legion of draugs," she said.

"It startled me and I had no proper defenses yet, Valkyrie!"

"Are you saying you'd react differently now?" she asked as they stepped back into the moonlight.

Aerelius shut the door behind them and resituated the branches, ensuring it was concealed before turning to face her. "Well, I can't say. As my betrothed, I suppose the chivalrous thing would be to protect you at all costs, even though you seem perfectly content to do the opposite for me." He slipped an arm around her waist and touched a finger to her chin. "Although, your feathers and witchcraft are far more useful on a vicious rat than my powers of persuasion."

"Powers of persuasion?" She laid a hand to his chest and nudged him back a step so that he released her. "Is that what you call it?"

"'My ability to lull victims into a lust-addled stupor' sounds odd when we're discussing rodents, don't you think?" He slid his hands in his pockets and began to walk beside her.

"I suppose that's a fair point, although it won't stop me from tossing you in the path of danger the first chance I get."

Aerelius laughed and draped an arm around her shoulder. "You are a horrible creature, Freya Balthana."

"And yet you hope to woo me," Freya said with a sigh as she leaned into him. "That's quite the conundrum."

"Oh, I don't have to hope." He put a hand on her hip, stopping her, then turned her to face him. "In all seriousness, though, I would like you to allow me to do what I can to make you happy with this arrangement, Freya."

Softening, she smiled. "I've never doubted that, even while I was away. I'm just reeling a bit from this new timeline." She laid her hands on his arms, testing the way the show of affection felt when they were away from gawking onlookers. "What about you?"

Sensing what she was doing, he looped his hands around her waist, linking his fingers together behind her back. "What about me?"

"Are you happy?"

"I am, although I think practicing some more of these 'shows of affection' our parents want from us might boost my mood a bit." He inclined his head toward a path that disappeared off to their right. "Right down there is the fountain we stood beside when you let me kiss you the last time you were here." He grinned suggestively. "We could take a trip down memory lane, if you'd like. That would *certainly* make me happy."

"You're insufferable, did you know that?" Freya shook her head, unable to keep from smiling at the memory. "I meant, are you content with this arrangement?"

"With making you my queen? Yes, without question. Our parents are pragmatic in all their decisions, political and otherwise, and this pairing was no exception." His arms tightened when she frowned, as though sensing her slight offense at his response. "As far as the arrangement... no, content is not the word I'd use. We were so close as children, and when my father told me you wouldn't return until it was near time for us to marry, I was furious. I know the girl you were, but not the female you've become. We should have spent the past six years getting to know one another, not half a world apart."

"Maybe." She bit her lip, then sighed. "I don't know. I think... I think growing on my own, living side-by-side with the people I'm going to rule, learning from them, will make me a better queen. I meant what I said earlier. Isolating myself from the outside world will only isolate me from my future subjects."

He gave her a soft smile. "See? Pragmatic, just like Byrric."

"Pragmatism is why I never fought this betrothal, at least not outwardly."

"And here I thought it was my wit and charm."

She let out an exasperated sigh. "Are you ever serious?"

"When the mood strikes," he replied airily. "Come, I'm sure the commander is eager to get you back to Aldridge."

Freya nodded, then the pair turned and began strolling back through the garden.

AFTER THE PRINCE escorted Freya back inside, Byrric insisted she ride back to Aldridge with him instead of her friends, citing the need to discuss a few things. Despite her protests and the female officer who now accompanied Rissen, he wouldn't budge.

When they were inside the carriage and the door was closed, Freya turned and glared at her father.

"You knew he was going to do that, didn't you?"

Byrric folded his arms and stared at her evenly. "I had an inkling, yes, and had I told you—"

"I wouldn't have come?" Freya finished. "Why does it seem like no one in this blasted city has any faith in me?" With a huff, she slumped against the wall of the carriage. "I've lost the ability to choose my own clothes, I'm incapable of choosing logic over desire, and the gods only know what else! Gods above, Father, has there ever been a time when you thought I might run from this? I know my obligations!"

"Is that all Aerelius is to you?" he asked.

"What's that supposed to mean?" Freya snapped.

"Is the prince simply a duty you must fulfill?"

"I'm not in love with him, if that's what you're asking, but perhaps if I'd been allowed to visit Iladel a few times over the past six years, I might be able to say otherwise!"

"You seemed quite enamored when you were dancing," he pointed out.

"Appearances can be deceiving."

"Meaning?"

"I threatened to stab him with his own sternum if he ever put me in a position like that again," she said flatly.

Byrric blinked, then burst out laughing. It took him several moments to collect himself, and when he did, his eyes were streaming with tears of mirth. "Freya! If Salazar heard you say that..."

"Well, he didn't." Freya folded her arms and glared out the window, sulking silently for several seconds. "And no, Aerelius isn't just an obligation. He was a good friend when we were younger, although I think it's safe to say that relationship could have been cultivated far better if we hadn't been separated the last six years. I look forward to becoming reacquainted, but I wish it weren't such a necessity." She met his eyes. "As for love... I can't say it won't happen, but we've got to learn about one another all over again. That takes time."

"You have more of a starting-off point than most betrothals," he pointed out. "Your mother and I met only three months before we were to marry."

Freya pressed her lips together and stared out the window, the blackness of night the only thing that stared back. Her parents' betrothal had been far more typical of such pairings, based purely on politics. Cina's mother, Selinda Cantor, daughter of the governor of Allanor, was betrothed at birth to Caelora's wealthiest Lord, Jora Enrieth. Selinda had been one of the most powerful witches to come from the Cantor line of witches, magic she passed down to Freya's mother in spades. Combining Cina's power with a male Valkyrie was sure to be a union that could potentially produce a powerful half-blood heir, which would prove to be a valuable partnership.

When it became clear that Freya was a true half-blood, her parents and the king and queen had drawn up the agreement for their betrothal. She'd always thought that was where talk of her marriage to the prince began, but now, according to the queen, that agreement had been in the works for years prior to her birth.

"I appreciate the chance to form a relationship with the male you've chosen for me," she finally said, meeting her father's eyes. "I can only hope he and I find that same friendship we had as children."

The smile he gave her held nothing but pride. "You did well, tonight, Freya, and despite what you might say, you two already show a clear united front. Based on your interactions tonight, I'd say you're well on your way to finding what you feel you've lost."

A smile flickered across her lips. "I certainly hope you're right."

22

"Are you certain you don't want to take a day or two off?"

Freya paused in the middle of tugging on one of her knee-high suede boots and looked at Lea. She and her friends had discussed in depth whether or not it was wise for her to dive right back into classes, with Laz and Collin falling a bit more on her side, while Lea and Aer tended to lean on the side of easing back in.

"Absolutely." She finished fastening her boot and let her foot thud to the floor. "I had to fight with the king to let me live on campus. I won't hide away because I'm worried about what some people might say."

A knock sounded, and Lea walked over to let Lazarus and Collin in before responding to Freya.

"I'm only saying that it couldn't hurt to let the... fervor die down a bit before subjecting yourself to all of that."

"Are you still trying to convince her to avoid classes?" Collin asked as he walked in.

"The suggestion isn't without merit," Lea said haughtily.

"She's got us," Lazarus said with a shrug. "And Aer will be meeting us for lunch before Combat."

"And let's not forget my two shadows," Freya added as she picked up her brush and began running it through her hair. "Rissen has a partner named Cecilia. It's utterly ludicrous. I've been wandering around here for two weeks without guards at my back. I've made myself a bet that I'll be able to slip them at least twice a day."

"I'll take that bet," Lea muttered.

"*You* still owe me money," Freya reminded her. Setting the brush down, she picked up her bag and slung it over her shoulder. "Now, shall we go?"

"I may be regretting this decision," Freya muttered when she and Laz arrived at Civics. Rissen and Cecilia, a small, brown-haired wolf shifter with a stern face that dared anyone to try something, had insisted on waiting until the hallways were clear of all students before escorting her through the building, so when they entered the room, all eyes were drawn toward them. Her previous class, Toxins, had been similar, except Professor Florian had set a tall atomizer of widow venom on the front table, a clear threat to any students who might interrupt. He dove into his lecture the moment she and Lea took their seats, giving the other students no time for whispers, lest they risk another poisoning.

She'd never been more grateful for a professor willing to poison his students in broad daylight until now.

"Are you referring to coming to class in general, or your insistence that we still sit in the back?" Laz murmured as he stepped through the door beside Freya.

Ignoring him, Freya kept her stride purposeful as she walked across the room and up the aisle to their seats. She could feel stares burning into her as she walked, so she forced herself to meet the eyes of a few students, smiling at a few as she hoped to put into practice her plan to let them all know she was still one of them and not the least bit intimidated.

Some returned her smiles, a few averted their eyes, while others held her stare with expressions ranging from reverence to contempt.

The sudden itch to let out her wings tingled along her spine.

Inadvertently, her eyes landed on Myria, who was staring down at her desk, absently tapping her fingers along the edge.

"She's quite furious," Laz whispered once they sat. Putting his back to the students who were watching them, he faced her. "Embarrassed as well."

"I feel a bit bad for her, you know?" Keeping her voice just above a breath, Freya shot another glance toward the pretty blonde. "Making that type of assumption about your future..."

"It's a shame, truly. I wouldn't be surprised if she challenged you in Combat soon."

Freya drummed her fingers against her desk. "Well, I wouldn't be opposed, honestly. She gave me quite a workout last week."

Just then, Professor Ildar entered the room, rapping loudly on the doorframe as he did, silencing the class.

"Texts out!" he shouted. "Chapter four, let's go!"

Laz turned to face front as Freya flipped to the start of chapter four, "Foreign Relations."

"At least it's not the chapter on the ascension of monarchs," she whispered to Laz.

He snickered. "That will be next week, don't worry. He's likely to ask you to present to the class. I'll be sure to bring snacks."

She scowled at him.

For the next half hour, Professor Ildar droned on about the importance of forming allegiances and knowing the strengths and weaknesses of your neighboring lands. A good deal was a basic review of Freya's lessons in primary and secondary school, but the more detailed information regarding their closest neighbors, Jotunheim and Dystone, was mostly new to her. Her father had kept her abreast of a good deal of Lindorothian politics, but as foreign relations were ever-evolving, there was plenty she hadn't yet been brought up to speed on. Mainly the shifting relationship between Jotunheim and Dystone. It had been tumultuous at best over the last few centuries, the two nations having had their fair share of small skirmishes and attempted reconciliations. Based on the more recent news coming from the Dystonian capital of Caldel, things were currently going well, a state which typically left everyone in the surrounding nations content.

According to a number of Lindorothians, though, that assessment was inaccurate.

"I heard the Jotnar want to take the humans as slaves again, and that's why they've been attempting to rebuild relations," Derron Wailend said, interrupting their professor when he began to speak of the importance of annually revisiting the terms of treaties. "That seems to go against any type of peace-keeping logic, I would think."

"Well, according to *my* father, they're allying with the humans in an attempt to conquer Lindoroth," Kira Leston, a friend of Myria's interjected.

"You're a fool, Kira," Myria groaned. "Everyone knows they simply want to open trade lines with them, and no army of Jotnar will ever be able to conquer Lindoroth, even with a human alliance."

"These are all perfectly valid concerns," Professor Ildar said, holding up a hand to silence them. "Although I won't believe a word of them until they come straight from the king or queen's own mouth."

"Well, what about our *future* queen?" Lady Leston asked, sliding a look at Freya. "Wouldn't *she* know?"

Freya rolled her eyes. "She is right back here and no, she doesn't."

"Easy," Laz murmured when he saw the surprised expression on the female's face.

Freya gritted her teeth, then smiled. "As much as I would love to contribute more to this conversation, only the sitting monarchs and their advisors would be kept well-informed on such detailed and classified information. I'm sure you can understand that, Lady Leston."

Kira smirked at her. "Of *course*, Lady Balthana. I just thought perhaps, since our relationship with Jotunheim has struggled a bit in recent years, you might know more."

Freya shrugged. "I'm sorry to disappoint."

Kira gave Freya a simpering smile. "I'm certain it won't be the first time."

Freya opened her mouth to respond, but Laz kicked her ankle.

"Careful, Kira," Myria warned, her tone falling somewhere between genuine and disdain. "She may start aiming feathers at your neck for your disrespect."

Kira shot Myria a shocked look, then her expression shifted into amusement. "Oh? Tell me, Lady Bryton, how has life been the last few days, now that the prince has left you in the dirt?"

Freya leaned toward Laz. "Why isn't Ildar saying anything?"

Laz kept his eyes trained on the front. "Just watch."

"You know, jealousy isn't a pretty color on you," Myria said airily, brushing a strand of hair from her face. "I may not have landed a prince, but at least I had a chance." She smirked. "Unlike some of us."

"Did you, though?" Kira arched a brow. "From what I heard at the ball, his highness and Lady Balthana have been betrothed since they were children."

Freya looked around the room at the rest of the students, most of whom were staring at the interaction between the two females with rapt attention. When her eyes landed on their professor, though, she saw what Laz meant.

Professor Ildar was standing silently at the front of the room, one finger on his chin as he watched the females continue to sling barbs at one another. She hardly knew him, but it was clear by the small smile on his face that he was absorbing their words, taking in the way they spoke.

"Alright." He stepped forward and clapped his hands once. "Let's halt there." Brows raised, he looked around the room. "What lessons can we take from the interaction between Ladies Bryton and Leston?"

Laz's hand shot up. "Lady Bryton wasted no time in showing an imbalance of power."

Professor Ildar ignored Kira's gasp of outrage. "How so, Lord Cailen?"

"Lady Bryton referred to Lady Leston by her given name, while

Lady Leston used both Lady Balthana's and Lady Bryton's proper titles. The use of given names in conversation is reserved for close relations, peers, or subordinates, but never social or professional superiors."

"Indicating?"

Freya raised her hand, waiting until her professor acknowledged her before speaking. "Despite her known disdain for me, Lady Bryton acknowledges the stratified nature of our society by using my proper title. She used Lady Leston's given name as a way to establish dominance. Second, because Lady Leston addressed Lady Bryton properly, she acknowledged the position of her house beneath that of House Bryton."

"What would you know about it?" Kira snapped.

Freya sent Kira a cool look. "My father was the leader of the Allanorian army for five decades, three of which your uncle served under him, and my great-grandfather was governor for two centuries. I am well-aware of your family's countless business contributions to the economy and well-being of both Allanor and Lindoroth as a whole. However, House Bryton is a governing entity. House Leston is not." She flicked a glance toward Myria, who seemed to be studiously ignoring her.

"Lovely!" Professor Ildar said, cutting off any response Kira may have had. "This is just one demonstration of the complex nature of our society. A bit of a tangent from our original lesson, to be sure, but an interesting sidebar, nonetheless." Grinning, he looked around the room. "Now, let us shift back to our discussion of our friends to the east. Lord Jarrison, what else can you tell us about the realm of Dystone?"

FREYA WAS THRILLED when she arrived at the training yard and learned that it would be the first day outside the sparring ring. As much as she enjoyed honing the skills Officer Ristheld had been working on, she was already well-versed in most of them and was eager to begin working a different set of muscles. Her group members—Collin, Gareth, Aer, and Myria—gave her a strong workout each day, but it was becoming repetitive. When she walked in on Monday and he directed them toward the targets set up at the end of the yard, her fingers itched to wrap around the handle of a knife and begin throwing.

"Care to make a wager?"

Her lips quirked at the sound of Aerelius' voice at her side. She'd just stepped up to the line of her assigned target, knife in hand, but paused at his offer.

"Alright." She twirled her knife between her fingers. "What's your wager?"

"Well, since you're insisting that I *woo* you, I was thinking a friendly bet." He tapped the flat side of his blade against his palm. "If I win, I get to choose our plans for Friday evening."

"And if I win?"

He gave her a wide grin. "You get to choose."

Freya pointed the knife in his direction. "Alright. Counter-bet. I'd wager we choose the same thing. If I win, I have free rein when it comes to our wedding plans."

"I'm sure my mother might object to that, but I'll bite. If I win?"

A slow smile spread across Freya's face. "You can choose my wedding gown. And..." she stepped closer and tilted her face toward his, "I might even let you kiss me."

Aerelius' mouth opened, then closed, momentarily stunned. "You could always lie," he pointed out.

"So could you. You won't, though."

"Won't I?"

"No, you won't."

Aerelius narrowed his eyes, considering. "Deal."

Freya flipped her knife in her hand and turned toward her target. "Shall we begin?"

Grinning, Aerelius stepped toward her and placed a hand on her lower back, then brushed his lips against her ear. "Plot twist—you have to do it with the eyes of all of our fellow students on you."

Freya gritted her teeth, then took a quick glance around the yard. Sure enough, their banter had once again drawn the attention of those around them.

Returning her focus to her target, she shrugged. "You underestimate my ability to work under pressure. Now, I'd take a step back, unless you'd like this knife to end up embedded in your chin."

"Have I ever told you how much I love when you threaten me?"

She smirked. "Have I ever told you that you're a twisted bastard? Now move."

The prince obediently stepped away, taking aim at the target beside her. "Ready, Valkyrie?"

"On your mark."

"I DON'T KNOW what you're so upset about," Freya said, sliding a nonvenomous feather from her wing. Idly, she began to clean her fingernails with the tip. "I told you not to underestimate me, and you *did* train with me when we were young." She looked up at her target, which now held a single, thick gash where all five of her shots had landed. "Although, hitting all five in the same spot is a feat, even for me."

Aerelius scowled. "Not only did you take advantage of your prince's ignorance of your skill *again*, you also took advantage of your future husband. It's insulting."

Setting the feather down on the fence beside her, Freya met his eyes. "Well, now we're even for the snake in my hair. And really, Aer, four out of five in the center of your target is quite good."

Stubbornly, they held one another's gazes for several moments before Aerelius spoke. "You know, I think we may need to revisit this wooing thing. You should be trying to entice me, not the other way around."

Freya laughed. "Oh, don't be such a poor sport! We can go for a rematch if you'd like." She hopped off the rail and rested her knife against his sternum. "Don't act as though you don't find my skill endearing."

His lips quirked, then he let out a quiet laugh. "Mildly endearing, at best. Also, pointing knives at me in public probably isn't what my father meant when he said we needed to appear unified."

"Well, referring to your future wife's skills as 'mildly' anything is a surefire path *away* from gaining her affection."

Grinning, he tapped her on the nose. "Ah, but I already have your affection, Freya. Your love is what I'm after."

Rolling her eyes, Freya couldn't help but laugh.

Grinning, she shoved him back a step. "If you'll excuse me, I'd like to go work on my archery." Biting her lip, she angled her head to the side. "I'll meet you at the palace on Friday, after my lesson with Florian."

The prince gave her an easy smile. "For our date?"

"Yes, Your Highness, for our date."

"I'll be waiting with bated breath."

Still shaking her head, she sheathed her knives and made her way over to the archery range, the thought of her date with her prince making her steps just a little bit lighter.

23

After classes ended for the day and Freya had bathed and changed, Rissen and Cecilia insisted on escorting her to the palace, consenting reluctantly to her request that they run in their shifted forms as she flew overhead. She'd grudgingly accepted that she would need to have guards nearby, but she wasn't quite ready to give up her personal freedoms—mainly, flying from Aldridge to the palace—any time soon.

"I need to stretch my wings now and then, you know," she griped when they attempted to usher her into a carriage.

Cecelia smiled pleasantly.

"Lady Balthana, the commander, the headmistress, not to mention the king, have all insisted we accompany you—"

"You may accompany me," Freya said. Facing her, she let her wings out, flaring them wide, and grinned. "From below."

"My Lady!" Rissen exclaimed as she leapt into the air.

"I'll alert you to any threats, I promise!" Freya called over her shoulder.

"The king will hear of this!" Cecilia shouted.

Turning, Freya folded her arms and flapped her wings, hovering in midair.

"All that will do is get the three of us in trouble. Me, for slipping you both, and you for allowing me to do so." Grinning, she did a quick loop above them. "It's in all our best interests to just let this go!"

Rissen and Cecilia exchanged a look, then Rissen turned a stony stare on Freya.

"Stay within sight, Lady Balthana, and don't go above twenty feet!"

"Thirty!" she called back, not waiting for an answer before ascending a bit further. Without another word, she took off toward the palace, hardly giving her guards time to shift into their wolf forms and charge after her. So as not to aggravate them entirely, she flew just slightly ahead, keeping her eyes trained on the road while also keeping her promise to maintain an altitude of no more than thirty feet.

A short time later, she touched down on the palace lawn just in front of the drawbridge. Hands on her hips, she turned and faced her guards who'd come to a stop just behind her, shifting back into their regular bodies.

"Now, that wasn't so bad, was it?" Freya's smile was wide as the thrill of finally getting to stretch her wings over a long distance coursed through her.

Cecilia huffed and smoothed back her hair while Rissen gave her a withering look.

"I see you both are doing a wonderful job keeping our lady Valkyrie in line."

"Yes, yes, they almost managed to keep up with me." Freya turned to face the prince. "Now, let's say we let these two relax a bit while you take me through all the tunnels you've discovered in my absence? I'm anxious to see that new one in particular."

"How did you know—" Aerelius clenched his jaw and sighed. "You know, for as often as you win bets, one might begin to wonder if you can read minds."

Freya retracted her wings. "People, Aer. I can read people."

Shaking his head, he glanced at Rissen and Cecilia. "You both can head inside if you'd like. There's about to be a shift change, so Maghda should have dinner on the table shortly."

"Yes, Your Highness," Ceclia said as she and Rissen each gave a quick bow.

Rissen tossed Freya a wink. "Enjoy your evening, my lady."

Once they'd disappeared through the gatehouse, Aerelius held out his hand to Freya. "Shall we?"

"Lead the way." She took his hand, lacing her fingers through his, and let him lead her across the drawbridge.

"So, how many have you found, anyway?" Freya asked, turning to him as they ambled toward the entrance.

"Since you left?" He frowned in thought. "Not many, as I've been searching on my own and my responsibilities have increased. Perhaps four entrances we never found, but a far greater number of passages and chambers stemming from some of the main ones."

"Have you really been searching this whole time?"

"Mostly. I stopped for a few years, hoping you'd return and resume the hunt with me." He gave her a wistful smile. "Once Byrric assured me for the fifth time that wasn't going to happen, I decided to start up again with the grand plan of impressing you with everything I found."

"Impressing me?" She gave him a curious look. "Aer, you know you could have come to visit me in Watoria. Written me, even."

"I asked, but my mother insisted I let you be. She said we'd already taken your future choices from you, and that the best thing I could do while you were away would be to let you live your life as you wished."

Surprised, Freya had no immediate response. She understood the queen's sentiment and appreciated it more than she could convey, but she'd also never argued the betrothal her parents had arranged for her, at least not once she'd grown old enough to understand their reasoning.

Despite only seeing him a few months out of the year, Aerelius had been her closest friend. Even at the age of thirteen, the idea of spending her life with someone whose company she enjoyed appealed to her a good deal. But she hadn't pined for him the last six years. Instead, she'd spent her time experiencing life outside the royal court as best she could. It was a gift she hadn't realized she'd been given, for which now she was incredibly thankful.

"That's... quite admirable," she said quietly as they approached the arched entrance to the hallway. "And much appreciated."

"As much as I may needle you, Freya, I still care for you," he told her. "I acknowledge that an arranged marriage may not be your preference, nor is it mine, but I plan to do what I can to make you happy. I'd never... force anything."

She gave him a shocked look, dumbfounded that he would think she'd think that. "I know, Aer. I've never doubted that. Even if I was unhappy with our arrangement, you weren't the one who chose it. I'm just thankful that we were able to become friends first." She wrinkled her nose. "If I met you for the first time now, I might kick up more of a fuss."

He laughed and put his arm around her shoulder. "As if you're so much more agreeable!"

Grinning, she elbowed his side. "One day, Aerelius, I'll make you come to regret crossing me."

He tightened his arm around her shoulder and touched his lips to her hair. "I'd love to see you try."

ONCE INSIDE THE GARDEN PASSAGE, Freya conjured up two balls of light and set them both floating in the air beside them, then gestured for Aerelius to lead on.

They'd gone about ten feet in silence before Freya spoke.

"Alright, I have a question," she said, looking up at him. "Your powers—what do you do with them? Joking aside, have you learned what practical uses you have for them?"

"Well, I can think of a few practical uses *we* could find for them," he joked.

Freya laughed, even as the idea sent wild thoughts through her mind. "*Aside* from the obvious, have you yet learned how to use them defensively? Offensively? You didn't use them much in combat."

"Some," he told her, turning serious. "Not as much as I'd like, though, which is part of the reason I insisted my parents let me spend the year at Aldridge with you. The ability to increase positive emotions is beneficial, certainly, but as for practical use? No. I've yet to have anyone teach me anything aside from fogging the mind, which can be tiring if I hold it for too long."

Freya pondered that for a moment. "Yes, but that's still quite useful, if you think about it. It's simple, and based on your show in Combat, would be quite effective."

He slid his eyes toward her and smiled. "Perhaps we should practice. Shall I fog your mind again, Freya?"

"Only if you'd like another feather at your throat," she replied sweetly.

"Again with the death threats!"

"My *endearing* death threats," she corrected. They continued down the passageway until they reached the bend, then stopped when they turned the corner and were faced with two tunnels jutting off in opposite directions, both much wider than the one they were currently in.

The pair looked between the passages for a moment, then Aerelius smiled. "Well, Valkyrie, which way should we go?"

Closing her eyes, she drew her shifter senses forward, then she inhaled deeply to take in the scent from each passage. The left carried the scent of dry air, nitre, and dust, while the right held the smell of cave slime and iron.

"The left," she said after a few moments, opening her eyes and pointing. "It's a bit cooler, so my guess is that it leads into the palace. The right is heavy with humidity, so it likely leads to one of the underground waterways in the mountain."

"Afraid of a bit of water?" Aerelius teased.

"I don't trust you not to toss me in," she said airily. "But perhaps another day."

As they navigated toward the left-hand tunnel, Freya let her fingers drift along the wall, adding two more balls of light to illuminate each side so they could watch for anything that might indicate a hidden chamber or passage.

They'd gone another fifty feet or so when a foreign scent pricked at Freya's nose, wafting faintly from the tunnel ahead.

"Do you smell that?" she asked, stopping.

Aer paused, then sniffed. "Is that... human?" He looked to her for confirmation, his expression perplexed.

She nodded. "Relatively fresh, too. I thought the king was addressing relations with Jotunheim. Why would a human be here?"

"Here in the palace, or here in this passage?" Aerelius asked.

"Both, I suppose."

"I don't have an answer for either," he replied, frowning down the tunnel where the scent seemed to be the strongest. "My parents meet with Dystonian ambassadors a few times per year, but they generally walk straight through the front door."

Freya followed his gaze, her curiosity slowly getting the better of her. Lifting her brows, she looked up at Aerelius.

"Well? Shall we continue our exploration, then? Perhaps we can find where he or she came from."

His confusion giving way to amusement, he smiled down at her. "You're a terrible influence, did you know that?"

She shrugged. "I wouldn't have been half as good at my job in Watoria if I hadn't had a strong sense of curiosity. Come, let's see where it goes."

More cautiously than before, they continued down the tunnel, keeping a closer eye out for latches or doors as they neared the bend just ahead.

When they rounded it, they drew up short as they faced a dead end.

Curiously, Freya approached the wall to her right and began examining the mortar between the stones, searching for cracks or openings. "Look around, see if you find anything."

For the next few minutes, they worked in silence on opposite sides of the passage, easily falling into the routine they'd developed when they were younger. Aerelius relied mainly on his sense of touch, while Freya used her heightened senses of smell and sight to find anomalies in the stones.

Freya turned when Aerelius made a small click with his tongue, signaling her to come close. Silently, she walked to where he stood.

He held a finger to his lips, then pointed at a spot on the wall. Frowning, Freya looked where he was pointing, and her eyes widened at what she saw.

"*A keyhole?*" she mouthed. Slowly, she bent at the waist to examine the small hole that looked to be cut directly into the stone. Touching her finger to it, she felt a faint draft, but when she attempted to peer through, all she saw was darkness. She gave a sniff, surprised when the only scent that reached her was that of baking bread. Running her fingers along the wall, she felt for cracks or seams where the door might be, but all she felt was stone.

Scratching her head, she straightened and looked at Aerelius, shrugged, then pointed back toward the entrance.

Quickly and silently, the pair returned to the garden, not speaking until they were outside and made certain there was no one else around.

"Come," Aerelius said, taking her hand. "To the drawbridge."

"Why?" she asked, tugging on his hand to stop him.

"So no one can listen to our discussion through spy holes in the wall."

Freya followed him through the halls of the palace, back out front, and across the yard onto the drawbridge. He sat down on the edge, legs dangling over the side, and held a hand out for her to sit beside him.

"What did you see?" he asked once she sat.

"Nothing," she replied. "A dark room. I could smell bread baking, though, so it seemed we were near the kitchens."

"A darkened room near the kitchens that unlocks from the outer side of a secret door?" He took on a contemplative look for a moment, then smiled. "Do you know what this means, Freya?"

She arched a brow. "What does this mean?"

"We've got a puzzle to solve."

She stared at him for a moment, then laughed. "We've also got school, Aer, not to mention all your princely duties, whatever they may be, and a *wedding* to plan. When, exactly, do you suppose we scour the castle for this puzzling room?"

"You could always revisit the idea of moving in," he said. "Your chambers are already prepared. Right next to mine, in case you were wondering. That would give us all the time in the world."

"Can you focus, please?" she groaned. "Why in heaven's name is a human sneaking about in the castle?"

"An illicit affair with one of the kitchen staff?" He laughed when she made to ruffle his hair, swatting her hand away. "Well, it could be! You never know."

"Utterly impossible," she huffed. "As future king, you should be far more concerned with what creatures are sneaking around your palace."

"*Our* palace, you mean," he said with a sly smile. "And why should I worry when I've got you?"

Her eyes widened. "You should *worry* because—"

He cut her off with a laugh. "Oh, Freya, relax! I plan to do a bit of investigating after you leave, but look at this objectively. If a human has been in the palace tunnels, it's quite likely my parents know about it and simply don't want it broadcast to the world. If we start asking questions, they will inevitably be alerted and, knowing my father, our tunnels will be sealed up." He touched a finger to her chin. "Trust me, we'll know soon enough."

She gave him a speculative look. "You seem quite sure of that. What kind of investigating are you planning?"

"What do you think?"

"Fine, but if the human returns..."

"I'll send word immediately. Now, let's head back in. Zeke is on duty in the kitchen tonight, so we may be able to persuade him to send extra dessert with dinner to my chambers."

Freya frowned. "You don't want to eat with your parents?"

"Heavens, no. My father's become insufferable half the time now that his reign is ending, and Mother is more concerned with our upcoming nuptials than keeping him happy. So, no, I'd much prefer dinner just the two of us." He jumped to his feet and held out a hand to help her up. "Now, let me woo you with my powers of persuasion."

Her eyes widened and she paused in the middle of brushing off her pants. "You aren't telling me you use your powers on the poor kitchen staff!"

He frowned, then laughed. "Gods above, Freya, what do you think of me? I meant my charm, my ability to persuade people with my words." Draping an arm around her shoulder, they began to walk back inside. "You should know a thing or two about that."

"It hasn't worked on me, yet," Freya pointed out. "Perhaps they aren't as powerful as you think."

"Hasn't it?" He wound his fingers through her hair. "You're here, aren't you? My arm is around you, my fingers are in your hair, and you thoroughly enjoyed our dance at the ball, no matter how hard you try to deny it."

"Did it occur to you that I'm simply putting into practice what our parents told us to do? You're to be my husband, after all. People might think I didn't care for you if I shoved your arm off my shoulders. They might question the truth of our feelings." Taking his hand, she turned and faced him, then laid her other hand on his chest. Gently, she curled her fingers in the fine fabric of his shirt and tugged him closer, tilting her face toward his. "And now? To those guards watching us from up on the ramparts, it might appear that I'm about to kiss you, pull you into a passionate embrace, unable to help myself, even though we're out in the open." She bit her lip, then let her eyes drift to his mouth before meeting his heated gaze. "Isn't that the kind of thing a queen should do with her king? Shouldn't we be eager to have those meddlesome guards tell everyone what they saw here?"

Aerelius swallowed, then rested a hand on her hip and drew her closer. "Then it would be a shame to risk rumors spreading about our lack of affection," he whispered, his lips now barely a breath away. "Shall we give them the show they're looking for?"

Freya smiled, then, though her mind huffed in protest, released the hold on his shirt and smoothed out the fabric. Standing on her toes, she put her lips to his ear. "Ask me again after our second date," she whispered.

With a groan, the prince let his head fall back, but he couldn't fight the smile that tilted his lips as he pressed a kiss to her forehead. Then, without warning, he lifted her up and tossed her over his shoulder.

She let out a squeal, then started beating her fists against his back as he strolled over the drawbridge into the palace.

"Put me down! You are an absolute *barbarian*, Aerelius Harridan!"

He laughed, then swatted the back of her thigh. "And one day, you'll love me, Freya. Mark my words."

She huffed. "We'll see about that," she muttered.

24

The following Thursday, Freya was summoned to the palace, her father instructing her to ride—not fly—with Aerelius after classes completed for the day, along with cryptic instructions to "be careful."

"So what do they want with you now?" Lea asked as Freya sifted through her wardrobe.

"The king and queen want me and Aer present to meet some foreign guest. Byrric was scant on the details." Freya sighed. "He tells me nothing and just sends an officer to order me here or there. I've half a mind to show up in my training clothes." Pulling a blush colored blouse from a hanger, she stepped in front of her mirror and held it up to see how it looked with the flowing black pants she'd chosen. Wrinkling her nose, she shook her head, then stripped down to her underclothes and started over.

"I'd go with a dress, personally," Lea offered. "Foreign guests almost always consist of emissaries or other high-ranking members of court. A dress would suit either." Frowning, she got up off her bed and walked over to Freya's wardrobe and began examining her dresses. "We need to make another shopping trip, Freya. You didn't purchase enough formalwear last time."

"Yes, another round of shamelessly spending the commander's money might be a good pick-me-up," Freya replied with a grin. "I could do with a bit more silk in my wardrobe."

"Seeing as you're our next queen, the prudent decision would certainly be to stock up on clothing worthy of royalty," Lea agreed, pulling out a calf-length dove-gray dress made of soft, gauzy silk. "Accessories, too, of course."

"Well, for tonight, I'm limited to what's here." Freya took the dress from Lea and looked it over, taking in the sleeves that tapered to her wrists, fitted bodice, and open back. Though understated, it had a classically flattering shape. "Yes, this will do."

After getting dressed and weaving her hair back away from her face into two small twists, she dabbed on a bit of lip rouge and a dusting of shimmer on her eyes. Stepping back to examine herself in her mirror, she gave a nod of satisfaction.

"Now, let's just hope it satisfies whoever it is I'm to be impressing tonight," she said.

Lea laughed. "The boys and I will be awaiting details later."

Blowing her a quick kiss, Freya draped a matching cloak over her arm and left.

When she stepped outside, she immediately opened her wings, flaring them wide in the late afternoon sun. Tilting her face to the sky, she considered flying the short distance to the academy gates, then, remembering the dress she wore, opted against giving the students of Aldridge a cheap show.

"Don't even think about it," a voice warned.

Freya paused, then let her shoulders slump.

"I'm only going to the gates, Rissen. Am I unable to do even that on my own?"

The tall male came to a stop beside her with Cecilia at his right.

"Forgive us, my lady," Cecilia said, "but for a moment, it appeared you were planning on flying off and leaving us."

Freya sighed. "No, I simply forgot you two were here. Please don't take offense."

Rissen grinned, flashing his bright white teeth. "None taken, my lady. Now, if you'll allow us to escort you, Cecelia and I will be riding behind you and his highness to the palace."

As the trio began to walk, Freya studied at each of them. They were a bit of a painting in contrasts—Rissen was tall, broad-shoul-dered, and dark-featured, while Cecilia was compact, with a pretty face that might fool one into thinking she had little to no strength about her. Like Rissen, her shifted form was a wolf, and a quick one at that, if what Byrric had told her was correct.

"Do you both truly believe guarding me this closely is necessary?"

Cecilia clasped her hands behind her back and exchanged a look with Rissen. "Perhaps not," she said slowly. "But as our future queen, we, along with our monarchs and your father, would prefer not to deal in uncertainties."

"Will you continue to be my guards after the prince and I are wed?"

"The Queen's Guard consists of eight officers," Rissen replied. "Whether we are included in that will require a discussion between you, your father, and his highness."

"Alright." Freya said. "If I'm to have some say, I'll rely on the both of you to assist me in gathering information on any guards who have potential."

"My lady, that's..." Cecilia exchanged a look with Rissen.

"A bit improper," he finished.

"Why?" Freya stopped and turned to face them both. "If you've been assigned to me already, I would imagine you're well-seasoned, correct? The commander never would've given you this assignment otherwise. That means you know the other guards, know who is in the pool from which my personal guard will be chosen."

"That's true, but—" Rissen began.

She held up a hand. "Do I seem the type to let my father and husband decide who will protect me, day-in and day-out? Who will follow me around, hovering at my back at all hours?"

"No, Lady Balthana," he said, bowing his head.

"Look at me," she ordered. When he did, she tilted her chin up and held his gaze. "I am the type to use all resources available to me in order to make good decisions. Your knowledge of the current guards will help me do that."

Cecilia frowned. "You wouldn't trust the commander's judgement?"

"As always, it's his intentions I'm wary of, so I'd prefer to have a counter-offer ready."

Her two guards were quiet for a moment, both seemingly torn as they looked at one another, carrying on some silent conversation.

Finally, Cecilia sighed and looked at Freya. "Alright, then."

"Just remember, regardless of what insight we give you," Rissen began, "it's unlikely you will have the final say."

Freya shrugged. "We'll see. Now, let's not keep my betrothed waiting."

When they reached the gate, they found a carriage there, the door propped open, and Freya could see the tips of Aerelius' brown boots visible beyond the doorframe. She drew in her wings, then taking Rissen's hand, she allowed him to assist her inside.

As she settled onto the seat across from the prince, he gave her an easy smile. "You look lovely."

"Thank you," she replied. "Care to tell me what this is all about?"

"An emissary from Jotunheim has come to call," he said, propping one foot on his knee. The carriage gave a jolt and began to move forward. "Empress Lessia's nephew, Jonas. He's relatively new to the position and has been making the rounds, meeting the rulers and governors of neighboring countries. My parents would like us there to get a feel for him, learn a bit more about the ruling family, and allow *him* to get an idea of what Lindoroth's next monarchy might be like. He'll be staying for a few weeks, possibly longer."

Freya's eyes widened. "I'm meeting a foreign emissary and no one thought to give me notice? I nearly wore pants!"

Aerelius smiled. "You look perfect, Freya, truly. It's just a formality, really. The king and queen want to present the future monarchs to the Jotnar now, and Jonas is one of Empress Lessia's most trusted advisors." Leaning forward he held out his hands for hers. When she took them, he smiled. "All we have to do is impress upon him the strength of our relationship, the solidarity between us, so he can return to his ruler and report on the future of the monarchy. What you choose to wear will have no bearing on that."

She gave him an amused smile. "Tell me, how do you propose we do that, considering we've barely had time to catch up with one another?"

"A kiss might convince him," Aerelius suggested, leaning forward.

She smiled. "Do kings and queens often kiss in front of foreign ambassadors?"

"What fun will our life be if we don't break molds, Freya?"

She laughed. "I'm happy to break molds with you, Aer, but let's avoid scandalizing the current monarchs."

"Speaking of catching up, I was thinking..." Aer gave her a sly smile. "After we meet with the Jotunn, would you be interested in a tour of the palace?"

"A tour?" She gave him a curious look. She'd spent nearly a third of her early years in the palace and had presumably seen almost everything. "Of what?"

"The areas you haven't seen, perhaps a quick stop by your future quarters."

"My future quarters?" She thought about it for a moment, considering, and was surprised at how excited she was at the thought. "Yes, I suppose I would be amenable to that."

"I thought you might enjoy it. Now, at the risk of ending up with a pierced lung, I thought you might want to know that my mother has been itching to begin planning our nuptials. There's a good chance she'll corner you soon."

"Well, I expected that to happen soon enough," Freya said. "Honestly, considering this has been arranged since we were children, I'm a bit surprised she hasn't already designed it down to the last napkin ring."

"My mother never had a daughter, Freya," he said quietly, staring down at their joined hands as his expression shifted toward serious. Smiling softly, he brushed a soft kiss across her knuckles. "Planning this wedding with you is something she's been looking forward to for years." Meeting her eyes, he gave her a gentle smile. "I know she could never replace Cina, but I hope you're able to find a similar enjoyment with her."

Tears burned Freya's eyes, forcing her to take a moment to collect herself. No, Ordona would never replace her own mother, but she'd never treated Freya as anything less than family. Freya could and would do all she could to return that sentiment.

Squeezing Aerelius' hands, she smiled. "I think I'd really like that."

THE LAST TIME Freya was at the palace when visitors from foreign lands were present, she'd been ten, and she and Aerelius had spent much of their time spying on adult conversations from a passage behind the fireplace in the dining hall. It had been a horrifically dull conversation involving extended talk of Dystonian parchment, the quality of their mead, and whether or not importing leather goods from Jotunheim was worthwhile. The main points she'd come away with were that the apple mead of Teid was unmatched, the only region worth purchasing parchment from was Leford, and the leatherworkers of Jotunheim couldn't hold a candle to those of Allanor, although they came in at a close second.

This time, Freya and Aerelius stood in the throne room beside King Salazar and Queen Ordona's thrones in their first appearance as a royal couple awaiting Lord Jonas Edrin of Jotunheim, nephew of and courtier to Empress Lessia. Freya prayed the conversation would be more riveting than the last she'd witnessed.

"You're fidgeting," Aerelius whispered. He brushed a hand soothingly down her spine. "Try to keep your hands still."

She let out a quiet breath, then opened her fists and let a bit of magic swirl around her fingers to release some of her pent-up energy. Being nervous was a thing she was unaccustomed to, and now, as butterflies rioted in her stomach, she began to realize that it was an emotion she'd need to learn to ignore. That fact alone had her back going straight and her chin tilting up with a forced air of confidence.

"Here they come," Aer breathed as footsteps sounded in the hall. He took a small step forward, positioning himself directly beside her but keeping his hand on her back.

For a moment, she expected him to stand just behind her shoulder, present her like the relative newcomer she was. When she realized what he was doing—telling any who saw them that she would be his partner, not his submissive—she could've kissed him.

Presumably, the prince already had power and the respect of foreign dignitaries. With that small gesture, he was telling anyone who saw them that she deserved both of those things, as well.

Yes, in that moment, she really and truly wanted to kiss him.

"Thank you," she whispered as the door opened and the king and queen walked in. She brushed a hand across the fabric of her dress, immediately feeling underdressed for the occasion. The queen's gown was resplendent in shades of yellow with white, glittering doves embroidered on the bodice. Her mantle, pale gray shot through with shimmering gold, was pinned to the shoulders of her dress, cascading in a waterfall of velvet to the floor. The king's doublet—white with gold buckles—was worn over a gray tunic cinched at the waist with a gold belt, and his mantle, identical to the queen's but trimmed in white fur, flowed behind him as he strode toward his throne.

Atop their heads sat gleaming gold crowns. King Salazar's was tall, made of thick gold and encrusted with rubies, while Ordona's appeared to rise from her black hair in a sunburst of rubies, canary sunstones, and topaz.

As Freya glanced at Aer, she saw that, while not nearly as regal as his parents, his outfit still spoke volumes of his status.

The soft makeup and pretty braids Freya donned suddenly felt childish.

Shaking off her doubts, she held her chin high and smiled as they approached.

King Salazar gave them both a nod. "Our visitor should be here shortly, then you can be about your business."

"And Freya, I was hoping we could talk later," Ordona said. "Come to my chambers once we're done here."

"Of course, Your Majesty," Freya replied with a slight bow of her head.

"I told you," the prince whispered teasingly as his mother and father settled themselves on their thrones.

Just then, the doors opened and two guards walked in, immediately taking flanking positions on either side. A herald with a mop of gray-streaked brown hair entered, then addressed the monarchs.

"King Salazar, Queen Ordona, I present the Jotunheim emissary and nephew of Empress Lessia, Lord Jonas Edrin." With a deep bow, the male stepped off to the side, making way for the lord to enter.

Lord Edrin had the typical appearance of the higher class of Jotnar—attractive, tall and lean, with skin so white it blended almost seamlessly into his light gold hair. His eyes were pale gray, nearly as colorless as his hair, his lips full. He'd dressed in vanilla-colored leather, a poor choice, considering his complexion, although it didn't hide the undeniable handsomeness that lurked in the cut of his jaw and broad shoulders.

"Your Majesties," he intoned with a deep bow. "It is a great honor."

"Lord Edrin," the king said. "I hope your trip from the north went well."

"Quite, Your Majesty." He flashed a smooth smile. "We made excellent time. Your hospitality during my stay in Iladel is much appreciated." Turning, he faced Freya and Aerelius and held out his hands. "And these must be our future monarchs!" He barely spared a glance at the prince, instead studying Freya. "Lady Balthana, is it?"

"It is," she said with a nod, keeping her expression neutral. "It's a pleasure to make your acquaintance, Lord Edrin."

"Your reputation precedes you, my lady," he said. A small, slightly unsettling smile curled his lips. "One of our emissaries visited Watoria two years back and heard a good deal about you from one of their senior marshals. Ashton Carinald, I believe was his name?"

Freya angled her head a bit and smiled. "Yes, Officer Carinald and his fellow marshals taught me a great deal."

"Indeed," he said, his lips twitching slightly.

Freya held his gaze, forcing her eyes to not narrow as she was, again, hit with the urge to flare her wings. "It's a shame you were unable to make the trip yourself. Allanor is a beautiful realm with much to offer."

"And now one of its fiercest protectors will be ruling all of Lindoroth." He gave them all an easy smile.

"The Watorian marshals are more than capable of protecting their lands, Lord Edrin," Freya replied. "They had a large hand in training me, after all. Much of what I know is thanks to them." She gave him what she hoped was a sweet smile. "Especially when it came to dispatching draugs who've slipped in to harass the locals. Their training in that regard was quite unmatched, truly."

Aer's fingers stiffened on her back.

"Ah." Jonas nodded knowingly. "Yes, the lesser creatures of Jotunheim often cause some headache or another. I hope they didn't make your job too difficult."

Only when they're robbing my citizens, she wanted to say.

"I've learned to hold my own quite thoroughly."

"Well, then I dare say your kingdom couldn't be more fortunate."

She smiled graciously. "I will do all I can to live up to such praise, my lord."

"How long do you plan to stay, Lord Edrin?" the prince asked. His tone had shifted, all sense of playfulness or easy taunts gone.

"That is yet to be determined, Your Highness," Jonas said, finally turning away from Freya to face the king and queen. "I was hoping to explore your markets a bit, see what new wares Jotunheim might be interested in acquiring from Lindoroth. There are a few other matters I'd like to address as well, but those can wait. I'd also just like to see the land," he added with a smile. "Iladel and its surrounding areas are famed for their beauty, something I'd like to explore for myself."

"We'd be happy to provide a guide who can give you a thorough tour of the city," the queen said. "My nephew Lazarus and his partner

Collin are well-acquainted with the area. I'll have it arranged for the day after tomorrow."

"Your Majesty, if I may?" Freya gave Ordona a small smile. "Your niece was so welcoming to me when I arrived. Perhaps Lady Calliwell and I could take Lord Edrin through the city? It would be a wonderful chance for me to revisit Iladel." She smiled as Aer brushed an approving hand down her back. "And it would give me an opportunity to get to know one of our closest neighbors."

A smile quirked the corner of the queen's lips, then she nodded her assent. "Yes, Freya, I think that's a lovely idea."

"It's settled, then," the king said. "The palace is open to you, Lord Edrin. My guards will escort you to your guest chambers, and I'll have the staff bring dinner to your chambers shortly."

"Thank you, Your Majesties," Jonas said. He looked over at Freya and Aerelius and nodded. "My lady, Your Highness. It was wonderful to make your acquaintance."

Freya smiled. "Likewise, Lord Edrin. We'll speak soon of our trip into the city."

With another bow toward the king and queen, Jonas left.

As soon as the door shut, Aerelius turned to face his parents. "I don't care for him. He reminds me a bit of a weasel."

Ordona gave him a chastising look. "Aerelius Harridan, you will bite your tongue!"

The king lit a cigar then took a long puff and smiled. "It's hard to disagree with him, though, Ordona, and I dare you to deny it."

"Insufferable," Ordona huffed. "Every last one of you."

25

After shooing off Salazar and Aerelius, Ordona summoned Freya to her chambers to discuss wedding preparations.

"We only need to get a few ideas flowing," the queen explained as she and Freya settled in her solar. Piles of fabric swatches, sketches of floral arrangements, and detailed menu options lay stacked on the table in front of them. "The planners can take it from there, although you and Aerelius will have to make final approvals, of course."

"Oh, Aer said I could have free rein over our wedding plans," Freya told her.

Ordona pursed her lips. "And what led my overly-opinionated son to such a decision?"

"He lost a bet," Freya replied, grinning.

Ordona sighed and shook her head. "You two... As much as I'd like to chastise you both for your foolishness, I can't help but be reassured by how quickly you seem to have fallen back into your old ways."

Freya smiled softly and ran her hand over the swatch of champagne silk in front of her. "I am, as well. We still have a ways to go, but we'll get there."

"Your guards and his have all reported that you seem to be establishing yourselves as a strong couple on campus," Ordona said, her voice full of approval. "While knife-throwing contests might not be my ideal choice for expressing your affections for one another, I suppose it suits you both."

"You've been receiving reports?" Freya couldn't help but feel a bit insulted, even though she'd likely have done the same thing in the queen's position.

"Of course." Ordona picked up one of the sketches, a detailed drawing of a tall vase bursting with roses and Saithian cornflower, and examined it. "And with the exception of your first day facing one another, I'm quite pleased." She handed Freya the sketch. "I don't prefer cornflower, but with Salazar's homeland being the source, it might be a good choice."

Freya took the page and examined the pretty bluish-purple blossoms, then looked over the piles in front of her. "On the way to Iladel, the ship's cabin I was in seemed to blend elements of all five realms. Do you think we could do something like that?"

Ordona nodded slowly, then began sifting through the parchment and bits of fabric. "Tradition is to represent the bride's heritage with the menu, so I would recommend carrying on with that. For the rest, though, yes, we could manage a theme of unity." She smiled at Freya. "I think that will speak volumes about the kind of monarchs you'll be."

"What about Solstice?" Freya asked. "Will we still have a ball?"

"After the wedding, dear," Ordona said. "For now, let's focus on your nuptials."

"Do you think the planners will be able to manage?" Freya asked.

"Oh, you've got nothing to worry about there. They're the best in all five realms."

For the next hour, the two of them sorted through the samples before them, tossing aside those they knew wouldn't work and setting the ones they felt would in a small box that would be sent to the planners.

There was a noise at the door, jolting Freya from her scrutiny of a sketch of a feathered wedding dress. Ordona's eyes drifted past Freya and lit up. "Ah, Aerelius! Have you come to join the planning?"

Before Freya could turn to face him, she felt his hands come to rest on her shoulders. "I've come to rescue my betrothed, actually," he said. "As scintillating as this conversation surely is, I'd hoped to steal her away for dinner."

Freya patted one of his hands. "It's fine, really. I can come find you when we're done."

"No, no," Ordona said, smiling at them both. "I think we've got a good starting point. I'll send our ideas over to the planners and they can begin working on it. We can meet again soon."

"Are you sure?"

"Of course she is," Aer said, sliding her chair back so she could stand. She scowled as he nearly pulled it out from under her in the process.

"Really, Freya, go on," Ordona said, smiling softly. "Enjoy yourselves."

Not needing to be told twice, Freya stood, hardly having time to push her chair in before Aerelius had taken her hand to drag her toward the door.

"So, where are you stealing me off to?" Freya asked as he led her down the hall away from Ordona's chambers.

"To wander," he told her, smiling mysteriously as he snaked an arm around her waist. "And I've got something to show you."

"Oh?" She arched a brow. "What might that be?"

"You'll see. Did you and Mother come to any decisions?"

"Several, actually." She smiled slyly up at him. "I was thinking a nice tangerine color for your doublet—velvet, of course—might go well with the beading on my dress. Cinderfish stew as an appetizer, topped with sun fruit—"

His eyebrows shot up. "Ah, so you think you're funny, then?"

"Think? I *know*—"

Her words cut off with a laugh as the arm around her waist tightened and he pulled her down a narrow, darkened hallway. She sucked in a sharp breath as he pressed her back to the wall and put his lips against her ear, his breath feather soft against her neck.

"Tangerine is a horrid color for me *and* you," he whispered. "And you're allergic to sun fruit."

Smiling, she leaned her head against the wall, putting a few inches of space between them. "You know, Your Highness, there was a time you'd slip bits of it into my porridge just to see what the result might be."

He gave her a slow, wicked smile, then ran a thumb across her cheek. "Try to dress me up as a piece of fruit and I may revisit that idea."

Shifting the fingers of one hand to talons, she walked the sharpened nails up his chest, then dragged one lightly across his chin. "I'd love to see you try."

He froze, then a slow smile spread across his face and his eyes danced with mirth. "You wouldn't dare mark your prince."

"No?" She pressed her talon harder against his chin. "Are you sure about that?"

Gently, he took her hand, then pressed his lips to her palm, smiling in satisfaction when her claws retracted. "Will you let me kiss you, Freya?"

She laughed. "That's quite a segue." Then grinning, she tapped her cheek. "Alright. I'll let you have one, right here."

"Hmm. I think I can work with that." His eyes hard on hers, he pulled her toward him, spreading his fingers against the small of her back as he lowered his lips to her neck. Her eyes widened in surprise at the press of his body, then she melted just a little as he ran his hand down her spine, teasing the soft skin just between the small ridges from where her wings spread. Softly, he trailed his lips up her neck and along her jaw, then grazed his teeth against her ear, sending a tingle shooting straight to her belly. Finally, he gripped her chin with his other hand and touched a soft kiss to her cheek that caused her insides to burn.

It took every ounce of willpower she had not to turn her head and let him take her mouth, as well.

"Satisfied?" she asked, her voice hardly a whisper.

Pulling back, he gave her a crooked smile and ran his hand up her back again. "Far from it."

She cleared her throat and took a steadying breath. "Were you using your power on me?"

"Of course not!" His surprised expression turned smug. "It's good to know I have such an effect on you, though."

She rolled her eyes and shoved him back, immediately feeling the loss of his body so close to hers. "I thought there was something you wanted to show me?"

"Ah, yes. Shame on you for distracting me so thoroughly." He took her hand and they began to walk down the wide, echoing hall at a meandering pace. "Now that you seem to be putty in my hands, I think you'll be far more interested in where I'm taking you," he said, turning down a side hall.

Stopping at a pair of heavy mahogany doors inlaid with swirling opal designs, Aerelius grinned. Pushing them open, he stepped inside and held out his arms.

"You chambers, my lady. I thought if you saw what you were missing, you'd reconsider your current residence."

Cautiously, Freya stepped inside. It was about the size one might expect of a princess' chambers—spacious, with carved wood paneling, high ceilings, and carpeting that was a thick, rich wool, the kind one could curl their toes into. A gas-fueled crystal chandelier hung from the white tray ceiling, the flames causing the gems to sparkle. In the center of the room was a massive bed flanked by two built-in bookshelves that were already stuffed full of books. Wood-framed glass doors patterned in gold inlay led through a wall made entirely of windows, perfect for a Valkyrie who cared little for being cooped up inside.

She could easily imagine herself here, taking breakfast on the veranda or in the four-poster bed, possibly curling up in front of the marble fireplace with a book.

With a sigh, she faced him, reluctant to show him how much

she'd just fallen in love with the room. It was perfect, and he damn-well knew it.

"I'll make a deal with you," she said, hating how easily the room had made her want to cave. "If it will get you and your father off my case, I'll compromise." She held up two fingers and wiggled them. "Two nights a week, I'll stay here."

Aerelius' answering smile was nothing short of dazzling. "Two nights sounds divine, my lady." He quirked his eyebrows suggestively and inclined his head toward a door off to the side that blended almost seamlessly into the paneling. "And in case you have any bad dreams, my chambers are just through there."

"In case *you* have any bad dreams, you mean," Freya said with a laugh.

"Whatever makes you sleep at night, Freya. Now, I thought we'd head down to the kitchens, rustle some dinner from the cooks." He strode across the room to the fireplace, then, grinning, he ran his finger on the underside of the rosewood mantel.

"Ah, there it is," he murmured. There was a soft *click*, then the bookshelf beside the fireplace moved, opening into the room just a few inches, revealing a darkened space beyond.

Freya's eyes widened. "I have my own secret passage?" With a quick skip of excitement, she hurried over and tugged on the shelv-ing, surprised to find the door opened without a sound. Curious, she examined the hinges that were sunken into the wall. She ran her fingers over the cool metal, then nodded when she felt the unmistak-able prick of silencing magic. "Where does it lead?"

"It leads straight to a linen closet two halls over from the servants' quarters on the lower floor."

"No wonder we never found it," she said. "I barely remember this room."

"In a palace with nearly three hundred rooms, that's unsurpris-ing." He held out his hand, smiling when she took it. "So, does this count as wooing, Valkyrie?"

Laughing, she pulled him into the passage and set a ball of light hovering in the air beside her. "Only you would think pulling a girl into a dark and dusty hidden passage would constitute wooing."

His hand tightened in hers. "Well? Does it?"

"Of course it does. Keep on like this and you'll have me in a puddle at your feet in no time."

Chuckling, he pulled the door shut behind them. "So, how are wedding plans *actually* coming along?"

Freya dragged her fingers along the dusty stone walls as they walked slowly down the passage. "Well enough. We've chosen a theme, so now it will be up to the planners to get it right."

"I'm eager to see how things turn out," he said, sounding sincere. "Although I wouldn't mind a bit of consultation along the way."

Freya shrugged. "A deal's a deal, highness. You lost, fair and square."

"Is this how the rest of our lives will be? Making bets to determine major decisions?"

She elbowed him. "Only if you're silly enough to think you'll ever win," she quipped. "Otherwise, no. Major decisions will certainly be a joint effort. Sixty-forty, at least."

Amused, he smiled down at her. "And let me guess. You'll be the one who gets sixty percent of the say, correct?"

"Or perhaps seventy. That's to be determined."

"Based on...?"

"The type of decision, of course," she said playfully. "We're expected to have children, so when it comes to naming our future offspring, for example, I may be willing to bend a bit."

Draping an arm around her shoulder, Aerelius laughed and kissed her hair. "Do you know how much I adore hearing you speak of our future children so causally?"

"It's an eventuality I came to terms with long ago." Pausing, she turned to face him. In the soft light, the golden highlights in his black-brown hair shimmered and the depth of his dark eyes seemed endless. "Taunting aside, I want you to know that I truly am alright with our... arrangement. If I'm to be paired with someone against my will, I couldn't ask for more than for that person to be one of my oldest friends."

"An arrangement you were forced into against your will, hmm?" Bringing her hand to his lips, he laid a soft kiss on her knuckles. "You've grown into quite the wordsmith."

She smacked his chest. "I'm being serious!"

"Oh, I know," he said with a laugh. "That's the best part."

"You know what?" She let her hands fall from his. "I take it back. I'm going to ask Byrric to rescind the agreement."

Linking his arms around her waist, he began to walk her backward down the hallway, his face tilted toward hers. "Good luck with that. The agreement was signed in blood."

"Not *my* blood. Nor yours. That was all our parents' doing." Turning, she continued ahead, allowing him to keep his arms around her waist as they walked.

They walked the rest of the way in silence, Aerelius pointing out a few narrower passages that broke off from the one they were in, explaining the different areas of the palace grounds they led to. She was surprised to find that the tunnel system was far more extensive than she'd thought, based on their earlier explorations. After a few minutes, they came to a stop in front of a wooden door. Freya put her hand to the door and closed her eyes.

"It's spelled, too," she whispered. "Soundproofing and anti-rot."

"That would make sense," Aer said with a nod. "This palace is five thousand years old. A wooden door wouldn't last that long in such good condition."

"No," Freya murmured, frowning. "But neither would a spell. Magic needs to be refueled every few centuries if a spell is to be truly ever-lasting."

"So this door is either a newer addition or we're not the only ones who frequent these tunnels," Aer finished. "Well, my mother *is* a witch blessed with earth magic. She's the one who told us of the passage system, so it wouldn't be terribly surprising if she's also the one refueling the spells within it."

"Perhaps," Freya agreed.

As one, they pressed their ears to the door, listening for anyone on the other side. After a few moments, Aerelius hooked his finger around the stone latch and pulled, slowly opening the door as silently as possible. Freya let her light wink out, then followed him through. When he pulled it shut, she saw that a stone facade had been mortared onto the wood, allowing it to blend seamlessly with the walls on either side. "Impressive," Freya whispered, running a hand across the rough surface. "Not a seam in sight."

The closet they were in was small, with shelving on one wall from floor to ceiling, all empty and covered in a fine layer of dust.

"It seems to be the quickest way to get from our wing to the kitchens," Aerelius replied. "In case you're ever in the mood for a late-night snack."

She gave him a wry smile. "Aren't I always?"

Taking her hand, he opened the outer door, sticking his head out and looking in either direction before exiting. He led her down a hall and past the main pantry before turning and taking her down a shorter, darker hall, then another, then a third. It was a dizzying maze, and had it not been for her strong sense of direction, she'd almost certainly get lost if she had to find her own way back.

When they came to the door at the end of the hall, he glanced back in the direction they came before pulling the latch and stepping inside.

"This is it?" Freya whispered, reigniting her light and looking around the small, dusty room. Free-standing shelves formed three rows in the room, each bearing empty wooden crates that may have once held root vegetables, but all they held now was a fine layer of dust.

For whatever reason, this room had been deserted.

"There's nothing here," Freya said, frowning as she turned in a slow circle. "Have you checked all the crates for a key?"

Aer nodded. "There wasn't one."

"So they either took it with them or someone in the castle has it, although a human with a key to the palace seems more than a bit far-fetched."

"Exactly," Aer said. He gestured toward the rear wall. "The keyhole we found is over there, barely visible, but I would assume someone locked the door from in here when the human left."

Freya bit her lip and frowned. "Did you—"

"I checked the hallways for passages we hadn't yet found," he told her, anticipating her question. "Unless I missed something, the closest one was the closet we came through, which has no less than a dozen branches. My assumption is this was just a stopping point, a way to get in from the gardens without being seen. It's a simple enough trek from the gardens to the forest from there."

Walking toward the hidden door, Freya touched a finger to the keyhole that was almost completely obscured by a small ridge in the stone. Glancing around the room, she frowned. "And your parents have said nothing about human visitors from Dystone?"

"None. I've attempted to bring human relations up with them both, mainly regarding their monarchs' attendance at our wedding, but nothing seemed amiss."

She bit her lip and stared down at the small hole in the wall. "It's strange, don't you think? If the human was here to visit one of your parents, as future king, you'd think they might tell you about it."

"You would think. I plan to keep looking, but unless he or she returns, I don't know that I'll find much else."

Annoyed, Freya sighed. It wasn't only the fact that a human was sneaking through the palace was odd, but more so that the king and queen, assuming they knew, hadn't mentioned a thing to Aerelius. Relations with Dystone had always been favorable, considering the Linds had been the reason for the liberation of their people, so a visit from one wasn't unheard of or even unexpected.

On the same token, Freya supposed there was a good deal about being a monarch she and Aerelius had yet to learn, including why visitors from foreign lands would be secreted in and out of the palace.

"You're going to drive yourself crazy if you keep playing what-if," Aer whispered. He held out his hand for hers. "We'll see what else we can find, but for now, let's eat."

They made their way in the other direction toward the main

kitchen, walking more slowly this time so Freya could do her own examination of the walls along the way. When they got to the kitchen, they found Maghda, the rotund female who commanded the kitchens like a captain did a ship, preparing dinner for the rest of the palace. Her assistants, all significantly younger and a good deal more sprightly, scurried about.

"Your Highness!" Maghda said, smiling when she saw the prince. "I heard you might be paying us a visit. And look at you, Lady Balthana! All grown up!"

Freya grinned and accepted the female's warm embrace. "Maghda, it's lovely to see you again."

Maghda gave her a warm smile, then gestured toward the long harvest table that ran the length of the room and where two servants sat at one end shucking corn.

"Sit, I'll fix you both something to eat." When they did, she picked up a second sack of corn and dropped it on the table in front of them, her eyes twinkling. "And while you're here, feel free to lend a hand."

The prince *tsk*ed and shook his head. "Maghda, if I were any other prince..."

"Ah, but you're not, and you know I don't tolerate idle hands in my kitchen." She moved toward a large pot that was bubbling softly on the stove. Glancing over her shoulder, she waved a hand toward the produce. "Go on."

"Would you order my father to shuck corn if he ventured down?" Aer asked.

Maghda barked out a laugh. "Your father knows better than to make his way down here, princeling."

Amused, Freya stood and pulled a basket off the wall, then sat down, arching a brow when Aerelius narrowed his eyes.

"You know, Valkyrie, it's bad form to let the staff order their future monarch around," he said, picking up an ear of corn. "Feel free to demand the most complex meals you can come up with for our wedding."

Freya tossed the stump from the end of her corn at him, leaving several strands of silk on his blue tunic. "You might want to be a bit more appreciative of the people who prepare your food, Highness, or you may end up poisoned."

He pointed at her with an ear of corn. "You've been spending too much time around Florian."

"Oh, don't mind him," Maghda said, stirring her stew. "He's down here twice a week peeling potatoes or coring apples. One time I even got him to truss a turkey."

Freya gave him a wide-eyed look of surprise. "Impressive. Even I can't do that."

He gave her a quick wink and reached for another ear. "If you're lucky, maybe one day I'll teach you."

"I'll teach her, you mean," Maghda shot back.

"Why in the world did you need to truss a turkey?" Freya asked, still a bit surprised.

"I'd gone hunting with my father," Aerelius explained. "I was about twelve or so? I'd always done well with hunting other fowl and larger animals, but this was my first wild turkey." He shrugged and tossed the cleaned ear of corn into the basket. "I knew how to dress a deer, but nothing of trussing a bird, so mother insisted I bring it down here so Maghda could teach me."

"Begged me to do it for him, too," Maghda said, then clicked her tongue. "'What will I ever need to do this for?' he'd asked. But I told him, you want to come into *my* space, you live by my rules." She pointed a spoon at Freya. "That means learning yourself a thing or two."

"I look forward to it," Freya said sincerely. "My aunt was the cook back in Watoria. I was always out, either at school or working for the marshals. Some days I hardly took the time to stop and eat."

"No wonder you're so small," the cook said. She sniffed. "Least you've got some muscle on you, though. Next time you visit, I'll have you lug some sacks of grain, keep you from getting soft."

Freya laughed. "I think I'd like that very much, Maghda."

26

Unsurprising to Freya, Lea was less-than thrilled to have been assigned to act as a tour guide for Lord Edrin. Freya had broken the news to her as they walked from the last morning class to the dining hall for lunch the following day. Despite Lea's eagerness to help Freya adapt to life in the capital, trotting a Jotunn through the Iladelian markets was, according to her, not her job as the prince's cousin to do.

"How exactly did I end up escorting him around?" Lea asked as she and Collin took seats in the dining hall with Laz and Freya after their morning classes. "Why not you?" She scanned the room. "And where is your betrothed? He'll get me out of this."

"Queen Ordona ordered it herself," Freya told her, taking up a spoonful of her chilled cantaloupe soup. "And I'll be with you."

Lea narrowed her eyes at her. "Don't lie to me, Freya. I know you had a hand in this."

"I'm insulted you would think so little of me," Freya said with mock outrage.

"I don't see why you're so upset, Lea," Laz said. "It's a city tour, not a betrothal. Save your upset for when she insists you allow him to escort him to the Solstice ball."

Lea gasped. "Bite your tongue!"

"Is it really that big a deal?" Collin asked.

"It takes time out of my day," Lea said haughtily. "And from what Aer said, he smells."

Freya rolled her eyes. "My sense of smell is far superior to his, and I can tell you, Lord Edrin smells like any other Jotunn warlock."

"We could meet up with you, if you'd like," Collin suggested. "For lunch, perhaps?"

"We could?" Laz asked.

"No, it's fine," Freya told him, sending a deprecating look toward Lea. "She's clearly being overdramatic."

"Oh, there's Aer," Lea said, sighing in relief as she stood. "He'll get me out of this. Cousin!" she shouted across the hall. "Come here!"

Freya watched as Aer made his way across the room, smiling politely as he declined multiple invites to sit with the other students. That he cared enough to even acknowledge them—something many royals wouldn't bother to do—spoke volumes to her about the kind of person he had turned out to be.

A few seconds later, Aer sat down next to Freya, his two hulking guards—Rodrick and Perinald, Freya had learned—taking up position behind him, their backs to the wall. "What is it?" he asked.

"Your mother," Lea began, pointing at him with a breadstick, "has offered me up as some sweaty dignitary's tour guide and I would like you to rectify that."

Aer shrugged. "She's the queen," he said simply. "What she says goes."

"I'm going to go *with* you, Lea," Freya repeated, trying to hide her frustration. "I can't do it on my own. It's been too long since I've explored the city."

"Is he handsome at least? If I'm to spend the day with this male, I'd at least hope he's nice to look upon."

Propping his chin on his fist, Aer looked at Freya, eyes twinkling. "I don't know, Lea. Freya, would you say our guest is handsome?"

"Well his skin *is* like a fresh fallen snow," Freya said dreamily, mirroring his position. "And his eyes—" She squealed as Aer tried to tickle her. Grabbing his wrist, she gave him a warning look, doing her best to ignore the teasing gleam in his eyes. "I won't hesitate to hurt you, *Your Highness*."

"A fact I'll never forget, my love," he said, gently dislodging her grip and lacing his fingers through hers, smiling when she didn't pull away.

"So that would be a yes, then?" Lea asked.

"He's mildly handsome," Freya said. "And for the last time, *I'm going with you.*"

"Don't trouble yourself, Freya," Collin said. "As you said, Lea is being overdramatic, as per usual."

Lea huffed but didn't deny it.

"It will only be a few hours," Freya told her. "Hardly a blip in time, really."

Lea groaned. "Alright, alright. But don't expect me to be happy about it!"

Freya held up her free hand and smiled. "I'd never ask that much of you."

Lea frowned at Aer. "And why aren't you insisting on escorting us?"

Aer shrugged, then plucked a bite of cantaloupe from Freya's plate, smiling when she scowled in response. "I'm quite certain Freya would kill me in my sleep if I ever attempted anything that resembled nannying."

Freya preened. "What makes you think I'd wait until you're sleeping?"

"So when will your excursion be happening?" Collin asked, shaking his head at their exchange.

"Tomorrow," Aer replied.

"To—" Lea huffed. "Freya, I pray you won't be so demanding when you're queen."

She frowned. "How am I to have any fun, then?"

"Lady Balthana?"

Freya flashed a quick look at Aer at the sound of Myria's voice. He gave her an amused look that clearly said, "Have fun and expect no help from me."

Turning, she found the sharp-eyed lady of Saith standing behind her, a look of resignation on her pretty face.

Freya kept her expression as neutral as possible. "Yes?"

Myria's lips thinned as she looked around the table, giving a tight smile to Freya's friends, before taking a deep breath and meeting Freya's eyes. "May we speak privately?"

"Ten sils she's here to grovel," Laz murmured quietly, enough for only Freya to hear.

"Thirty," Aer replied, popping a grape into his mouth and leaning back in his seat, grinning at Freya.

Fighting back a smile, Freya stood. "Of course. Let's go outside." She held up a hand when Rissen and Cecilia made to follow. "I'll just be a minute," she told them. Then, brushing past Myria, she strode toward the door, leading the way out.

When they emerged onto the patio, Freya turned to face her. Standing together, Myria in her pretty floral dress, with delicate blond curls cascading over her shoulders, and Freya in her leather pants and light gray blouse, her hair pulled back in a wispy braid, their differences were impossible to miss. Even still, Freya found herself hoping she and the girl could eventually find some sort of common ground, form an amicable relationship. Freya never liked the thought of having an unnecessary enemy, and a governor's daughter was a good ally to have.

So, she offered up a smile as she addressed her.

"What can I do for you, Lady Bryton?"

Myria wiped her hands on her silk dress nervously. "It's—please, call me Myria."

"Alright. What can I do for you, Myria?"

Myria took a deep breath, clasping her hands together in front of her and giving Freya a meek look. "I wanted to apologize for the way I treated you initially. While I couldn't have known your true identity or status, it was wrong of me to assume so little of you." She took a deep breath. "I hope you can accept my apology and that we might be able to move forward as friends."

Freya angled her head and eyed Myria speculatively, hardly able to contain her amusement. The poor girl looked as though having a molar pulled might be more fun than her current circumstances, and she was doing little to hide it. Freya had expected this soon enough and assumed she'd get similar apologies from Myria's friends who'd joined in her taunts. Petty as it might've been, Freya took a small pleasure in Myria's discomfort.

Doing her best to keep her face neutral, she let Myria suffer in silence for a few seconds before responding. "I appreciate your words, Myria, but there's something you should know about me."

Myria gave her a wary look. "What's that?"

"I don't tolerate forced apologies." Before Myria could offer a rebuke, Freya held up a hand. "I find them quite pointless, to be honest. I can only assume your father instructed you to apologize after you so brazenly threatened and insulted me on multiple occasions. Do I have that right?"

Myria opened her mouth, doubtless to deny Freya's claim, but instead, her shoulders slumped and the false look of contrition she'd worn shifted to defeat.

"Yes. Well, more my mother than my father. But—"

Freya shook her head. "While I can understand their reasoning and yours for obeying, your apology means little to me if it's insincere."

Myria's jaw tightened. "I admit that I viewed you as competition for the prince's affections and wanted to scare you off. I did what I felt necessary to eliminate you as a threat."

Freya gave her an amused grin. "In other words, you aren't actually sorry?"

"No," Myria replied. "I am not. But I *will* be moving on. I may hate you for landing the prince, but I'm not pathetic enough to try to sabotage your betrothal." She took a deep breath and her expression turned sour. "After seeing you and Aerelius together, I can acknowledge any chance I had may have been slim, and I have too much self-respect to try to convince someone to love me when his sights are so clearly set elsewhere."

Freya's brow shot up in genuine surprise, then she laughed. "Self-awareness. That's something I can appreciate far more than a politically-fueled apology."

"I—truly?"

"Of course. While I disagree thoroughly with your actions, I understand your motivations. And, as I'm no stranger to a parent making choices for me, I can even sympathize a bit."

Hopefulness flashed in Myria's eyes. "You're unhappy with the choices your parents made for you?"

Freya smiled wryly. "No, Myria, not in this case. I care for our prince a great deal."

Myria folded her arms and looked out across the sunny quadrangle of the campus, then sighed. "That's rare, you know. Being content with a betrothal."

"I know how fortunate I am, and I take nothing that has been offered to me for granted," Freya told her.

Myria wrinkled her nose. "I was assuming you'd laugh in my face, call me names, possibly even spit on me for my disrespect. Thank you for not doing any of those things."

Freya laughed. "Has anyone told you that you're quite skilled at backhanded compliments, Lady Bryton?"

Myria's lips twitched, then she frowned. "May I ask you a favor?"

"Of course."

"If my father or mother asks..."

Freya gave her an understanding smile. "You groveled at my feet?"

Myria let out a relieved breath. "Thank you."

"Believe it or not, I also know a thing or two about frustrating parental expectations." She smiled sincerely. "My lips are sealed."

JUST AFTER LUNCH, Freya received notice she was to report to the headmistress' office before heading to her next class. When she arrived, she was surprised to find her father waiting for her outside.

"This can't be good," she said wryly as she approached. "Don't you have soldiers to order about?"

"Queen Ordona informed me you'll be acting as a guide to the Jotnar emissary," Byrric said, ignoring her jab. "I'd hoped to speak to you privately about that before you go."

Freya looked around the busy campus and frowned. "Alright. Let's go to the lake."

She sent a nod toward Rissen and Cecilia to let them know she'd return, then let out her wings and took off, looping once in the air as her father joined her. Side-by-side, they flew across campus, and as Freya watched the students roaming about below, all of whom were oblivious to the thrill of soaring through the sky, she had to admit she enjoyed having someone to fly with for once. Byrric taught her how to fly long ago, but after he left Watoria, she was largely on her own, teaching herself most of her evasive maneuvers and aerial moves.

When he picked up speed, tucking his wings tight to his sides, she grinned, accepting the challenge. With a sharp flap of her wings, she burst forward, overtaking him just before they crossed the line of trees that surrounded the lake.

"You're getting slow in your old age," she teased as they touched down.

"Or I let you win," he countered.

"Uh huh." She sat down on the sand. "Now, what did you need to speak with me about?"

Byrric sat down beside her as well and rested his elbows on his knees. "When you and Lady Calliwell take the Jotunn to Iladel, I want you to be wary of everything he says. Be cognizant of everything you tell him and report back to me with anything you find worth noting."

Freya was surprised—and a bit insulted—he thought she'd do anything less. "Might I ask why you feel the need to forewarn me?"

"Our relationship with Jotunheim is tenuous enough as it is. Considering your position, you need to be aware that all you say and do will be turned over and dissected. You haven't yet had the experience to gain any political savvy, so this will be a test of your abilities."

"That's why I offered to do this," she told him. "I could've easily suggested Laz and Collin take this on, but Lea will have a softer approach, and he's already quite curious about me."

Byrric nodded, his face serious. "Alright. As a monarch-in-training, I will trust your judgement on this."

Freya arched a brow. "But not as your daughter?"

He laughed. "My daughter would do her best to make me look a fool. A future monarch, however, would want to create a strong image for herself."

"Which I'm attempting to do."

"I heard you nearly got into an argument with Kira Leston in your Civics class. Is that what you consider making a strong image for yourself?"

"The girl needed to be put in her place, and I merely provided thorough answers to a question our professor asked. It isn't *my* fault if she took offense to the truth. And do you and the king and queen truly have spies on me everywhere I go?"

"Yes," he replied without an ounce of shame. "So you should behave as though every word you say will be reported directly to the king, himself."

"I do! But I'm not going pander to some opportunistic brat who finds it acceptable to belittle people—including her future queen, no less—for her own amusement." She frowned. "And considering it was Governor Bryton's daughter whom I defended, you'd think I might get a bit of credit for that, considering how vile that girl has been to me since I arrived."

"Speaking of Lady Bryton, you were seen speaking with her outside the dining hall earlier." He gave her a pointed look. "I trust it was a civil conversation?"

"Quite," Freya confirmed. "Her false contrition was almost convincing."

Byrric sighed and lifted his eyes skyward. "And I'm sure you told her just that."

"Honest, Commander," she said, smiling sweetly. "I was honest with her, and she appreciated that. We won't be braiding each other's hair any time soon, but at the very least, her looks toward me should be a bit less venomous. I don't know about you, but I consider that a good thing."

"Yes, I suppose it is." Standing, he held out a hand to pull her to her feet. "Ah, I nearly forgot. I was also told to tell you that you 'promised the prince two nights at the palace and tomorrow will be the first.'" Arching a brow, he sighed. "Care to elaborate?"

Freya rolled her eyes. "My fiancé is using fancy bedrooms and hidden passages to convince me to move to the palace. Two days a week are my compromise for now."

"Yes, I suppose that might ease his mind a bit," Byrric said with a nod. "Salazar's, too. Good work, Freya. That's one less annoyance we'll have to deal with."

"For now," she amended. "Aer will likely back off, but the king will take it as an opening. I'm fully expecting him to push back."

"It's only for a few more months," he replied. "There are more than enough precautions in place for you to remain at Aldridge until the winter holiday. After the wedding, though, you won't have a choice."

She waved off his warning. "I know, which is why I'd like to get as much time here as I can. I've cooled down a bit now, but I'm still quite furious that I won't get even a full year here as I was promised."

"You can thank your prince for that," Byrric responded dryly. "But you and he are a distraction enough as it is. Why he insisted on attending and his parents allowed it is beyond my comprehension."

"For the same reason you and King Salazar allowed me to," Freya said simply. "To learn from the best and potentially form friendships with the children of the more influential citizens of the realms."

"Forming alliances is not the main reason Salazar invited you to attend or why I agreed to send you," Byrric told her. "He knew your strengths and wanted you in an environment, at least for a time, where you could hone those strengths before becoming bogged down by queenly duties."

"He could have just as easily had that done at the palace," she corrected. "He saw my talents at a young age, certainly, but the reason he wanted me *here* was for the relationships I could form and the influence I could garner, pure and simple." She gave him a tight smile. "I meant what I said after the ball. I want the citizens of Lindoroth to revere me based on who I am, not the title I hold. As a student here, I would've been able to take more steps to ensure that. Without knowing who I am, they'll see me as a female whose species landed her a betrothal with the prince and nothing more. That may have been true when I was a child, but I want to prove that I'm worthy of their respect."

Byrric was silent for a moment, and Freya could tell he wanted to refute her claims, despite their accuracy.

"You are quite perceptive, daughter," he finally said. "And you'll find another way. If there's one thing you got from your mother, it's her persistence. Don't let this one setback cause you to falter."

She laughed. "You know, I think that's the most fatherly advice you've ever given me, Commander."

27

A s per the queen's instructions, Lea and Freya met Lord Edrin at the market entrance the following morning, their guards following quietly behind.

"You really should have worn a dress," Lea whispered as they waited for Lord Edrin's carriage which slowly rattled down the road toward them.

Freya flicked her a glance from where she leaned against the pillar that framed the market gates. She'd opted for more casual attire, her normal leather pants replaced with a pair made of loose, black muslin, and a fitted, sleeveless blouse the color of blueberries. Her hair was pulled back in a tight braid that fell over one shoulder, keeping it off her neck and making the color a bit less obvious. "I'm going to be trudging through a hot, crowded city all day. If I need to take flight, I'd prefer not to flash my underthings to all of Iladel."

"You won't need to take flight, my lady," Cecilia told her. "Not while we're around."

Freya bobbed her head side to side, considering. "I will if my aim is to evade you."

Rissen arched a brow. "We're under strict orders from our commander and the prince to report back if you choose to fly off."

"That's certainly not a hassle you'd want to face on your return, is it?" Cecilia gave her a knowing look.

Freya narrowed her eyes. "You're basing that conclusion on the assumption I find no joy in irritating my father or my fiancé."

Rissen folded his arms and stared at her evenly. "Yes, but do you enjoy the resulting reaming Cecilia and I get each time you evade us purely to spite them, my lady?"

"He's got you there," Lea sing-songed, smiling smugly when she saw the look of guilt on Freya's face.

Freya sighed. "You're lucky I've taken a liking to you both."

Lea smirked up at her own personal guard, Iska, who continued to maintain his typical stoicism. "And here you thought *I* was a difficult child."

He gave her a reluctant smile. "Never, my lady."

"Ha!" Lea snorted.

"I'm not difficult!" Freya exclaimed as Lord Edrin's carriage rolled to a stop in front of them.

"Problematic, then?" Lea suggested. "Ornery, perhaps?"

Before Freya had a chance to retort, the carriage door swung open and Lord Edrin was beaming down at them, his bright white teeth flashing in the sun, the pale skin of his face already showing a tinge of redness at the heat.

"Ah, Lady Balthana! So lovely to see you again!" He stepped down from the carriage and sent a dazzling smile to Lea as the coachman pulled the carriage off into a waiting area. Smartly, he'd chosen to wear a lightweight tunic and loose-fitting pants, ideal for walking through the city on a hot day.

Turning to Lea, he gave her a deep bow. "And you must be Lady Calliwell."

"Yes, but please, call me Lea," she replied with a small curtsy. "It's lovely to make your acquaintance, my lord."

"Please, it's Jonas." He looked between them both expectantly. "Now, shall we? I'm eager to see what treasures await."

"You haven't brought any guards?" Lea asked, frowning at his carriage.

He laughed. "When I've got a Valkyrie queen to protect me? No, I think I'd prefer this tour without a cadre of guards lurking behind us." He cast a somewhat annoyed look at the stoic guards that had accompanied Freya and Lea, the three of which stood a respectable distance away. "Although I suppose that was unavoidable."

"You'll get used to them, don't worry," Lea whispered conspiratorially. She gestured toward the market. "Shall we?"

"Where would you like to go first?" Freya asked as they ambled toward the gates. "Were there certain wares you were hoping to examine?"

"Jotunheim is interested in expanding on its mineral imports," Jonas said. "Stones and metal, mainly. "

"It might be worth a stop in Caelora on your return trip, then," Lea advised. "Iladel holds a great deal of their forged metals, but if you're hoping to acquire raw materials, you'd be better off going to their source."

"Is there a reason for a renewed interest?" Freya asked. "I was under the impression the Jotnar had no use for importing those types of goods because of your own mines."

"We didn't, but the labor involved in extracting minerals from our own mines has become a bit cost-prohibitive in many areas," Jonas replied. "Many of our people have been traveling across the border to Lindoroth for them instead, so Empress Lessia would like to provide them within our own lands, if possible."

Lea gestured down an aisle that appeared to hold what Jonas was looking for. "Let's start with minerals and make our way around. Then we'll find ourselves a bit of Iladelian cuisine for lunch."

Letting the two of them walk slightly ahead, Freya scanned the crowded market, already bustling despite the early hour. Rows upon rows of stalls stretched out in all directions, offering fragrant spices, potions, and other magical goods, along with Allanorian leather, Edhillian jewels, Caelorian weapons, and Saithian silk. Its hurried feel reminded her a bit of Watoria's market, despite being easily quadruple the size.

For the next few hours, their group wandered through the

avenues of stalls, sampling foods and examining gems and various metals. Jonas took notes in a small notebook along the way, taking particular interest in the quality of blades made of Caelorian alloys. As Lea and Jonas continued along the row, Freya lingered for a few moments at the stands of jewelers, her eyes drawn to the lovely pieces created by the artisans of Edhil and Caelora. A witch, her smooth skin beginning to soften with age, smiled at Freya when she saw her admiring a pair of rose stone earrings.

"Do you like them?"

Freya nodded. "They're lovely." Gently, she touched the stones, their facets causing them to flash in the sun. "How much would you like for them?"

The witch eyed Freya, taking in her features and narrowing her eyes a bit. Freya saw them shift the moment recognition hit. "For you, my lady, a gift."

Freya held the female's gaze, unsure of how to proceed. She could almost hear Byrric whispering in her ear, telling her to accept the gift with grace.

"Alright, I'll take them," she said after a moment. "But only if you sell me the matching necklace."

The witch gave her a knowing grin as she plucked the necklace from the velvet-covered table. "Your father is a stubborn one, too, you know."

Freya laughed as the female packaged the pieces in small velvet bags. "So I've told him."

"My name is Rosina," she said, handing Freya the two bags and accepting the gold fifty-sil coin Freya dropped in her hand.

Freya's eyes brightened with recognition. "Oh! I believe Kallan procured a few pieces from you for a dinner and ball I recently attended."

Rosina smiled and nodded. "Yes, he brings me a good deal of business. Should you have need of any other pieces, my lady, I would be honored to have your patronage."

"Thank you, Rosina. I'm sure you'll be seeing me again soon." With a final wave, she went on to join the others, who'd move on to a vendor's stand that sold flatware and heavy serving dishes. She found Jonas turning a gold serving spoon over in his hand as he examined the designs etched into the metal.

"Are you in the market for new place settings, my lord?" Freya asked when she approached.

"Ah, there she is!" Jonas grinned. "As I was just saying to Lea, the metals we mine for jewelry and flatware aren't as strong as yours, which are seemingly ageless. Although I'm sure there's a bit of magic involved."

Freya gave what she hoped was a bashful smile. "Unfortunately, I'm not well-versed in the methods of our craftspeople," she said. "They're unmatched, however, whatever they may be."

"Indeed," he murmured, flicking a glance at her leather boots. Then, smiling, he set down the gold serving spoon he'd been looking over. "Shall we eat, then? I'm quite famished."

"Of course," Lea said, drawing his attention away from Freya. "There's a cafe just inside the gates to the city I think you'll enjoy. We can walk a bit more after that, unless you're eager to get back, of course?"

"No rush at all, Lea," Jonas replied.

As they made their way toward the gates that led from the market into the main part of the city, Freya fell into step beside him.

"So, how was your trip from Jotunheim, Jonas? I've never been that far north, but I've always heard it's a lovely trek."

Jonas clasped his hands behind his back and smiled at her. "I live on the eastern edge of Rodrun Lake, and since we don't have a canal system like yours, the trip took about a week on horseback. The lands between here and there are majestic, to say the least."

"I'd love to see it someday," she said wistfully, not having to fake her sincerity. "Dystone, as well. I'm told the human lands are a good deal different than our continent."

"Indeed," he said with a nod.

"Have you been, then?" Lea asked him.

"I have." He gave them both a rueful smile. "Sadly, they're still a bit wary of my kind across the sea."

Freya had to bite her tongue to keep from telling him she under-stood the humans' reticence. To the Linds and the Jotnar, the three centuries since the war were barely a blink, something the humans knew all too well. Many of the Jotnar who'd attempted to overtake the humans were still alive, still holding onto their old prejudices and animosity toward the beings they saw as lesser. In the time since the war, international sea travel had been severely limited for the Jotnar, enforced by both the Lindorothian and Dystonian navies. Even still, the Jotnar hadn't done much in the way of curbing their tendency toward battle over discourse. The draugs and lower beings of their lands often snuck into Lindoroth to wreak havoc, and little seemed to be done on the part of their empress to quell their behaviors.

As she examined Jonas now, a fair-haired son of Jotunheim and barely thirty, it was difficult to tell if he carried those same prejudices and violent tendencies. He seemed more open, more willing to accept those from outside his homeland, but Freya knew better than anyone how deceiving appearances could be. Even still, she didn't want to live her life under a cloud of cynicism, so she made herself a promise not to write off a person simply because of the history of their lands. Being open to those whom others would consider beneath her was largely the reason she'd spent most of her life in Watoria instead of the capital, after all.

"Has there been discussion of reviving international travel between your countries?" she asked as they stepped through the door to the small cafe Lea had led them to.

He sighed and let his eyes run over the busy market as he responded. "I've pressed my aunt a good deal to work on building friendships with the Dystonians, but both parties seem quite reluc-tant. She's made some headway since the new monarchs arose, so my hope is we might be able to try once more."

"Your aunt was a commander in that war, though, correct?" Lea asked, ignoring Freya's silencing look as they sat, their guards taking up residence at the table beside them. "I would imagine that would make it difficult to trust her intentions to be noble."

Jonas gave her an understanding smile. "Which is why she sent me as her emissary. Even still, King Willem insisted I was to be the only one to disembark from my ship and refused to meet me further inland than the palace in Caldel."

"At least you were still able to see the land," Freya said.

"Indeed." Smiling, Jonas rubbed his hands together, then picked up his menu. "Now, what do you recommend?"

Lea gestured for Freya and Jonas to set their menus down, then beckoned toward the female who'd been hovering to the side, waiting to approach. "Clarissa, could you bring us a bit of everything, please? Lady Balthana and I would like to show our guest the best Iladel has to offer."

"Yes, my Lady," the small brunette said, smiling. She gave Freya a quick curtsy, then dashed through a door to the kitchens.

Freya threw Lea an amused look. "A bit of everything?"

Lea shrugged. "She knows what I prefer, and what I prefer is superb, so I'm certain you'll both enjoy it all."

Jonas laughed and looked at Lea. "Have you lived in the capital long?"

"We began summering here three years ago," she said. "I moved here from Edhil just before the start of term this year."

"Ah, the southern lands! Tell me, which regions do you prefer?"

"Oh, I quite love them all," Lea gushed. "Even the desert is nice to visit in the cooler months. The canyons are such a treat to see."

"Yes, I hear they're quite lovely. Perhaps over the summer I'll make a visit."

Lea smiled. "I'm sure my father would welcome you warmly."

Shifting, he turned his attention to Freya. "Freya, I'm eager to hear more about you. When I heard Lindoroth's next queen was the daughter of Byrric Balthana and Cina Enrieth, I was quite stunned, to say the least."

"Why is that?"

"I've found female monarchs often have—need, even—an air of submissiveness. Forgive my bluntness, my lady, but I don't see that in you at all."

Lea coughed back a laugh as Freya angled her head curiously.

His eyes darted between her and Lea briefly, and whatever he saw in their expressions had him backpedaling immediately. "I meant no offense, of course. I simply assumed you would follow in your father or mother's footsteps."

"Both chose to serve their land, protect its people," she countered. "Isn't being queen doing just that?"

"Forgive me, I thought—"

"That a betrothal means I'll be a reluctant queen?" Freya's lips slid into a slow smile. "I can assure you, my lord, that couldn't be further from the truth. Aerelius and I are quite fond of one another."

Lea rested her elbow on the table, propping her chin in her fist as she watched on in amusement.

Jonas held up his hands in apology as a slight flush mottled his pale skin. "I'm sorry, my lady. Truly, there was no offense intended."

"Then none will be taken," Freya replied coolly. "Now, my father mentioned you might want to see Aldridge while you're visiting. Is that correct?"

"Ah, yes!" He smiled, seemingly relieved at the shift in topic. "I enjoy comparing the teaching methods in other education systems to our own. It's wonderful to think outside the proverbial box, so to speak, and I've always had an interest in the field."

"You should come visit this week, then!" Lea grinned at Freya before continuing. "Our last class each day is Combat, so you might even get lucky enough to see our Valkyrie take on her prince."

Jonas' eyes widened. "You fight your betrothed? With weapons?"

"Of course!" Freya smiled wickedly. "Sometimes I even let him win."

He stared at her for a moment, shocked, then gave her a bewildered smile.

"That, my lady, is something I'd like to see."

AFTER LUNCH, Lea led them on a tour around the city, showing Jonas the sights as Freya nostalgically recalled the times she'd spent walking the streets with her parents as a child. She'd always seen Iladel as the best place to go if one wanted to see what the whole of Lindoroth had to offer, and it seemed that hadn't changed at all. The scent of spices mixed with fresh flowers, the quiet hum of magic, and the cheerful sound of street performers had always left her with a feeling of contentment as a child, and now that she was grown, the additional knowledge that this was now her city and these would soon be her subjects gave her a sense of added pride.

"You seem quite happy here, my lady," Jonas commented to Freya when Lea stepped into a tea shop for refreshments. "At home, even."

She gave him a curious look as they took seats at a small table. "That surprises you?"

"Indeed. I can honestly say I wouldn't adapt so well if I were pulled from my homeland and dropped into a distant realm."

Freya frowned. "Had that been the case, I can assure you I might have struggled." She held a hand out, gesturing around the busy plaza. "This was the place I called home for four months each year up until my teen years. It may not be my homeland, as you say, but calling it my home now is something I feel blessed to be able to do." She couldn't help feeling irritated that she felt the need to explain herself so frequently to him, but it was all she could do not to thoroughly chastise him for his presumptions.

"Ah, I was unaware you were so familiar with Iladel," he said with a tense smile. "Again, I fear I've offended you."

She appraised him for a moment, taking in the slightly uncomfortable expression he wore, then sighed. "Can I offer you a bit of advice, Jonas?"

"It would be well-received, I assure you," he replied, letting out a relieved breath.

"If you'd like to know something about me, all you need to do is ask. No matter how you phrase your questions, my answers will be the same. My status as Aerelius' bride gives me both pride and happiness, as does my future as a leader of Lindoroth. If you hope to unearth some discord in my heart, you'll find yourself disappointed."

Jonas studied her for a moment, a look of slight consternation on his pale features. After a moment, he shifted his gaze away from hers and across the plaza. "I must say, Freya, I'm surprised at that. I've never known a female to be content to be traded away from her family into another."

"Traded?" Her brows shot up in warning at his bitter tone. "I would be careful how you proceed, Lord Edrin. Insulting my parents and our monarchs isn't something that would lead me to look upon you favorably in the future."

His eyes widened, then he blinked and a wide smile broke out on his face. "Ah, you do sound like a queen, don't you? Allow me to take a step back. I only worded my statement as I did because Empress Lessia—and *only* Empress Lessia—arranges her family's marriages, and she does so in a way that is only advantageous to her, no matter the cost. Power, wealth, and political affiliations always weigh more heavily in betrothals than compatibility of the individuals." He sighed and looked out across the square, silent for a moment before continuing. "My parents were always in strong agreement with her on that, along with her husband, Crispin, before they all passed. Once they did, Lessia took over as a mother figure, or her version of one, at least, continuing to raise me and my sister at court."

"I'm sorry," Freya said quietly. "That kind of loss... I know only a fraction of it, but my sympathies are with you, nonetheless."

The ghost of a smile flickered across his face. "I watched my own sister, who was in love with another male, get betrothed to someone she'd never met, a person who was neither handsome nor kind, and who lived far from her home. She'd grown up in the capital, so when she was forced to move from Madrya, she was quite heartbroken. She had no choice in the matter and has lived a life filled with unhappiness and, though she'll never admit it, pain ever since."

Freya frowned in confusion. "The mating bond doesn't help with that?"

Jonas shook his head. "Most of my kind don't want to be tied so... deeply. Many believe they're a detriment, a falsehood disguised as love."

"But the gods will only grant bonds to those they believe are stronger for it, those who will become better people because of it," Freya argued. "They make for stronger unions, not weaker."

"On that, my lady, we are in solid agreement," he said. "That said, I'm sure you can imagine why it's difficult, knowing what I know of other arrangements, to understand another female being happy with hers. Perhaps if the mating bond had been an option, she would be happier and he would be more kind, but that's not for us to know."

Freya's heart twisted a bit at the thought of his loss and another female finding herself under such unfortunate circumstances. "I'm sorry, Jonas," she said quietly. "For your sister's plight."

"I hope you can forgive me for projecting feelings of her experience onto yours." Laughing, he shook his head. "Gods above, I think that might be the fifth apology I've handed you today, my lady. I'll have to work on removing my foot from my mouth before our next visit."

"We all have slips of the tongue now and then, Jonas. I understand a little of how you feel, but just know that your sister's circumstances are not my own."

"Here we are!" Lea sang as she emerged from the tea shop with three tall glasses of iced tea. She set them down on the table in front of Freya and Jonas, then sat down, taking a glass for her own.

Relieved that Lea had interrupted what was becoming an increasingly uncomfortable conversation, Freya picked up her glass and took a long sip. The tea, cold and refreshing, tasted of mint and raspberry and helped quell the discomfort of the city heat. It had become stifling, so much so that Freya longed to open her wings and fly off, cooling herself in the mountain air overhead. Instead, she touched the glass to the pulse points at her wrists and neck, hoping to find some bit of relief.

Jonas began to inquire about Lea's home realm of Edhil and what it was like to be a governor's daughter, so Freya leaned back, content to let them chat while she observed the comings and goings of Iladel's busy square. She was eager to return on her own one day soon so she could wander about the city without the inquisitive eyes of a foreign emissary on her. It was exhausting, knowing Jonas would likely be retuning to his empress and reporting every detail of Freya's actions, interpreting or misinterpreting them one way or another.

She'd just finished her tea when Cecilia leaned over.

"My lady? The commander instructed us to have you back to Aldridge by late-afternoon." She gestured toward the sun, which was making its slow descent to the west. "We should leave soon."

"Ah, yes, the monarchs are expecting us for dinner!" Jonas said, breaking off from his conversation with Lea. "I should begin making my way back, as well. Will you be joining us this evening, Lea?"

She flashed him a regretful smile. "No, I've promised Lazarus and Collin I'd catch up with them for dinner."

"Another time, then?"

Lea exchanged a quick look with Freya, then smiled at Jonas. "Another time."

28

F reya wasted no time loading herself into the carriage Byrric had called for her, unsurprised when she found him already aboard, waiting for her.

Once settled in and on their way to the palace, she gave him her report.

"He seems to be looking for a reason to question my desire to be queen," she began. "He found half a dozen ways to inquire about my happiness, my level of contentment, whether or not I felt like a piece of chattel who'd been traded at market."

Byrric arched a brow at that. "Do you?"

She gave him a withering look. "It seemed he was projecting his feelings toward his sister's unfortunate circumstances onto me. It took a bit of convincing, but I think he sees that I'm happy."

Byrric nodded, a look of consideration furrowing his forehead. "Yes, Lessia's methods of choosing betrothals are advantageous to her and her alone. I can see why he might question your happiness when his own family has had such a dissimilar experience."

"He also has quite an interest in acquiring Lindorothian metals and stones for import into Jotunheim. He claims their mines are no longer as fruitful as they once were."

"We've gotten reports to that effect," Byrric replied, nodding. "Importing would make sense, although we're not fond of the idea of them having increased access to our raw materials. Anything else?"

Freya frowned. "Yes, there was one thing, although it might've been nothing at all. He mentioned in passing the beauty of Dystone, but when he discussed meeting their monarchs, he claimed they wouldn't allow him further inland than Caldel. I thought perhaps I'd misunderstood, but when I mentioned how fortunate he was to have seen the land, to see if I'd misheard, he didn't dispute it."

"Hmm. What are your thoughts on that discrepancy?"

She tapped her foot on the floor of the carriage as she thought. "I think it's possible he exaggerated a bit about his visit to Dystone when it was first mentioned. That, or he was lying, either about seeing the country at large or only being allowed to see a small sliver. I'm not entirely certain what the purpose of that would be, though."

"Your overall assessment, then?"

"He's a bit odd, perhaps warranting some suspicion. At the very least, I'm wary of him."

"Good," Byrric said brusquely. "It's smart to be wary. Now, Salazar wants me at the northern border of Caelora for a bit, so next week I'll be leaving to head north. I'll trust you to keep an eye out for anything else worth mentioning."

Freya frowned. "What for? I thought border security was more than adequate."

"It is, but after I told him about the draug attack in Watoria, he's become hell-bent of finding out how to prevent them from getting in."

"They come in through the bay," she told him, shaking her head. "He doesn't need more security at the border; he needs it on the western shores."

"I'll be looking into that as well. I'm of the opinion that both need to be shored up a bit, so we'll see."

Freya nodded. "Alright. Now, aside from his inquisitive nature, is there a reason you're so suspicious of Jonas? He seemed genuinely interested in bettering relations between the humans and Jotnar."

"His intentions may be perfectly valid, but I struggle to trust anyone with an aunt like his," he replied. "She was brutal in the last war, but she was also incredibly effective."

"Is there a difference?"

"Brutality breeds little more than fear," he told her. "Effectiveness in battle and government tends to breed respect and admiration alongside that fear."

Freya leaned back in her seat and stared out the window, turning his words over in her mind. She supposed it wasn't all that different than what she hoped to achieve as queen—respect based on her actions and achievements, as opposed to just her title. The war stories she'd heard of Lessia, however, were nearly always violent in nature. The empress had been uncannily skilled at ousting her enemies, and when she found them, their executions often lasted days, during which time she'd extract information regarding others who opposed her desire to enslave the humans of Lindoroth.

Violent tendencies aside, Freya had to admit that when it came to torture, Lessia seemed more adept at gaining knowledge from her prisoners than many others. In a way, Freya respected that, a thought which horrified her more than a little.

She'd never given much thought to how she would handle criminals or those who opposed her. She knew her father had probably had a hand in many interrogations over the years, something she tried not to think too heavily on, but any consideration of how she might be involved in those kind of things had never been at the forefront of her mind. Governing, civics, politics, and history had always been the subjects drilled hardest into her during her schooling, all necessary things, to be sure; but while facts and figures could help increase her ability to make informed decisions and think critically about issues, they were lacking greatly when it came to the nuances of governing a country.

"Freya?"

She dragged herself away from her own thoughts and looked at her father. "Hmm?"

"I asked if you enjoyed getting out into the city today."

"Oh." She forced a quick smile. "Yes, it was lovely. I bought more jewelry," she added with a grin.

"Gods, help me," he muttered. "Well, I suppose supporting local merchants isn't such a bad thing."

"She tried to give them to me," Freya told him. "The earrings, anyway. I insisted she sell me the matching necklace, as well."

Byrric gave her a curious look. "May I see?"

Opening her satchel, Freya pulled the small velvet pouches out of her bag and handed them to him. "She noticed me admiring the earrings and recognized me," she explained as he emptied the gems into his palm.

Nodding absently, Byrric turned the earrings over in his hands. "Who sold these to you?"

"A woman named Rosina."

"Ah," he said knowingly. "Yes, Rosina is lovely, if not a bit of a pistol."

Freya smiled. "I'm assuming part of the reason she gave them to me was to likely ensure my repeated business?"

"And that you'll tell everyone you know about the generous, reverent shopkeeper with the beautiful jewels," he added, grinning as he handed them back to her.

"Well, her work speaks for itself, so I can't take too much offense." She gave him a silencing look when he opened his mouth to speak. "And before you say it, no, I won't be putting those things anywhere on my person until I confirm they aren't laced with poison. There's no magic on them that I can feel, but I'll do a few more tests in order to confirm."

Byrric laughed. "Suspicion is in your blood, isn't it?"

She smirked. "One of the better qualities I inherited from you, I'd say."

As THE NIGHT was unseasonably warm, Salazar had the kitchen serve dinner on the veranda off the dining room. Jonas joined them, eager to talk about his day in the city. He spent a good deal of time discussing his many finds with the king and queen, falling into a deep discussion with Salazar and Aer regarding a potential partnership between Jotnar leatherworkers and Caelorian steel mines.

After a meal of roast lamb, sugared carrots, and crisp potatoes, the conversation shifted toward Freya and Aerelius' upcoming wedding.

Jonas was equally as inquisitive at dinner as he'd been in the city, his questions now focusing a good deal on the prince and Freya's marriage—who would be attending; what details had been planned; and so forth.

"Has the guest list been finalized yet?" Jonas asked the king and queen.

"Not yet," Salazar replied, taking a puff of his cigar and shooting a look of annoyance at the queen and Freya. "The females seem to be taking their time on that front."

"Ah, yes. My younger sister's wedding took quite some time to plan and involved a good deal of arguments and tears. Although I can't say I see your Freya as the type to break down over a floral arrangement." Jonas winked at her.

She felt Aer stiffen beside her.

Smiling, she inclined her head in acknowledgement. "You are quite perceptive, Lord Edrin."

"Indeed," Salazar murmured. "We do hope your empress will be able to attend, of course. It's been some time since her last visit."

"I'm certain Lessia will be quite eager to come," Jonas replied. "Our past is mottled, certainly, but times have changed, and she acknowledges the benefit of moving forward as friends. There's no reason we can't all join together in such a happy time."

Ordona's face broke into a smile that seemed to Freya a bit forced. "I couldn't agree more, Lord Edrin. We plan to invite the human monarchs, as well. Perhaps we can consider this a new beginning of sorts."

Freya and Aerelius exchanged a look, but both remained silent.

"That's wonderful to hear!" Jonas exclaimed, his smile brilliant.

"As I was telling Lady Balthana and Lady Calliwell on our stroll today, Jotunheim is eager to attempt a solid reconciliation with Dystone. We would welcome the opportunity to join together to see that happen."

"Interesting you say that, Lord Edrin, as Freya and Aerelius have chosen a theme of unity for the event," Ordona replied. She smiled at Freya. "I thought it was a lovely idea."

"A true partnership is important to us," Freya said, taking Aer's hand and smiling at him, glad when he returned it with a warm smile of his own.

"Something we fortunately already have," he replied, brushing a thumb across her knuckles.

"We'd like that to carry over into our relationships with the other realms and lands," Freya finished.

"A sign of a good reign, that," Jonas said with a nod toward Freya and the prince. "I'm sure the Dystonians will feel the same. In the brief time I spent with King Willem and Queen Isadora, they seemed quite open to cleaning the slate, at least somewhat."

"Well, I suppose we'll find out soon, won't we?" Salazar said, stabbing his cigar out in an ashtray, his dark eyes focused on Jonas. "The guests will be arriving in eight weeks."

Freya watched carefully to see Jonas' reaction, but all she noticed was a slight tightening around his eyes. It seemed he and Salazar were having some kind of stare-down.

"Will they be staying through until the wedding, then?" Jonas asked, his tone easy.

Salazar nodded. "They will. We'll be inundated with guests for the entire week leading up to the wedding."

Jonas flashed a smile at Freya. "I'm sure they're just as eager to meet you as I was. Isadora is a lovely woman, quite openminded, as I was telling Freya earlier. The king seems to be a tougher nut to crack, though, so hopefully your Freya will be able to soften him up a bit. "

Freya smiled. "Well, I look forward to meeting them both." Angling her head, she gave him a curious look. "Are you planning on staying until the wedding, Jonas?"

He gave her a somewhat bashful smile. "The king and queen have offered their hospitality, I've chosen to accept."

"That's lovely to hear," she replied. "I look forward to learning more about your lands while you're here."

"Perhaps another trip into the city will be in order, then," Jonas said. "Lady Calliwell indicated there was far more to see than we saw today."

"Oh, it would take days to see all the city has to offer," Ordona said with a smile. "Any time you need a guide, please don't hesitate to ask."

"Lea and I would be happy to plan another trip if you'd like," Freya offered.

"And I would be happy to accept," he told her with a grin.

"Well, on that note," Aerelius said, his voice carrying a hard edge as he stood. "I think it's time we retire for the evening. Freya?"

Freya looked up at him, surprised at the commanding tone he used, but stood to follow his lead, taking the hand he offered. When he brushed his thumb over her fingers, she relaxed a bit.

"Jonas, I had a lovely time today," she said as he stood to bid them farewell. "Lea as well. I hope you enjoyed seeing all Iladel has to offer."

"Indeed, my lady." He gave a short bow, and she didn't miss the way his eyes flicked toward their joined hands. "Thank you kindly for taking the time to familiarize me with your city."

"It was my pleasure," she replied.

After saying their goodnights to the king and queen, Aerelius touched a hand to Freya's back and led her from the room.

He'd hardly shut the door behind them when she whirled to face him, annoyance vivid on her face.

"Wait." He held up a hand. "Hear me out."

"You all but ordered me to follow you, Aerelius. You know I won't—"

"Tolerate that, I know." He ran a hand through his hair and scowled in the direction of the dining room. "He's been staring at you all night."

"So? I have no interest in him." Smirking, she cocked a brow and folded her arms. "Are you jealous?"

"No, but I also don't care for some entitled royal thinking he can ogle—"

"So help me, if you say '*what's mine*' I will throttle you."

Aerelius paused, clearly taken aback. "I was *going* to say 'my fiancee,' but point taken."

"Aer!" Freya groaned as she realized how harsh her words had sounded. "You know that's not what I meant."

"You're not my possession, Freya. You never have, nor will you ever be." He seemed to be struggling to control the irritation in his voice. "But you will be my wife, and I won't tolerate other males staring at you as though you're a prized mare!"

"Oh, don't you take that tone with me," she snapped. "I'm more than capable of handling a drooling male, if that's your concern. Which he isn't, by the way."

"Your ability to handle yourself is the least of my concerns and you damn well know it."

"What are you so worried about, then? You know I don't have feelings for him, so why not just let me deal with any potential advances? Really, Aer, do you think he's the last male who will ever look at me?"

"Of course not! But how would it look if I sat back and allowed other men to gawk at you? Especially when it was clear you were being too polite for your own good?"

"I was being polite because he'll be going back to his empress and reporting every small detail about you, me, and our relationship so far. He doesn't need to tell her that you're jealous and territorial and that I'm more than willing to verbally castrate him if need be. Not yet, anyway." Softening a bit, she took his hands. "Unity, remember? We just need to show we're happy and strong together, not that we're going to bite the heads off anyone who looks at either of us the wrong way. We're stronger than that."

Squeezing her hands, he leaned down and rested his forehead against hers, then closed his eyes and sighed.

"You're right," he said quietly. "I'm sorry."

"Hey," she whispered, waiting until his eyes met hers before continuing. "We've got plenty of time to show them who we truly are. You know better than to think I'd let someone walk all over me, and you know you can trust me not to feed into someone else's advances. Right?"

"Of course."

"Good." Keeping hold of his hand, she stepped back. "Now, I don't know about you, but I'd like to get some sleep."

Hand in hand, they started to stroll through the marble halls toward their rooms. When they arrived, Freya's heart skipped a few beats as she eyed the set of doors not twenty feet away from hers that led into Aerelius' chambers, trying not to think about how easily he could slip into her room, or she his. She'd been thinking more and more about their relationship, the expectations that fell on their shoulders because of it, and the fact that neither of them seemed to have any reservations about where they were headed as a pair.

"Have Rissen and Cecilia brought up my things?" she asked.

"Yes," Aerelius replied. "I told them to leave putting them away to you."

"Thank you." They stopped at her door and she turned to face him.

Smiling, he leaned down and kissed her cheek, then her neck. "You are most welcome, my love. If you have any bad dreams, you know where to find me."

Rolling her eyes, she laughed and pushed his chest playfully, then stepped into her room. "Good night, Aer."

Grinning, he blew her a kiss. "Good night, Freya."

29

Freya tossed and turned for hours before finally giving up on sleep. After living for so long in a bedroom a third the size of this, her new one was too big, too open for her to sleep comfortably. The longer she lay awake, the more she thought over her circumstances, her upcoming nuptials, and the life that had been thrown at her feet a good deal sooner than she'd planned. She wasn't opposed to a life with Aerelius, of course, but the other changes she was facing, the larger ones, weighed on her mind and rattled her nerves more than she'd anticipated.

There was so much she could do with her role as monarch, more than what would ever have been possible as a typical Lady of Iladel, regardless of her family ties. She could speak for the lower classes, using her experience living in a rural area as a voice for the citizens who would largely go unheard otherwise. In doing so, she could help unite the citizens of all five realms and bring them together in a way that would make Lindoroth stronger as a whole.

She could and *would* be a good leader, a strong one who her people would look to for guidance. One they would *want* to look to for guidance.

But she'd no longer be Lady Freya Balthana of Allanor. In just two months, she'd become Princess Freya Harridan, and once Aer took his crown, she'd become Queen. Her name would become her husband's, remaining only partially her own. She could keep her family name if she wanted, but she'd have to fight a good deal for it, considering her role. Although, the thought of not sharing her king's name turned her stomach almost as much as losing her own.

Eventually, she would be expected to produce an heir, something she tried not to cringe from. Females only cycled once every few years starting around the age of sixteen, and even then, it could take decades or even centuries for some Linds to become pregnant, as had been the case with both her and Aerelius' parents. Multiple children were even more of a rarity. It would happen, though, and she needed to get over her nerves about becoming a mother long before then. She'd been fortunate to have three wonderful mother-figures in her lifetime and knew all she had learned from them would help shape her into a good mother to her own children.

Then there was Aerelius, who'd fallen effortlessly into the role of fiancé, leaving her to catch up with feelings that were so clearly well-established in his mind. She could only assume his parents had done more to prepare him over the years than hers, not to mention her father had fed Aer information on Freya regularly. Byrric had given her updates on the prince now and then, but Aer's level of familiarity with her felt much deeper than hers with him.

Her annoyance at her running mind had nearly led her to slip from her room for a late-night walk, but she paused when she heard the door that connected her and Aer's rooms open. A moment later, he slid into bed beside her.

Turning to face him, she smiled. In the dim moonlight that shone through the window, she could see his dark hair was mussed from sleep, somehow adding to his handsomeness. "Hi."

"I heard you tossing and turning from the other room," he whispered. "What's wrong?"

She tapped her temple. "It's just a bit noisy up here tonight, that's all."

His mouth curved into a crooked smile. "Would you like me to distract you?"

She laughed. "Whatever you've got going through you mind will most certainly not put me to sleep."

Placing a hand on his heart, he looked at her in mock outrage. "I take offense to such assumptions, my lady."

"Alright, then. What do you propose?"

Idly, he took her hand, linking his fingers through hers as he pondered her question.

"Well, I suppose we could sneak to the kitchens for a snack, although at this hour, Maghda might have us helping prepare tomorrow's breakfast." Smiling, he kissed the back of her hand. "You could tell me about your life in Watoria."

Propping herself up on her elbow, she frowned curiously. "I thought Byrric kept you informed on how I was doing?"

"Of your training, education, and social standing, certainly. Tell me about all the rest. The things he didn't see on his brief and infrequent visits."

"You mean my work with the marshals?"

"I'll be honest, Freya, I questioned Byrric's sanity a bit when he allowed you to work for them." Tucking a piece of hair behind her ear, he smiled softly. "I'm glad he did, though. You seem stronger for it."

She laughed. "One might've thought, considering who my parents were, that the marshals would've brought me on without testing my mettle first. But after I went through their training regimens, I was thankful for it."

"What did you like most about working with them?"

Freya pursed her lips as she thought for a moment. "Helping people. Knowing I was playing a part in keeping the city safe."

"You said you faced another spirit user once. What was that like?"

"Twice, actually, but one was part of the marshal's training program. He was more skilled with negative emotions, true mental manipulation. He helped train us on what to expect and how to combat their power." She bit her lip, almost embarrassed to continue.

"The second one—he was like you, able to put his victims into a stupor. I found him with a knife at the throat of a female who'd just left a nearby tavern, and, well, you saw how I reacted to you that day in combat. It threw me off my guard enough that it took me a few moments to realize what he was."

His eyebrows shot up in surprise. "So what happened?"

"I dragged him to the roof so the girl could run, then he stunned me before I could get my magic up to block his," Freya said, cringing at the memory. "Nearly dropped him, the fool. He hit me here and here—" she touched Aerelius' sternum and temple "—and I just barely got my wits about me when he made to kick me back down to the street."

"You killed him, then?"

"Bit him and loaded him into a marshal's wagon." She touched a finger to one of her incisors, which were slightly longer than the rest of her teeth. "My fangs have just enough venom to stun, but not kill. One of the officers worked him over a bit at my request, then he was sent to a labor camp for a few months."

"Do you think he learned his lesson?"

"I certainly hope so." Frowning, she bit her lip. "Aer, can I ask you something?"

He smiled softly. "Of course."

"This." She held up their linked hands. "When you hold my hand, put your arms around me, say the things you do... is it all for show?"

He blinked, surprised. "Do you really have to ask?"

"I like to think we're both getting very good at playing our parts, but you've been at this far longer..." She trailed off, feeling suddenly silly that she'd dragged the conversation here.

"I'm not playing a part with you, Freya," he said quietly. "Certainly not here in this room. I've always admired you. Even when we were children, you were one of the strongest people I knew. I suppose I didn't acknowledge that as any sort of true feelings until you were gone and I knew we'd be separated for so long. Consider things like this..." he held up their hands "...as my way of testing the waters."

Kissing her palm, he asked, "What about you? You've seemed quite... receptive."

She smiled. "I am. Even though it's been a few years since we spent any amount of time together, I've compared every new friendship I've had since to ours. I missed our banter, the ways we used to trick one another. When I came back, I'd hoped we could fall back into what we had, but then I saw the way you fought me in combat, the look you gave me when I saw you the first night in the dining hall..."

He laughed quietly. "That was shock, Freya, and nothing more. I expected to see you for the first time at the palace before first term started, so I was a bit caught off guard when my betrothed arrived in the dining hall in full leathers, with no notice, wearing a glamour disguising her as a commoner. Had my magic not been so strong, I don't think I would have recognized you. Even though Byrric always kept me updated of your progress, the strength of your magic surprised me."

"It surprises me sometimes, too," she murmured.

"Why don't you use it more often in Combat?"

She shrugged. "I prefer physical fighting to using spells. Using a spell in the midst of a physical fight would end things too soon, giving neither of us a true challenge." She propped herself up on her forearms and grinned. "It's quite versatile, though. Would you like to see?"

He arched a brow. "I'm not sure. Would I?"

She drummed her fingers lightly on his chest, then pulled her hand away. Aer tensed and his eyes widened as phantom fingers began to crawl up his torso.

"Freya—" His words were cut off when her magic drifted around his neck, the tendrils of power dragging lightly across his skin. Another invisible hand of magic ran its fingers through his hair, weaving through the dark strands and giving a solid tug.

"That is... something." He swallowed hard and stared at her. "What else can you do?"

Smiling, she pulled the magic back in, releasing his neck and hair.

Holding out her hand, she focused her power in her palm, forming it into the translucent blade of a dagger. "This kind of thing came in handy when I had to handle more than two assailants."

Reaching out a hand, Aer touched his finger to the razor-sharp blade, gently caressing her magic. "It doesn't feel sharp," he whispered.

"Because I don't want it to hurt you," Freya replied. "If I did, that would've taken your finger off." In demonstration, she tossed the blade upward, embedding it in the high ceiling.

He gave her a chastising look. "I don't think either of my parents will be fond of knife gouges in the ceiling."

"What little you think of me," she said, laughing. She held out a hand, calling the magic back inside. Once the blade disappeared, she flicked her fingers, instantly repairing the damaged wood. "See? No harm done."

Laughing, Aer turned his head to look at her. "Will you show me something else? Something that doesn't involve physically tormenting your fiancé or damaging palace property?"

Narrowing her eyes, she thought for a moment, then rolled onto her back and faced the ceiling again. She waited for him to do the same, then with a wave of her hand, the ceiling disappeared, revealing the night sky above.

Biting her lip, she smiled at him when she saw his eyes go wide. "My mother taught me not long before she died. On days when the weather was bad, it was our way of spending time outside. To anyone walking past, all would look normal."

Aerelius smiled as he gazed up at the open sky. "You still hate the rain, then?"

"Almost as much as I hate being cooped up inside." She waved her hand one more time, causing the outer walls to fade away, revealing the gardens that her chambers were adjacent to.

They laid there for a few minutes holding hands in silence as the night sky passed overhead. It wasn't something Freya had shared with anyone before, not even her aunt, but something about sharing it with him felt right.

"Aer?"

"Hmm?"

"Are you nervous?" she asked quietly.

He was quiet for a moment, then he shifted to face her, propping his head on his fist. "I'm on the edge of terrified," he admitted. "I don't know the first thing about being a husband, and I know there's a good deal you probably want to do before becoming tied down." Smiling, he brushed a thumb over her chin. "What I *do* know is that I'm thankful we were able to get to know one another without the pull of a mating bond holding us together."

Freya took his hand in hers, placing them palm-to-palm.

"What do you think it will be like?" she asked quietly. "The bond, I mean?"

"It's a blood bond, so I'd expect it to be... intense," he said. "My father said it's different for everyone, though."

Frowning, Freya examined where their palms were joined. In just over two months, a royal priest would score each of their palms with a knife, then they would join hands as they spoke their vows and an incantation would be recited. It was simple, but also nerve-racking, considering it would be done in front of hundreds of people.

Aerelius touched a finger to her forehead. "What is it?"

Frowning, she tried to gather her thoughts, struggling with the best way to answer. Discussing deep emotions didn't come naturally to her, so putting into words the things going through her head was more difficult than she expected.

"Being nervous is... not a thing I'm accustomed to," she said slowly. "Yet I've experienced it at least a dozen times since I've arrived in Iladel and it seems there's a good bit more of it to come. It's a bit off-putting."

He gave her an understanding smile. "You don't always have to be tough as nails, Freya. Not with me."

"It goes against my nature a bit," she admitted, smiling wryly.

He considered her for a moment, then put his hand on her hip and slid closer.

"Can we make each other a promise? Here and now, not in front of all the people who will be watching us marry?"

"What kind of promise?"

"To allow ourselves to be vulnerable with one another. Our lives as monarchs will sometimes require us to be cold and harsh. I've watched that bleed over into my parents' marriage, and I would prefer not to follow that same path. You and I were friends before anything else and that's something I'd like to maintain." His eyes softening, he brushed a thumb across her lower lip. "At least, until you're so desperately in love with me that all feelings surpass those we have now."

Closing her eyes, Freya breathed a sigh of relief. *This* was why she knew he would be good to her, why he'd be a good husband, why she knew he would be a person worth spending her life with. He cared about her, about her happiness, and about their happiness as a couple. There was little more she could ask for in her situation.

"Alright," she said with a laugh. "I promise to saddle you with all of my doubts and worries for as long as we live. And when you're so desperately in love with me *you* can't see straight, I promise not to taunt you too mercilessly."

He laughed. "Likewise." Pausing for a moment, his face turned serious. "Do you trust me to do all I can to make you happy?"

"Always," she whispered. "Do you trust me?"

Running his eyes over her, he brushed a stray lock of hair off her face. "Maybe... On one condition."

She rolled her eyes and groaned, but a retort had barely formed on her tongue when he touched his lips to hers. Surprised, she froze for a moment, then smiled, her mouth curving against his.

"That's your condition?" she whispered when he pulled back. "A kiss?"

"Or two," he murmured, his eyes dancing. "Is that alright?"

For the first time since they'd kissed six years ago, she saw uncertainty in his eyes.

He truly thinks I'd turn him away, she thought.

Not trusting her voice, she nodded.

A quick thrill zipped through her as he leaned in and kissed her again. She let her body soften against him, molding her lips to his. He moved his mouth to her jaw, then neck. "Perhaps three?"

"Three is good," she said quietly. She struggled to keep her breathing steady as she tilted her chin up so he could brush his lips against her throat.

He gripped her hips and shifted her onto her back. Bracing himself on his elbows, he smiled softly as she ran her hands up his arms.

As his fiery gaze bore into hers, she felt a sense of calm wash over her. At first, she thought he might be using his power on her, but after a moment, she realized it for what it was.

Contentment.

She arched against him, running her fingers in his hair as he deepened the kiss, letting out a small hum of approval when he hitched her leg around his hips.

Her heart fluttered when his hand skimmed up her thigh, pushing up the hem of her nightgown as he drew her against him. His hand continued up, splaying his palm flat against the soft skin of her side as she ran her hands across the smooth planes of his chest.

Everything around them seemed to disappear.

After a few moments, she pulled back, breathless. "I think there are some things that should wait until our wedding night, don't you?"

"Perhaps," he whispered, brushing another soft kiss across her lips. Then, meeting her eyes, he grinned wickedly. "Although word of our premarital relations would *thoroughly* scandalize our parents."

Freya let out a shaky laugh but struggled to form any kind of witty response. She'd been kissed before, but never with such... intensity.

After one last, lingering kiss, he shifted so he was lying next to her and pulled her close. She wrapped an arm around his waist and snuggled against him, resting her head on his shoulder.

"Thank you," she whispered. "For distracting me."

He kissed her head. "I'll happily distract you again if you'd like. Our second kiss was more than I could've hoped, but I think we could stand to practice a bit more."

"You're incorrigible," she said, unable to keep from smiling. Waving a hand, the walls and ceiling reformed, then she tugged the blanket up over them.

Tightening his hold on her, she felt his breath against her hair when he asked, "Does this mean I get to stay the night?"

"So long as you behave," she murmured, already succumbing to the warmth of his body and the weight of the heavy blanket on top of them. "I may even let you come back tomorrow."

He chuckled softly and began running his hand up and down her spine, slowly lulling her to sleep. "I'm going to hold you to that."

30

After classes let out on Monday, Freya, Aerelius, and the others took dinner at the lake. As they all settled on the blanket Collin had laid out, Freya didn't miss the amused expression on Lea's face as she sat down beside Aer.

"Wedding planning is going well, then?" Lea asked, accepting the plate of food Lazarus handed her.

"It is," Freya replied, swatting Aer's hand away when he tried to steal some of her chicken. "Ordona and I spent most of the day yesterday working out the details. We've got a guest list nearly down and the planners have been working night and day on everything else. The only thing left is—"

"Your dress!" Lea squealed and clapped her hands. "Oh, and *my* dress! I'm so excited for this part!"

"Gods above, not more dresses," Laz groaned.

Collin laughed. "It's the most important part, didn't you know?"

"'Feathers and orange beading' was what I heard last, isn't that right, my love?" Aerelius said, wiggling his eyebrows at Freya.

Lea gave her a slightly murderous look. "*Please* tell me he's joking."

Freya laughed. "No, I'll be going with something a bit more traditional than that. My first fitting will be the weekend after next if you want to come."

"Are you kidding? I wouldn't miss it!"

"Kallan will be arriving at the palace first thing the Saturday after next," Aerelius told her. "I'm sure my mother would love to have you." He smirked. "And your opinions."

"My opinions are well worth having," Lea replied. "Speaking of which, and not to change the subject, but what are your thoughts on Lord Edrin coming to tour the school?"

Aerelius slid Freya a look before responding. "I don't see any harm in it. After all, seeing how vigorously the students are trained here isn't a bad thing."

Lea arched a brow. "He's expecting to see you two fight in combat."

"I've been thinking about that, actually," Collin said, frowning. "Do you truly think it's the best idea?"

Freya gave him a curious look. "Why wouldn't it be?"

"It's a show of strength," he explained. "If one of you loses, the strength of that person could be questioned."

Freya and the prince exchanged a look.

"The logic is sound," Laz agreed slowly. "Although I might take it a step further and say that *neither* of you should spar with anyone. If you fight each other and one wins, the other looks bad. If you fight someone else, one might question whether that person allowed you to win."

"Better to let others demonstrate the skills they've acquired here," Collin finished. "Display the quality of the education at Aldridge rather than put on a spectacle."

Freya frowned, annoyed. "We're not a spectacle," she grumbled.

"You're a half-blood with a twelve-foot wingspan and you kill your foes with your own feathers," Lea pointed out. "To an outsider, that's quite a spectacle."

"Don't worry, Freya," Aer said. "I'll let you get in a win or two before—" He cut off with a grunt when Freya shot her elbow into his side.

"Cinderfish and pixies will marry before you have to *let* me win anything, highness."

He quirked a brow. "Care to make a wager on that?"

"Seeing as I always win our wagers, certainly," she shot back.

"I wouldn't, Aer," Laz cautioned. "She'll have you standing at the altar dressed as a chicken."

"I pray that, one day, I find love the likes of which you two share," Lea said wistfully.

"Impossible," Aer said around a mouthful of food. "You'd have to be willing to accept the occasional death threat, something I don't see you doing, cousin."

"So overdramatic," Freya grumbled. "It happened once."

"Twice, actually," Aer said. "Since you've arrived, that is. That's not counting the amount of times you threatened to toss me off the ramparts when we were children."

Collin coughed. "Perhaps while Lord Edrin is here, you two should refrain from that kind of... talk," he suggested. "Your parents want you to appear unified, and I highly doubt that will send the right message."

"We're unified." Aer grinned and put an arm around her and kissed her temple. "Aren't we, Freya?"

"Absolutely," she said, patting his cheek. "But Collin has a point. We shouldn't send Jonas home with any bit of negativity to report."

"Perhaps *Jonas* should find himself a sense of humor during his visit."

Freya sent Aer a chastising look. "While I may not think either of you are wrong, considering Jonas will be spectating, I think it's safe to say someone *will* challenge either Aer or me."

Collin frowned. "Well, just be careful in how you handle them. Don't hold back, but don't make it seem as though you're pandering, either."

Freya snorted and Aer laughed.

"What about either of us tells you we would pander?" Aer asked.

"Just be careful," Collin said with a sigh.

Freya grinned. "We're always the epitome of careful, aren't we, Aer?"

"Always, my love. Always."

As per the king's instructions, Freya met Jonas in front of the headmistress' office on Wednesday after breakfast. She shared her first class that day with Lazarus, so he accompanied her to meet Jonas on their way to Civics. Rissen and Cecilia followed close behind, and for once, she wasn't the least bit perturbed by their presence. Something about Jonas still seemed off, although she couldn't quite put her finger on what it was or if it was even something worth worrying over.

"Lea told me he likes to pry a bit," Laz said as they crossed the quad. "Is there anything else I should know?"

Freya thought for a moment. "He doesn't seem to like direct acknowledgement of his inquisitive nature. I believe he feels as though he's more sly than he actually is."

Laz nodded thoughtfully. "What do you suppose his intentions are?"

Freya shrugged. "It seemed clear he wanted to suss out whether or not I wanted to marry Aer, presumably so he could return to Lessia and inform her of potential weakness in our monarchy. He truly appeared shocked when I told him I was perfectly content with my lot in life."

Laz gave her a knowing smile. "Perfectly content, hmm? Does that mean you're finally giving in to my cousin's advances?"

"Give in," she scoffed. "Do I strike you as the type to give in to anything that doesn't appeal to me if given the choice?"

He pressed his lips together as his eyes twinkled with amusement. "So he appeals to you, then?"

"Of course, he does," she said. "As I appeal to him. It doesn't mean we can't or won't antagonize or infuriate each other now and then."

Laz laughed. "No, but I would think it would mean you'd try to avoid doing those things."

"Not possible," she replied. "Any partnership, romantic or otherwise, always involves pushback. If there are no disagreements, no
arguments, it would indicate one or both parties simply placates the
other while suppressing their own wants or needs." She frowned at
him. "Are you telling me you and Collin never argue?"

"Oh, frequently. Not intentionally, though."

"Aer and I—" She sighed, then turned to face him as they reached
the door to the main building. "It's sort of a... dance that we do. It's
always been that way. An acknowledgement that I won't put up with
his nonsense and he won't put up with mine."

"You must've driven your parents mad when you were children,
then," he said with a laugh.

"And yet they still chose to tie us to one another." She grinned.
"I'm not quite sure what that says about their judgement."

Laz pulled open the door to let her pass through. "I think it
speaks highly of it, quite honestly. Despite your how much you nip at
one another, it's clear you share similar minds."

Freya gave him assessing look. "You know, Laz, I think Collin has
rubbed off on you. You're quite insightful."

He grinned. "Or perhaps *I've* rubbed off on *him*. Did you ever
consider that?"

Freya snorted a laugh as they stepped through the office doors.
Scanning the room, her eyes landed on Jonas, who was talking
quietly with Headmistress Dyren, a look of deep concentration on his
face. When he saw her, he brightened and smiled.

"Ah, Lady Balthana! So lovely to see you!" He gave Laz a curious
look before shifting his attention back to her. "I was just telling your
headmistress how eager I am to see the famed Aldridge professors at
work!"

Headmistress Dyren flushed slightly and smiled. "Yes, well, I do
hope you enjoy yourself."

"Oh, I'm sure we'll have great fun," Freya said, beaming at them
both. "Lord Edrin, this is Lord Lazarus Cailen, a good friend of mine
and cousin to the prince. He'll be with us for the first class of the day."

"Lord Cailen is a wonderful guide," the headmistress assured him. "You'll be in good hands."

"Good to hear!" Jonas said, his eyes appraising as he looked at Laz. "Shall we go, then?"

After bidding farewell to the headmistress, Freya and Laz led Jonas into the hall.

"Our civics class is a bit of a walk, but it will give you a fair look at what our facilities look like," Freya explained as she led him toward the cavernous rotunda.

"Has this building been here long?" Jonas asked. "It's quite beautiful but certainly has an aged feel."

Freya inclined her head toward Laz. "I think I'll let Lazarus handle that question. He's a bit of a history buff, so he's far more knowledgeable than me in that area."

"Is he, now?" Jonas' brows lifted. "Well, Lord Cailen, what can you tell me?"

Laz gestured toward the high, coffered ceiling of the rotunda as they came up on the fountain. "The academy was constructed a millennium back, with this building being the first. The ceiling here tells the history of our kind, long before the Jotnar and Linds separated and formed their own nations."

Intrigued, Jonas stared up at the ceiling, taking in the detailed carvings that depicted the major events of the history of Lindoroth.

"Fantastic," he murmured, seeming nearly as struck by it as Freya had been when she first laid eyes on it. He pointed toward a far corner at the burst of red flame and the nearest corner, where the flowing blues and gold tones showed Lindish creatures traveling into the halls of the gods that awaited in the afterlife. "The Great Beginning and the Final Death. Those are always my favorite pieces to look upon. I've yet to see a representation I dislike."

Freya smiled. "Likewise. I've never been a big fan of history, but the stories of our origins were always some of my favorite."

"It must have taken years to create," Jonas replied, still staring up at the ceiling.

"Dozens," Laz confirmed. "A fair few died during its construction."

"Pity." Jonas looked back at them. "As striking as it is, death for the sake of art has always been something that flummoxed me."

"If you've got an interest in art, my aunt and uncle have quite a collection in the palace," Laz said. "But for now, we should continue on. Class starts in a few minutes and Professor Ildar is harsh when it comes to tardiness."

"Even with your future queen?" Jonas asked, surprised. "That seems highly improper."

"Shouldn't I be held to the same standards as the rest of the students here?" Freya asked as they made their way down the crowded halls.

"Forgive my honesty, my lady, but no, I don't believe you should. As the future monarch—"

"I should set an example for those I'm to lead," Freya finished. "Not flaunt any entitlements I may have."

Laz pursed his lips and slid her an amused look.

"Fair enough. Tell me about you two," Jonas said, his shrewd eyes darting between them. "Have you been friends long? You seem quite close."

"Only since the start of the year," Freya replied, smiling fondly at her friend. "Sometimes it feels like longer, though."

"Freya saw the immediate benefit of a friendship with me," Lazarus teased, throwing an arm around Freya's shoulder. "Nearly begged me to befriend her, didn't you?"

Freya rolled her eyes and smacked his chest. "Liar," she chastised. "Now you'll have our guest telling his empress I've got to beg for friends."

Jonas laughed at that. "Not to worry, my lady. Your secret is safe with me."

Jonas, much to his dismay and Freya's relief, had to excuse himself just before her combat class, citing an appointment he'd forgotten about with the king.

By the time she'd left Jonas at the front gates before heading to her room to change, Freya was a bit exhausted from playing tour guide. He was inquisitive nearly to a fault, wanting to know about professors, talking at length with them after class, and asking questions that required painfully long responses throughout. Freya had to hold her tongue several times to keep from telling him to just *observe*, as he said he would, but thought better of it. The questions a person asked could reveal more about them than they intended, although his tended to border on tedious and tiresome more than illuminating.

As she entered the training yard, though, she was eager to let out some of her pent-up energy. She'd no sooner walked through the door when she felt Aer's arm snake around her waist from behind.

"Hello, my love," he murmured, brushing his lips against her ear. "Care to show a bit of unity?"

She rolled her eyes and turned to face him. Kissing the tips of her fingers, she touched them to his cheek. "I think that's sufficient, don't you?"

He took her hand and kissed her palm. "I was hoping for a bit more, but I suppose that will have to suffice for now."

Smirking, she let out her wings, holding them high enough to partially conceal them both, then stood on her toes, drawing his mouth toward hers. His lips curved into a smile as he accepted the offered kiss, but when his hand moved to tighten on her waist, she pulled back.

"We don't want to put on too much of a show, do we?" She glanced around, happy to see only a few students seemed to have noticed their exchange.

"Don't we?" Grinning, his hands slipped around to her lower back, thumbs hooking in the waistband of her pants. "Personally, I think it would please people to see just how fond of one another we are."

She grinned when she saw Collin making his way over. "I'll show you my fondness another time. Now, shoo. My warmup partner is here."

Aer glanced over at Collin, then back at her. "You never want to warm up with me. Why?"

"Collin doesn't try to flirt his way into winning," she said.

"And as a wolf, I'm quicker than you," Collin said, coming to a stop at Freya's side.

"Exactly." Freya grinned.

Aer narrowed his eyes at Collin. "I feel as though I should take that as an insult."

Freya patted his cheek. "You'll get your time with me later. Go find Lea. I think she mentioned something about practicing her tackling maneuvers on you today."

"Of course she did," Aer said with a sigh. He gave her a quick peck on the cheek. "Have fun."

After he walked off, she faced Collin. "So, what'll it be today?"

"Blocking," he said, holding up his arms. "I need to work on my speed when I'm not in my wolf form."

Freya jerked her chin toward the far side of the yard. "There's an open spot over there."

Once in position, Freya and Collin wasted no time falling into the rhythm they'd found as partners. He was very serious about his training, so the flirting or joking she endured when she fought Aer or Laz was entirely absent, replaced instead by solid focus. He put her in mind of her father, in a way, with his determination to perfect moves and timing before shifting to something new, often dominating their sessions. She'd asked him once if he'd ever considered a military career, but his only response was that Maddix males were educators and innovators, not soldiers or politicians.

As it seemed that was a topic he didn't care to elaborate on, she hadn't brought it up again.

For the next thirty minutes, they alternated taking hits at one another, using arms, legs, and shoulders to block hits. As a wolf, Collin was sleek, his gray-brown fur a perfect natural camouflage. His speed was superior to Laz's, although Freya would never admit that aloud, but it was clear he hadn't had sufficient training while on two legs prior to his arrival at Aldridge. So, each day, he focused on a different skill, and Freya did her best to drill it into him.

When Officer Ristheld began calling out their first round of sparring partners, Freya sighed. For whatever reason, he'd been pairing her with Myria at least twice a week. She wasn't sure if it was Byrric's doing or because he felt they made good partners. Whatever his reasoning, Freya had to admit that, despite how irritating the girl could be, she was proving to be a challenging enough partner. The grating nature of her voice combined with her smug looks each time she landed a hit were both things Freya could stand to live without, however.

"You know, I've been meaning to ask you something," Myria said now, narrowing her eyes at Freya as she took a sip of water between rounds. "Why don't you ever use your magic? Or your feathers? You could beat me easily with either, as much as I'm loathe to admit it."

Freya shrugged. "Those tend to be the easy ways to end a fight and I'm already well-aware of how to use them. Physical fights are different. No two people have the same skill, so I prefer to learn how others work instead of ending a fight quickly."

Myria arched a brow. "I see. Although perhaps you should start requesting to beat on your prince now and then and give me a break."

Freya glanced over at Aer, who was laughing with Laz. "I've got the rest of my life for that. For now, variety is what keeps me sharp. And I'm not the one who assigned us as partners."

"You're going to be *queen,*" Myria lamented. "Surely you have some say over who you train with."

Freya gave her an apologetic shrug just as Ristheld began rattling off new assignments, sending half the group toward the archery range and the rest toward target practice. Myria flounced off without so much as a goodbye when her name was called, but Freya was stopped in her tracks by Byrric.

"Come with me," was all he said.

Frowning, she silently followed her father outside. When they reached the grassy quad, he spread his wings and took off. Freya sighed, gave a quick wave to Rissen and Cecilia who were waiting outside the building, then flew after him, following him in the direction of the lake.

"I'm going to be leaving tomorrow," he told her once they landed on the beach. "I want you to be on your guard, Freya. Jonas' interest in you seems to have grown, enough that he's been heard asking about you at the palace."

"That shouldn't come as a surprise," she said matter-of-factly. "If I were in his shoes, I'd be doing the same."

"No, it doesn't." He sighed and ran a hand over his face in what Freya saw as an embarrassed gesture. "He's also expressed suspicion that there might be something between you and Lazarus."

Freya's eyes widened, then she laughed. "Clearly, his observation skills are quite lacking if he thinks I'm Laz's type."

"Regardless, please refrain from walking around with another male's arm around your shoulders, no matter whose company he may prefer. I'd rather Jonas not race back to his empress with troubling reports of your behavior."

"Troubling reports," she huffed. Noticing his silence, she narrowed her eyes. "There's something else. What is it?"

Byrric leveled a stern gaze at her. "I know you and Aerelius have been sneaking around those tunnels again."

"Is there a law against that I'm unaware of?"

"No, but it would behoove you, considering your position, not to betray the secrets of your palace to a foreigner we know very little about. The Jotnar are crafty, Freya."

"Something you've drilled into me since birth. Why do you suddenly seem so uncertain about my ability to be discreet?"

"When you and the prince share a thought, you tend to lose your heads a bit, focus only on a whim and not the surrounding circumstances. All I ask is that you take more care with your actions now that there is a guest in the palace." He frowned. "And no more joking about breaking your betrothal, either."

"We don't lose our heads," she said stubbornly. "Just because we're fond of one another and share the same sense of fun doesn't mean we're incapable of rational thought."

"Humor me?"

She smirked. "Alright. Aer and I won't go galivanting through the tunnels while Jonas is around."

He gave her a knowing look. "Until he *leaves Iladel*, Freya. Don't try your word games with me."

Scowling, she huffed. "Fine. We won't go galivanting through the tunnels until Jonas leaves Iladel."

"And returns to Jotunheim."

She groaned. "Gods above, you ruin all my fun!"

He patted her cheek and grinned. "It's what fathers do best, Freya. I should be back in a few weeks. Mind Rissen and Cecelia while I'm gone."

"Mind them," she grumbled. "I'm going to be queen, in case you've forgotten."

"Meaning you'll soon have even *more* guards, so you'd best get used to the ones you have now."

"Alright, Commander. I'll mind my chaperones while you're away. Satisfied?"

"Perfectly."

31

F reya woke the morning of her first dress fitting with butterflies rioting in her stomach. Once the planners had taken over the logistics of the wedding, she and the queen had been going back and forth with Kallan on ideas for Freya's wedding gown, but today was the first day Freya would see his concepts on her. Until now, each of their sessions consisted of swatches of fabrics, samples of beadwork, and scraps of lace. Kallan had taken down her measurements but done little in the way of testing out his designs on her. With the exception of the corset and slip, both of which were obscenely revealing, she hadn't seen any aspect of the dress at all.

The only thing that sent her a bit of calm was how excited Lea was to go with her to the castle. The queen had arranged for Kallan to fit Lea for a gown, too, something Lea had been nearly climbing the walls in excitement over.

As they rode toward the palace in the carriage after breakfast, Lea's excitement continued to grow, but Freya's nerves started to rattle her again.

When her parents first told her that she and Aer were to be married once he came of age for the crown, she was five and he was a boy whose favorite activity was tugging on the pretty twists her mother liked to weave through her hair. He was very often dirty and was almost always getting hollered at by his governess or the queen. Freya didn't care that marrying him meant she'd be queen one day—the gravity of that fact was completely lost on her.

As they grew older, they also grew closer, slowly moving out of the stage of their lives where boys were icky and girls were stupid, until eventually, they became friends. By the age of ten, summer vacation in the capital was the thing they both looked forward to because it meant exploration through the tunnels, climbing on the ramparts, and traipsing through the forests.

The summer Freya turned thirteen was when she realized how much she'd come to care for him. The start of the school year had been upon them when her father sat her down to tell her she wouldn't be coming back until it was time to go to Aldridge. She'd get a year there, he'd told her. One year of studying with the children of politicians and ruling families, learning from the finest educators in Lindoroth, before it would be time to set aside her studies and take her place at the prince's side.

The night before she'd left for Watoria, she and Aer went on a walk through the gardens where they shared their first kiss. The kiss itself was awkward, a bit sloppy, and altogether strange because it shifted their relationship from friends to something more. Aer wasn't just her friend anymore—now she knew what his lips felt like when he kissed her, how his hands felt when he curled his fingers around hers, and how, when she was that close to him, he smelled just a little like vanilla.

Freya couldn't help but smile a bit at the memory. It had been a test of sorts, a way to see if there was any kind of attraction. Or as much attraction as was possible at that age.

She'd noticed the moment she'd arrived that season that Aer had filled out a good deal since her last visit, but, while she could see the budding strength in his arms and torso, he hadn't quite outgrown the lankiness of youth. And based on how he'd taken her in when she set foot in the palace, he'd noticed the way her body moved differently than it had just a year before, the way it had shifted from the parallel lines of childhood, to the arcs and curves of adulthood.

Not for the first time, he had taken her hand as they walked away from the palace and along the hedgerow that encircled the garden. They'd meandered along the paths, drinking in the warm summer sun on what would be Freya's last day in the capital for six years.

"*I was thinking,*" Aer had said thoughtfully as they came up on the fountain. "*Seeing as we're to be married... perhaps you should let me kiss you just once before you leave.*"

Never one to shy away from a challenge, Freya had shrugged in feigned indifference and sent him a sly glance.

"*Perhaps I should, although I'm not quite sure what would be in it for me.*"

"*Shall I show you, then, my lady?*"

Stopping, he'd taken her by the waist and turned her toward him. The touch of his fingers on her hip had been gentle, his eyes, hesitant. The confident arrogance he wore so well now was only just beginning to peek through back then.

"*I think... I might like that,*" she'd admitted. Her voice had come out more sure than she'd expected, a fact that she had been proud of, considering her utter lack of experience with the opposite sex. She could see a bit of nervousness hovering in his eyes, and she had the sudden urge to ease it. So, curling her fingers through his, she'd leaned up on her toes and touched her lips to his.

His mouth had curved against hers in a laugh, and she'd nearly shoved him back as she felt her face flush with embarrassment. But he'd tightened one hand in hers and cupped her cheek in the other, then drew her mouth in for another kiss. A real kiss.

As she stared out the carriage window now, watching as the mountains grew taller and the sun rose higher, she thanked every deity in existence that she and her prince had been able to make their way back to that. She thought of Jonas' sister, the female who'd been forced to marry someone cruel, and acknowledged just how lucky she was that her prince was kind, caring, and invested in her happiness.

"Freya?"

She was jolted from her thoughts by Lea's voice. "Hmm?"

"Are you alright? It seemed I'd lost you for a moment there."

Freya smiled. "Yes, I'm fine. Just a bit..." She wrinkled her nose. "Something."

Lea eyed her dubiously. "You aren't getting cold feet, are you?"

Freya's eyes widened. "No! Not at all!"

"Then what were you thinking about?"

"Honestly?" Freya smiled ruefully. "I was thinking about how fortunate I am. When Jonas and I spoke that day we were in Iladel, he mentioned his sister. She was forced into an arranged marriage with someone she didn't care for, one who wasn't kind. That could very easily have been me, had my parents chosen someone else."

Lea gave her an understanding smile. "My cousin is a good person, isn't he?"

"He really is," Freya murmured.

"May I ask you something without you getting angry?"

Freya looked at her warily. "Possibly."

"Are you in love with him?"

Freya frowned, considering her response. Her first reaction was to deny it, but that didn't feel quite right. To confirm it felt a bit odd, too, considering they'd only just begun to get to get reacquainted.

"I think... if he were gone, I would feel like a large part of me had gone missing. We've got a synchronicity that I know I wouldn't find with anyone else." She met Lea's eyes. "I was devastated when my father told me I wouldn't be returning until it was time for Aldridge. I felt like I was losing my closest friend. Coming back and finding out we could still have that friendship was more than a little relieving."

"You didn't have close friends in Watoria?"

Freya shook her head. "Not who I connected to like I did with Aer. He just... understood me, shared the same mind as me. I tried to find that with the people I went through school with in Watoria but it was never quite the same."

Lea's expression softened sympathetically. "That sounds a bit like love to me."

"Maybe," Freya said, smiling as they approached the drawbridge into the palace. "All I know is that I want him in my life."

"Well, I've seen the way he looks at you," Lea said. "All joking aside, it's clear he feels the same way."

"I wish it had been under different circumstances, though," Freya replied. "Yes, we got to know each other long before we were expected to get married, and I'm grateful to our parents for it. It would've been nice to see how things would've unfolded had that not been the case."

"Has it ever truly felt forced, though?" Lea frowned curiously. "You two finish each other's sentences, seem to share the same thoughts half the time, and your interests align quite a bit. You can't fake those things, especially considering you haven't seen each other in so long. That type of connection is innate."

"Yes, I saw it in my parents at times." Sighing, she looked down at her hands. "I don't know. I suppose we'll find out soon enough. The mating bond is supposed to be easier for people who already care for one another, or so I'm told."

Lea nodded. "My mother told me when she and my father had their bonding ceremony that it felt like they were being stitched together, like a connection was being repaired. There was a rightness to it that she's always struggled to explain. It was strong, intense, but not painful in any way."

"Yet Aer said his parents' was more difficult, took more magic to seal."

Lea laughed. "Well, Aunt Ordona and Uncle Salazar may love each other now, but to hear my parents tell it, they were a long time getting there. I don't see that being the case for you and Aerelius."

"Nor do I." Freya waited a moment while Rissen opened the door for them, then smiled at Lea. "Thank you for the talk."

Lea grinned. "Anything for my future cousin."

Freya laughed, then rolled her eyes when she saw Aer trotting across the yard toward the carriage.

"If you think you're getting a peek at my dress, you're sorely mistaken!" she called to him, allowing Rissen to help her hop to the ground.

He grinned as he approached. "As it so happens, I've got plans with Laz and Collin. For some reason, Collin thinks now would be a good time to teach Laz to hunt pheasant. As my hunting skills are impeccable, I've offered to oversee their excursion." Touching a finger to her chin, he tilted her face toward his and kissed her. "Hi."

Smiling, she kissed him again, then frowned. "Laz doesn't know how to hunt?"

Lea let out a bawdy laugh as she came around the side of the carriage. "Oh, Freya. That might be the funniest thing you've said since we've met."

"My cousin has always preferred indoor activities," Aer said. "Collin is quite the opposite. It's taken two years, but he's finally convinced Laz to let us take him hunting."

Freya looked between them, wide-eyed. "But he's so good at archery!"

Aer shrugged. "A hobby." He held out his hand for hers. "Come, Kallan and my mother are waiting."

Holding Aer's hand with her left, Freya let Lea link her arm through her right, and the three walked into the palace together.

Despite the mid-autumn chill that hung in the air, the windows in the halls were all flung open, the deep blue drapes billowing in the breeze. The leaves on the trees in the gardens had begun their melt from green to shades of gold and red. Freya could tell from the slight bite in the air that the nights would soon be getting colder as the seasons began to shift.

"They've set up in your chambers," Aer said as they turned down a hall in the direction of their rooms. "Rini and Tyna arrived not long ago and plan to offer all manner of opinion on your hair and makeup."

"*And* your mother?" Freya huffed. "With all of this input, will I have any say at all?"

"If you'd like, I can just agree with everything you say," Lea offered.

"Perfect solution," Aer agreed with a firm nod. "Do that."

Freya slid a sly look at him. "Even if it involves bright orange feathers?"

Lea chuckled. "You know I won't let you get away with that."

They came to a stop outside Freya's bedroom door, and Aer sent a pointed glance at Lea. Without a word, Lea slipped into the room with a quick "see you at dinner" to her cousin.

"Are you sure you don't want me to stay?" Aer asked. "I could be a buffer between you and all those people who think they know best."

Freya feigned shock. "You mean you *don't* think that?"

He twined his fingers through hers, then kissed the back of her hand. "I think that I know you better than anyone in there. I think if you come to me on our wedding day, bogged down by frills and lace, it won't have been your own decision."

"Do you also believe I'm not the type to speak up for myself if they tried to force it on me?" Gripping his lapels, she leaned up on her toes and lowered her voice to a whisper. "As it so happens, I do plan to wear a bit of lace."

Aer stilled, then laughed quietly. "We've still got nearly two months before our wedding, yet you're already tormenting me." He brushed a hand through her hair, then cupped her cheeks and kissed her. "Have fun. I'll see you tonight."

"You, too. Try not to get shot with an arrow."

He grinned. "I'll be sure to tell Laz how strong your faith is in his skills."

Laughing, she shoved him back. "Goodbye, highness."

He blew her a kiss. "Goodbye, Valkyrie."

Once he'd turned the corner and was out of sight, she opened the door to her chambers and went inside, hoping to find some semblance of calm, despite the number of occupants she knew it would have.

The organized chaos she saw awaiting her when she stepped inside made her stop short.

Kallan had set up his dressing pedestal in the center of the room, his design case and stack of papers on the table he'd pulled from beside Freya's vanity. Rini and Tyna had drawings of hairstyles and makeup combinations strewn across the table where Freya would normally take her meals, their collection of cosmetics piled nearby. Ordona and Lea were sitting beside each other on the bed, poring over the surrounding stacks of detailed sketches of the floral arrangements the planners had come up with.

"Ah, my lady!" Kallan said, grinning when he saw her. "Come, come, we've got much to do!"

"Oh, good, you're here!" Ordona rose, a sheath of papers clutched in her hand, and approached. She'd donned a lavender dress, a simple cut made of soft muslin and silk. The color was perfectly accented by her golden skin and dark hair, which had been tucked into a chignon at her neck. "We've gotten some preliminary ideas back regarding flowers and decor, so I've asked Kallan to try a few different designs based on the ones I think will best suit our theme."

Kallan gestured toward the pedestal. "If you'll just strip down and hop on up, we can get started."

Freya forced a smile and nodded. "Of course."

Noticing her mood, Lea cleared her throat. "How about I call for some refreshments? A bit of wine might get the ideas flowing a bit more freely, don't you think?" Without waiting for a response, she pulled the cord for the servant call bell beside Freya's bed.

"That sounds like a lovely idea," Ordona replied.

Bless her, Freya thought as she began tugging off her pants. By the time she'd stripped to her undergarments and stepped onto the pedestal, a bird-like female servant—Dina, Freya recalled—had arrived and been given an order for three bottles of wine and a charcuterie board of meats and cheeses.

Kallan had just finished retaking her measurements a short while later when Dina returned pushing a cart into the room.

"We can take it from here," Ordona said. "Thank you, Dina."

With a small curtsy, Dina left, and the queen began pouring glasses for everyone. When she handed Freya her glass, she arched a brow. "Once we're using real fabric, the only liquid allowed in the room will be water. Understood?"

Smiling, Freya nodded. "Understood."

"Now, I know you were thinking white for a dress," Kallan began, looking at the queen. "But with Freya's hair and coloring, I think unbleached silk might complement her a bit better."

Ordona tsked. "I think we'd like to stick to something traditional, wouldn't you, dear?"

Freya bit her lip and examined the pieces of fabric Kallan held out for them to inspect. While part of her wanted to agree with the queen about sticking with tradition, Freya's eye kept being drawn toward the slightly darker, more neutral-looking shade that was sure to bring out the rose tones in her hair.

Recalling her discussion with Aer about breaking molds, Freya knew what her choice would be, but not wanting to shut Ordona's opinion down entirely, she suggested trying both. "It's really impossible to make a choice like that without seeing the full picture, don't you think?" she asked.

"Agreed," Lea said firmly. "The white might be a bit too stark a contrast against that hair, no?"

Ordona's eyes slid between the two of them, then she sighed. "Alright, we can see them both."

"Perfect!" Kallan laid out six sheets of blank design paper. "I've got a few different shapes and styles in mind, so let's get started."

Freya took another gulp of wine, then handed the glass to Rini, who set it down on the table. Once she'd fluttered back to Tyna's side, she magicked a notebook and pencil from thin air and nodded at Kallan.

For the next several hours—days, in Freya's mind—Kallan dressed and undressed her, sheathing her in one design after another, wrinkling his nose and shaking his head at some, nodding and making hums of approval at others. Now and then the queen would give a suggestion, and Freya quickly learned that her and Ordona's ideas of what a wedding dress should look like varied quite a bit.

When Freya asked about a mermaid cut, Ordona sniffed and insisted a ballgown was more classic. Later, when Freya suggested a beading design similar to the one Kallan had put on the dress she'd worn to the Commencement Ball, with a fade of diamonds, the palest rose opal, and pearl, he'd drawn up the design, only for Ordona to say the design "should be more tasteful and elegant and less of a statement piece."

Freya tried very hard to disagree as politely as she could, offering up the option of trying multiple patterns before deciding, but it was Rini and Lea who finally began to steer the discussion in the direction they could tell Freya wanted to go.

"I've been frequenting the city markets quite a bit in recent months," Rini began. "A great many of the modern wedding gowns incorporate beading, very often in combination with the more traditional lace styles."

"She's right!" Lea said, clasping her hands together and beaming at the queen. "Oh, I saw one that was just *so* lovely that I'm considering a similar design for my own gown."

Ordona sighed, eying Freya's current ensemble—a mermaid silhouette in silk the color of sand, with beading that started at her left hip and burst out in swirls across her torso, breasts, and down her thighs. "What if we added a bit of lace or chiffon to this one? Perhaps a cream overlay?"

Freya and Lea exchanged a look, then Lea gave a small shrug.

Smiling at the queen, Freya nodded. "Alright, let's see how it looks." When she looked at Kallan to tell him to begin, the expression on his face told her he was about at his wits' end. "I think after her majesty's suggestions, this design might be the one to go with."

"As a starting point, my lady," he corrected, his small nose scrunching as he scrutinized the beading he'd just added. "This is the rough draft. We've several more to go before we have a final product."

Freya blinked. "I—how many more fittings do you think there will be?"

Angling his head to the side, Kallan began to tick them off on his fingers. "Well, there's this one, of course. Next will be for proper length, but before that, we need to choose footwear. My suggestion would be a flat style, but females these days often like a bit more height. Although with his highness' height... well I do suppose it's a matter of what you're comfortable with, isn't it? Then we'll do another to properly fit the back against your wings, which will likely take a few hours, at least..."

As he continued to drone on, Freya smiled and nodded in what she thought were appropriate places, hoping Lea, Tyna, or Rini were taking notes.

She was surprised some time later when she looked through her open veranda door and saw that the sun had begun to slide behind the mountains. A yawn sneaked its way up her throat too quickly for her to stifle, causing Rini, who'd just been comparing blush samples to the beadwork on her dress, to pause.

"Oh, my lady, you must be exhausted," she lamented, tucking her palette into the tool belt at her waist. "We should stop for the day, don't you think, Your Majesty?"

Ordona frowned from her place a few feet away from Freya, her finger resting on her jaw as she watched Kallan work, her expression telling Freya she'd stay there the rest of the night if possible.

"Yes, I suppose we could all do with a bit of dinner and rest." She let out a heavy breath and smiled tiredly at Freya. "You've been a real champion about this, dear. I know how hard it is, being poked and tugged at for so long."

Kallan transferred the final version of the design onto a piece of paper, then stacked it on top of the other versions that had variations in beadwork and cut. He smiled at them both, his eyes a bit less bright than they'd been that morning, no doubt due to exhaustion.

"Quite right, Your Majesty. I'll work on the overall design, then once that's set, we'll get to work on properly fitting the back."

Freya's eyes widened slightly in Lea's direction at that. Lea shrugged. "Perhaps next time we'll switch from wine to mead. I think Aer said several casks of apple mead just came in from Dystone last week."

Rini let out a noise that sounded a bit like squeak mixed with a snort. "You'll need a bit more than that, my lady. I know Kallan, and he'll have you extend and retract your wings twenty times before the day is over."

Freya couldn't hold back her grimace at that.

"It will all be worth it in the end, my lady." Kallan gave her a reassuring smile and began packing away his tools in a small leather case.

"I don't doubt it," she murmured, stepping off the pedestal and accepting a robe from Lea. As she shrugged it on, she smiled at the queen. "Thank you for all of your input, Your Majesty. It was nice to have you here to share this with me."

The queen pulled her into a hug. "I've waited for this day for a long time, Freya," she whispered. "I'm sorry if that's made me a bit over-opinionated."

Laughing, Freya hugged her tighter. "I wouldn't ask for it to be any other way, I promise."

And despite how tiring, and at times, irritating the day had been, Freya meant it with all her heart.

32

The next month slipped by in a blur of classes, fittings, discussions of wedding details, and time with her friends. Most days at the palace were spent with the king and queen discussing what her duties would be once she and Aer were crowned, meeting visitors, or working out details of their wedding. Later, after the palace had gone silent, Freya and Aer would often spend hours traipsing through the tunnels in search of new passageways or chambers, careful to avoid the notice of anyone who might report their movements back to Byrric. When Freya had expressed her concern over her father barring them from the tunnels, Aer had simply laughed and reminded her that he was the prince and therefore outranked her father by quite a good deal. It was one of the few times he pulled rank as a royal, but Freya couldn't say she minded.

They'd been unable to find anything more about the human they'd scented in the garden passageway, and as nearly two months had passed since, they'd set that curiosity aside for other, more readily available things.

More enjoyable, though, were the times he would pull her close when they laid down to sleep, kissing her silly late into the night. They'd spend their time getting to know one another in ways Freya hadn't expected so soon, and despite what she—and Aer, although he refused to outright say it—wanted, they'd agreed to wait until their wedding night to cross the final line.

While intimacy before marriage was hardly frowned upon in their world, Freya knew exactly what was expected of them. She'd also heard plenty of rumors about maids checking bedsheets the morning after weddings in an attempt to confirm the wife's virginal status, the mere thought of which made Freya's lip curl in annoyance. Busybodies had always been one of her greatest peeves, but as queen, she knew she'd have to put up with things like that and much worse.

When she'd griped about it to Lea one afternoon while they had tea by the lake, Lea's only response was, "If you become pregnant on your wedding night or shortly after, the last thing you want is someone questioning whether the child is Aer's or not. Physical proof of your virginity is the only thing that will keep that from happening."

Freya considered pointing out it would be simple enough to forge said evidence, but considering how many secret passages wound through the palace walls, it would *also* be very simple for someone to catch her in the act of doing so.

So for now, they settled for enjoying one another in other ways. And, if Freya was being honest with herself, just waking up beside her prince each morning gave her more flutters in her belly than she cared to deal with. The utterly girlish nature of her feelings made her feel more than a little odd, but she also thanked her lucky stars that she had them at all.

When she traveled to the palace for her third dress fitting, she was surprised when she touched down in the yard to find Salazar himself waiting for her. He wore a white tunic under a tan suede vest, with dark brown pants and suede boots. His black hair was tied back at his nape, giving him an unexpectedly casual appearance.

"Good morning, Your Majesty," she said with a small curtsy.

"Freya," he said with a nod. "Before my son whisks you off, I was hoping we might have a word."

"Of course." She retracted her wings and waved goodbye to Lea,

Laz, and Collin, who'd just pulled in behind her and would be spending the weekend at the palace, then silently followed the king through the palace to his personal quarters. In the rear was the area where he conducted most of his personal business dealings—those he didn't care to share with those outside of his immediate circle.

That he was leading Freya there made her instantly wary.

He gestured toward a chair in front of his desk before settling himself behind it. It was wide, likely five feet of space sat between them caused by the broad surface of the desk alone. Legs carved from Allanorian oak in the shape of Lynx rearing up on their hind legs, paws held aloft, held the heavy top up. A smaller man, one who didn't wear Salazar's power or his shifted form as boldly as he did, would've been swallowed up by the massive and ornate piece of furniture.

Once she sat, he folded his hands on the desk and smiled. It was a soft smile, very similar to Aer's, only with a slightly harder edge. Again, she was struck by how much Aer had grown to resemble him. The king's face was slightly more aged, although not nearly as aged as Professor Florian's. Soft lines formed at the corners of the king's eyes when he was amused, and the scruff of his beard showed just a touch of gray near his temples, easily belying his age, which Freya put at about four hundred. Everything else—the sharp cut of his jaw, the dark, wavy hair, and the wide brown eyes all perfectly reflected those of his son. His harsher temperament and the cool indifference he often exuded were where their similarities ended, as Aer had gotten his warmth largely from Ordona.

"So, Freya. How have you been getting on now that you've been spending more time here?"

Freya let out a quiet breath as she turned over appropriate responses in her mind. It was such a simple question, but one that, if answered incorrectly, could cause her a good deal of annoyance. If she gushed about how much she loved being in the palace, he might revisit her living arrangement. If she did the same regarding Aldridge, the outcome would likely be similar. Despite how much she'd come to enjoy her time at the palace, she wasn't quite ready to be away from the rest of civilization just yet.

"I feel as though I've found a good balance, at least for the time being," she replied cautiously. "I enjoy getting to know the students there while also easing myself into life at the palace. I've formed good relationships at Aldridge that are both pleasant and could potentially be beneficial in the future."

"How so?"

"I've become close with Lea, Lazarus, and Collin, as you know. Myria Bryton and I seem to be getting on a bit better than when we first met. I understand her mother is a friend of the queen's, so an amicable relationship with her daughter will likely make dealings with Governor Bryton a bit smoother. I've acquainted myself with several lords and ladies of various social strata, all of whom have taught me a good deal about how the areas of society outside those I'm already familiar with function. It's been quite an illuminating experience, to be honest."

"And would you consider these individuals your friends?"

Another loaded question.

"If I were not becoming queen, the answer to that would likely be simple—yes, I think I could consider them friends, or acquaintances at the very least. As it stands, I believe I must be wary of all individuals who hope to befriend me, both now and in the future. I consider myself a good judge of character, Your Majesty, but even still, I'm always deliberate in my words and actions."

"There are no exceptions to this rule you've written for yourself?"

"None," she said firmly. "Even now, speaking with you, I'm weighing every word as carefully as I can."

He angled his head and eyed her curiously. There was a glint of something there, something he was about to let slip that Freya was certain would cause her hassle.

"What about Lord Edrin? Are you careful with your words and actions regarding him?"

She didn't bother hiding her surprise at such a shift. "Of course,

Your Majesty. There isn't any need to doubt my caution around someone I know so little about."

"Hmm." He leaned back and steepled his fingers in front of his lips. "He seems to believe you're reluctant to become queen. Do you have any thoughts as to *why* he might think that?"

Freya's mouth dropped open in outrage, but she quickly recovered herself, drawing in a quiet breath through her nose to reel in her emotions.

"Lord Edrin spent a good deal of our trip into the city subtly interrogating me on my feelings for Aerelius and my status as future queen," she replied calmly. "He made multiple attempts to get me to admit my reticence, none of which were fruitful because I have none. He questioned how I felt about being traded off, to which I told him he should watch his tone if he expects an amicable relationship with me. He also divulged that his sister was forced into an unhappy marriage, giving him a biased view of how betrothals work."

"He told you of his sister?" Salazar actually seemed surprised at that fact.

Freya nodded. "He did, and assuming he was being forthright, I can understand why he might feel the way he did when he questioned me." She frowned. "Your Majesty, I am not in *any* way reluctant to marry Aerelius, nor do I hold any reservations about the path you, the queen, and my parents have chosen for us. Aerelius and I are fortunate to have been able to form a friendship, to become a team long before our wedding. I care for him a great deal and plan to do all I can to make him happy, both as my husband and as a king."

"And as a father?"

Her mouth went a bit dry at that. "Bearing his children will be a great honor."

He raised a single dark brow. "Will it?"

"*Yes.*" She didn't have to force conviction into her tone; it was there, clear as a bell. Even if she still questioned whether what she and Aer had was love, she knew, when they were ready, he would be a wonderful father. Their children would be strong and capable and *loved* because of the true partnership their parents had.

She and the king stared at each other for a moment as he assessed the truth of her words. She held his gaze, refusing to let him see how much she was rattled by his subtle accusation that she may not want her place at her prince's side.

After a moment, he nodded. "Alright. Do not mistake me, Freya. I know you care for my son, and he, you. It's clear the affection you show when others are around isn't simply for show. I hope you realize how beneficial that will be to you both."

"I do, Your Majesty. Betrothal or not, I know exactly how lucky I am. Aerelius is more than I could've hoped for in a mate, and I know that will help make us effective rulers."

"Indeed. Now, there was just one other matter I wanted to address."

She frowned. "Your Majesty?"

"You and Aerelius have been poking about those tunnels again, despite Byrric clearly telling you not to," he said, his voice full of disapproval. "I don't give a damn if my son outranks him."

Her eyebrows shot up. "I'm sorry—"

"We've got a foreign guest in the palace, one from a nation that has been hostile to us in the past and whose intentions I only barely trust now. I've already spoken to my son about this, but I'd like to make it clear to you as well. The tunnel system is one of the aspects of this palace that does not need to be broadcast while we have guests. If by chance you two stepped into a hall as a guest walked past, you'd risk piquing the curiosity of someone who is best left in the dark. Do you understand what I'm saying?"

She pressed her lips together and nodded. "Yes, Your Majesty."

"Good." He rapped on his desk twice and stood. "Well, I think we're done here. I'm sure Aerelius is eager for you to go to him, so I won't keep you any longer."

She stood and smiled. "It was good speaking with you, Your Majesty. I don't ever want you to feel I have doubts about your son or our future together. The responsibility you've placed on my shoulders is one I will never shirk or take lightly."

He gave her a sharp nod. "I'm glad to hear it."

IRRITATED, she strode through the castle, nodding stiff greetings at the servants and staff she passed along the way to Aer's chambers. Lord Jonas Edrin was truly beginning to get under her skin, something that was incredibly difficult to accomplish. That he'd achieved such status in such a short amount of time irritated her more than his actions.

"Finally!" Laz muttered when she stalked into Aer's room. "Aer made us wait for you to eat."

She sent a chastising look at her prince. "Entirely unnecessary, but appreciated, nonetheless."

With a tug on her wrist, he pulled her down into his lap and gave her a lazy smile. "And how do we show our appreciation, my love?"

Grinning, she stuffed a strawberry in his mouth and kissed his forehead. "With a simple show of affection, of course."

Narrowing his eyes, he bit the fruit and pulled the stem from his mouth, scowling at Laz when he snorted a laugh. "That wasn't quite what I was going for."

"Well, it's all you'll get for now," she said, picking up a fork and spearing a slice of cold turkey.

"So what did the king want?" Lea asked, pouring them each a glass of iced tea.

Freya frowned and tore off a small bite of meat. "It seems our visiting friend thinks I'm feeling a bit reticent about becoming queen, or so he told the king."

Lea gasped. "He said *what?*"

"Bastard," Aer muttered, tightening his arm around her waist. She slid her hand over his and squeezed. As annoyed as she was with Jonas and his insistence on stirring up trouble, she felt worse about the fact that his meddling might cause Aer to think she was unhappy.

"All of those questions he asked that day in Iladel? I was right when I said he was fishing for information. I didn't give him the answers he wanted, but he still went to the king, regardless."

"I'm assuming your presence here so soon means you were able to convince Uncle Salazar otherwise?" Lea asked.

"I was," she confirmed.

"It's so odd," Collin said, frowning. "First he believes you're having relations with *Lazarus*, of all people, and now this."

"It's just so infuriating! I don't care what his motives are. I've never —*never*—fought this!"

"Well, that's not entirely true," Aer said, his annoyance shifting to amusement. "You threw a knife at your father once, when he insisted we dance at my nameday ball."

"Gods above," Laz muttered.

"It was a butter knife and I was *eight*," she groaned, exasperated. "Once I was old enough to understand the importance of it all, I was far less difficult!"

Collin cleared his throat. "Did he have any other reason to think you might be unhappy?"

"None," Freya said, breaking off a piece of bread angrily.

Aer kissed her shoulder. "Is it safe to assume you also received the same scolding I did regarding the tunnels?"

"Yes," she sighed.

"You aren't truly planning to listen, are you?" Lea asked incredulously. "We may not have known each other long, Freya, but I think I know you and my cousin better than that."

Aer gave her a look of mock confusion. "My dear cousin, whatever do you mean? You think *I* would go against my father's wishes?"

"Without question," Laz replied, laughing.

"Perhaps this once you shouldn't?" Collin suggested, sliding a slice of bread from the tray.

"Perhaps," Freya agreed, giving him a bright smile as Aer chuckled quietly. "I suppose we'll see."

KALLAN, the queen, and the pixies arrived a short while later, shooing off the males so the dressmaker could set about fitting Freya's wedding dress around her wings. As Rini had forewarned, Freya was required to extend and retract her wings at least a dozen times, shifting them up, down, spreading them wide, and pressing them together as Kallan took copious measurements of her back and shoulders with each movement. By the time Kallan decided he'd taken enough measurements and notes regarding the placement of her appendages, she was quite ready to collapse in bed to let her muscles rest until the following day.

Freya was just seeing Kallan out when Aer knocked on her door. He waited until the dressmaker had left, then stepped toward Freya and took both of her hands.

"Did you have a good day?"

Grinning, she wrapped her arms around his waist. "Oh, yes, Highness. My wings were in dire need of a tediously uncomfortable workout. Quite fun, that."

Leaning down, he kissed her slowly. "Well in that case, I think I'd like to claim you for myself for the rest of the evening. Cheer you up a bit."

She gave him a slow smile. "As it so happens, I was hoping for the same." She'd been turning an idea around in her mind, letting it percolate a bit as she went about getting fussed over, until it became fully formed.

"Were you, now?"

Circling her arms around his neck, she nodded. "There's something I'd like you to help me with."

He paused, narrowing his eyes as his hands hooked around her waist. "Why do I feel this isn't going in the direction I was hoping?"

She sent him a dazzling smile. "Because you're incredibly perceptive and know me too well?"

Letting her go, he dropped down on the end of the bed and braced his hands behind him.

"Alright, my love, what do you need my help with?"

"I think Byrric and the king are hiding something," she said.

Aer's laughed. "And this surprises you?"

"No, of course not," she said, waving a hand. "But I think they're hiding something that they specifically don't want *us* to know about."

"Is this because they don't want us in the tunnels?"

She nodded. "Because they both went out of their way to specifically tell us to stay away. Doesn't it strike you as a bit odd that Byrric's warning came only a few weeks after we scented a human in the tunnels, and more than ten years after they all but encouraged us to explore them?"

"What do you think it might be?"

"I don't know," she said slowly. "I suppose it could be something as simple as a surprise wedding gift, but I don't think it is. My father was far too serious."

"Byrric is *always* far too serious," Aer pointed out. Smirking, he curled his fingers, beckoning her forward. When she stepped toward him, he rested his hands on her hips. "In nineteen years, I don't think I've ever heard him make a joke."

Freya's rested her hands on his shoulders and her eyes drifted toward the door to her passageway. There were nearly two dozen tunnels that branched off from it and dozens more from those. By her estimation, she and Aer had explored maybe half of those in their lifetimes, but each time they found a new one, it seemed five more appeared. Whether it was due to magic or feats of architecture, it was becoming increasingly clear to her that, despite how certain they had been as children, they were unlikely to ever map out the tunnel system in its entirety.

"You're quite suspicious, you know that?" Aer observed. "Did you consider that their reasoning could be exactly as they stated?"

"I suppose..." She shook her head. "No, it seems entirely unlikely Byrric and your parents would be completely unaware of a human slipping through the palace in the middle of the night. It has to have something to do with that."

Aer nodded slowly. "Yes, I suppose that's a reasonable assumption."

"And how often were foreign guests in the palace when we were snooping about as children? They never seemed to care then"

He narrowed his eyes. "Another fair point."

"I have them now and again." Cupping his face in her hands, she leaned down and kissed him. "Humor me?"

His hands slipped down to the backs of her thighs. "On one condition," he said. With a tug on her legs, he pulled her down so that she was straddling his thighs.

Draping her arms over his shoulders, she lifted her brows in question. "You and your conditions." She sighed. "What is it now?"

He laid a soft kiss to her collarbone. "You tell me more about these lacy things you plan to wear on our wedding night." He laughed when he saw her deadpan look. "Alright, alright. We'll investigate a bit tonight if you'd like."

"Thank you."

She tried to ignore the feelings that shifted at his mention of their wedding night. No matter her confidence in him or their pairing, romantic relations were one thing she knew little about. She and Ashton Carinald had a few stolen kisses here and there back in Watoria and she'd played her share of kissing games in secondary school, but anything beyond that, especially true, raw emotion, was not something she'd ever learned to handle well. Put a knife or bow in her hand and she'd be able to handle it a thousand different ways, but a naked male was something she knew little and less about. Just the thought of stumbling through their first time made her stomach roil a bit.

As if sensing her unease, Aer brushed her hair behind her shoulders and pulled her closer, his eyes smoldering as they gazed into hers.

"Are you thinking about lacy underthings?" he teased.

"A bit," she conceded.

He was silent for a moment, his expression conflicted as he seemed to struggle to work up the nerve to say something. "I'm nervous, too, if that's your concern," he finally admitted.

She started, surprised at his admission. "As a male, shouldn't you be overly confident in your prowess?"

"I think *our* exceeding levels of confidence are why we feel so compelled to be honest with one another, don't you?" He gave her a soft smile. "But... as much as I'm loathe to admit it, I worry that I may not be able to make you as... happy as I'd like."

With a sigh, she averted her eyes. "And my concerns are just the same as yours. I like to think that because it's *us,* it will be perfect, but reason tells me it will be anything but."

"Freya," he whispered. "Look at me." He waited until she dragged her gaze back to his before continuing. "Nothing about you will ever make me unhappy." He took a deep breath. "This marriage may be arranged, but I would've picked you a hundred times over if given the choice."

She let out a relieved laugh, unable to keep a smile from curving her lips as his words sunk in, searing themselves in her mind and heart. "I'd have picked you, too, Aerelius Harridan, without a moment's hesitation."

33

Much to both her and Aerelius's disappointment, there was little to be found when they began their hunt for information about what their parents might be hiding. Their trips into the tunnels hadn't provided anything terribly interesting aside from the occasional, mildly curious conversation topics. Maghda had brought out a switch on one of her kitchen boys for stealing chocolates that were reserved for the wedding. King Salazar had taken to requesting marmalade instead of sun fruit preserves. The maids were scrambling to ensure proper accommodations were ready when wedding guests began arriving. And Jonas, according to kitchen gossip, was a shameless flirt and had already managed to bed two of the female staff members. The only thing that rang with any bit of suspicion was a hushed conversation between Salazar and the head of his guard, Sir Ervic, but they'd disappeared down a hall before any of their words could be made out.

Freya was beginning to wonder if she was grasping at straws, searching for something deep and interesting to occupy her mind when so much of it was being forced full of fittings, tastings, seating charts, and background information on the more important guests who would be attending their wedding.

Despite their lack of luck thus far, however, Freya could feel it in her bones that there was something they would find, some clue as to why their fathers didn't want them in the passages that snaked through the palace and its grounds. The more she thought about it, the more she became convinced Byrric and Salazar's reasoning, while valid, didn't fit with their past behavior. Ordona had shown Freya and Aerelius the passages when they were only eight, the summer after Freya discovered the door under the drawbridge. No one had ever paid them any mind when they would pop out in the middle of a hallway, startling the staff, or worse, one of their parents.

No, something about this warning had Freya's hackles up and she wanted to find out why.

It was four weeks after their first venture, and the weekend before their final exams week, before they finally found anything.

They'd gone only about one hundred feet into their sixth trip into the tunnels when Freya's ears perked at the sound of footsteps in the distance. Aer put his hand on her back, then she extinguished her lights, bathing them in darkness. As her eyes adjusted to the lack of light, she cast a cloaking spell over them, blocking their presence from passers-by.

As the footsteps moved closer, she and Aerelius inhaled simultaneously, drawing in the scent of the person coming toward them.

"Human," Aer whispered in the same moment the scent registered with Freya.

The steps became louder, clearly coming down the same passage they were in. Soft light bobbed toward them a few moments later, setting the tunnel aglow. Freya double-checked her enchantment, then waited as the human came around the corner.

He was tall and broad, but his face and hair were obscured by a dark hood and mask that covered his nose and jaw. He wore an olive tunic topped with a sleeveless gray jerkin and tied with a brown leather belt. His gait was swift and purposeful, telling her he was clearly familiar with the layout of the tunnels. Any other features that might help her identify him in the future—hair or eye color, age, scars—were completely obscured under his clothes.

As he got closer, she felt Aer grip her hand. When she gave him a questioning look, he inclined his head toward the human's waist. Frowning, Freya followed the direction of his gaze, then her eyes widened slightly when she saw a small, ancient-looking brass key hanging there glinting in the light of the small lantern the man carried.

They waited in silence until he'd passed, but Freya didn't dare lift her enchantment. She waited until the glow of his own light vanished before reigniting her lights.

"Tell me that wasn't a human with a key to our castle," Freya said, her mouth feeling a bit dry.

Aer's expression was hard as he stared off in the direction the human had gone. "Let's go find out."

Freya tightened her magic around them, silencing their steps and voices as they followed the human's scent. She was beginning to think the human might be lost, when Aer put a hand on her arm, stopping her at the end of a narrow tunnel that the human had turned down.

"This leads to my mother's chambers," he said thickly, concern over what he might find if they continued on this path etched clearly on his face.

Freya was at a loss for words, unsure of what she might say that would dissuade him from thinking the worst. The thought of the queen carrying on with a human... considering where the tunnel led, she couldn't blame him if that's where his mind had leapt.

"It may not be what you think," she finally said, peering down the narrow branching tunnel. "Let's not jump to conclusions yet."

He sent her a dubious look. "There's a door about forty meters down that opens into the rear of her sitting room."

Freya stared warily down the corridor, hesitant to go any further. The queen was a gifted witch, one who would no doubt hear right through Freya's spell. So she touched a finger to her lips, then her ear, and closed her eyes, extinguishing her lights once Aer gave her a nod of understanding.

Once they were bathed in darkness, Freya shut off all but her sense of hearing, straining to hear any bit of sound from their position.

She felt Aer touch her hand just as the words reached her ears, so quiet she would've missed them had she not been straining to hear.

"*She has become a problem for us,*" a male voice was saying. "*You must trust me on this.*"

"*Is that so?*" The queen's voice carried softly down the corridor. "*Please, tell us. Why should we trust you when your king has made his disdain for us so clear?*"

"*I may not have several centuries of espionage under my belt, but I know my king! He is not the man today—*"

The king's voice joined the conversation next, and Freya felt Aer's body relax a bit.

"*What are you implying?*"

"*As I told you last time, it's worse. I worry for what may happen to Willem—*"

"*We are aware of what you're asking of us,*" Salazar replied. "*We aren't prepared to commit to anything without seeing what you speak of. With our own eyes.*"

"*Do you not trust your own commander's judgement?*" the man's voice rang with shock followed by a low, dark chuckle. "*And here my belief was you thought him infallible.*"

Freya bristled a bit at the insult to her father.

"*I've advised them to await further proof before helping you commit what might amount to treason,*" Byrric replied cooly.

Freya's eyes widened at the sound of her father's voice as she felt Aer's hand tighten around hers.

"*What proof?*" the human asked. "*You saw—*"

"*I know what I saw!*" Byrric shot back. "*It was enough to warrant suspicion, I'll grant you, but nothing more!*"

"*Nothing has changed,*" Salazar snapped. "*Our answers remain the same. It was foolish of you to come here tonight. You put us all at risk.*"

"*Risks are necessary, Salazar!*" the human hissed. "*This cannot go on much longer! Please, consider our offer. We only want—*"

A soft knock sounded in the queen's chambers, barely audible in the dark tunnel.

"Ah, finally," the king said.

The words became quieter, telling Freya the monarchs and their guest had moved too far from their location to hear. Taking Aer's hand, they jogged back to her room, not speaking until they were safely inside, and even then, she didn't lift her enchantment.

For a moment, they stared at one another, unsure what to say.

Finally, Aer exhaled and rubbed a hand across his chin. "Well, I suppose I should be happy my mother isn't having an affair."

She shot him a chastising look. "What do you think he meant by 'consider our offer'? And what proof?"

Aer dragged a hand through his dark hair and sat down on the edge of the bed. "Willem and Isadora have only been in power in Dystone for three years. Perhaps there's a bit of unrest and they'd like help in exchange for..." He shook his head. "No, that wouldn't make sense, not if there's something wrong with the human king."

"Jonas said King Willem seemed... odd," Freya said. "'A tough nut to crack'" were his exact words. Maybe their king is ill? This man we followed seems to know him."

"We don't even know who that man was, Freya," Aer said.

"Whoever he is, he's important enough to have unfettered access to the castle," she pointed out. "My father has taken him seriously enough to bring his concerns to the king and queen. Although how he knows him is beyond me."

"Your father spends a good deal of time traveling, so it's not unexpected that he'd have associates abroad," Aer murmured. "I wish we could've heard who joined them."

"Agreed." Freya sighed, then bit her lip. "When will the humans be arriving?"

"Next week," Aer replied. "But Freya, now that we know this man, whoever he might be, seems to have unrestricted access to the tunnels, I think it might be best if we stay out of them."

Freya huffed out a breath and sat down next to him. She didn't realize it until now, but this hadn't been something she truly thought would amount to anything serious. Or, at least, not so serious as a human consorting with the monarchs and having late-night discussions regarding the stability of his own king. Whether King Salazar and her father had been honest in their reasoning or not, didn't matter; there was clearly something afoot.

"You're right," she said after a moment. "Perhaps we should've listened to them all along. If that man had seen us…"

"Your enchantments are flawless. He never would've seen us." Aer slid his hand into hers and kissed it. "And I don't think we were wrong to pursue this. You were right; something was amiss. Maybe we should be privy to it, maybe not. If nothing else, we know to be wary."

"Wary of what, though? Every human who walks through the palace doors? Lindoroth and Dystone have a strong relationship, last I checked. Am I suddenly to assume the worst?"

"We're to be king and queen of Lindoroth one day, Freya." Aer said gently. "You should always assume the worst."

Her eyes searched his, determined to see the facetiousness in his words hidden there. When she didn't, she frowned. "That's a horrifically pessimistic outlook to have, Aer. Do you truly believe that?"

"Do I believe everyone is out to harm us?" He shook his head. "No, certainly not. Lindoroth has always been kind to our neighbors, so they have no true reason to harm us. It doesn't change the fact that there will always be someone out there who believes they can do our jobs better than we can or want the power we have. Those are the ones to be wary of."

"And because they don't have 'traitor' scrawled across their foreheads…" Freya leaned forward and rested her elbows on her knees, then pressed her fingers to her temples. In the span of just a few minutes, the enormity of the life she was about to dive into was laid out for her. Despite knowing they would do all they could to be good monarchs, kings and queens always had to worry about opposition or outsiders who wanted to take what was theirs. Some monarchs had it worse than others, of course. Jotunheim was a prime example—the only reason Lessia never lost her crown was because she was ruthless when it came to dissenters, of which there had been many of over the centuries. Untested monarchs like Willem and Isadora would still be considered weak by many, especially those whose reigns were long, like the Linds and Jotnar.

Freya didn't want to live out her reign distrusting of everyone. Her mind revolted at the mere thought of carrying that type of burden on her shoulders. She wanted to say Aer was being overdramatic, that it couldn't possibly be that bad, but as he ran a calming hand up and down her spine, soothing the tension from her body, she knew that wasn't the case.

She took a deep breath and sat up, then looked at him. "So what do we do?"

"All we can do right now is wait," he replied. "The humans will begin arriving next week, and I'd bet my crown that man will be among them. Once he's here..."

Freya gave him half of a smile. "We boldly ask him why he's been sneaking around the palace in the middle of the night?"

"I was thinking I could get him roaring drunk and hope he spills his secrets," Aer suggested. "Or enlist Lea to seduce them out of him."

"I'm not quite sure which of those ideas is worse," Freya replied, shaking her head. "And I have a feeling Lea might have a thing or two to say about you offering her up as seductress."

Aer laughed. "Clearly, you don't know my cousin all that well. She'd jump at the chance. Truly!" he added when he saw Freya's dubious look. "Just ask her!"

34

Breakfast the following morning was a test of patience and restraint for Freya and, if the tight set of his shoulders was any indication, the prince, as well. Salazar and Ordona both seemed perfectly at ease, neither appearing as though they'd had a late-night rendezvous with a mysterious human. Instead, they were casually buttering toast and cutting into their sausages as though there wasn't a care to be had.

They'd made it halfway through the meal when Aer sent a cursory glance at his father as he took a bite of egg. Swallowing, he asked, "Have we any word on when guests will begin arriving?"

Not a flinch, not a flicker of emotion was to be seen between the monarchs.

Salazar took a sip of his coffee, then set it down. "Next weekend, so long as no one is delayed."

Aer nodded, then busied himself portioning fruit onto his, then Freya's, plates. "Accommodations are nearly ready, then?"

Ordona smiled knowingly. "Don't worry, we've housed all guests in the eastern and northern wings. You'll have your western wing all to yourself."

Freya paused, her fork full of egg halfway to her mouth as Aer blinked.

Freya recovered herself before he did and put on a smile for the queen, trying hard to conceal her mild mortification. "It's kind of you to consider our proximity to the guests on our wedding night, Your Majesty."

"Of course dear," the queen replied. She patted Sal's hand. "We remember how it was."

Aer cleared his throat and set his fork down. "Right. Well, I believe Freya and I had a few things we wanted to take care of before she leaves this afternoon, so if you'll excuse us, I think we'll be on our way." He dabbed his mouth with his napkin and stood. "Freya?"

Smiling at the king and queen in a way she desperately hoped wasn't awkward, Freya took Aer's hand and stood.

Salazar narrowed his eyes shrewdly as he looked back and forth between them. After a moment of tense silence, he nodded. "Alright. Best of luck with your exams this week."

"Oh, and darling?" Ordona smiled at Freya. "Don't forget you've got your final fitting Sunday morning. You may want to return to the castle with Aerelius Friday afternoon instead of Saturday morning. You'll want plenty of time to get settled in, because the last week before the wedding will be a busy one. Lea and the boys will be coming then, too."

"Yes, of course," Freya replied. "Will they be staying here through Solstice?"

"They will, along with the governors and their families," Salazar said. "I've ordered your guards to organize moving all of your things up here."

"Thank you, Your Majesty," she replied.

Aer gave her hand a quick tug, then nodded at his parents as he led Freya out of the dining hall.

When they'd made their way down several corridors and were on their way back to Freya's chambers, Aer finally broke the silence.

"I'm not quite sure I've ever had a more awkward encounter with my parents."

Freya huffed out a laugh. "Because they're keeping something from us, or because they've taken steps to ensure we aren't *heard* on our wedding night?"

Aer frowned, considering. "Both. Now, what shall we do for the rest of the day?"

Freya leaned against the wall outside her door and considered. "I really should study a bit, although I'm not sure how I'll be able to focus."

He inclined his head down a hall that led to the library. "Come, I'll quiz you." Grinning, he added, "You can repay me with various physical shows of affection."

She rolled her eyes and smacked his chest, hardly able to contain her amusement at the scandalized look on the faces of the servants who were methodically cleaning the windows nearby.

"Idiot. Let's go."

Freya and Aer spent several hours in the palace library that day brushing up on what they thought they'd need to know for their final exams, which would encompass most of the following week. Freya left feeling confident that she'd absorbed the necessary material over the course of the term that she would need to do well in each of her classes.

There would be an exam the first four days of the upcoming week, starting with Civics and ending with Toxins, which was the test she was most wary of. She was confident in her grasp of the content, but Florian's methods of testing students were something she wouldn't expect to encounter in any other course. Indeed, her literature, civics, and history courses all consisted of lengthy written exams, but Toxins would be a practical examination that would require a deep and detailed recall of all they'd covered over the course of the term.

Rissen and Cecilia attempted to give her and Lea a pep talk on their way to class, but Freya felt it fell a bit short in terms of motivation.

"He'll call you in one at a time," Cecilia explained when they arrived and saw all their classmates milling about in the hall. "There's less chance of other students getting hurt if something goes wrong."

Freya grimaced. The mercurial old warlock was brilliant, to be sure, but in the three-and-a-half months since the term began, he'd stoked the inherent skepticism within Freya more than she ever would've anticipated from a university professor, former assassin or not. She'd come to the point where, after seeing Lord Sindel suffer burns after failing to check his desk chair for poisons, she'd begun contemplating standing for each class.

You're good at this, Freya, she told herself.

"Try not to worry, my lady," Rissen said. "You either, Lady Calli-well," he added when he saw Lea's slightly blanched expression.

"Easy for you to say," Lea muttered. "You're not at risk of losing your tongue if you go in there."

He chuckled. "Professor Florian may be unique in his ways, but he would never allow a student to suffer death or permanent disfig-urement for failing an exam."

As one, Lea and Freya gave him incredulous looks.

"Do you realize, Rissen, how utterly absurd that sounds?" Freya asked.

He grinned as he and Cecilia took their places against the wall. "As I said, neither of you have a thing to worry about."

"Listen to him," Cecilia added, sliding a smirk at her partner. "On occasion, he can be quite a good judge of things like this."

Freya and Lea exchanged a wary look, then faced the classroom door. Freya smiled when she saw Gareth standing a few feet away, squinting down at a brown moleskin notebook.

"Getting a bit of last-minute studying in?" she asked him.

Gareth laughed, then dragged his gaze away from his notes and looked at her. "It's likely pointless, I know, but my eldest brother had Florian for Toxins and still can't speak his name without shuddering."

"Goddess, help me," Lea muttered.

Freya's eyebrows winged up. "That's... unfortunate. Would you like some help?"

He smiled gratefully. "It would be much appreciated, Freya. I can only quiz myself so much."

With a shrug, she took the proffered notebook and looked down at the page he'd been reading. "It will help Lea and me as well." Casting a glance behind Gareth, she noticed Myria looking through her own notes and trying not to appear as though she was eavesdropping.

Knowing better than to ask her to join, Freya positioned herself a bit closer and began going through Gareth's notes.

"THIS IS BEYOND ABSURD!" Lea hissed thirty minutes later, after the fifth student had torn out of the classroom, sobbing as she clutched her eye. "We can go through these notes a dozen times but there's no way—"

"Oh, stop complaining, Lea," Myria snapped.

"Oh, go back to studying on your own, *Myria*."

Freya rolled her eyes. "Will you three stop acting as though this is the first time you're seeing this? At least one of our classmates has been poisoned on a weekly basis. This is no different."

With a groan, Myria slumped back against the wall beside Gareth.

"Saithwater," Freya said, looking at Gareth. "Describe it."

He sighed and rubbed his fingers against his forehead.

Shaking her head, she closed the book and gave him a disparaging look. "You were poisoned with this not one month ago, Gareth."

"A fact I've worked hard to block out," he replied sourly. "Saithwater... is clear, but when held to the right light, flecks of silver can be seen floating in it."

She nodded, then handed the book to Lea as Lord Edmund Raster was called into the room. "My turn."

They'd gone a few more rounds before Edmund emerged, seemingly in one piece, if the smug grin on his face was any indication.

Myria sent him a smirk. "It went well, I take it?"

He sent her a sly look. "Come visit me later and I'll tell you all about it," he crooned.

Myria face contorted with disgust. "Pig."

Before Edmund could respond, Gareth was called in. Edmund clapped his friend on the back and Freya and Lea wished him luck.

Once Gareth disappeared inside, she looked at Edmund in question. "You passed, then?"

"I did," he confirmed, his voice dripping with superiority. "There will be a celebratory end-of-term party in our dormitory if you ladies would like to attend."

Myria sniffed. "I'm sure Freya has her own duties to attend to."

Ignoring her, she smiled graciously at Edmund. "As much as I would love to join you all, Myria is right." She tilted her head toward Lea. "We're expected at the palace once exams are completed." *Assuming I come out in one piece, that is.* She gave Myria a curious look. "I was under the impression you would be as well."

Myria sneered. "Yes, yes, I'll be there with bells on," she muttered. "Another time then, Edmund."

They waited in silence for a few minutes, hoping Gareth would emerge from the class relatively unscathed.

Freya couldn't help but wince when he stepped into the hall bearing a smattering of vicious red burns across his forearms and a boil the size of a golden sil on his cheek.

"I got the saithwater right, at least," he muttered, wincing as he prodded the jagged edge of one of the burns.

"Freya Balthana!"

Freya felt a chill skitter down her spine at the sound of her name, but she refused to be cowed by a simple test.

That's all it is, she told herself. *A simple test.*

Taking a deep breath, she sent a wave to her friends and tried to ignore her thundering heart as she walked through the door, running through her toxins one last time, from plant-based poisons to venoms found in all manner of fauna.

Lindberry root causes stomach pain or death.

Eitr will kill anything instantly.

Sintrial petals can be used as perfume or a paralytic.

"Lady Balthana, so nice to see you!"

Taking a deep breath, she met her professor's eyes and dragged up every ounce of confidence she had.

You will not poison yourself.

You know all of these things. You've used half of them.

You're going to be queen. You can handle a damn test.

Your father and Aer will never let you hear the end of it if you don't score perfectly.

That thought alone was enough to shake some of her nerves.

Florian gestured toward a stool that sat in front of the table at the head of the classroom. "Please take a seat."

Setting her satchel on the floor beside the stool, she casually wiped the seat with her sleeve and sat, then watched warily as the man who so casually poisoned his students on a daily basis sat across from her, a friendly smile gracing his lips.

"You get that sense of cynicism from your mother, don't you?"

She let out a breathless laugh. "One of her finer qualities."

"Indeed. Now, before we begin, do you have any final questions for me?"

Only about a thousand, Freya thought. Mainly, she wanted to know why he felt poisoning his students was the most effective method of teaching,

There was a tug of magic, then words slipped from her lips unbidden. "All of the students this semester—" Freya bit the inside of her cheeks and pulled her own magic forward, forcing her tongue to stay quiet.

He smiled, not seeming the least bit surprised she'd used her own power against him.

A test, she thought.

"Ah, yes." He nodded. "The ones who so frequently fell victim to my whims. You see, Freya, those students have been raised in a world that doesn't cause them to question their surroundings, protected by others but never protecting themselves. Once they arrive in my class-room, all certainty is removed, replaced entirely by *un*certainty. Suspicion."

"And the need for self-preservation," Freya said quietly. She shook her head and grinned. "I have to say, I've been torn between horrified and impressed all semester."

"And now?"

"Truthfully? I think it's brilliant."

"Interesting," he murmured. He studied her thoughtfully for a few moments, and she was struck by the depth of his eyes. They were both ancient and sharp, cunning and curious, expressive yet vacant. She found herself trapped under his scrutiny, felt him *inspecting* her like a new purchase. Curling her hands to fists, she focused on the bite of nails into skin, waiting until he finally spoke.

After a few tense moments, Florian waved a hand and a half dozen vials appeared on the table, all small and seemingly innocu-ous. "The first part of your exam is simple. Identify these poisons and describe their uses."

She let out a quiet breath. That was easy enough.

Stepping off the stool, she crouched down so the vials were at eye-level. Pulling her fountain pen from her bag, she touched the end to a few, shifting them so she could see how they swirled and danced in the sunlight that streamed through the windows. After a few moments, she nodded.

"Saithwater is a paralytic," she began, touching her pen to the first. Then, she began moving down the row. "Hemlock will kill its victim instantly, as will ore powder. If administered in small doses over time, ore powder will also cause catastrophic organ failure that might appear as another, more common illness. Lindberry root extract can cause illness or death, depending on dosage, widow venom mimics death but doesn't actually harm the individual," she touched her pen to the last vial, then set it down. "And Eitr will kill anything that draws breath."

"Good." Florian waved a hand, causing the vials to disappear, then inclined his head toward the back of the room, where he'd set up a mannequin. "I've just given you a vial of eitr and a needle. How many pin pricks would it take to kill a creature of that size?"

She opened her mouth to respond, then let her jaw snap shut as she considered her answer more thoroughly. "None. Eitr would be administered orally. A fatal dose for a creature of that size—" she did a quick calculation "—would be two thimbles."

Florian arched a white brow and folded his arms across his chest. "Incorrect."

Freya's mind raced over her answer and the variables in front of her. She knew she was correct because she'd used just that method to take down a huldra, a female seductress demon who liked to frequent the seedier parts of Watoria, not six months past.

Florian was tricky, though, and would very well dose her with a bit of whatever poison she seemed ignorant of, just to teach her a lesson.

Quietly, she eyed the mannequin, then walked over to it and gave the shoulder a small nudge with her elbow.

Hollow, not solid wood as she'd expected.

"A quarter thimble," she amended. Turning her head, she looked to Florian for confirmation.

He nodded slowly. "Correct. I'm curious, Freya. You've done quite well in my class, but you've clearly come to me with an edge. Where did you come by such a thorough understanding of toxins?"

She sat back down on the stool. "My mother taught me a good deal when I was younger and we covered the basics in secondary school, but I've always found it to be a fascinating field. As I got older, I sought out any literature I could find on the subject."

"Interesting." He tapped his thumb on his sharp jaw. "Why is that, I wonder?"

"My mother... she was killed in the field after being poisoned with ore powder by a Jotnar separatist." She pressed her lips together and averted her eyes. "He'd been a prisoner of Empress Lessia's who'd escaped and thought my mother was attempting to send him back for punishment."

"Was she?"

"According to the commander, no. She was willing to bring the Jotunn south, but he tossed a fistful of ore powder in her face." She sighed and looked to the window, saddened as she recalled the day so many years ago when her father came to her, his eyes showing more emotion than she'd ever seen, to tell her that her mother had passed.

"Your mother was killed near the northern border," he'd told her in a simple, brusque tone. *"We've dispatched the person responsible."*

Not long after, Freya was informed she would no longer be summering in Iladel with him or the royal family. Byrric would continue to live in Iladel, and Freya would go live quietly with her aunt, unnoticed and relatively unknown on the other side of Lindoroth.

Returning her attention to Florian, she forced a shrug. "Ever since, learning all I could became a bit of an obsession, I suppose."

Florian nodded, and Freya thought she saw a bit of under-standing in his aged eyes.

"It's good to take some things on yourself," he said. "As queen, I imagine a thorough knowledge of all subjects will be of use, especially those that can be used against you."

"Indeed," she murmured, a bit horrified at the thought.

"Well, Lady Balthana, it is my honor to tell you that you've passed with flying colors," Florian said.

Freya frowned. "Even though I got the dosage wrong on my first guess?"

A small smile played at his lips as the lines that framed his eyes crinkled. "Because you didn't poison yourself in the process. You missed the firebloom serum, but your keen sense of suspicion saved you."

"Fire—but there were only six vials!"

"Yes, and it would have burned straight through your skin had you touched them."

He inclined his head toward the pen she'd used to prod the vials, which she'd set on the table.

Her eyes widened when she saw that the instrument she'd used to maneuver the vials had been reduced nearly to ash.

35

As there was no final exam for Combat, Freya and the others set out for the palace right after she and Lea completed their Toxins exam.

"I'm going to fly," Freya told Aer as they walked toward the carriages the palace had sent. Laz and Collin had already boarded one, and Iska was helping Lea in beside them. The second carriage behind them was loaded down with Freya, Lea, Laz, and Collin's belongings, which would be taken to the chambers assigned to them by the royal family. Their parents would be arriving over the next few days, with Collin's making the trip down from their home in Kildin, the capital city of Caelora, with Lazarus' parents.

"Why don't you ride with us for once?" Aer asked, taking her hand.

She shook her head. "No, I'm still too antsy to be cooped up in a carriage. I'll meet you there."

"Alright. Fly safe." He leaned down and gave her a slow kiss. "If you happen across any marauders, give a shout."

"I hope you realize how much of a possibility that is," she told him, dismissing his nonchalantness.

Being away from the castle and unable to do any more investigating into what mysterious threat the human had been talking about
had been bothering Freya all week, to the point where she was on
edge with nearly everyone. She and Aer had decided not to involve
the others for the sole purpose of plausible deniability on their part,
but not telling their friends what they overheard was beginning to irk
her. She'd also wanted to confront her father all week about the
conversation she and Aer had overheard, but for once, he didn't
appear at school. As irritating as he could be at times, she didn't
necessarily dislike his presence. He was her father, after all, and had
always done what he thought was best for her.

Whatever he was doing now, whatever he was hiding, she had to
trust it was for good reason, whether it had anything to do with her
or not.

"I'm sorry." Aer held up his hands in surrender. "No more jokes, I
promise. Be safe, though, please."

Smiling, she kissed him one last time as she opened her wings.
"Aren't I always?"

"Would you truly like me to answer that?"

With a quick grin and a flap of her wings, she was in the air,
blowing him one last kiss as she aimed for the mountains, Rissen and
Cecilia running in their wolf forms beneath her.

The palace was abuzz with activity when they arrived, with
servants rushing to and fro in their final preparations for the arrival
of the first round of guests the following day. Freya and the others
had decided to take the night to themselves, giving them a few final
hours where they weren't all required to put on their most poised and
courtly facades.

This was the part of court life Freya didn't miss. The occasional
dinner here and there didn't bother her, but the day-in, day-out
manner of existing at court was exhausting. Between mingling with
the guests and the final preparations for the wedding, their sched-
ules were packed to the brim leading right up to the event. Had she
and Aer wanted to continue their investigation of what they'd overheard in the tunnels, there would be little time for it, and even if

there was time, it would be foolish to snoop about now that there were going to be so many guests in the palace. They could easily slip past a single guest unnoticed, but it would be foolish to think the same of the dozens of guests who would soon be filling the palace.

"Who's turn is it to raid the wine cellar?" Laz asked, his eyes scanning the busy entry hall. The air inside had a heavy chill to it, as all of the windows and doors in the guest wings had been thrown open to let in some fresh air after having been closed up for several months.

"I'll have three casks delivered to my chambers," Aer said. "That should last us for the next week."

Freya eyed him askance. "We do actually need to be presentable for our guests, Aer."

"Trust me," he told her. "You'll be thankful for it."

"Lady Balthana? Your Highness?"

Freya and Aer turned to the servant who'd addressed them, one of the queen's personal attendants. He was average height, a bit thin, with a mop of brown hair that flopped across his forehead. His pointed chin was tilted up just a fraction, giving him a look of superiority.

"Yes, Oscar?" Aer replied.

"Their Majesties await you both in the queen's solar."

Laz patted Freya and Aer on the shoulders. "And the fun begins," he said, grinning. "We'll try not to drink all the wine before you're released."

Freya blanched and a sudden sinking feeling settled in her stomach as Lea, Laz, and Collin followed the servants carrying their luggage toward one of the guest wings.

"Lovely." Aer sighed and pinched the bridge of his nose. "Alright, tell them we'll be along shortly."

Oscar gave him a quick bow before turning and disappearing down the busy corridor.

"Why do they need to speak with us already?" Freya hissed.

"Because there's a royal wedding in a week and we've still got a fair amount of preparing to do," he replied, taking her hand. "Come on, the sooner we get there, the sooner we can hide ourselves away for the rest of the night."

They wound their way through the halls, gradually encountering fewer and fewer staff as they neared the southern wing where the king and queen resided, far on the opposite side of the palace from the guest wings. Freya welcomed the silence and calm, knowing both would be in short supply in the coming days.

Aer knocked on Ordona's doors when they arrived, and a few moments later, she ushered them inside.

"We won't keep you long," she promised, leading them to her solar. "We just wanted to talk to you both a bit before the guests start arriving."

"Ah, good, you're here," Salazar said when they stepped onto the veranda, where one of Ordona's enchantments was keeping the chilly air at bay. He gestured toward the empty seats at the table. "Sit."

Once they were all settled, the queen smiled at them both. "There are a few things we need to go over before the guests begin arriving tomorrow," she said. "Nothing extravagant, just some things we should be clear on."

Aer arched a brow. "Such as?"

"The Jotnar will be arriving in the morning," Salazar said, tapping a fat cigar against a glass ashtray. "The humans will be arriving later in the afternoon. I want you both to make them feel welcome. Take this opportunity to get to know your foreign neighbors now, because you won't get a chance like this any time soon."

"Of course," Freya replied. She gave the queen a curious look.

"Take tonight to brush up on who's who one last time." Ordona smiled. "Have you been studying the list of Dystonian and Jotnar royals who will be attending?" Ordona waited until Freya nodded, then looked at the prince. "Aerelius, you and your father will be leading a hunting party the day before the wedding with the higher-ranking males of each nation."

Aer sighed and ran his hands through his hair. "I suppose that will be my opportunity to demonstrate my ability to lead a rabble-rousing group of royalty and nobility?"

"Consider it your bachelor party," the king said dryly. "And I don't think I have to remind you both, but I will anyway. Keep the jokes and snark at a minimum while we've foreign guests here. Your versions of propriety are much different than what outsiders would expect."

Aer raised his hands in acknowledgement. "Not to worry, Father. I'll only gaze upon my future queen with total adoration."

Salazar sent him a warning look, but Aer's response seemed to mollify him.

"And what will I be doing?" Freya asked.

The queen smiled. "You'll be plenty occupied, don't you worry."

Fittings, Freya thought. *More fittings and seating charts and tastings.*

The king and Aerelius began discussing the planned hunting trip, so Freya and Ordana moved to the cushioned chairs in the sitting area and spent the next hour discussing menu options and the final details for the wedding.

"I have to be honest, Your Majesty," Freya said, inserting a bit of regret into her tone, "I still feel a bit underprepared to meet the other royals. Your notes have been incredibly helpful, but is there anything else you feel I should know? Lessia doesn't have much family, but it seems the Dystonian royal family is quite extensive."

Freya thought she saw the queen narrow her eyes a touch, but it was hard to be sure because her face slipped into a lovely smile almost immediately.

"Yes, those humans do take advantage of their ability to reproduce like rabbits, don't they?" Picking up a jug of wine from a nearby table, she poured a glass for them both. "What would you like to know?"

"Well, you've provided a good deal of information about their history, family, and so forth, but I'm curious how I might be able to connect with the more high-ranking members of the court on a personal level." She watched the queen carefully. "Interests, that sort of thing."

"Ah." The queen nodded, then leaned back in her chair and rested her elbow on the arm, goblet poised near her lips. "Well, if it's gossip you're looking for, I've got plenty of that. There's always a thread of truth to every bit of tongue-wagging, Freya. You'd do well to remember that."

Freya laughed. "Then I suppose you'll need to fill me in on all you can."

"Alright, then." Ordona took a long sip of her wine. "Where to begin?"

36

The first thing the following morning, Freya and Aer received word from the king and queen that Lessia and her cadre had arrived earlier than intended. When Aer went into his room to dress, Rini helped Freya into a sky blue gown made of soft linen that sat just off her shoulders and tapered to her waist, with several layers of tulle under the skirt to add a subtle curve to her hips. Once she was dressed, Rini braided her hair in a simple coronet, leaving the rest pin-straight. Freya was worried it all sent too meek of an image, but the pixie merely shook her head.

"Let them see your softer side, my lady," Rini had said as she dusted Freya's cheeks with blush. "Don't let them see your fierceness just yet." Pausing, she gave Freya a considering look. "I'll leave it to you to decide whether to let out your wings or not."

A short while later, Rini left and Aer arrived to escort her to the throne room. He wore a deep blue shirt under a black suede jerkin with gold fastenings, and brown pants tucked into black boots with gold buckles. It was a step above his normal casual, but just below what she might expect for receiving foreign royalty.

As they walked, he flicked a glance at Freya's shoulders and frowned.

"I'd let your wings out."

With a sigh, she released her wings, letting them flare out behind her and Aer as they walked. It was a freeing feeling, one she hadn't allowed herself often enough since she'd arrived in Iladel.

As though reading her mind, he tapped the edge of one. "You should leave these out more often, Valkyrie. Byrric does."

"Byrric is a giant peacock," Freya quipped, flexing her wings to flick his hand away playfully. "I prefer subtlety. And besides, Rini suggested I keep my 'fierceness' concealed for this meeting. I've been debating what kind of message I want to send."

"Your wings aren't what make you fierce, Freya," Aer told her, his words carrying a mild undertone of surprise. "Neither is your magic. They're just a part of who you are."

She stopped, then turned to face him, angling her head as she studied his face.

"Do you mean that?" She put her hands on his chest. "That my wings—my magic—they're just a part of who I am?"

He gave her a confused look. "Of course."

She sighed, feeling a bit silly that she'd even brought it up. Despite the treatment and even deference at times she received from others around her due to her heritage, Aer had never once treated her as anything other than his equal.

He gave her a crooked smile, then ran his hands down her arms until they came to rest on the curve of her waist. "Freya, have I ever given you any reason to think I hold you on a pedestal because you're a half-blood? Because of who your parents are?"

"No." She smiled. "It's just nice to hear you say it, I suppose."

He brought his hands up to cup her face, then stared into her eyes. "You set yourself apart from others, not because of a lucky heritage, but because of what you do with the power you were given. You don't squander it, you don't look down on those who have less than you. You're a good person, but that comes from here," he said, putting a hand just above her heart. Gently, he brushed his other hand along the arch of her wing, and she closed her eyes at the softness of his touch. "These? They just come with the package."

"I think," she said slowly as she opened her eyes, "that I would very much like you to kiss me."

He laughed quietly, then tilted her chin upward. "And I would be happy to oblige."

$\sim$

WHEN THEY ARRIVED at the throne room, Freya saw that two thrones had been placed to the queen's right side. Freya couldn't help but smile when she saw that hers had been carved to suit a pair of wings. They were a bit smaller and not nearly ornate as those on which the king and queen sat, but their purpose was clear.

She and Aer would no longer be standing to the side.

The king and queen were dressed in their typical finery. Ordona's fawn-colored silk and chiffon dress was a shade Freya felt would look boring on herself but somehow managed to highlight Ordona's natural beauty by bringing out the golden tones of her skin. Salazar wore his typical black pants and boots, today topping them with a dark gray vest and cravat with a fitted red jacket that hung to mid-thigh. Pale gray mantles trimmed in gold hung from both royals' shoulders, and their crowns sat firmly atop their heads.

Jonas stood slightly to the side of the dais where their thrones stood, clad fully in the white leather he'd worn when he first arrived in Iladel, awaiting his aunt's arrival in silence, hardly acknowledging them as they made their way forward and took their seats beside the queen.

Byrric stood at the right hand of the king, hands clasped behind his back, wings hovering at his shoulders. He gave Freya an approving nod when he saw her.

The room was silent for a few moments before a herald opened the doors and announced the arrival of Lessia's court. She'd brought at least two dozen courtiers with her, each of whom were escorted in before her, one by one. With each arrival of the tall, slender Jotnar, the tension in the room seemed to mount, no doubt a type of power play on the empress' part.

When the empress herself finally walked in, her courtiers all kneeling in a line on either side of the wide red carpet that led to the thrones, she looked just as Freya had always pictured.

The first thing Freya noticed was the depth of Lessia's dark eyes. They were piercing, calculating, and more than a little unsettling. Jet black hair fell to her thighs and her skin, despite her flushed cheeks, appeared white next to the stark contrast of her hair. Like most Jotnar, she was tall and thin with a sharp-featured face, a regal nose, high cheekbones, and full, red lips. She wore a charcoal gray silk dress that was fitted through her waist and flared out at her hips. A diadem made of Jotnar gold—a white metal that had a tell-tale iridescence that differentiated it from simple silver—rested on top of her head. A single, egg-sized diamond was set in the center of the piece. Though none of her individual features were terribly striking, and as a whole, Freya wouldn't call her beautiful, something about their combination made Lessia seem otherworldly.

Jonas strode forward and dropped to one knee, bowing to his aunt when she came to a stop in the center of the room.

"Empress," he said, not looking up from the floor. "Well met."

Lessia remained silent for several seconds, allowing the tension in the room to build a bit more before she spoke. Freya fought back the urge to shift in her seat.

"Well met, nephew. You may rise."

Jonas stood in a single smooth motion, then stepped to Lessia's side. Her courtiers remained kneeling.

Ordona and Salazar, who'd seemed to have perfected the art of mimicking statuary, remained seated in their thrones. After a thorough talking to the previous day regarding demeanor among royals, Freya forced her expression into one of indifference, ensuring that no hint of what was going through her mind was apparent on her face.

"Queen Ordona, King Salazar," Lessia crooned. "The moment I saw your invitation, I just knew I had to come."

"We're pleased you were able to make the trip," Salazar said. "It wouldn't be a proper celebration without our neighbors in attendance."

Turning her smile on Aer and Freya, Lessia said, "I've been so eager to meet your successors. Your future princess is... lovely." She ran appraising eyes over Freya, assessing her as nearly everyone who just met her did.

In talking with Ordona, Freya learned that Lessia liked to push and pry, to lure others into verbal traps, belittling themselves in some way or another. She hadn't been entirely sure what Ordona meant when she explained it—she couldn't fathom belittling herself due to the words of another—but now, as Lessia ran cold eyes over her, she understood.

Lessia liked to suss out weakness and to exert dominance.

Freya met her eyes with a somewhat disinterested stare, then gave her a small smile. "Well met, Empress. I've been looking forward to meeting you as well."

"As have I," Aer said, giving the empress a nod. "Lord Edrin mentioned you preferred northern exposure, so we've made accommodations for you and your party in the north wing of the palace."

Lessia smiled. "That's quite kind of you, Your Highness. Now, I hope you don't mind, but it's been a long trip and I would very much like to get some rest."

"Of course," Ordona replied. "Your luggage has already been brought to your rooms, and Syndra will be happy to show you where you'll be staying."

The small brunette servant stepped forward and curtsied. "If you'll just follow me, Empress, I'll show you to your rooms."

When the room had emptied of all but Freya, Aer, Salazar, and Ordona, Freya blew out a breath.

This was going to be a very long week.

AFTER THEIR INTRODUCTION TO Empress Lessia, Ordona and Salazar sent Freya and Aer off to help with the arrival of the other guests who would be staying at the palace for the remainder of the week. For the better part of the rest of the morning, they were tasked with greeting the governing families and helping to ensure accommodations were all in order. When they were called back to the throne room several hours later to greet the human monarchs, Freya realized that it was quite possible the man they'd overheard with the king, queen, and Byrric would be within the palace walls in a short while.

They'd hardly had time to greet the king and queen and sit on their thrones before a herald announced the Dystonian court. Despite bringing a slew of guards, they'd brought only a handful of royal guests, perhaps half of what Lessia had arrived with, relieving a bit of the tension before it had even developed.

Freya wasn't entirely sure what she expected the human monarchs to look like, as it had been a fair number of years since she'd actually *seen* a human. What she recalled most about humans was that, compared to Linds and even Jotnar, humans had always seemed a bit plain. Maybe it was due to lack of magic or supernatural abilities, or maybe it was because they just didn't hold the same spark Freya so often saw in her own kind.

King Willem's siblings were the last to enter just before the king and queen. His youngest sister, Rosie, was sixteen and betrothed to a wealthy lord in the southern human province of Leford. She was a small girl with golden hair and a soft face. Reginald, the brother, was a broad-shouldered man with blond hair and a gentle smile, who looked to be only a few years older than Freya and had yet to choose a wife. His other siblings—two more brothers and another sister—had stayed behind in Dystone.

Though attractive by human standards, Willem Ristner's siblings were plain enough, which suited her memory of humans as a whole. She was a bit surprised, then, when Willem and Isadora entered. They both held a beauty that seemed unnatural for humans. Isadora had golden hair that flowed to her waist in a wave of soft curls. Her face had delicate features, her lips full, and her cheeks held a natural flush. She was slight, coming hardly to her husband's shoulder, with a tiny waist and kind eyes.

The moment Freya looked at Willem, she saw what Jonas had

been referring to when he'd insinuated the Dystonian king was a bit odd.

He had short-cropped brown hair and a face that bore high cheekbones and wide, almond-shaped eyes, giving him a strong, attractive appearance. The slightly shifty expression on his face, however, and the way he carried himself—as though ready to bolt through the door any moment—along with the way her senses went on high-alert the moment he looked her way, told Freya there was certainly something a bit off about him. She inhaled quietly and was unsurprised to scent a good deal of anxiety oozing from the man.

Aer placed a hand over hers.

"Your Majesties," Salazar said, standing to welcome them. "It was so good of you to come."

"We're thrilled you'll be celebrating such a joyous occasion with us," Ordona added.

"Your Majesties," Willem said with a bow. "Thank you for the invitation."

Isadora's smile was striking, a thing that no doubt brought her a fair share of male attention in her life, as she gave the king and queen a deep curtsy. "It's so lovely to finally meet you, Your Majesties," she said sweetly. "I've been so eager to visit your lands."

"Indeed," Willem said, his deep voice suggesting he'd been anything but eager.

"Is there anything you'll have need of during your stay?" Aer inquired.

"No, no. We'd just like to settle in, check things over," Willem murmured, his eyes scanning the room. "You can never be too careful, you know."

"I'm sure you'll find it all to your liking," Ordona replied. "We've prepared a room for you in the eastern wing, away from the other guests."

Frowning, Willem looked at Freya. The sudden eye contact had her hackles rising instantly. "Does your future queen not speak?"

Freya's brows flew up and she was momentarily at a loss for words. "I—"

"No matter." Willem scratched his chin, cutting her off as he faced the king and queen. "Would you be so kind as to have someone show us to our quarters?"

Salazar gestured toward Syndra, who'd just appeared at the doorway. "Syndra will see you there. Should you need anything, please don't hesitate to use the call bells in your rooms."

"Thank you most kindly," Isadora said, smiling prettily at them once more before following her husband as he strode from the room.

Freya smiled tersely as they left, her jaw clenched so tight she thought it might break.

Once the massive doors clanged shut, Ordona sighed and relaxed in her seat. Salazar followed suit, then snapped his fingers. Seconds later, a servant was handing him a cigar and match.

"Well," Aer said, lacing his fingers through Freya's. "This ought to be fun."

Freya was fuming by the time they left the throne room.

"'Does your future queen not speak,'" she grumbled, her stride brisk as they made their way back to Aer's chambers. "Bastard."

"Pay them no mind," Aer told her, taking her hand to slow her pace. "Humans will always be jealous of our kind and some will, therefore, try to belittle you in any way they can."

She huffed. "And we're to spend the next week with these people?"

"And get along famously the entire time," he said with a grin as he opened his door. "Don't worry, Valkyrie. You'll win them over within a day."

"The queen, maybe—"

"Ah, there they are!"

Freya and Aer froze at the sound of Jonas' voice, which was coming from inside Aer's bedroom.

Again at a loss for words, Freya took in the sight before her. Lea, Laz, Collin, and Jonas all sat around the table just to the left of the veranda doors. Three charcuterie plates and four jugs of wine sat between them. As half the food was eaten, it appeared they'd been there for some time.

She and Aer exchanged a wary look before he finally spoke.

"It appears I missed an invitation to a party in my own room," he commented, shutting the door with a snap.

"Well, we ran into Jonas on our way down from our own rooms," Lea said, plucking a grape off the plate in front of her and giving Freya a wide smile. "He's been here for weeks, so we thought it hightime he spent some time with us."

"My aunt decided to retire early, and I can't quite bear the company of her entourage," Jonas added, indeed looking far more at ease in their company than he had in the throne room hours earlier.

"So we asked him to join us for the evening," Laz finished.

"Did you, now?" Freya asked, amused.

"I hope you don't mind," Jonas said, sipping his wine. "I believe your friends saw how eager I was to avoid returning to the frigid temperatures that tend to accompany Lessia everywhere she goes."

There was a surprising amount of bitterness in his voice, as though the mere presence of his aunt in the palace had sucked a bit of life from him. In the two months since he'd arrived, Freya had only seen him a few times outside his visits to Iladel and Aldridge. He'd been present at dinner only twice when she stayed at the palace and spent his days either exploring Iladel or in his room. According to Aer, he enjoyed frequenting the palace library and galleries, examining ancient tomes and artwork from the long Harridan line. It seemed a bit surprising that he now wanted to join in with the five of them, be more social than he had been. But, she supposed, now that she knew a bit about the kind of company Lessia offered, she couldn't really blame him.

While she still hadn't gotten over the insinuations he'd made to the king and Byrric about her, she also wasn't prepared to risk a relationship with a foreign emissary over a mere annoyance. So, she and Aer took seats, thanking Laz as he handed them each a glass of wine.

"You're always welcome, Jonas," she told him.

Aer glanced dubiously at the three wine casks that were set against the wall behind the table. "How far into our stores have you four gotten?"

Scrunching his face, Laz leaned back and looked at the four jugs on the table. "Half a cask or so." He tapped one of the jugs. "This is only our first round."

Freya arched a brow and sipped the wine, its vibrant, summery flavor bursting across her tongue. "Only your first, hmm?"

Laz patted Jonas on the shoulder. "Our new friend here is quite the drinker, it seems."

Aer flashed Jonas a smile. "Understandable, considering."

"So what have you all been up to today?" Freya asked, sliding one of the plates of food forward. "Gods above, I'm starving."

"Hiding from our parents, mainly," Laz said. "My mother keeps on me about my attire for the wedding. I'm the cousin of the groom, for heaven's sake. No one will be looking at me."

"You're also a governor's son," Collin said, his tone implying this wasn't the first time they'd had this discussion. "You can't stand beside your parents at a royal wedding dressed for a dinner party."

Laz waved a hand in annoyance. "Yes, yes, I already know. Can we talk about something more interesting, please? Freya, Aerelius, how was your meeting with the humans?"

Aer and Freya exchanged a quick look, one that wasn't lost for a moment on Jonas.

"Ah, King Willem is quite... something, isn't he?" Jonas asked with a knowing smile. "How long did it take him to insult you, Freya?"

"What makes you so sure he insulted me?" she asked, blinking in surprise.

"The man is quite the misogynist, if I'm not mistaken, and a bit of a bigot," Jonas said. "He wouldn't speak down to your betrothed, but seeing as you're not a royal yet, he wouldn't hesitate to do so to you." He picked up a piece of bread and dipped it in jam. "Other monarchs will test you, my lady. He's just not very good at it."

"How do you mean?" Aer asked.

"When I visited Dystone a while back, he saw me as he likely sees

Freya—a peripheral royal, if you will. He tried several times to get me to... snap, perhaps?" He shook his head. "No, maybe that's not the right word. It just seemed he wanted to be irksome, get a rise out of me."

Freya couldn't help but notice how similar Willem seemed to Lessia in that regard, although something told her that Lessia's centuries of experience weighed heavily in her favor when it came down to the effectiveness of such a tactic.

"Did it work?" Lea asked, smirking as she rested her elbow on the table and propped her chin on her fist. "I can't imagine it did."

He gave her a brilliant smile in return. "Not in the least." He looked to Aer and Freya expectantly. "Will we be having dinner in the main dining room this evening?"

"No," Aer said. "Guests are still arriving and getting settled in. Tomorrow, though." He jerked his chin toward the call bell near his bed. "I'll call for dinner now if you'd all like to stay. With so many to cook for, it will take a bit for them to get up here."

"I'd be delighted," Jonas replied.

As Aer stood to call the kitchen, Freya rested her forearms on the table and smiled at Jonas, trying to put her lingering annoyance with him aside. "So, did you meet many of the human royals when you were in Dystone? I feel as though I know so little about them."

"I did. While the king and queen have no children yet, their families are quite extensive. Willem has three younger brothers, two of whom have a handful of children each, and two younger sisters. Isadora has just the one brother but a whole horde of cousins. They had a dinner with the entire family while I was there, and needless to say, I and my escorts were vastly outnumbered," he said with a laugh.

Freya's eyes goggled at the thought of such a large family, and she couldn't help but feel a twinge of jealousy for how easy the humans seemed to have it when it came to offspring. Linds and Jotnar alike were, as a rule, slow to procreate. The thought of having six children in such a short time frame was mind boggling.

"Were you in Dystone long?" Collin asked, seeming genuinely curious.

Jonas paused, then looked around the table and laughed. "If I didn't know better, I'd think you only invited me to stay to pump me for information."

"Not at all," Freya said easily. "It's a benefit, surely, to have someone who's familiar with our guests here tonight, but we're all friends here." She tipped her glass in salute. "Let's get to know one another a bit better, what do you say?"

Tipping his glass in return, Jonas nodded. "I think that sounds wonderful."

37

F reya and the others were up until late into the night talking, getting to know their new friend and each other a bit more. Jonas was far more enjoyable to spend time with than she'd expected, and she was surprised to find he shared a number of common interests with them.

While admittedly fun, Freya was feeling the aftereffects of a late night of drinking fairly hard the following morning, when she grunted at Dina to leave breakfast on the table and tugged the pillow back over her head.

She wasn't sure how much later it was when she felt Aer flop into the bed beside her and begin stroking her back.

"Time to get up, sleepyhead," he crooned. "The day awaits."

Rolling onto her back, Freya rubbed at her eyes, then turn toward the window, where the sun was blazing.

"You let me sleep in," she murmured.

"Not so much," he replied, tucking her hair behind her ear and smiling down at her. "It's nearly nine. The ship carrying the rest of the humans has just docked, so they'll be here in a few hours. I thought you might want to take some time to yourself before they arrived."

She groaned. "Why not let me sleep, then?"

He grinned. "The younglings are in the training yard with Ervic and a few others." He tapped her nose. "You've been tense and I think tossing some knives about might help. Perhaps show the children a thing or two?"

Her heart leapt at the idea, but her stomach's answering grumble stopped her.

"Food first," Freya replied, sitting up and gesturing toward the tray Dina had left. "Then yes, I'd love to."

After wolfing down a breakfast of eggs and sausage and taking a quick bath, she tugged on a pair of fur-lined leather pants and topped them with a long-sleeved ivory tunic trimmed in silver. She touched a few dabs of rouge to her lips and cheeks and brushed out her long hair, then tied it back in a loose braid that hung over her shoulder.

"You look quite lovely," Aer commented. "Not at all like you're planning on chucking knives at targets for the next hour or two."

"That's the point," she told him, pulling her weapons case from under her bed. "Strong yet delicate is exactly the image I'm going for right now."

"You're anything but delicate, Freya."

"True, but I don't want to come on too strong." She a sheathed knife at either hip. "Especially with children."

"I hope the irony of you saying that as you strap daggers to your belt isn't lost on you," he said, grinning. Stepping forward, he slipped his arms around her waist. "And you *are* strong. That's not something that should be concealed."

Smiling, she laid her hands on his chest. "I know, but we're not at school anymore. I've got a different sort of impression to make and I want it to be one that shows balance. I won't wander around all day in fancy dresses, but I can't very well wear my leathers all the time, either."

"But I like your leathers." He hooked his thumbs in the waistband of her pants at the small of her back, then dragged his teeth along the shell of her ear. "Especially these."

She released a quiet breath as shivers ran through her. "We should go," she said reluctantly.

"We will," he whispered, brushing his lips along her jaw. "In a minute."

When she tilted her head to the side, he continued placing soft kisses down the column of her neck, then he slipped his hands down to cup her backside, pulling her closer.

She sighed contentedly as his lips found hers again, all too willing to stay away from the throngs of people who would soon be flooding the palace for just a little while longer.

Reluctantly, she nudged him back. "As enticing as this is, we've got guests coming here for us, so we need to be visible."

"They're coming here because they were invited, and to deny a royal invite would be in poor taste," Aer murmured, nipping at her ear. "But I suppose I see your point."

He gave her one last kiss. Then, letting his hand drift down her arm, he wrapped his fingers around hers and tugged her toward the door.

"So, has there been any word on our mystery guest?" she asked quietly as they entered the hall.

"No," Aer said. "But all things considered, I would imagine there's a good chance he's already here and will likely be at dinner tonight."

"That won't be a bit awkward," Freya muttered. "Any thoughts on who it might be?" She'd been going over the faces of the human monarchs' party since she'd met them, but none seemed to stand out to her and their scents had been too muddled for Freya to tell if the human they'd scented was present.

"None. I haven't seen hide nor hair of the humans since yesterday, so the only glimpse I got of them was in the throne room. Most will be at dinner tonight, so it's quite probable he'll be there."

"And how do you expect either of us to keep a straight face if that happens?"

"You're a good actress, Valkyrie, even if you don't know it." He elbowed her lightly. "I almost believed you wanted nothing to do with me that first day in combat."

She gave him a deadpan look. "That's because I wanted to throttle you quite thoroughly."

Wrapping his arm around her shoulders, he kissed the top of her head. "You've been in love with me since we were children, just admit it."

"Perhaps," she said with a slow nod. "I suppose you'll have to wait until after our wedding to find out."

He tsked. "Typical Valkyrie, stubborn as always."

She slid him a look. "I'm fairly certain that's one of the main reasons you've fallen hopelessly in love with *me*."

His lips quirked into a smile. "Just wait and see, Freya. Wait and see."

FREYA'S STEPS felt a bit lighter when they arrived at the training yard, where the palace knights were working on skills with pages and apprentices who hoped to become squires one day. It was a familiar place, one in which she'd spent a lot of time during her summer visits having duels and archery contests with the others. Some of the children there now were as young as ten, shifters, witches, and warlocks who, like Freya, had begun training to become castle pages not long after they could walk. Others were into their teen years and would soon be getting their official title of squire. The excitement she knew they felt just now was one she'd often been envious of when she'd been working alongside the others her age when she was younger. She'd never actually wanted to be a squire or knight, necessarily, but the idea of having such an exciting assignment at a young age—even if it did require things like polishing armor and gathering firewood for patrols—was something she wished she could experience.

That was long before she'd been given the opportunity to prove her worth with the marshals, putting the skills she'd learned into practice in ways many of the squires didn't get until they'd reached knighthood.

When the children and knights saw Freya and the prince walk in, all movement ceased as they turned to face them

"Sir Ervic!" Aer called to the guard in charge of the group. "My betrothed has an itchy hand today. Would you mind if she worked with you a bit?"

"We would be honored, Your Highness," Ervic said with a bow.

"Sir Ervic," Freya said in greeting, smiling broadly at the knight. "It's lovely to see you again."

"Likewise, my lady," he said. "I've been telling this lot stories of your skill as a child. Are you here to give us a demonstration?"

"I'd just like a bit of exercise," she said, tapping her blades. "So long as I'm not intruding?"

"Never, my lady," he said with an easy smile. "It would be nice for the children to see someone else's technique for a change."

Freya looked around the yard, suddenly realizing all eyes were on her now, not her prince.

"Alright, then," Aer said after a moment, his eyes twinkling. "I'll leave you to it."

"You aren't staying?"

He shook his head. "My father needs to see me about something, so I'll see you at lunch."

"That sounds lovely." Gripping his forearms, she stood up on her toes and kissed him. "Thank you."

With a final wave at Ervic, the prince walked off.

"Was there anything in particular you'd like to do, my lady?" Ervic asked once he'd gone.

"I'm interested in the Valkyrie's knife skills, myself," Jonas called from the other side of the yard, an easy grin on his face as he met Freya's eyes. He'd appeared seemingly out of nowhere, although with the dark overhang he was standing beneath, it was more likely he'd been observing the whole time.

Ervic's jaw tightened. "My lady?"

Freya narrowed her eyes appraisingly at the children, all of whom seemed a bit uneasy in her presence. "I think a bit of knife work sounds perfect, actually," she told Ervic. "Although I'd love to see how your charges are coming along first, if it's not too much trouble?"

"It would be an honor to have your feedback, Lady Balthana. Your father has spoken highly of the skills you acquired while in Watoria, and these will be your knights soon enough."

She blinked, a bit taken aback at the unintended boldness of the statement. All her life, the knights under her father's command had been *his* knights, despite being in the king's army.

Even more dizzying—and laughable—was the idea that, not only would they be her knights, her father would also be under her command.

Unable to hide the smile that thought pulled forth, she nodded at Ervic. "If that's what you'd like, I'm happy to do so." Spying an empty space beside Jonas on the side of the archery lanes, she added, "I'll just go stand with our friend for now."

Ervic's lips twitched in amusement. "Thank you, my lady."

As he turned back to his charges, Freya made her way over to where Jonas stood. Though she still held a good deal of annoyance regarding the presumptions he'd voiced about her to the king, he'd been an enjoyable guest the previous night. While she wasn't quite sure she was ready to move past his more... irritating tendencies, she was willing to give him a chance.

"Good morning, Jonas," she said, offering up her friendliest smile. "How has your day been so far?"

"Quite lovely," he said. "Although I have a feeling the peace and quiet we've managed to enjoy in recent weeks is going to be shattered quite soon, wouldn't you agree?"

"Yes," she said with a sigh. "I suppose you're right." Freya turned her attention back to the pages and squires who'd picked up their weapons and gone back to their training. "I'm surprised you aren't with your aunt. Is she with the king and queen?"

"Indisposed, as she often is after a long trek." His jovial demeanor from the night before seemed to have vanished at the mention of Lessia. "She'll be in her chambers until dinner, most likely."

Freya nodded, not quite sure what the most appropriate response would be. He didn't seem overly thrilled that his aunt had arrived. Freya would even go so far as to say a bit of melancholy had befallen him, so she could only assume that he was no stranger to Lessia's harsh demeanor, despite being her blood.

"What brings you down here today?" she asked him.

"Now and then I come down to observe the various teaching methods of the knights. It's quite fascinating to see how their varying techniques can change the way a lesson is taught."

"Do you have an interest in teaching?"

"I do." He gave her a wistful smile. "Alas, I was placed directly into my aunt's employ once I came of age."

"You don't enjoy acting as emissary, then?"

"At times," he allowed, folding his arms as he focused his attention on the young squires. "I get to see foreign lands and meet new people, which is nice, and the Lindorothian lands are far more hospitable in most areas than Jotunheim."

She gave him a curious look. "Your words sound certain, but your tone implies something else."

"It can be a lonesome duty," he admitted. "I visit these wonderful places, but I share them with no one."

Freya was surprised at both his honesty and forlornness, even going so far as to feel a bit sorry for him as she realized that loneliness might play a part in why he'd chosen to stay in Iladel for so long. Compared to the cold, harsh lands in Jotunheim, Iladel was a dream. It held the best of what Lindoroth had to offer and none of the dreariness so often found in the northern lands

"May I ask why you've decided to come here today, of all places?" Jonas asked after a moment. His tone held genuine curiosity, not incredulity or confusion, as she might've expected. "I know why I've ventured out, but I expected you to stick close to your prince and friends."

"This was one of my favorite places when I was a girl, especially when I felt the need to release some pent-up energy, as is the case today." She inclined her head toward where Ervic stood helping a young boy adjust the height of his throwing arm. "Ervic was one of the first to teach me proper swordsmanship."

"I'm impressed, Freya," he said, his face expressing as much. "Not only can you throw knives and fire an arrow with precision, you can also handle a sword."

"I can," she confirmed. "Although I can't say it's my favorite weapon. A bit bulky." She touched a hand to the knife at her hip. "I prefer something more easy to maneuver."

"Too true," he mused, flicking a glance at the two bone-handled daggers she wore. They stood in silence for a few moments watching as two students picked up blunt-bladed tourney swords and began practicing. The ability of palace knights to teach their students swordsmanship immediately became evident as the small children, ten if they were a day, dashed and ducked about the ring with rapid precision, a young knight alongside them calling out moves.

"I believe I owe you an apology, Freya," Jonas said after they'd watched the boys parry for a few minutes. "It's been on my mind since we spoke last night and I'd like to fully clear the air, if I can."

"How so?"

"I misjudged you at first," he admitted. "You're not at all what I expected as the prince's betrothed."

"What was it you expected, Jonas?"

"To be quite honest, I expected a doe-eyed female hovering silently at his highness' shoulder. When I saw you were nearly the opposite, I struggled to believe it." His face was unabashed as he continued. "Knowing what I do of King Salazar, I expected his successor's spouse to be one to follow her prince, not stand beside him, and it made me instantly wary of you."

She tried to rein in her shock at such a statement, biting down hard on her tongue to keep from pointing out the insult to her queen. Salazar was certainly a male set in his ways, but Ordona held nearly as much authority and respect as he.

"Do you know what I've learned about you in the short time we've spent together, Jonas?" Freya gave him a reluctant smile. "You're quite adept at backhanded compliments and are a bit of a busybody."

He barked out a laugh. "And you, my lady, possess a brutal honesty that will get you far in this world. I believe your kingdom will thank you for it one day. I do hope we can be friends."

"My lady?" Ervic called. "Would you like to join us now?"

Grinning, Freya nodded, then turned to Jonas. "I respect your honesty, Jonas, and appreciate your apology. I hope we can be friends as well."

"It was overdue," he said. "Now, let's see the famed Valkyrie's weapon work, shall we?"

38

Two hours later, Jonas had left to dive into a book and Freya was crouched beside a tow-headed young page, demonstrating her technique for properly gripping a knife for throwing. Holding her own blade at chin-height, Freya flicked her wrist and sent it sailing down the lane toward the bullseye, then gave the boy an encouraging nod. The page took a deep breath, then pulled back his arm and aimed for his target ten feet away, far closer than the one she'd hit, and threw. When his knife landed on the outer edge, his shoulders slumped in defeat. Freya patted him on the shoulder and went to get his knife.

"Did you know, Barin," Freya said as she handed it back, "that when I was your age, I almost never hit the center?"

"It's true," Aer said, stepping into the yard. "She nearly took my ear off *twice*."

The boy frowned up at them. "Why did you have your head so close to the target?"

Aer slid a look at Freya, who was biting her lip in amusement. "My dear friend seemed convinced she could hit an apple atop my head, and I was smitten enough to believe her."

The boy's eyes widened, then he laughed. "Do you have a scar?"

Leaning down, Aer tilted his head to the side, tapping the edge of his ear. "Just there."

"But Your Highness—why—" he cut himself off, seeming hesitant to voice his next question.

Aer laughed. "Why did I let her try a second time?"

Freya's lips trembled with laughter. "As it happens, his highness has a fondness—perhaps a weakness—for bets. All I had to do was promise him a kiss if he won."

Aer smiled fondly at the memory. "Sadly, I had to wait several years before winning that one."

Freya inclined her head toward the target. "Would you like to take a few more throws, Barin?"

When he nodded, Aer stepped back and allowed Freya to help Barin line up his throw once more. After a few attempts, Ervic came over to relieve Freya.

"Productive day?" Aer asked as she walked toward him.

"Quite," she said, smiling. After she and Jonas had spoken, she'd jumped in with Ervic and had gotten her hands into archery and a bit of swordplay, something she always felt to be a bit lacking in. She indulged a few of the students who offered to show her proper technique, allowing them their assumptions that her difference in methodology was due to inexperience and not simply a nontraditional technique. Even still, she was surprised and pleased to find that the upcoming generation of knights seemed quite promising.

They'd hardly made it down the corridor from the training yard when a voice called out to them.

"Your Highness, my lady!"

Turning, they paused when they saw Isadora heading their way. Freya was surprised to see Lessia at the Dystonian queen's side. Eight guards—two Jotnar and six human—trailed behind them. Freya couldn't help but smile at the humans' abundance of caution. She understood it, but even they had to know that six humans, no matter how well-trained, would be no match for Lindorothian and Jotnar guards.

The two females were a study in contrasts, one lovely and delicate, the other cold in both appearance and demeanor. Lessia's gown was, again, a stormy gray, with a long skirt that trailed behind her, the train whispering over the stone of the corridor. Her black hair was worn loose, some hanging over her shoulders, the rest trailing down her back. On some, the style would've seemed messy or too casual, but paired with her dress and the confident, almost condescending tilt of her chin, it looked stunning.

Isadora, though, looked every bit the fragile human queen she was. She wore a pale blue wool dress with a white fur stole, and her hair fell in soft golden ringlets around her shoulders much the way a porcelain doll's would. Her cheeks were flushed a delicate pink in the chill that filled the open walkway, and her lips were red against her light skin.

Though she couldn't be more than five years Freya's senior, she carried herself with a certain grace that spoke of years of painfully formal training on how to be perfectly proper. There were no sword fights or patrols in her background. No, she'd been born and bred to be beautiful and, if Freya wasn't mistaken, obedient.

"Your Majesty, Empress," Aer said with a bow. "How are you this morning?"

"Quite well, thank you," Lessia said. She gave Freya an assessing glance, one that lasted all of one second but spoke volumes of what she thought of her. "My lady."

Freya gave her a small nod. "Empress."

Isadora smiled prettily, although there was a tight set to her jaw. "I just needed a bit of fresh air," she said. "After being on a boat for the last three days, it's hard to stay closed up inside." Smiling at Lessia, she continued. "I ran into the empress on my way to the gardens."

"Her Majesty's mind and mine seem to have traveled along the same path," Lessia said, brushing a stray hair from her cheek. "I was looking for a bit of the same."

"Well, the gardens are lovely this time of day, and as it happens, that's where I was headed myself," Freya said, quickly making up her mind. "Would you like me to show you? I've got a bit of time before lunch."

"That would be much appreciated, Lady Balthana," Lessia replied smoothly.

"Indeed," Isadora said, her shoulders sagging slightly. "I only saw the gardens from above, but they look quiet dizzying. A guide would be welcome."

Aer gave Freya a curious look as he leaned down to kiss her good-bye. "I'll let our parents know you'll be along shortly."

Freya smiled when he pulled back, letting him know she was fine to be on her own with the two monarchs. "Thank you."

After Aer and his guards disappeared around a corner, leaving Rissen and Cecilia to follow behind Freya silently, she gestured toward the hall that would take them to the main gardens. "It's not a far walk from here."

"Lady Balthana, I'm actually quite glad I ran into you," Lessia said, hooking an arm through Freya's as they began to walk. Freya's instinct screamed at her to step away from the empress, but she held her ground, refusing to let Lessia see that she was unnerved by her proximity. "I was hoping perhaps the three of us, and Ordona of course, might be able to sit together at dinner tonight." She patted Freya's hand and smiled at Isadora.

"I'd have to confer with Ordona, but yes, I think I would enjoy that very much." Freya turned to Isadora. "Your Majesty?"

Isadora's answering smile came a beat later. "Yes, my lady, I think I would enjoy getting to spend time with just the females."

Lessia sent Freya a reproachful look. "Now, my lady, as the incoming queen, I would expect you would be the one to make deci-sions on when and where you seat yourself."

Freya gave her a calm, level look. "This is still Queen Ordona's palace and she's far more knowledgeable than I when it comes to planning events, so for now I'll continue to defer to her."

"It's quite logical and certainly makes things easier," Isadora said with a smile.

Lessia made a small "hmm."

Recalling Lessia's husband had passed away several years ago and that this might be a poor topic of conversation, Freya moved to change the subject.

"How long will you both be staying in Iladel? Do you have plans to travel more, now that you're here?"

Lessia sighed. "It's been some time since I've been this far south, but I haven't yet decided how long my stay will be."

"I've told Willem I'd like to visit the other realms, or Edhil and Saith, at least, because I've heard they're quite beautiful," Isadora said. "He's hesitant, so I suppose we'll see."

Freya didn't miss the slight curl of Lessia's lip at Isadora's obvious submissiveness to her husband. Something told Freya that Lessia didn't have a submissive bone in her body.

A male appeared in the corridor before them, his thigh-length green cloak identifying him as one of Lessia's servants.

"Empress, Lord Edrin has asked a word of you, if you may," he said, keeping his eyes trained just past Lessia's shoulder.

"Oh, bother." Lessia sighed loudly. "Alright, tell him I'll be right along." Turning to Freya and Isadora, she smiled sweetly. "I suppose our walk in the gardens will have to wait, unfortunately. Apologies Lady Balthana, Your Majesty."

"Not to worry," Freya replied. "I look forward to dinner."

Lessia gave her a curt nod, then swept off, her long gray skirts trailing behind her.

"Shall we continue on?" she asked Isadora, noting her slightly relieved expression.

"Yes, please."

As she and Isadora continued walking, Freya struggled to come up with an innocuous conversation topic. *Do you happen to know of any of your king's men who might want to commit treason against him?* didn't seem the best tactic for sussing out information, especially considering she knew little and less about the woman. Isadora seemed meek and mild, but any good actress could feign such things.

They traveled for a few moments before Freya broke the silence.

"Have you made any other plans for your stay in Iladel, Your Majesty?"

"I hope to explore the main city while I'm here. I've heard such wonderful things about it, and the cities in Dystone are quite small compared to yours." Isadora clasped her hands behind her back and sighed contentedly as they neared the garden entrance. "This is such a beautiful space," she commented.

"It's always been one of my favorites," Freya told her. "You should see it in spring and summer."

"I think I'd very much like that," Isadora said as Freya led her down the main path. "You and Aerelius have known each other for a long time, correct?"

Freya smiled. "Yes, we've been friends since we were children." She bit her lip before continuing. "Did you and King Willem not know each other prior to your wedding?"

"Not well," Isadora said with a sigh. "The betrothal was made when we were infants, but we only saw each other once a year at summer solstice before that. A week-long visit and no more."

"And your parents?"

"I hail from the governing house of Vindarria, the easternmost province of Dystone. We have the strongest army in the land, so Willem's father saw a benefit in uniting our families." There was an odd note to her voice, something that told Freya she'd likely recited those lines many times in her life, perhaps to convince herself why a betrothal to a man she didn't know was a good thing.

"It's always about power, isn't it?" Freya said ruefully.

"Too true," Isadora murmured, her words carrying a clear undercurrent of resentfulness.

Feeling the conversation deteriorating, Freya shifted direction. "I haven't yet had the pleasure of visiting Dystone," she said. "Do you have a favorite region?"

Isadora brightened. "Oh, yes! I'm partial to the eastern lands, myself, but when I moved west to take my place at Willem's side, I fell in love with both the land and its people. It was so... different than what I was used to, but in such a good way." She smiled at Freya. "Has it ever been like that for you?"

"A bit. I spent most of my life to the west of Lindoroth in Allanor, not far from Iston, where the rest of my kind still live. That's where my father grew up. We summered here every year up until I was thirteen." She smiled softly. "Iladel was my second home."

"But not after?"

Freya shook her head. "After my mother passed, the choices were to either bring me here and have others raise me at court or have my aunt raise me in Allanor." She shrugged. "My father chose Allanor."

"It doesn't sound as though that is what you would've chosen," Isadora said softly.

"No, I can't say it is." Freya sighed. "I know why my father chose the way he did for me, and in many ways I'm thankful. I may have even done the same in his shoes, but I think I would have liked a bit more time here as just a girl, the prince's friend." She gave the young queen a slightly embarrassed look. "Does that sound silly?"

"Not in the least!" Isadora linked her arm through Freya's. "But what I *will* say in your father's defense is that he gave you a gift most women in our positions never receive."

"A gift?"

Isadora nodded. "You got to be perfectly ordinary, if my guess is correct. Or, perhaps, not *ordinary*, but I'd be willing to bet you weren't stuffed and trussed like a turkey on a daily basis while you were living in Allanor." She cast a pointed look at Freya's pants.

Freya laughed at that. "No, Watoria wasn't the type of place you saw many stuffed and trussed females."

"I think it will help you bring your own unique spark to your throne," Isadora said with a firm nod. "People will expect great things from you, Freya, but something tells me greatness will be anything but difficult for you to achieve."

Momentarily stunned, she stared at the woman. It was the highest compliment she'd ever received from someone who wasn't already familiar with her, not to mention the delivery had far more wisdom than the young queen looked to possess.

"Thank you, Your Majesty. Your words are very kind."

"Well, I wouldn't speak them if they weren't true," Isadora said matter-of-factly. "I may not seem like much, my lady, but I like to think I'm a good judge of character." She patted Freya's hand and looked around the garden. "This reminds me of the gardens in Caldel a bit. Lovely, even in the colder months."

"The prince and I used to escape here often when we were children," Freya told her, smiling at the memory.

"The other children and I used to play games in them often, during our visits at court," Isadora told her. "Willem has five siblings, so we were often getting ourselves into trouble."

Freya laughed. "It sounds like you were very much like me as a girl. Aer and I always found ourselves in a bit of trouble." She frowned. "Almost daily, I'd say."

Isadora laughed, a high, tinkling sound that reminded Freya a little of bells. "Ah, yes, Willem's younger brothers were the troublemakers of their family. Rosie and Anabeth, their sisters, they were sweet, but the boys... yes, they were trouble."

"You're close with the whole family, then?" Freya asked.

"A bit," Isadora replied. "More so now than back then. I only saw them once a year for about a week, just long enough to allow Willem and I to spend a bit of time together. It was hardly enough time to form meaningful relationships," she said, her tone carrying a touch of bitterness. "Willem was often with his father and the governors, so most of my time was spent with his siblings. They were a fun group, those five," she said fondly.

Freya smiled wistfully, wondering what it must've been like to grow up with siblings, who she'd always thought might be like having live-in friends. She enjoyed her privacy and had never been the social butterfly her mother had been, but she was always fine with that. She didn't realize until she'd met Lea, Laz, and Collin and reconnected with Aer that she'd been missing out on a great many things by maintaining that privacy.

It was weird having close friends. She'd had acquaintances back in Watoria, her closest friend being Ashton, who'd befriended her on the first day of her ninth year of school. Aside from him, though, she hadn't allowed herself to get overly close with anyone. She'd been social enough, going to dances and parties, but that had more to do with her desire to get to know the people she'd soon be ruling and let them get to know her.

Having friends without that hanging over their heads was... nice, even if, technically, they had been provided to her by the crown.

Regardless of where they'd come from or how they'd appeared in her life, she couldn't imagine her life at court without them.

39

R ini arrived two hours before dinner to help Freya dress. After presenting her with two options for dinner attire, they decided on a peach A-line cut gown with sleeves that tapered to her elbow that was, as the pixie put it, "understated but deliciously flattering." She chose gold combs inlaid with green opals for Freya's hair, using one at either temple to pull her hair back from her face, then touched her lips with a bit of pale pink lip rouge and dusted her cheeks with shimmering pink blush. It was a style she often chose, one she felt brought attention to the vibrant color of Freya's hair without making it the focus, which it often was when Freya wore her typical brown or black leather.

Rini had just finished the laces on the back of Freya's gown when there was a knock at the door. Freya called for them to enter, and Byrric strode in, shutting the door behind him. Before speaking, he waited to the side of the door until Rini had finished and given him a farewell curtsy—a thing Freya might expect to look odd, being done in midair like it was, yet somehow Rini managed to make it look graceful.

He wore his formal black uniform, wings held high at his shoulders. He'd taken to keeping them out in recent days, Freya had noticed, whereas he normally kept them retracted while indoors. His gait seemed stiffer than normal, too, which, considering his typical surly demeanor, was saying something.

"Lessia has asked the queen permission to sit near you at dinner tonight, so I wanted to speak with you before we go."

Freya frowned, then nodded. "Yes, she mentioned wanting to sit near one another. Who else will I be sitting with?"

"Ordona and Isadora, so far as I can tell. I'd recommend doing what you can to strengthen your budding friendship with Isadora so that you have one royal ally who isn't your own queen while she's here."

"Budding friendship? I've gone on *one* walk with her."

"She hardly has any female companions in Dystone, and you spoke for quite awhile today, especially after Lessia left you both. Presumably that means you got on well enough."

She nodded, utterly unsurprised he knew she'd been with Isadora and Lessia earlier. "Alright, fair enough. Is Lessia truly that bad?" Freya had heard stories of Lessia's hard demeanor and violently strict way of governing her lands, but stories were so often exaggerated. So far, all Freya had seen of the empress' contrary demeanor were a few seeming-attempts to irritate her, and poor ones, at that.

"She's... tricky," he said slowly. "I'd planned to take some time with you before her arrival to discuss the best ways of handling her, but as we've been a bit short on time, for now I would recommend avoiding time alone with her. She's an opportunist and has no qualms manipulating others if there's something she wants."

Freya turned back to the mirror and leaned forward to examine her makeup. "Are you afraid I might give up the keys to the kingdom before they're even in my hand, Commander?" She flicked a glance at him in the mirror, but the smirk faded on her lips when she saw the serious expression on his face.

"No, Freya, but there are a fair number of aspects of ruling you are not well-versed in yet. She knows that and will attempt to exploit that ignorance, perhaps call your abilities into question, drag your weaknesses to the surface. You need to be prepared for that."

Anger sparked within her as she spun to face him. "My ignorance, as you put it, is through no fault of my own. You are the one who kept me away!"

"A decision I stand firmly behind," he told her smoothly. "Don't mistake me, Freya. I know there is a good deal you could have gleaned from your time here had I brought you to live with me, but the time you spent living among your people will be invaluable." His tone began to shift toward irritation. "You know that, have always known that, so I would appreciate a bit less petulance and a bit more gratitude for the fact that you were *allowed* to live a normal life!"

"A few months per year wouldn't have diminished that experience!" Stepping off her dressing pedestal, she put her hands on her hips. "I would still be who I am, but I wouldn't be as likely to need these pep talks before dining with foreign royalty!"

His gaze remained cool and level despite her anger, something that only served to infuriate her even more.

Forcing herself not to let him get to her any further, she sat down on her divan and tugged on the slippers Rini had chosen for her, ignoring him as she settled herself.

Once her shoes were in place, she sat up straight and let her hands rest in her lap, forcing a calm composure.

"I'm sorry," she said after a moment, looking up at him. "As much as I'm loathe to admit it, I've been quite nervous these past few months. Ordona has given me heaps of information on the royal families, but it's quite a lot to absorb, especially on top of my studies and all of the other preparation I've done with the king and queen." She shook her head and looked out the window. "You and Mother taught me so much growing up, but handling things like nervousness and unease has never been a thing I needed to concern myself with."

He folded his arms across his chest, but he didn't bother offering words of comfort, nor did she expect him to.

"Lessia can be difficult, but Isadora is not. You've spent time with her on your own and got along well. Being as shy as she often can be, that tells me you managed to find a good place with her. Keep fostering that, because it will be valuable in the future."

Freya nodded slowly, recalling that Isadora had opened up considerably once Lessia had left them in the gardens earlier. "And Willem? Isadora seems quite lovely, but Jonas said he was a bit... different."

A small muscle feathered in Byrric's jaw before he answered. "Willem is a bit more difficult, yes. That's why getting in with Isadora will be a great benefit. While he may be a bit off-putting on his own, if she favors you, he will, too." He gestured toward the door. "Come, dinner will be starting soon."

Standing, she double-checked that her hair was still in place, then allowed her father to offer his arm. Taking it, she bit her lip, working up the nerve to push a bit further.

"And what of the other royals?" she asked as they stepped into the hall. "Who else will be dining with us tonight?"

"Willem's siblings, Isadora's cousins, and Jonas, of course, as well as the governors and their families. The courtiers who've arrived with the other monarchs won't be joining us."

Freya let out a quiet breath. Then, focusing on the smooth marble floor before her, she decided to push her luck just a bit harder. "You've told me a fair bit about Lessia and her methods of ruling, but you haven't said hardly a word about Willem and Isadora's methods." She looked up at him, painted curiosity on her face. "Do you feel they're good rulers? Strong?"

Byrric looked straight ahead, his own expression like stone, betraying no hint of what might be going on in his mind, then nodded. "As they are relatively new to their thrones, it isn't easy to make that determination from afar, but I believe they are as strong as humans can be. Their reigns are pitifully short compared to ours, and they have far less time to create an heir, so there is always someone chomping for the throne. Willem is cold, but Isadora balances him, as I'm sure you've noticed. Their subjects seem happy, more or less, and any internal strife has been nearly nonexistent. On the whole, Dystone is a fairly calm country and a good ally to have."

Nothing to indicate an unstable monarchy, then, Freya observed.

Byrric was never one for small talk and Freya couldn't think of anything productive that might fill the gap in conversation, so they walked the rest of the way in silence.

When they arrived at the dining room, Aer and his parents were just arriving. He seemed to have gotten word of what Freya would be wearing, as his cravat and the jeweled fastenings on his white velvet doublet complemented the shades of peach that were woven throughout Freya's gown. His dark hair, so often tousled these days, had been brushed back for once, the ends just touching his ears. He extended his arm toward her, giving Byrric a short nod when he handed her off.

"You look lovely," he whispered as she curled her hand around his forearm. "You really should keep Rini on as your personal assistant after the wedding."

Freya drummed her fingers on his arm. "Hmm. That's quite enticing, actually."

They waited for a servant to announce the royal family before going in. The sight of all of the guests—perhaps forty in total—either bowing or curtsying when they walked in was a bit unnerving, as Freya was used to being on the other side of shows of deference.

Once they were inside, she and Aer turned and faced the doors, stepping off to the side and bowing to their king and queen, who strode in together behind them. The king waited several beats before allowing their guests to rise.

"You get used to it," Aer whispered, a small smile on his face, noting her discomfort.

Before she could respond, another servant came in and announced dinner was to be served. As everyone made their way to their places, each marked with a place card, Freya scanned the guests to see who'd been placed where. Ordona and Salazar sat at opposite ends of the table, facing one another. The queen, as Byrric had suggested, had seated Freya to the left of Isadora, who sat at Ordona's left. Lessia had been placed at Ordona's right, directly across from Isadora. Freya had hoped she'd be beside Aer, assumed it, even, so she was surprised to find herself placed between Isadora and Myria, with Aer to Salazar's left at the other end of the table. Byrric sat to Salazar's other side.

Aside from the governors, there were a few other guests Freya hadn't yet met—a tall blond male who bore a striking resemblance to Myria, and two females with hair the same titian shade as Collin whom, Freya assumed, were Governor Maddix's daughters. Human, Lind, and Jotnar guards of each house were stationed at intervals around the room.

Freya wasn't quite sure what purpose Ordona's seating arrangements served, but knowing the queen, each decision had been very deliberate. She was happy to be beside Isadora, at the very least, although she could've done without Myria to her left. Despite their somewhat amicable relationship of late, Myria was still quite tiring to be around.

Dinner was a fairly simple affair. Freya made small talk with Isadora, discussing plans to possibly take a trip into Iladel in the upcoming days. Lessia, resplendent in a glittering teal gown that would've put the finest of the queens' gowns to shame had its owner not worn such a dour look, spent most of the meal talking with Ordona, relieving Freya of the need to include her in conversation. Freya tried to watch them, see how they interacted, hoping she might glean some lesson on dealing with alpha females, but Isadora seemed intent on avoiding being included in their discussion, and Myria kept insisting on speaking to Isadora over Freya's lap.

By the time dessert was served, Freya was inwardly cursing Rini for lacing her corset so tightly and the queen for seating her beside Myria, whose simpering had hit a new level of irksome.

"My goodness, I don't think I can manage any more!" Isadora said with a laugh, touching a hand to her stomach.

"It's these dreadful corsets," Myria complained. "I think Lady Balthana should enact a law when she's queen, outlawing them entirely." She gave Freya a sweet smile. "Wouldn't that just be lovely?"

"It will be my first order of business, Lady Bryton," Freya said, forcing a smile.

Ordona smiled graciously at Isadora. "Maghda has been with us for some time now and has a tendency to outdo herself on occasion."

"I'm certain she's got quite the feast planned for your wedding, then," Lessia said, lifting her golden goblet to her ruby lips.

Freya smiled her thanks to the server who set a plate of lindberry sorbet in front of her. "Maghda is one in a million, I can assure you."

It wasn't until they'd exhausted all polite topics of conversation that the version of Lessia her father and Ordona had warned her about emerged. It seemed odd, as though the empress had been waiting for an opportune moment to strike, diving in for insult almost instantly when Isadora began to talk of Freya's nuptials.

"Now, Ordona, speaking of the wedding..." Lessia smiled at Freya and took a small sip of her wine before continuing. "What *is* the deciding factor for determining betrothals in Lindoroth? Practices here seem a bit different than before."

Ordona angled her head and gave the empress and easy smile. "Well, Lessia, it's quite the same as in Jotunheim, you know that. There isn't simply one factor that decides who will marry whom." She set her goblet down and gestured down the table toward Salazar. "Take Salazar and myself, for example. My father was a wealthy lord-turned-governor in Saith and was renowned amongst his citizens. My mother, bless her, was highly intelligent and beautiful. King Avinald and Queen Lynda saw a beneficial alliance there, so they sought my hand when I was hardly walking."

Lessia gave Freya a curious look. "What of your son, then? Lady Balthana is quite beautiful, to be sure, but she is, after all, the daughter of a military man."

"Oh, my," Myria muttered, taking a large sip of wine. Freya shot her a glare before addressing the empress.

"My father is a highly respected commander and long-time friend to the royal family," Freya corrected Lessia. "My mother was the strongest witch of her time." She laced her tone with a bit of syrupy sweetness. "Also, as I am sitting right before you, I would appreciate it if you took some care before attempting to insult me, my family, or the decisions of my king and queen."

She didn't risk a look at Ordona, but she could feel her approval from where she sat beside her.

"My lady, I meant no offense, of *course*. I only ask because betrothals typically involve powerful alliances and, well, to be quite honest, I don't see where you fall." She picked up a pastry and eyed it. "You're a half-blood, which makes you a good fighter and a powerful witch, but what can you do for Lindoroth? So far, all I've seen is two younglings enamored of one another. I might expect someone of your... lineage to become a knight, perhaps continue working with the marshals."

"Aerelius and I were fortunate enough to form a strong relationship in our early years," she said, keeping her words clear, precise, and as deliberate as possible. "So if you're insinuating that my monarchs and parents chose me for the prince due to our feelings for one another, please allow me to put that concern to rest."

"That's all well and good, dear, but what of the royal lineage? What will you do when it comes time to bear his young?" Lessia turned the pastry over in her fingers, examining it as though expecting spiders to crawl out. "Have you even checked her fertility, Ordona?"

Isadora and Myria gasped, and Freya's eyes widened in shock. But Ordona, to her credit, remained cool.

"That barbaric practice was abandoned centuries ago, Lessia," Ordona replied, a touch of weariness to her voice. For several millennia, females, especially those of high-ranking families, were often subjected to invasive magical procedures to ensure their fertility. One of the first things Ordona had done when she and Salazar took their crowns was to outlaw the practice entirely. It was something that had caused a good deal of controversy, but by and large, the citizens of Lindoroth favored the decision.

There was a moment of tense silence as Lessia took in Ordona's refusal to be cowed by Lessia's insinuations. Freya racked her brain for a response, for anything to say, but all she saw was red.

Isadora cleared her throat, dragging the empress' attention away from the queen.

"Well, I for one think emotional ties will make for a stronger marriage," she said. "If you already know one another as well as you two seem to, well, I dare say you've got it better than any of us did!"

"Indeed," Ordona murmured.

There was a bit of an awkward silence before Myria spoke. "Lady Balthana, I've been meaning to ask how preparations for the wedding are going. Are they nearly complete?"

Isadora beamed. "Oh, the planning part is so fun, isn't it?"

Freya sent a grateful look at Myria, who didn't show so much as a flicker of emotion in response, then faced Isadora. "It truly is. If my dressmaker weren't such a genius, I'd worry I wouldn't fit into my dress after all of the tastings I've endured!" Freya gave her a conspiratorial grin, then picked up her wine. "Aside from that... we've just finished seating arrangements this morning."

"Oh, I do hope you haven't seated me with anyone dreadful," Myria griped. "I just can't bear sitting next to someone for four hours who's unable to hold a conversation."

Isadora bit her lip and smiled. "And your vows? Have you written them?"

"*Are* you writing them?" Lessia asked, seeming to thaw slightly. "They always seem like such a waste of breath to me."

"No, we're going with the traditional incantation," Freya replied, softening her words as best she could.

Lessia nodded. "Yes, simple is often best. Crispin, bless his soul, wanted us to write our own, but I simply couldn't be bothered." Her lips curved into a small smile. "Isadora, you seem the type to write your own prose." It was a simple statement phrased as a question, yet her smile implied something more, something Freya couldn't quite put her finger on.

The human queen smile bashfully. "Yes, Willem and I composed sonnets for one another. It was quite romantic, really," she said dreamily, but Freya thought she detected a note of discomfort in her tone.

"Empress, how are your accommodations?" Ordona asked.

"Apologies for the change in subject, but I meant to ask when you arrived, and it just slipped my mind. Is everything to your liking?"

Freya tried to get her aggravation under control as she waited for the other guests to be served their desserts. Shifting her focus, she watched as her friends and the highest-ranking officials in Lindoroth, Dystone, and Jotunheim talked and laughed. The din had become considerably louder in the hours since dinner began, thanks largely to the many jugs of wine that had been served, but as plates were placed in front of guests and everyone began to tuck into some of Maghda's finest desserts, the noise level dipped lower than it had during the meal.

She'd only gotten a few bites in when she heard Aer laugh at the other end of the table. Something about it had her curious, so she looked over, assuming all of the males had fallen half into the bottle by now. She was surprised to find Aer looking back at her. He gave her a crooked smile, then tilted his head to the side in a seemingly affectionate gesture. The glint in his eyes told her it was more, though, so she followed the tilt of his head until her gaze landed on the man who sat to his left. King Willem's brother Reginald, if her memory served. Handsome, by human standards, he was broad and blue-eyed, with blond hair tied back with a leather cord, wearing a jovial grin.

"I don't know that I should risk another bite," Aer said to Reginald, his jaw set as he laid his napkin on the table. "Our chef has outdone herself this time." As the other guests were currently devouring their desserts, his words carried easily down the length of the table. He was trying to send her a message, that much was clear, because Aer would never skip dessert, nor would he say he couldn't "risk another bite."

"Oh, darling, don't be silly!" Ordona called back. "This is your favorite, after all!"

Reginald grinned and elbowed Aer. "Well, I'd say it's a necessary risk, Your Highness. Worth popping a button or two, don't you think?" Then he laughed. It was low, full of amusement, but carried a tinge of something else.

Freya nearly choked on the small sip of wine she'd just taken, recovering herself with an embarrassed wave of her hand when Ordona sent her a slightly disapproving look. A flicker of relief flashed across Aer's face.

The words weren't exactly the same, but they were close enough.

But that voice...

Her anger toward Lessia and her idiotic attempts to belittle her were instantly forgotten.

Yes, Freya was certain the man in the passageways they'd heard speaking of treason was the Dystonian king's brother.

40

F reya could hardly keep her wits about her for the rest of dessert. Myria, bless her, seemed only to notice Freya's lack of interest in conversation, taking the opportunity to fill the lulls herself, asking Isadora and Lessia about the fashions of their lands and gushing over the sonnets Isadora had recited that she and Willem had written one another. By the time dinner let out, Freya all but ran to Aer's side, grabbing him by the hand and dragging him into the hall.

"I tried to get your attention a dozen times!" he hissed the second they'd gotten back to her room and she'd cast her silencing spell. "We really need some kind of signal, Freya."

"Perhaps if your mother had seated us together that wouldn't have been an issue!" With a huff, she started digging through her armoire for something more comfortable to wear, desperately needing to be rid of the confounded dress she'd been tied into for the last five hours.

"Well, I don't know what you wanted *me* to do about it! And how do you think I felt? I was seated next to the man!" He dragged a hand through his hair. "Gods above, I'm supposed to go hunting with him."

"You'd best get your wits about you now, then," she warned,

tugging her pants on under her dress, then turning and indicating for Aer to loosen her laces. "Where are the others?"

"Meeting us on the ramparts near the southern turret," he replied, his tone so serious he didn't even bother—or didn't think to bother—with innuendos as he helped her out of her gown. She breathed a sigh of relief as the corset released, then held it against her chest as he handed her the shirt she'd chosen. He turned his head, giving her a bit of privacy as she tugged it on, letting the gown fall to her feet.

"Did you tell them anything?" she asked.

"Just that there was something we needed to discuss." Quickly, she finished getting dressed, ignoring his impatient looks as she did.

Once she was finished dressing, he said, "The quickest and most discreet way is through the tunnels."

She bit her lip, considering, then nodded. "I'd rather deal with a scolding than anyone following us."

"Agreed."

Quickly, they made their way through the tunnels, Freya maintaining her cloaking spell the entire way through. When they emerged from the passageway, they were in a chamber at the foot of the southern turret, the shortest and least guarded of the twelve that rose above the palace. A spiral staircase wound upward, leading to the ramparts on the top of the palace walls.

They emerged a few moments later, high above the palace grounds. Guards were stationed along the walls every twenty feet or so, each standing stock-still as their eyes and senses roamed over the grounds, watching, listening, smelling for any hint of danger.

They found Lea, Laz, and Collin sitting on a section of the wall that jutted out over the mountain in a spot where terrain was so rough it would be nearly impossible for anyone to scale or breach the walls in any way. Laz and Collin sat against one side, their backs against the merlons, Laz's head on Collin's shoulder, their fingers laced together between them, while Lea sat across from them.

"*Finally,*" Lea grumbled when she saw them. "You know I don't like being the third wheel, Aer, and Lazarus has had too much wine. He keeps making moon eyes at Collin."

"Well, we could *leave*," Laz told her. "Aer insisted we needed to meet up here under cover of darkness *immediately*." He frowned at Lea. "And now you're the fifth wheel. We really need to find you someone, cousin."

She sneered at him, then looked at Aer and Freya expectantly. "Well?"

Aer looked around at each of them. "What we're about to tell you three doesn't leave this spot, do you understand?"

"Of course," Lea replied as the others murmured their agreement. "What is it?"

Freya tightened her enchantment, then, as succinctly as possible, they told the others of scenting the human in the garden tunnel and of all they'd overheard of the conversation in the queen's chambers. Aer added in a few more details about information he'd gleaned when Freya wasn't at the palace, mainly a few conversations that had stopped when he entered a room or came around a corner, along with odd looks between the king and queen. It was hardly more than curious behavior, but seemed worth noting.

When they were done, Laz wore a confused look, Lea looked stricken, and Collin's expression had slipped from suspicious to simply curious.

"Do you think King Willem is unwell?" Collin asked, drumming his fingers on his thigh.

"It's difficult to say," Aer replied. "This man sounded concerned, perhaps a bit scared, but we only heard a small portion of the conversation."

"Who do you think joined the conversation, then?" Laz asked.

"I've seen Ervic and my father talking a few times in the past few weeks," Aer said. "The conversations always came to halt when I stumbled on them, though."

"Does this mean King Willem's brother wants to stage a coup?" Lea blew out a breath. "That's... quite unfortunate, considering the timing."

"If he knows he'll have the backing of Lindoroth, what better time than when all three nations are in one place to do it?" Aer asked, then shook his head. "I was so sure it would've been someone else. A guard, even an opportunistic cousin. The moment I heard that voice, however..."

"A coup is quite a leap," Collin said dubiously. "Nothing either of you have told us indicates something that treasonous."

"And even if that were the case, he won't do it at your wedding," Laz said.

"You sound awfully sure of that," Lea told him. "Wouldn't a large, enclosed gathering where everyone's guard is down and their intoxication levels up be the ideal time and place?"

Collin shook his head. "No. If he wants to overthrow his king and hopes to use the help of Lindoroth to do it, he won't risk destroying an alliance by disrupting a royal wedding that's been planned for nearly twenty years. Even if Ordona and Salazar have agreed to help, they wouldn't allow it." He gave Aer a questioning look. "You were next to him all night—how did he seem to you?"

"Friendly, to be quite honest. He seems to be the more pleasant of the two. Willem only spoke to my father, ignoring any other attempts at conversation, but Reginald seemed to want to engage with everyone."

"Did he say or do anything to indicate he might want to overthrow his brother?" Collin asked.

"No, but I wouldn't expect him to, either," Aer replied.

"And Willem?" Laz asked. "What was he like?"

"Standoffish. Aloof. He didn't seem at all concerned with what I may think of him, despite the fact that I'll be king in just under a year." Aer thought for a moment. "He and Reginald hardly spoke to one another, now that I recall."

Lea narrowed her eyes and chewed on her lip, twirling a lock of her curly black hair around her finger. She'd worn it down tonight, letting it cascade in tight curls over her shoulders. "Perhaps this is a silly question, but do you think it might be time to confront Uncle Sal and Aunt Ordona? Or at least the commander? You two have a right to know if something could threaten your wedding."

Freya shook her head. "No, Collin's right. With the amount of planning they've—Ordona, especially—put into this, there's no way they'd risk something happening. It's too risky."

"Exactly," Collin said. "*If* your suspicions are accurate and *if* they've got a hand in helping Reginald, I'd bet my family's fortune they've agreed to help him *after* their successors are wed."

"The reception, then?" Laz asked.

"More likely in the following days," Aer replied, frowning absently at a spot on the ground. "Not at a point when both current and succeeding monarchs are shut in one room. It would be too easy to destroy our lines as well." He gave a heavy sigh and ran a hand roughly over his face. "My parents are putting us on a ship for Errest the day after the wedding."

"They're *what?*" Freya asked, stunned.

"That's what my father wanted to discuss with me earlier," Aer told her. "Our 'honeymoon' is a trip around the continent, greeting our future subjects and seeing the land."

Freya blew out a long breath, then shook her head. "You'd think they would've discussed that with us first."

Aer shrugged. "Not necessarily. It's a valid reason to send us off and it's something we would need to do, or at least should do, anyway."

"This is all assuming that you two are correct in your assumptions," Collin said, holding up his hands in a calming gesture. "During the conversation you overheard in the tunnel, did anyone explicitly state that he wanted to usurp his king?" He lifted his eyebrows in question, waiting until Freya and Aer shook their heads. "Then perhaps we're all blowing this out of proportion. The 'she' he spoke of who is dangerous—we don't know who he was referring to, but it's quite possible he's seeking out aid to dispatch whoever this female is because Willem is being reticent. The logical assumption, of course, is that he's talking about Lessia, but it could just as easily be an opportunistic human who is close with the royal family."

Freya nodded slowly. "Yes, good point." She hadn't realized just how much of a leap she and Aer had made based on what they'd overheard, which was admittedly very little. She let out a quiet breath and exchanged a look with Aer. "It's entirely possible, probable, even, that we're mistaken."

Aer nodded. "I certainly hope so, although based on the tone and urgency..." He rubbed a hand across his chin and shook his head. "It wasn't something simple, that much is certain."

"Well, whatever it is, the king and queen want evidence, meaning a rash or quick decision is likely out of the question," Collin continued.

"And if said evidence makes itself apparent during their stay here?" Laz asked. "There's still nearly a week until the wedding."

"Even if this was about a coup," Collin added, "or some other significant move against the crown, which I'm still not convinced of, and even *if* they made their choice today to back Reginald, neither of them are stupid enough to do it *before* your wedding. It's just not logical."

As they continued to volley theories and reasoning back and forth, Freya leaned against Aer and focused her attention on the mountains that rose up behind the palace. She tried to settle her nerves by telling herself that their parents were smart people and would never do something they didn't wholeheartedly believe in. With her father involved, she believed that doubly so. Considering his involvement, though, the reasonable assumption would be that this...whatever it was, would require some type of military support.

Still, she struggled with why they would conspire with a foreign royal to act in any way toward their monarchs, especially during such an important time for Lindoroth. Monarchs were limited to three centuries' rule, after which time they would pass the crown to their successor, which was, in most cases, their eldest son. If they had no children, they would appoint a successor in much the same way the governors of each realm did—through a long and extensive vetting process that required the consensus of all four sitting governors. As Aerelius was the only royal son, Ordona and Salazar wouldn't be foolish enough to risk harm coming to him or the female they'd chosen to rule with him.

Aer's words from the previous week—that she should always assume the worst—came back to her as she considered the damage that could be done to her kingdom before she even had a chance to rule. Whatever the king and queen were planning, or potentially planning with Reginald, it could be catastrophic if their actions truly went against the human monarchy. Whether it was a coup or not didn't matter in her mind; if it was subversive in nature, it could lead to poor foreign relations at best, and full-out war at worst.

41

The following morning, Freya was awakened by a knock at the door. Aer, bucking propriety entirely, had continued to sleep in her room each night, neither of them caring all that much what their guests might think of their sleeping arrangements. And, as they hadn't gotten direction from their parents to change their habits, neither thought it necessary to do so.

Although, Freya realized as she looked at him when she rolled over, she should probably have started insisting he wore a shirt.

"Go away!" he hollered, earning himself a light backhand to the chest from Freya.

"Shush, you!" she hissed as she got out of bed. Then, raising her voice, she said, "Coming!"

"Perhaps you should kiss me," he mumbled into the pillow. "That might make me a bit more hospitable."

She tugged on her robe over her nightgown and wrinkled her nose. "Your breath is atrocious."

He opened one eye and glared up at her. "And yours is like fresh spring daisies?"

Lifting her hair from under her collar, she grinned. Then, tightening her robe, she walked to the door and opened it, barely managing to conceal her surprise when she saw Isadora on the other side.

"Your Majesty! What brings you out this morning?"

"Apologies, my lady..." she trailed off, momentarily at a loss for words when she caught sight of the shirtless prince, who'd sprawled out the moment Freya had left the bed.

Noting her slight discomfit, Freya stepped into the hall and gestured toward Aer's chambers.

"Come, we can talk in here."

Isadora nodded, then followed Freya as she padded barefoot to the prince's doors. Rodrick and Perinald remained stationed outside of her room, while Rissen and Cecilia followed the short distance to Aer's room, taking up flanking positions on either side of the entry.

When Isadora's guards made to follow them inside, she waved them off. "I'm perfectly safe with Lady Balthana. There's no need to hover."

Once Freya and Isadora were alone, a bit of the stiffness the queen seemed to carry in front of the others eased a bit.

"What can I do for you, Your Majesty?" Freya asked as they settled on a divan beside the veranda doors. She was completely flummoxed as to what could've brought the queen to her doors so early in the day.

"I was hoping we might talk a bit in private before we have any further gatherings..." She twisted her hands in her lap. "Oh, I'm feeling a bit improper now!"

"Whatever you have to say won't leave this room," Freya assured her. As discreetly as she could, Freya cast a silencing spell over the room, leaving a small gap only at the door that separated her room from Aer's.

Isadora flushed and averted her eyes, looking suddenly embarrassed again. "It's just... you'll probably think me such a fool!"

"Only if you don't speak your mind," Freya told her, softening her words with a smile.

Isadora let out another breath. "It's so rare that I'm around creatures with magical abilities, and while you and Ordona seem quite lovely, Empress Lessia...she..." She closed her eyes. "Well, she puts me at unease."

"Ah." Freya nodded, immediately understanding Isadora's reluctance to share her thoughts. Despite being a queen, she was still a human, and when placed beside a creature as strong and cold as Lessia, it would be foolish *not* to be fearful.

Freya eyed her curiously. "Did something happen? You seemed relatively comfortable with her at dinner and when we spoke yesterday."

"Nothing overt," Isadora said carefully. "Just a discomfort, I suppose." She huffed. "The reason Lessia and I ended up together yesterday—and she found us before dinner, too—was because she just happened to be leaving her rooms at the same time as me. Willem didn't seem concerned in the least, so I followed his lead when we saw her before dinner. But yesterday, when I saw her in the hall... it was as though she'd been waiting." She shook her head, pursing her lips. "Perhaps my imagination is becoming overworked."

"Your Majesty, you don't need to explain yourself to me," Freya said gently. "I understand that our lands and our people can be a bit of an adjustment. What do you say about a signal, of sorts, when we're all together, something you can do to tell me that you're feeling uncomfortable? Perhaps running your finger on the rim of your glass? If I see you do that, I'll steer the conversation elsewhere."

The queen let out a relieved sigh. "That would be *much* appreciated." She cast a furtive look toward the hall, then looked back at Freya. "I apologize if I interrupted earlier." She bit her lip. "I didn't realize—in Dystone, well, we don't share rooms with our betrothed until the wedding night. I just—I suppose I just assumed..."

Gods above.

Freya held up a hand to stop the poor woman's embarrassed rambling. Sweet as she was, this was becoming so tiresome, Freya was beginning to think it was an act, and that was *not* a road she wanted to venture down when she'd hardly been awake ten minutes. "You've nothing to apologize for, truly."

Isadora deflated a bit, looking as though she wanted to say more.

"Speak your mind, Your Majesty. Please, I won't be offended."

"Oh, it's not offensive! At least, I hope it isn't." She bit her lip again. "I was just wondering... what is it like? Being able to so openly show your love for your betrothed?"

Freya blinked, surprised at the brazen nature of the question.

Before she could respond, Isadora rushed to speak. "I suppose a more accurate question would be, what is it like to be in love with the male you were told you had to marry? Willem and I had an amicable enough relationship, although I am—*was* much closer to his siblings. To be quite honest my lady—"

"Freya please," Freya murmured.

Isadora flashed a smile. "To be quite honest, Freya, I'm a bit jealous of how easy it seems for you."

"While our circumstances have never been easy, so to speak, Aer and I have always—well, almost always—had a strong relationship, and our parents have been close for centuries." She gave a small shrug. "He's always been a part of me, a part of my family. I consider marrying him as just a way of making that official. It isn't an easy lot in life, to be sure, but being so close already is a bit freeing, to be honest."

"Well, as I said, I envy you." Isadora smoothed her hands over her pink wool gown. "You've already surmounted a hurdle many of us never do."

"Leaving room for far more, I'm sure."

Isadora laughed. "Indeed, my lady, indeed."

A SHORT WHILE LATER, Freya bid Isadora goodbye and shut the door behind her. With a sigh, she walked to the door that connected her room to Aer's and opened it, one hand on her hip, eyebrows raised expectantly. Sure enough, she found her fiancé standing there, shirtless and still disheveled from sleep.

"Eavesdropping is quite a nasty habit, you know."

He pointed a finger at her and took a step into the room, his eyes dancing with triumph. "You didn't tell her she was wrong when she said you were in love with me." His lips tilted into that infuriating smirk he always wore when he caught her at something.

Her heart quickened as she realized what she'd done—or *not* done, as the case may be—during her conversation with the queen.

She took an involuntary step back, matching the two he'd taken forward, then tilted her chin up stubbornly. "Didn't I?"

He grinned triumphantly and began backing her into the room. "You did *not*." Leaning down, he kissed her, long and slow, leaving her just a bit breathless as the backs of her legs hit his bed. "Just admit it," he whispered, pulling back so his lips were barely a breath from hers. "I want to hear you say it."

"Say what?" And damn the gods if her voice didn't quaver as she spoke.

Lifting her up, he laid her back on the bed, falling on top of her and caging her between his arms. "That you're in love with me."

"You first," she murmured, arching her back as he started kissing the column of her neck.

"Oh, I'm quite in love with myself," he said with a laugh. "I think that's a well-established fact."

She couldn't help but laugh, despite the situation she'd landed herself in.

Infuriating fool.

"Tell me you love me, Freya," he murmured.

She ran her hands up his back, shifting her nails to talons and dragging them lightly across his skin.

"You. First."

He grinned, but before he could reply, there was a knock at the door.

"Goddess, help me," he muttered, turning his head toward the door. "What?" he shouted, not bothering to hide his annoyance at whatever poor soul had interrupted them.

"Apologies, Your Highness. Her majesty has sent me to retrieve Lady Balthana, but she's not in her room."

"She is currently indisposed, Oscar! Tell my mother she'll be there in an hour!"

Freya laughed and sat up, shoving the prince off of her. Before he could grab her, she danced away from the bed and made for the door. When she opened it, she found a red-faced Oscar on the other side.

She smiled brightly. "Please tell her majesty I'll be along shortly. I just need to get dressed."

"Of course, my lady. The dressmaker will be here in thirty minutes." He cast a glance over Freya's shoulder to where Aer lay on the bed, scowling, most likely. "She also wished for me to tell you she would have breakfast waiting for you, so there's no need to have Dina bring it here."

"That's quite thoughtful of her. I'll get dressed and hurry down."

He gave her a quick nod. "Yes, my lady."

She shut the door and faced Aer, who was on his side, propped on his elbow. "Our sleeping arrangements will be the talk of the palace today. We should've considered that before the guests began arriving."

Aer gave her a lazy smile. "I can live with that, especially now that you've lost our little wager."

"I've done no such thing. I was merely... avoiding interrupting. She is a queen, after all. It would've been rude."

He narrowed his eyes. "You'll break before me, Valkyrie. Mark my words."

FREYA'S final fitting was a blessedly short event. Kallan only needed to take a few final measurements, and as he'd grown noticeably tired of the conflicting opinions between Freya and Ordona, he did his work quickly. After going over a few details regarding tea with the queen and empress that was set for the following day, Ordona had other matters to attend to.

"You did wonderfully last night, Freya," Ordona told her as she was seeing her out. "I know Lessia can be quite troublesome at times, but I wanted you to know you handled yourself well."

"Thank you, Your Majesty." Freya leaned against the doorframe, her shoulders sore from the multiple wing movements Kallan had insisted on as he finalized her measurements. "My father told me she would try to push, but I didn't realize in what sense. She was so..."

"Conniving?"

Freya frowned. 'Conniving' wasn't exactly the word she'd have chosen to use to describe Lessia. Vulgar, perhaps, or even predictable, but conniving implied a subtlety that Lessia hadn't seemed to possess.

The flicker of a smile flashed across Ordona's face when Freya didn't answer. "Lessia is a creature of habit, darling. She wants to size up potential rivals and ensure they know their place beneath her." She smiled. "Which you've demonstrated you are not."

Freya gave her a small smile. "Thank you. That means a lot."

Ordona patted Freya's arm fondly. "I know this is difficult for you, being rushed into your marriage. I wish we could've given you your full year at Aldridge, because I know that was something you looked forward to."

Freya sighed. "It was, but I think it's for the best. After my father kept me away for so long, I just feel as though there's so much I need to catch up on here."

"In good time." Ordona pulled her in for a tight embrace. "You're going to be a wonderful queen, Freya. Know that and believe it." She pulled back, keeping her hands on Freya's shoulders as she spoke. "Other leaders will try to test you and you've already shown that you will not be cowed. That's something to be proud of."

And she was proud, if Freya was being honest with herself. She'd had her doubts over the years, as would anyone with a lick of sense, but Lessia seemed to have been Freya's first true test of how she would handle those who aimed to insult her or question her abilities.

If anything, it made her more determined to prove wrong any who might try.

42

The next few days rushed past in a blur of final preparations, accommodating guests, and, when they had time, attempts to suss out what Reginald might be trying to accomplish on his stay in Iladel. By the time the eve of their wedding arrived, Freya, Aer, and their friends still hadn't been able to uncover anything untoward, despite three more dinners with the visiting royals and a luncheon in the gardens.

Freya was woken the morning before her wedding by Dina delivering breakfast, followed shortly after by Oscar requesting her presence in the ballroom.

"When you are princess," Aer mumbled as she got dressed, "I do hope you'll make a law stating no one is to wake you before nine."

She smiled. "As the crown prince, shouldn't you have already done that? And isn't your hunting trip supposed to leave in an hour?"

He opened one eye and glared at her. "I've half a mind to cancel."

"You can't cancel, Aer."

"I'm the prince. I can do what I want."

Once she'd dressed—she opted for black wool leggings and a green tunic with black boots, aiming for comfort for what would surely be a busy day—she blew him a kiss goodbye and made her way down to the ballroom.

She'd just reached the end of her wing when she paused. Spending the day with Ordona would be tiring at best, and after the past week, Freya was in desperate need of a buffer. So, she stopped at the junction of her wing and the main hall and turned to her guards.

"Cecilia, could you tell the young Lady Calliwell that I've requested her presence in the main ballroom, please?"

"Yes, of course my lady," Cecilia replied, smiling her understanding. "Right away."

Freya watched as Cecilia strode off toward the guest wings, hoping Lea would already be ready to start her day.

"A wise choice, my lady," Rissen told her. "Lady Calliwell is quite skilled at turning a conversation."

"That she is," Freya murmured. "Come, let's take the long way."

When Freya arrived at the ballroom, walking a bit slowly to delay her arrival and give Lea time to make her way there, she found Ordona already fussing over its state of disarray.

"No, no, no, the tall vases are to flank the *doors!*" she shouted at two servants who were in the process of hefting a shoulder-height marble vase.

"Goddess, help me," Freya muttered as she made her way across the room to the queen. She offered smiles to the servants she passed, hoping they would see that she, at least, wasn't overly concerned with the proper placement of flora.

"Freya!" Ordona smiled as she saw her approach. "Good, I'm glad you're here." She gestured around the room. "Doesn't it look so lovely?"

Freya nodded as she looked around the room, happy to see that her vision of a theme of unity had been fully realized.

There were long tables set up around the perimeter of the dance floor, each clothed with linen of deep emerald reminiscent of the pine forests of Allanor. The goblets and settings were made of gold, mined from Caelora and studded with Edhilian emeralds. The space that remained open down the center of each table would hold vases bursting with cornflower and lilac, both native to the king's ancestral homeland of Saith. Curtains the color of fresh snow draped the windows, replacing the gold ones that normally hung there. A handful of the palace's pixies were fluttering about fussing with varying colors of light that would illuminate the the red and brown parquet dance floor, the wood of which had come from Allanor centuries ago and was laid out in a dizzying pattern of circular designs.

"Your first dance will begin just over there," Ordona said, pointing at the star that made up the center of the floor. "Then you'll receive guests at the head table, where you'll be seated with Sal and me, along with the visiting royals."

At that moment, Lea appeared beside them, giddy with excitement. "Oh, this all looks so lovely! Aunt Ordona, you've really outdone yourself!"

Ordona gave her niece a small smile. "Thank you, dear. I wasn't aware you'd be joining us."

Lea clasped her hands against her chest as she turned and took in the whole room. "Oh, won't you please let me use the palace planners when I'm to wed?"

Freya bit her lip, trying not to laugh as Lea laid her praise on a bit too thick.

Pursing her lips, Ordona sent Lea a chastising look.

"Grevillea, if you think I don't know why you're here, you're *quite* mistaken." She gave Freya a pointed look.

Lea's face soured at the queen's use of her full name. She gave Freya a shrug that simply said, "I tried."

"May I stay, though?" Lea asked. "This really is quite exciting."

Ordona sighed but didn't send her away, which, in Freya's mind, counted as a win.

The three of them paced around the room for the next few hours, watching and, at times, commenting on the decor or placement of certain things.

"The flowers will be brought in tomorrow morning," Ordona said as she watched servants walk in precariously balancing stacks of gold charger plates. She angled her head toward the entryway. "Come, let's leave them to it. I'll check the progress of the arrangements once Kallan arrives to start preparing you."

Freya and Lea exchanged an amused look at Ordona's choice of words. Freya was beginning to feel a bit like a piece of game being prepared for roasting. As they reemerged into the hall, they began to make their way back toward the main hall.

"Now, if you two would excuse me, I'll be heading off—"

Ordona's words cut off as they turned a corner and ran into Reginald. Freya, quite literally, was stopped short, stumbling back a step as his broad body made contact with hers.

"My lady!" Reginald Ristner exclaimed, gripping Freya's arms to steady her. "Apologies, I wasn't watching where I was going."

Freya took several steps back, straightening her stance and meeting his eyes as she did. "Not to worry, Your Highness," she said with a smile, smoothing her tunic.

"Prince Reginald!" The queen gave him a bright smile, one that seemed a bit forced. "Shouldn't you be off hunting with the rest of the males?"

He gave her a quick bow. "I wasn't feeling quite myself this morning, so thought it best I remain behind, lest I slow them down." He appraised his surroundings, seemingly confused. "I took a stroll to clear my head, and now I think I may have gotten a bit turned around getting back to my room. Perhaps you could direct me?"

Before the queen could respond, Lea cut in.

"Freya and I are actually headed in your direction now, Your Highness. We'd be happy to escort you."

Ordona opened her mouth, surely to object, but Freya spoke first.

"Yes, it's no trouble at all." She smiled up at the queen, feigning innocence as best she could. "If it's alright with you, Your Majesty?"

For the first time in her life, Freya saw Ordona falter, giving her all the confirmation she needed that something untoward was going on between her queen and Reginald Ristner. Indecision warred in Ordona's eyes for the briefest of moments before she gave a quick nod.

"Yes, of course. As it's on your way, it only seems logical." Her eyes lingered on Reginald a second longer than was proper, considering the distant relationship most would presume they'd have. "Freya, I'll see you at dinner." She turned and began to walk down the hall, her four guards following closely behind.

Once she was gone, Lea turned to Freya and Reginald. "Oh, dear. My apologies, Freya, but I just recalled my mother requested me for lunch!" She touched Freya's arm and smiled. "I'll come find you later, then?"

Freya's eyes widened a fraction, unsure why on earth her friend would leave her with the man they thought may be contemplating treason against his own king.

Recovering herself quickly, she nodded. "Yes, of course. We'll speak soon."

As Lea scurried off in the direction of the residential areas of the palace, Freya turned to Reginald. "Well, Your Highness, shall we?"

Hands clasped behind his back, Reginald nodded and they began to walk. Freya racked her mind in an attempt to come up with a topic of conversation.

"I'm glad we ran into one another," he said. "I was hoping we might speak the other night after dinner, but it seemed you and Prince Aerelius slipped out before I had a chance to catch you. May we talk a bit?"

"Of course. What can I do for you?"

"I know you're quite busy, so I won't take up much of your time, but as Willem's newly-appointed emissary to Lindoroth, I just wanted to introduce myself to you personally."

"Newly appointed?" Freya gave him a curious look, gesturing down a hall for him to turn.

"Yes, I've only just come into the job. Willem's previous emissary recently passed away, so I was given the position." His eyes scanned the corridor ahead, for what, Freya wasn't sure. With Rissen and Cecilia behind her, and guards stationed every fifty feet throughout the castle, she didn't know what type of threat he could possibly be looking for.

"I see." She paused a moment. "Is this your first trip to Lindoroth, then?"

"It is," he said with a nod, the lie flowing effortlessly from his lips. "I've been to the lands east of Dystone many times but have never made a trip to the west."

"You've been to the elvish lands?" Freya asked, surprised, her annoyance and suspicion instantly forgotten. The elves—creatures farther east than she'd ever hope to travel—were private, mercurial beings that rarely left their continent and were notoriously inhospitable to outsiders. To hear that a human man, so fragile in his mortality, had visited and returned was shocking, to say the least.

"I have," he replied, smiling at her reaction. "Avorell was an interesting land."

"And you lived to tell the tale," Freya said, not bothering to hide how impressed—and slightly horrified—she was at that. "That's quite an accomplishment."

"So I've been told." His eyes continued to take in their surroundings, the framed portraits in gilded frames, richly draped windows, and gleaming marble floors. "This is a lovely place to call home, my lady. Are you eager to make your place here?"

Shoving back her desperate desire to grill him on his travels abroad, she kept her words level and attempted to gauge his meaning. "I am. I've always enjoyed my time in Iladel, and I've become quite close with the royal family over the years, so I'm eager to call it my home permanently."

He nodded slowly. "Yes, I was told you and the prince have been friends for some time. It must help to already be so familiar with the region."

"It certainly is," she replied.

He flashed her a smile. "I must confess, I've heard some rumors about you, my lady. I wasn't sure if I believed them, but I happened to see you in the training yard earlier this week with the children. Your skill with a blade is quite impressive. Did you really work with the marshals in your home city?"

"I did," she said, noting the odd shift in topic. "They took me on when I was fifteen."

Reginald's eyes widened. "Fifteen... that's, I'm sorry, my lady, but that's so young!"

"Human women aren't taught to fight, then?"

"Oh, they are, and quite well in many cases. None are recruited as law enforcement at fifteen, however." He gave her an appraising look. "Was it your Valkyrie blood or your witchcraft that made them choose you?"

She slid him a glance. "As I'm a half-blood, I would venture to guess it was both."

Another confused look. "A half-blood?"

"Yes, Your Highness, a half-blood." A bit of annoyance slipped through in her words. She was unsure why he was pretending to be so dense. As emissary, he would know her background backward and forward. It would be foolish and irresponsible of him not to. "I inherited equal power from my mother and father."

"Is that not—well, wouldn't that be the case for everyone born of both races?"

She shook her head. "Witch blood nearly always wins out in mixed-race pairings. Valkyrie are strong, but rare, male Valkyrie even moreso, so it wasn't much of a shock that I have the power I do." She smiled up at him. "Now, I know my species isn't why you've asked to speak with me."

"Not entirely, no. I only wanted to get to know the future queen a bit, see what kind of mind you have." He scrunched his face in chagrin, then let it relax into a smile. "I was also hoping to pick your brain a bit about your time with the marshals."

She gave him an amused look. "Was there anything particular you wanted to know?"

"Your methods, mainly. They're quite unlike anything I've ever seen. Did your technique come from training with law enforcement?"

"My father and mother taught me most of what I know, but my mentor in Watoria helped hone my technique to fit my duties there." Once her father had given her permission to join them in a professional capacity, Ashton had ensured she was put through the most rigorous training they could manage. She'd often hated him for his indifference to her innate abilities, but as she grew, she acknowledged that his methods, while different than Byrric's and Cina's, were just as effective.

"I noticed you didn't seem to use your magic when working with the children yesterday. Is that standard practice for you?"

Smirking, she looked up at him. "If I didn't know better, I might think you were trying to suss out my secrets."

He chuckled. "Not at all, my lady. I only hope to take advantage of my experience here, learn what I can from a different land to hopefully better my own. As you are to rule this land, I'd like to get to know you."

Not thinking twice, Freya took the opening.

"Better your own lands? Forgive me, but I haven't heard of any difficulties in Dystone. Has something happened?"

"No, no, of course not," he said, his smile coming a fraction of a second too late. "But a nation can always better itself, wouldn't you agree?"

"Only a fool would think otherwise," she agreed. "My parents raised me with that very mindset."

Reginald gave a short nod. "Yes, your father seems good at his job, doesn't he?"

"He certainly does," Freya replied, a bit disappointed when she saw no real reaction at the mention of her father. "If you've got an interest in discussing techniques, I'd be happy to set up a time for you to visit the training yard and speak to the knights there. I'm sure Sir Ervic would be happy to show you around."

"If it's not too much trouble, my lady," he said.

"None at all. Now, tell me about Dystone. Your queen has said lovely things about the lands, but it sounds as though you've traveled a bit farther."

"Yes, as the youngest, I've had the good fortune of time to myself," he replied. "Willem spent most of his life under our father's thumb learning how to be king and my sisters and brother spent their time learning to find spouses, so I used my time to get to know my country." He gave a shrug. "Many think it's a lonely existence, but I quite enjoy it."

Freya nodded. "Having lived among the citizens of my own country, I can certainly see why you would feel that way. The anonymity I had these last few years was quite freeing. I look forward to my future here, but I'll always be thankful that I was able to have the opportunity to be normal. Not Lady Balthana or the future queen."

He smiled his understanding. "Just Freya?"

She laughed. "Yes, just Freya.

43

The walk to Reginald's wing took longer than Freya had intended, but as he seemed open to discussion, she chose a roundabout way to get to their destination. As they walked, Freya asked questions about where he'd traveled, while he asked her about her time in Watoria. It seemed a perfectly innocuous conversation, but Freya committed every word, every topic to memory to examine later.

Much of what she learned she already knew. He'd grown up in Caldel, the capital of Dystone, with his parents and siblings. He enjoyed to travel and hunt, was well-read, and despite being nearly thirty, had yet to find a wife or express any interest in furthering his family's line. It was unclear how his parents felt about that fact, and though she tried to push a bit, all she could glean was that he didn't care for the belief that one had to be settled by a certain age.

"What's the need?" he'd asked. "As a human, I've got a short life. Why on earth would I spend it with a woman who only makes me mildly happy?"

She tried to get him to slip, to mention something that might indicate true strife within his country or his family, but he maintained a smooth composure throughout. He seemed a nice enough man, and if she didn't know better, she never would've thought to question his motives or meaning.

After seeing Reginald to his chambers, she returned to her room to find Aer lying on her bed, hands folded behind his head.

"Back so soon?" She'd expected his hunting trip to go on several more hours, at least.

"The game seemed intent on eluding us, so we ended our day early." He grinned. "I heard a rumor about you."

She kicked off her shoes and dropped down on the bed beside him. "Oh? Does it involve me and a certain human taking a leisurely stroll through the palace?"

"Indeed it does," he said, propping his head on his fist. "Lea informed me she abandoned you, leaving you to dig for information once my mother was gone. So tell me, what was dear Prince Reginald like?"

"Handsome," Freya replied airily. "And quite charming. With a face like his, I could almost forget his potentially nefarious intentions."

"Ah, so now I have to worry that you'll leave me for a human, then?" Aer put his arm around her waist and pulled her down to lay beside him. "Shall I find a few reasons to convince you why that would be a terrible idea?"

Laughing, she turned to face him. "That human has nothing on you, even if his eyes *do* crinkle when he laughs." Her own eyes ran over his face, his mussed hair, and the sly smile that graced his lips. "Not even close," she said quietly, brushing her hand down his cheek.

His smile faltered a bit, then widened. "A valiant attempt to distract me, but that's a fact I am already well-aware of." With a nudge against her hips, he shifted her onto her back and rolled on top of her. "Now, let's see... how best to convince you that you shouldn't prefer a human to a handsome Lind prince?"

He braced himself on his arms, then dipped his head toward hers, smiling as she lifted her head toward him, eagerly accepting the offered kiss.

Contentment settled over her as it commonly did when they

shifted their focus to one another, to kisses and caresses and whispered words.

"Do you love me yet?" he murmured.

"How odd," she said with a grin. "I was just about to ask you the same thing."

"There's only one more day," he whispered. "It's alright if you want to just give in and admit it."

Sliding a hand up her thighs, he drew her legs around his waist, rolling his hips against her as he took her mouth again, his lips scorching against hers.

I love you.

"I could say the same for you," she said breathlessly as his hands continued to roam across her body, one slipping under her shirt, caressing her skin.

"Have you ever known me to admit defeat, Valkyrie?"

She let out a contented sigh as he ran his lips and teeth along her neck.

"We've got an hour before we have to meet our parents for dinner." Leaning back, he brushed his thumb across her cheek and grinned wickedly. "How much more convincing do you need?"

"To admit my love, or to abandon my hopes of a human consort?"

He laughed quietly, a low, dark sound that rumbled against her body. "Both."

"I suppose that would take quite a good deal of convincing," she whispered. "So what will you do?"

One more day, she thought.

A fact that no longer brought forth rattling nerves. Now she only wished for the hours to speed up.

Slowly, he slid down her body, lifting her shirt and feathering slow kisses across her stomach. His eyes met hers and he hooked his fingers in the waistband of her pants. "I think I'd like to try something new." Slowly, he began to undo the fastenings, causing her heart to kick up a notch. "Prepare properly for tomorrow, you know."

Keeping her eyes on his, she lifted her hips, allowing him to slide her pants down her legs.

She shuddered out a breath as he began to kiss his way up the inside of her leg, dragging his teeth along the sensitive skin of her thigh.

"I think I might like that."

THEY WERE LATE TO DINNER.

After they seated themselves at the long table in the king and queen's private dining room, pointedly ignoring the varying looks of disapproval being sent their way, a servant poured them each a goblet of wine while several others began setting dishes on the table and spooning food onto plates.

"Now that you're both here, there's a good deal we need to cover before tomorrow," Ordona said, her lips still turned down in annoyance. "Starting with the ceremony."

"What about the ceremony?" Freya asked.

"We've had to change officiants," Salazar said as two servants began to set dishes on the table before them. "Carigan has become indisposed, so Andreus will be filling in."

Aer paused, his goblet poised at his lips, and sent his father a disbelieving look that matched the one Freya wore. "The officiant of a royal wedding has become indisposed the night before we're to marry, and *Andreus* is your replacement?" He set his goblet down. "Are you mad?"

"Who is Andreus?" Freya asked. The name didn't ring any bells.

Byrric gave her an odd look. "Andreus Florian, your professor. He was a judge for several centuries prior to his current position and is a powerful warlock, as I'm sure you've noticed."

Her eyes widened in shock. "He poisoned nearly every friend I made at Aldridge this term and you expect him to *marry* us?"

Salazar sighed. "For educational purposes, Freya, and he's performed mating bond rituals for a good many royals, including myself, so I can assure you of his qualifications."

Aer arched a brow as he began cutting into his venison. "And what exactly led to the sudden absence of our former officiant?"

"He's fallen ill," Salazar replied.

"We've sent the castle physician to tend to him, but he is in no state to perform a wedding," Byrric said. "It appears he's come down with a case of food poisoning."

Freya and Aer exchanged a look across the table. Based on the way his eyes shifted when he looked at her, she could tell he believed their reasoning about as much as she did, which was hardly at all.

"Now, moving on." Ordona began cutting into her meat, abandoning the topic of their wayward officiant. "Freya, Kallan and the girls will arrive at your room promptly at nine tomorrow, so please be ready for them."

Freya smiled, but before she could speak, Ordona shifted her attention to her son.

"Aerelius, your attendant has retrieved your attire from Kallan already, so I'll expect you in your father's chambers and set to go by three o'clock. Guests will begin congregating at half-past, and Freya will enter the chapel at precisely four o'clock."

"I'll be at the door to escort you," Byrric added.

"You'll do the traditional mating vows and Florian will perform the incantation," Ordona continued. "Just do your best not to let on how much it's affecting you. The dizziness and other... feelings can make it difficult to control your reactions to the magic, especially when you're already in love, making the mating pull feel..." she wrinkled her nose and looked at Salazar, then Byrric. "Tighter?"

Aer grinned suggestively at Freya across the table at his mother's words and she almost smiled.

Admit it, he seemed to say.

She grinned back. *You first.*

"Hurried, more like," Byrric corrected. "More demanding."

"If you're unable to keep your wits about you, you'll appear weak to those in attendance," Salazar added. "A show of weakness is not an option."

"Agreed. Best to keep your eyes on one another."

"It will help keep your focus on remaining steady."

"The focus should be on one another, regardless."

"True. Yes, eyes drifting *could* indicate disinterest and we certainly don't want that."

"Their hands will be joined, so that will help."

As their voices blended together, one instruction or bit of advice melded into the next with hardly a breath in between. How to look at one another, how to appropriately show affection, proper hand placement while dancing, proximity while sitting, while walking, while speaking. Freya could feel her temper spiking with each suggestion, each instruction, feeling as though she'd gone from bride to a pet in need of training.

After several minutes, Aer let his fork fall noisily to his plate.

"I think we've got it," he said flatly. "Don't trip, frown, swoon, or faint and be sure to keep our groping on the dance floor to a minimum." He gave his parents and Byrric an expectant look. "Anything else?"

Byrric sighed. "I know this seems like a lot, but you must understand the importance—"

"I think we understand perfectly fine," Freya interrupted. Frowning, she looked at the three of them. "Do you all believe Aer and I have been putting on a show these last few months? That when we hold hands or look fondly at one another it's because we want others to think we're eager to wed?"

"No, of course not, dear," Ordona said softly. "But you two have your own way of doing things, of expressing your feelings, and on a normal day that would be fine—"

"I'm sorry, but how many times will we be chastised for inappropriately showing affection?" Aer frowned at Freya. "Four? Five?"

"Knife-throwing contests, death threats, and jokes about breaking your betrothal are not considered 'showing affection' by any stretch of the imagination," Salazar snapped.

"Your Majesties, we're well-aware of the importance of painting a picture of unity and love at our wedding," Freya said, knowing *that* wasn't an argument worth having. "Your presumption that we may not be able to handle a bit of magic is, quite frankly, insulting."

"A bit of magic?" Salazar laughed darkly. "You're demonstrating just how little you know, girl."

She sent him a glare. "Do you believe your son to be weak? That *I* am weak?"

"Freya," Byrric warned. "Enough."

Aer set his napkin on the table and leaned back in his chair. "It's a fair enough point. If you truly believed we were too ill-prepared to accept a mating bond during our wedding, you wouldn't have insisted on moving the wedding up." His eyes narrowed in speculation. "So you either regret changing the timeline, or you're more concerned than you normally would be about how a minor faux pas might paint a picture of our monarchy. Which is it?"

"We need to ensure you are both prepared for any potential missteps," Byrric said slowly, as though speaking with a child. "That no one will have cause to question the strength of your union."

Freya held her father's stare for a few seconds, torn between laughing and a desire to toss another butter knife at him for his deflection. Tension was radiating off Aer but starting a fight with their parents wasn't worth doing, not when they had so many other things to worry about.

She let out a quiet breath, then turned to the king and queen, looking at them each in turn. "Your Majesties, you've both spent a good deal of time preparing me and Aerelius for this wedding. The things you're telling us to do tomorrow are already things we would've done. We can assure you that you've nothing to worry about."

Ordona appeared somewhat mollified by her words, but there was no mistaking the meaning behind the tight set of Byrric's and Salazar's jaws.

"I think I'm full," Aer said after a moment. He smiled at Freya. "Walk with me?"

"Oh, and that's another thing," Ordona said, not seeming to get the hint that her son wanted out of the conversation. "Perhaps for your last night, you should maintain separate rooms—"

Aer held up a hand to cut his mother off. "No. We're adults. We aren't sleeping in separate rooms to create some ridiculous facade of propriety that was shot to hell weeks ago. The only creatures in this palace who could possibly consider premarital relations uncouth are the humans, and I doubt my betrothed and I enjoying each other behind closed doors will damage foreign relations."

"Gods above," Freya muttered, rubbing a hand across her forehead, surprised at the bite to his words.

"Perhaps a walk would be a good idea," Byrric told them, sending her a look. "Settle yourselves, get a good night's sleep."

Ordona cleared her throat. "Yes, tomorrow will be a long day. You should certainly rest up."

Salazar lit a cigar, staring at them both as he puffed on the end. He blew out a long plume of smoke, then tapped it on a glass dish, the ruby on his ring glinting. "I hope, Aerelius, for your sake, that when you have children, they aren't nearly as tiresome as the pair of you."

"You know, it's funny," Aer said, smiling. "I actually hope they turn out just like us."

44

A short while later, they found themselves staring out over the dark mountains as they settled down on the ramparts at the rear of the palace where the crenelated walls rose highest over the grounds.

"What can I do?" she asked, holding out her hand for his.

He hesitated for a moment before linking his fingers with hers, then tightened his grip as he let out a quiet breath. He'd hidden his anger well enough at dinner up until the end, but Freya could see it continuing to seep through now. The annoyance and aggravation of dealing with his parents—she could only assume he'd had similar discussions with them before—was wearing on him.

"I don't know," he replied, not taking his eyes off the dark forest. "I truly have no idea how to make my parents less demanding, less... irritating. I can't fathom why they think we'd need to be told how to handle the most basic of tasks."

"I would imagine they're just as nervous as we are," she said, then put her fingers to his lips when he opened his mouth to protest. "We're all nervous, Aer. There's no shame in admitting it."

An argument sparked in his eyes, but his shoulders relaxed, so she let her hand fall.

Freya bit her lip, thinking. "Aer, look at me." When he complied, she took his other hand. "Have I given you any reason to doubt my feelings for you? Any reason to think I would have to *force* an air of contentment with you on our wedding day?"

He averted his eyes. "No, Freya, it's not that." With a sigh, he let go of her hand and draped his arm around her shoulders, then pressed a kiss to her hair. "I've always felt as though my life was chosen for me," he began. "You are something I would've chosen, if given the chance, so please don't mistake my annoyance now with reluctance in regard to you. You *know* that isn't the case. But this pressure, this need for our parents to control it all, down to the way I *look* at you—" He huffed out an annoyed breath. "If it were up to me, I'd toss the crown aside and tell you we should run off together, choose our own path, and be done with it all."

She smiled to herself. Though it was something she'd kept to herself, she'd often felt the same way. It would be simpler, she thought, if she could go back to the easy life her father had given her in Watoria and just bring Aer with her. She'd cast glamours over them both and they could live however they pleased in perfect anonymity, making their own choices with no crowns weighing down their heads.

Freya thought for a long moment, then, before she could second-guess herself, she climbed into his lap, straddling his hips. Ignoring his suggestive smirk and the slide of his hands on her legs, she let out her wings, wide and dark in the moonlight, and slipped a feather from the lower, non-venomous edge of one.

"Give me your hand," she whispered.

He looked down at the feather, then gave her a curious look. "What—"

She paused. "Do you trust me?"

His response came without hesitation. "Of course."

"Then give me your hand," she repeated.

Still eyeing her warily, he released his hold on her thigh and wrapped his other arm around her waist, steadying her on his lap as he held out his hand.

She kissed his palm and stared into his eyes. "Ever since we were children, I've wanted you in my life. You fit, even when you made me angry, even when you were nothing but a gross little boy," she said with a wrinkle of her nose. "You were what I looked forward to every time I came to the capital, and when my father took me away, it hurt to be apart from you."

The anger in his eyes softened and he smiled. "I knew you'd come around eventually. Does this mean I've won our little bet?"

She took a deep breath, then before she could think twice, she scored his flesh with the tip of her feather, ignoring his sharp hiss of pain. Quickly, she did the same to her own hand, then dropped the plume and pressed their wounded palms together.

Touching a finger to his lips to silence him, she met his eyes determinedly and spoke the words she'd memorized weeks earlier. "I, Freya of House Balthana, pledge myself to you, Aerelius Harridan. I give myself to you fully in mind, body, and soul, to be your faithful wife, confidant, and friend." Trembling, she pressed a kiss to the back of his hand, then met his gaze, wide-eyed. "On this day, I give you my heart freely and take you as my mate."

He stared at her, stunned, then tightened his hand around hers as he wasted no time reciting his own vows.

"I, Aerelius of House Harridan, pledge myself to you, Freya Balthana." He took a deep breath before continuing, his expression full of excitement. "I give myself to you fully in mind, body, and soul, to be your faithful husband, confidant, and friend. On this day, I give you my heart freely and take you as my mate." Not taking his eyes from hers, he touched his lips to the back of her hand. "Do you know the incantation?"

Still shaking, she nodded. She touched a finger to where their blood had mixed on her palm, then drew a thin line along his collarbones, a bonding mark intended as offering to the gods. Taking his other hand, she dipped his finger in the blood on his own palm, then offered her neck to him.

"Wait," he breathed. "If we perform the ritual now—"

She shook her head. "The gods will see it as a renewal of our bonding vows when we wed." Slowly, she guided his hand toward her collarbone. "They'll accept the offering then, just as they will now."

His lips curved in a soft smile, then he closed the distance between his hand and her neck, tracing the same offering marks on her skin as she had on his.

"I call to the gods to bind us eternal," she whispered, letting her wings curve around them. "I beseech the Mother to accept this offering and grant us this favor. Allow our souls to join as one..." She took a deep breath and closed her eyes. "From this moment on, until the worlds choose to crumble, we swear fealty to our mate and no other."

Chest heaving, she opened her eyes, and her gaze crashed to his. She opened her mouth to speak, but the words were sucked from her throat when her call was answered.

A fiery hook tore through her, dragging her thoughts, feelings, emotions, her very essence toward him. His hands tightened around her waist and she gripped his shoulders as they pulled each other closer in tandem, the tug of their souls merging nearly overwhelming. The magic swirled within her and around them as it pulled them closer, fitting them tighter against each other.

Tears of relief sprang to her eyes as she realized the bond wasn't forging something new, as she'd expected—it was blowing oxygen to a fire that already burned deep in her heart. Pieces she didn't know were missing clicked into place, and she knew without question that this bond transcended all feelings of love.

Moments—possibly hours—later, the magic began to ebb, and she thanked the gods she hadn't had to feign any sense of calm as the magic had sealed their bond.

"Freya—" he rasped, his breaths coming in heavy pants.

She loosened her grip on his shirt. "Hmm?"

"It was... everything I feel... it was—"

"Already there?" she whispered.

He stared at her, wide-eyed. "For you, as well?"

Resting her forehead against his, she laughed. "Thank the *gods* we didn't do this in public."

He gazed up at her, then ran his hands through her hair and pulled her face toward his in a slow, heart-pounding kiss.

She put a hand to his chest, marveling at the way their hearts now beat in perfect rhythm. Breaking the kiss, she ran a finger along his clavicle, smiling when she saw the bonding marks had vanished—their offerings to the gods had been received.

"It's amazing," she murmured. "I can feel you..."

"That will certainly take some getting used to," he replied, then let out a quiet growl when she slammed her lips to his again. His hands slid under her skirt and up her thighs, fingers curling around the bare skin of her waist as she rolled her hips against his.

A small whimper escaped her lips when he pulled away.

"Not on the roof, my love," he said, his eyes tender. "The gods only know who's already been watching us."

Smiling, she dragged a finger across his lips as she retracted her wings. "Take me to your room, my prince."

Keeping her legs tight around his waist, he stood and carried her toward the stairwell. "Taking advantage of me so soon? I'm beginning to question your motivations, Valkyrie."

"As though there's nothing in it for you," she teased, laying a kiss to his neck. His pulse beat against her lips, echoing her own.

When they reached the bottom of the stairs, he pushed a large section of stone inward, revealing a dark passage.

Moments later, a latch clicked and he was pushing open a door into his chambers. Kicking the hidden panel shut behind them, Aer pressed her against the wall, his mouth plundering hers. She tore at his doublet, then his shirt, the fabric tearing as she revealed the smooth skin of his chest. In that moment, all she wanted was to explore every inch of his body, all of the most intimate places that might've made her blush just to think of a few months ago.

"Bed," she breathed, gasping when his lips found her throat once again. Her nails dug into his skin. "Now."

"So impatient," he murmured, setting her on her feet. Slowly, he dragged his hands down her sides. "Turn around."

She did as he asked, turning and bracing her hands against the wall, taking several deep breaths to steady herself. When he ran his hand down her spine, her eyes fluttered shut. With gentle fingers, he began to undo the laces that held her dress up, pausing now and then to kiss her bare shoulder and back.

When he was done, Freya let her dress fall to the floor in a puddle of pale green silk, leaving her in only her undergarments as she turned to face him, her heart thundering in her chest. She'd never been ashamed of her body, had always liked the way she was shaped well enough, and he'd seen her in various states of undress in recent months, but her heart still pounded as she let her prince take her in fully for the first time.

This was all so new. The way he looked at her, pupils dilated as he ran his eyes over her body, was so very, very new.

Taking a deep breath, she stepped toward him, shoving her dress aside.

"Gods above, Freya," he breathed, cupping her face in his hands. "You are *everything*."

Wordlessly, he scooped her off the ground, his fingers digging into her thighs as he brought her to his bed and laid her down, then gently slid her undergarments down her legs. Before he could settle himself on top of her, she put a hand to his shoulder and sat up.

With trembling fingers, she began to undo the laces and fastenings on his pants, then slowly drew them down his hips. When all of him was bared for her to see, she met his eyes, surprised at the amount of boldness she felt. Leaning forward, she pressed a kiss to his stomach. She wanted to touch and taste, please him in every way possible. Seeing her intent, he touched a finger to her chin, tilting her face toward his, and gave a slow shake of his head.

"Later," he murmured. "We've got all the time in the world and I think we've waited long enough."

Kneeling on the mattress, he caged her body between his arms, then brushed his lips across hers, down her neck, lingering at her collar bones where the bonding marks had been. She arched her back and gasped when he took her breast into his mouth, her fingers curving around his shoulders in response.

The bond that had awoken in her soared.

"I've always been yours, Freya. I hope you know that now," he whispered just before he brought his mouth back to hers.

"Show me," she breathed against his lips.

His eyes found hers, wide and dark in the moonlight, as he slowly eased their bodies together, joining them as one. She breathed through the sharp burn, focusing instead on the way his body fit against hers, the scrape of teeth against her neck, the taste of sweat when she dragged her lips across his shoulder, her nails as they dug into his back.

Slowly, the pain ebbed, replaced by the thrum of their hearts, the thrill of his skin against hers, and, finally, as pleasure worked its way in, anticipation.

Never in her life had she been happier, more content, than she was in that moment.

Later, when he collapsed on top of her, chest heaving, she closed her eyes and smiled, then gently ran a hand up and down his back.

He laid a soft kiss to the dip of her shoulder, then laughed.

"What—are you *laughing* right now?"

"Shh... no," he whispered. "I'm just... a bit in shock. When you said you'd break molds with me..."

"Ah," she murmured, her body relaxing. "Sealing a blood bond on the roof of your palace the night before our wedding wasn't what you planned?"

"I would've expected it to be my idea, not yours. I'm a bit perturbed you thought of it first, to be honest." He paused a moment, then laughed again, harder this time. "Gods above, Freya. Our parents are going to *murder* us."

45

"Goddess help me, they really did it!"

"*Clearly*, you imbecile. It *reeks* in here."

"All of you need to go away," Aer groaned.

"No, you two need to get up now," Lea said firmly as Freya rolled onto her back, pulling the blanket up around her chest. "Right now before anyone sees you! It's your wedding day, for heaven's sake, and Freya is expected in her room in less than an hour!"

"What were you two *thinking*?" Collin asked. "Ervic said he saw you both on the ramparts last night and something... happened."

The room was silent for a moment, then Laz let out a snort. "You two completed your mating bond, didn't you?"

Tightening the blanket around her chest, Freya tilted her chin up. "Yes, we did."

Collin groaned.

"Technically, we haven't done anything *wrong*," Aer said. "A bit unconventional, maybe."

"Maybe, he says," Collin muttered. "Your parents are going to kill you both for keeping them in the dark, you do know that, right?"

"You're lucky Ervic came to me and not the king or queen," Lea said with a tsk. "Kallan will be here in an hour, Freya, so you'd best get in your room before Dina brings your breakfast. I've already told her you requested something outlandish, although I'm sure Maghda has seen straight through that excuse."

Still holding her blanket up, Freya arched a brow. "A bit of privacy, then?"

Collin sent them another mildly disapproving look, then sighed. "We'll tell your guards to make sure no one comes down this way until you're both presentable."

The moment he left, Freya threw back the covers and made to climb out of bed, only to be stopped by Aer's vise-like grip on her waist. He pulled her back down, immediately pinning her to the mattress. Smiling, he brushed her hair, still mussed from sleep, from her face.

"What is it?" she asked quietly.

He kissed the tip of her nose, then ran his eyes over her face. "You. Waking up with you like this... it's different than I expected."

"In a good way, I hope."

"Very good," he murmured. He trailed a hand down her side, his heat-filled eyes boring into hers. "Tonight," he whispered as his hand drifted lower, stopping at her hipbone, "I'm going to kiss you everywhere."

A sigh slipped past her lips as he lowered his mouth to hers and slowly began to use his hands on her. She felt his heart quicken against her chest, mimicking the rhythm that beat there.

Perfection, she thought, her mind going to mush as she went pliant against him. *Absolute and utter perfection.*

There was a pounding at the door.

"Time is of the essence, you two!" Collin called.

"Ignore him," Aer whispered. "We've got a few minutes and I'd like to start our wedding day off on a high note, wouldn't you?"

Biting her lip, she nodded. Casting a glance toward the door that led into her room, she gave a quick flick of her wrist, locking the outer door.

Grinning, Aer rolled on top of her, then paused a moment, his face turning serious as his eyes searched hers.

"What is it?" she asked.

"I love you, Freya." He brushed a kiss against her lips. "If last night didn't make that abundantly clear, I just wanted to say the words aloud. I don't care if it means I've lost our bet."

Her heart soared and she couldn't help the silly grin that lit up her face. "I love you, too, Aer."

"ONE MOMENT, I just need to make sure she's decent!"

Freya bolted upright at the sound of Lea's voice in her room.

"Shit!" She scrambled out of bed, shoving Aer's arm off when he laughed and tried to pull her back under the covers. They'd gotten so wrapped up in each other that they'd lost track of time, and now the clock was moments away from chiming the ninth hour.

"You're about to become royalty, Freya," Aer mumbled. "People wait for you, you don't rush to them."

Scowling, she tugged on her robe. "That's easy for you to say. You aren't about to be fussed over and prodded for—" she checked the time on the clock on his mantel and groaned "—the next six hours."

The door to his room burst open. Freya was just about to duck when she saw Laz and Collin.

"Into your room, Freya," Collin said, glancing back into the hall. "Get cleaned up. The queen is on her way now."

"Yes, yes, I'm going," she said, just as there was a light knock at the door that connected Aer's room to hers.

"Freya!" Lea hissed through the heavy wood. "Now!"

Checking to make sure her robe was straight, she leaned down and gave Aer a quick kiss, then rushed into her room.

"Come on in, Kallan!" Lea began ushering Freya toward her washroom. "She's just taking a quick bath!"

"Thank you," Freya mouthed as she shut the door behind her. She heard the quiet rumble of Kallan's voice, along with the bell-like tones of Rini and Tyna's. More voices filtered in, so Freya picked up a rag and dipped it in her water basin and began bathing herself, scrubbing her skin with rose-scented water until she was sure Aer's scent was all but washed away. She paused as she brought the rag across her collarbone, then gently touched her fingers to the spot where her and Aer's blood had been the night before. The voices in her room faded away as she thought back on the sheer insanity and boldness of what they'd done. She had no regrets, nor did it seem Aer had any, but the fact that they'd bucked tradition so thoroughly surprised even her. When she told him she wanted to break molds together, she'd meant it with all her heart, but she'd never, not in a million years, thought that this would be how that began.

Her small smile turned into a grin.

There was a quick rap at the door, then it opened and Lea stepped in, shutting it immediately behind her.

"You look like the cat that ate the canary, Freya," she said. "I hope you'll be able to keep your head out there."

Freya set down the rag and slipped her robe on. "It'll be fine, Lea. You worry too much."

"Oh?" Lea arched a brow and folded her arms. "Tell me, how do you plan on hiding the fact that you're already bound when the priest performs the ceremony later?"

"Aer is going to meet with Florian beforehand," Freya said, ignoring her friend's chastising look as she started running her brush through her hair. "It's a bit unconventional, but we're going to treat it as a bond renewal. The guests will be none the wiser, and our wedding vows will remain the same."

"I'll go out on a limb and assume you've already discussed when you'll try for children?"

"I won't cycle again for another year, at least, but regardless, we both started taking a tonic a few weeks ago."

"Well, you two have thought of everything, haven't you?" Lea gave an amused shake of her head, then froze. "Wait, did you say *Florian?*"

Freya laughed. "Yes, according to their majesties, our officiant has come down with a case of food poisoning. As Florian has performed many weddings and mating bonds for the Harridan line already, they've chosen him as the replacement."

"I'm going to assume, based on your expression, that you find that as questionable as I do?"

"I do. I'm not concerned that he'll try to harm us, but I *am* a bit concerned that he's here to prevent us from being harmed." She set her brush down. "I didn't think the king or queen would allow anything to happen at our wedding, but to replace the officiant suffering from food poisoning with a poisoner is a bit... odd."

Lea bit her lip in consternation. "Understandable, but Florian isn't the type to poison someone just so he can officiate a wedding. If anything, I would say he's not a bad person to have looking out for you, so I suppose that's something." She cocked her head toward the bedroom. "Come, there's someone here to see you."

Frowning, Freya tightened the belt on her robe and followed Lea into the room. When she saw who was waiting for her, her eyes widened in delight.

"Aunt Ana!" she exclaimed, launching herself into her aunt's open arms. "Oh, I was worried you were going to miss it!"

"Never, dear!" Ana squeezed her hard, then pressed a kiss to her cheek. "My ship was a bit delayed, so I had to fly most of the way. It took a good deal longer than I'd hoped."

Freya grinned, then bounced on her toes. "Oh, I'm so happy you're here!"

Ana smiled fondly and laid her hand on Freya's cheek. "I wouldn't have missed this for the world, Freya," she said softly. "Now, let's see what contraption your dressmaker has come up with, shall we?"

Recalling that her room was currently occupied by several other people, Freya stepped back and smiled in greeting at the queen, who now stood beside her aunt. She held a look of wistfulness, and, if Freya wasn't mistaken, a bit of melancholy.

"Your Majesty, I'm so happy to share this day with you," she said sincerely. "The last few months planning... I can't thank you enough for all you've done."

Ordona smiled. "You've given me more than you know, Freya."

Ana took in the exchange with a bit of surprise, but she quickly masked it. Considering her last conversation with Freya had involved not wanting the royal court to change her, her surprise was understandable.

It hadn't been that way, though, Freya realized. She'd adapted, learned from her queen and her experiences living at court, but she didn't feel as though she'd been inherently changed. True, she'd only been back a few months, but the way she'd fallen so effortlessly into her new friendships and her relationship with Aer made her feel as though her concerns, though valid at the time, were unwarranted.

Taking a deep breath, she smiled at both females. "Well, where do we begin?"

"Hair and makeup first, of course," the queen said. "I'll be going back to my own chambers to prepare, but you'll be in good hands here." Stepping forward, she held out her hands, waiting until Freya took them to speak. "I've waited for this day for a long time, Freya," she whispered. "I hope you know how thrilled I am for you to truly join our family."

"Thank you, Your Majesty," she whispered.

Tears burned in Freya's eyes as she let Ordona pull her into a hug. When she pulled back, Freya thought she detected a hint of sadness, despite the warm smile that graced her lips.

Her heart sank a bit as she realized the queen had likely figured out what she and Aer had been up to the night before. This wedding—seeing her only child joined with his mate—was something Ordona had been looking forward to for years and, perhaps selfishly, Freya and Aer had taken away a part of that experience.

It was for us, Freya reminded herself. *No one else.*

"I think it's about time you started calling me Ordona, don't you?"

Freya gave her a small nod as she thumbed a tear from the corner of her eye. "I would like that very much."

She squeezed Freya's hands one last time, then rattled off a few more instructions to Kallan, his assistants, and Rini and Tyna before leaving. Once she was gone, Freya turned her smile on the pixies. "Are we ready to begin?"

"Yes, yes," Rini said, gesturing toward a chaise. "Sit, your breakfast should be here soon."

Lea picked up a bottle of wine and sat down next to Freya, then filled glasses for all of them. Once they were settled, she sent Freya a pointed look. "So, Freya, would you care to fill your aunt in on your activities of late?"

Eyes narrowed, Freya took the proffered glass and sipped, avoiding Ana's eagle-eyed gaze as she sat on the edge of Freya's bed arching a blond brow.

Glancing at Kallan and the pixies, she sighed.

"It's alright, my lady," Kallan said, barely suppressing a smile as the pixies tittered their small laughs. "You'll find no judgement here."

"What—" Squinting, Ana leaned forward and sniffed. "Freya Balthana! You didn't! Whose idea was this?"

Seeing the accusation in her aunt's gaze, she tilted her chin up an inch. "Mine, actually, so there's no need to go rushing off to verbally castrate the prince."

Ana rolled her eyes and gulped down the glass of wine she'd just been handed. Pointing at Freya with the hand that was holding the glass, she shook her head. "Your father will be beside himself if— who am I kidding—*when* he finds out. Traditions exist for a reason, Freya! Did you even consider the possibility that mating vows are the type of thing a parent—or an *aunt*—may want to witness firsthand?" Ana sighed and shook her head. "I'm not worried about your father's disapproval, Freya, I'm worried about hurt feelings."

Freya looked down at her hands and let out a breath. "I understand, truly, but Aunt Ana, this was for me and Aer. The rest of the day—it's not for our benefit, it's for everyone else. We needed something just for us." She stared at her aunt, beseeching. "Please don't tell him."

Ana and Lea exchanged wary looks before a look of resignation filled Ana's face. "Did he at least remember to hide the sheets?"

"Oh dear god," Freya groaned as Kallan gave an uncomfortable cough and Lea and the pixies snickered. "Yes! Now, let's move on before poor Kallan has a fit."

"It's quite alright, my lady. This isn't my first wedding, after all."

For the next several hours, Kallan put the final touches on Freya's dress as Rini and Tyna busied themselves with her hair and makeup. They'd gone through several rounds of fittings, deciding which look would be most appropriate for the dress Kallan designed—a thing he'd yet to show Freya in its entirety, but Rini and Tyna had finally come up with a plan for her hair and makeup. As the hairstyle Tyna had chosen to go with was a complex one, she started on it first thing.

Dina delivered lunch around midday, which Lea and Ana insisted on spoon-feeding to Freya so she wouldn't muss her makeup.

"This is utterly absurd," she groused around a mouthful of roasted lamb. "I'm perfectly capable of feeding myself!"

"Shush!" Rini chastised. "You move far less when you aren't fussing with forks and knives, and I need you sitting perfectly still if Tyna and I are to manage what Kallan has put us up to."

Freya narrowed her eyes at the small pixie hovering in the air in front of her, her tiny teeth digging into her lip in concentration as she gently applied a shimmering pink rouge to Freya's cheeks.

"You're lucky I like you, Rini, or I would've chucked you through the window by now."

Rini's expression didn't falter as she muttered a quiet "Mmm-hmm" before flitting to Freya's side to adjust the coloring at her temples.

"I like her," Ana commented as she watched Rini continue her work. "She's sassy."

"Why do you think I plan to keep her on as my attendant after the wedding?" Freya said, exchanging a grin with Lea as Rini fluttered around to face her again, her eyes wide in shock.

"Truly, my lady?" She clapped her small hands in glee, all irritation forgotten. "Oh, thank you so much! Tyna will be with Lea for the remainder of the academic year, and I was so hoping you'd become a permanent assignment." Clasping her hands against a cheek, she did a quick twirl in the air, her gossamer wings fluttering. "I've got *so* many plans for that hair of yours!"

"Well, if we're discussing assignments, Freya," Lea said, sliding a look at Ana, "I believe your aunt has some news you may find quite interesting."

Curious, Freya turned to her aunt, then winced when Rini tapped her cheek with her brush to keep her still.

"I can still fire you," Freya warned before looking back to Ana. "What news?"

Ana sat down beside her on the sofa and took her hand. "Well, your father and I have been talking the past few months about my plans now that you're gone and I've moved back to Iston. Since we have a Valkyrie queen coming to power, your father feels your employ should have at least one of your own kind." She grinned. "As your current palace physician intends to retire when Salazar and Ordona step down, would you do me the honor of allowing me to replace him?"

Freya's eyes widened, and it was only fear of another flick on the face by Rini that kept her from leaping into her aunt's arms.

"Aunt Ana, I would be *honored* to have you here. Elated, even!"

"Please, my lady, don't make her cry," Rini lamented to Ana. "Her makeup is nearly done!"

"Shush, you," Lea hissed. "They're having a moment, can't you see?"

"And this is why I do hair," Tyna muttered from behind Freya.

IT TOOK another hour before Rini and Tyna completed their work. In that time, two more pixies arrived to help Lea and Ana prepare, needing far less time to finish their hair and makeup than Rini and Tyna had needed on Freya.

Once they were done and everyone was fed and hydrated, Kallan announced it was time to dress.

"We've just a few finishing touches to add before I let you see the finished product." He inclined his head toward Rini and Tyna. "If you don't mind?"

Tyna tapped the center of Freya's back. "Wings out, my lady."

Frowning, Freya complied, letting her wings snap out and flare wide. She waited impatiently as Rini pulled out a small, soft brush and began brushing her feathers, ensuring none were out of place, while Freya tried very hard to hide her discomfort at someone else touching her wings. When the pixie was done, she dusted a bit of something across Freya's wings, then she, Tyna, and Kallan helped Freya into her dress.

"No veil?" Ana asked, surprised.

Kallan shook his head and smiled at Freya. "Meek and submissive are two things our lady is not."

When they finally moved away and Rini gestured for Freya to turn around, she nearly wept.

Kallan had kept the original off-the-shoulder, form-fitting cut that they'd decided on in silk that fell somewhere between cream and white, a shade that suited Freya's coloring while also appeasing the queen's insistence on maintaining some semblance of tradition. A smattering of rose stones and opals so pale they were nearly white began at her breasts and faded downward to her skirt. The back, nearly scandalous in its absence, was completely open to her tailbone, where a lace train fell to the floor, flowing out a dozen feet behind her.

Tyna had woven her hair into twists in a style that made the pink tones of Freya's hair stand out without taking over her appearance. She'd twisted the lower half into a thick, loose braid that hung down her back just between her wings, while the other half was braided into a coronet woven through with gold webbing. Webbing that took, to Freya's dismay, a horrendously long amount of time to affix to her hair.

Her wide wings, smoky gray shot through with pink, were glowing.

"How?" Freya whispered, marveling at the way they shimmered.

"Pixie dust," Rini whispered. "We don't share it freely, either, so don't get used to it."

"It's..." Freya shook her head, unable to tear her eyes from what Kallan and her pixies had created. "Perfect. It's just perfect."

46

As she made her way through the palace with her entourage of females, her train held aloft in the air behind her by Rini and Tyna, her heartbeat sped with each step. She'd been raised to be confident, sure in all of her dealings, and to never second-guess herself or question her own abilities. By and large, she was successful at those things. Yet, being the center of attention had never been something she wanted or particularly cared for, and today, she was being shoved in front of a crowd of hundreds for all to see and, of course, judge.

Her skin must have looked as green as she felt, because a cool hand slipped into hers, squeezing it in comfort. She smiled gratefully at her aunt.

"Thank you," she murmured.

"Why are you so nervous?" Ana asked. "You love Aerelius, don't you?"

"More than, if that's possible," Freya said with laugh. "I think... I think I'm used to attention being lavished on me after I've accomplished something, not mid-action."

Lea linked her arm through Freya's on her other side. "Well, you look like a goddess, so at least you don't have to worry about what the guests will think of your appearance."

"*And*," Ana said, shooting Lea a look, "I would be willing to wager that once you see your prince at the end of the aisle, everything and everyone else will disappear."

"It's true," Lea said, patting her hand. "My mother said something similar. She saw my father and *poof*." She fluttered her fingers in the air. "Suddenly, it was just the two of them."

"Well, I certainly hope you're right," Freya said. "Jittery isn't a good look for me."

Ana gave her a sidelong look. "Just focus on your prince, Freya. Ignore everyone else."

Easier said than done, when a large portion are probably expecting me to fail, Freya thought.

She forced back her doubts, reminding herself that she didn't care if they thought she would fail. She didn't care if people questioned her status as a non-royal, if they thought she was too rough to be queen. They were all wrong, and no amount of dubious looks would take that knowledge away.

She let those thoughts swirl in her mind, supplanting her nerves with determination.

No, she wouldn't fail. Not at this. She and Aerelius were connected on a level that most could only wish for. As individuals, they were strong, but as a mated pair, they would be unbreakable. Neither would allow the other to falter or flounder.

And that thought, that fact alone, put her at ease.

When she saw Byrric, wings hovering at his shoulders, waiting outside the door to the palace's chapel, she steeled herself for a new list of dos and don'ts for walking down the aisle.

Instead, her father smiled warmly, a sight so shocking she nearly stumbled.

"Well that's something you don't see every day," Lea murmured.

"Isn't that the truth?" Ana replied, laughing. "We'll see you inside, dear," she said as two guards opened the doors for her and Lea to pass through.

Lea gave her a quick kiss on the cheek and followed Ana into the chapel.

"Freya," Byrric said quietly once they'd gone. "You look lovely."

"Thank you." She gave him a tight smile.

He patted her shoulder. "Try not to worry. Just focus on your prince and you'll be fine."

"Fatherly advice," she said with a nod. "That's twice in the past two months, I believe." She grinned. "It might be a record."

He gave her a withering look, but the corners of his mouth tilted slightly in amusement.

Once Ana and Lea had stepped aside and Kallan ensured the train of her dress was flowing properly behind her, Rini did a final check of her makeup, hair, and wings.

"Perfection, my lady," she said with a sure nod. "Your prince is sure to swoon."

Taking a deep breath, Freya straightened her shoulders and smiled up at Byrric. His dove-gray wings dwarfed hers and he stood nearly a foot taller than her, but she knew, side-by-side, they showed the strength of the Balthana line, a clear indication to any naysayers of what Freya would pass down to her children.

Byrric gave the guards at the door a curt nod, and the doors swung open, revealing hundreds of guests, all turned to face her.

"Holy hells," she breathed. She shifted her wings, holding them just a bit higher at her shoulders.

The chapel was a dream. Pixie lights dotted the aisle and hovered in clusters above the guests who were seated in long rows. Roses and lilac hung from the crystalline windows, filling the room with their sweetness.

"Smile," Byrric murmured. "And look at Aerelius."

She forced her lips to curve upward as she sought out her prince.

When she found him standing at the end of the aisle, his own grin expectant, it was just as Lea said.

Poof.

He looked more beautiful than she'd ever seen, in black pants with a pale green brocade vest with gold and opal fastenings. His pale gray mantle trimmed in white fur, the one that matched the one she'd soon wear, hung from his shoulders, brushing the backs of his black pants just below his knees.

If it hadn't been for Byrric's hand on her arm, she would've sworn they were alone, just her and her mate in a beautiful room filled with the scent of flowers.

Hurry up, Aer seemed to say, his eyes filled with pride and anticipation, twinkling with the knowledge of the secret they shared. *I'm waiting for you.*

She grinned, sharing a smile with him that was only theirs, one only they knew the meaning of. In that moment, Byrric was no longer her escort. He was simply a hanger-on, an interloper that she wished to shed so she could run to her mate, onlookers be damned.

Instead, she forced her steps to remain slow and even, matching her father's pace as they traveled the endlessly long petal-strewn aisle until, finally, *finally,* they reached the altar. The prince wasted no time in holding out his hand for hers.

"My lady," Florian said. The poisoner had donned a black robe embroidered with whorls of onyx and gold, his white hair slicked back. His eyes, cunning as ever, met hers, a small smile gracing his lips. Freya's discomfort at the fact that he was the one to officiate their marriage still lingered, but something about the way he looked at her told her she had nothing to worry about.

He gave a small nod to Byrric, who took Freya's hand and placed it directly into Aer's.

"Byrric Balthana, do you give your daughter to his highness Prince Aerelius of House Harridan of your own free will?"

Byrric nodded. "I do."

Florian shifted his black eyes to Freya. "And do you, Lady Balthana, come to your prince of your own volition?"

Taking a deep breath, she smiled at Aer. "Yes, I do."

"Then let us begin."

Florian droned on for a good while about the sanctity of a mating bond and the importance of a strong marriage. He talked of past kings and queens who'd strengthened Lindoroth by absorbing and respecting their bonds. A sign of a truly strong monarchy, he said, would be indicated by the strength of its monarchs, the depth of their devotion to one another, and the vows they swore on their wedding day.

When at last he turned his attention to Freya and Aer, she was nearly out of her skin wanting to get on with it.

"His highness has explained your... situation," Florian murmured, low enough that he wouldn't be overheard. "You've nothing to worry about."

She gave him a nod of thanks.

He looked at Aer expectantly. "Your Highness, her mantle?"

The gray mantle Kallan had created for her was folded in the waiting hands of a nearby page.

When Aer beckoned him forward, he lifted the soft material and turned to Freya. It was a beautiful piece crafted from the same smoky gray velvet as Aer's, with patterns of leaves and swirls woven with glittering threads of silver.

Straightening her shoulders, she turned to face their guests. It was a struggle not to let the small, restrained smile she wore shift to beaming as she retracted her wings, allowing Aer to fasten the mantle around her shoulders.

"As you take on the mantle of House Harridan, so, too, do you take on the weight of its legacy," Florian intoned.

"I accept it with an open heart and with no ill-intent," Freya replied. She faced Aer once more and took his hands.

"And now, please repeat after me."

They repeated the words they'd said last night, replacing the words "accept this offering" with "accept this new offering." If the guests picked up on the slight deviation in verbiage, she didn't know, but even if they did, there was little within the addition of a single word that would indicate they'd done anything inappropriate. The magic that a vow renewal sent through them was strong, but not nearly enough to elicit the same reaction as last night, so their parents' concerns in that regard were eased.

Florian had hardly finished his declaration that their bond was complete when Aer had her in his arms. He smiled broadly, then gripped her chin in one hand and kissed her in a way that was, to her mind, a bit inappropriate for mixed company.

Cheers rang out around them from their families and friends and from the hundreds of subjects whom they would soon rule over.

"I love you," Aer breathed against her lips. "Princess."

"So, nineteen years later, and here we are," Aer murmured as his hand curved around Freya's back, resting on the bare skin at her waist. The musicians began to play a slow, lilting waltz that was tradition at Harridan weddings, and slowly and smoothly, Aer began to lead her around the dance floor. "Did you know there was a time I thought you might never return?"

Freya gave him a shocked look as he spun her past their guests, who stood in a wide circle around them. "But I promised you I would. Even if I didn't have a duty to my kingdom, I would've returned, Aer."

He sighed, then gave her a quick spin before pulling her back against his chest. He cradled their joined hands beneath them and rested his cheek against her hair.

"Are you happy, Freya?"

It was the second time he'd asked her since she'd returned to Iladel, but the question carried much more weight now. When he'd asked her at the ball, she'd only just found him again, had only begun to dip her feet back into life in the capital. Her betrothal, a thing that had hovered in the back of her mind for years, had just been pulled front and center once again and she hadn't been sure she still knew the male she was going to marry.

Now, months later, after spending time rediscovering each other, she couldn't imagine finding anything or anyone that could make her happier.

"I love you," she said simply. Tilting her face toward his, she took in his expression, the hard lines of his jaw, the deep chocolate hue of his eyes that was encircled with just a touch of green. "Nothing about you could make me unhappy. I would've been just as content without the trappings of tradition to make that apparent."

"I think you should let me kiss you," he murmured, smiling when she tilted her chin up just a bit more, her lips slightly parted. He leaned closer, and when his lips were just a breath from hers, he whispered, "Nothing about you could make me unhappy, either."

The kiss was outwardly chaste, appearing to those who stood a dozen feet away as a simple kiss between husband and wife, a bit of a show to put on for their guests. They didn't see the slow brush of his tongue over her lower lip or the way his hand clenched against her back when he pulled her harder against his body, the way the thumb of his right hand, which was still wrapped around hers and cradled between them, brushed along the bare skin just below her collarbone.

"Scandalous," she whispered when he released her mouth, a bit breathless.

"What do you think they would do if we disappeared now?" He laughed quietly. "All the rest is for them, anyway."

"I think we've defiled tradition enough in recent weeks, so perhaps we should stay the course just this once."

"Indeed." He pressed a kiss to her forehead, then touched his lips to her ear. "I thought you should know that I managed to steal a few moments with my cousins and Collin," he whispered. "They're going to be on the lookout for anything... questionable."

Freya bit her lip, closing her eyes and smiling as though he'd just whispered the most romantic words. "Has there been any indication something might happen?" After being held hostage by Kallan and the pixies for half the day, she'd hardly had time to worry about sneaking humans or devious plots, nor had she had a chance to check in with Aer to see if he'd found anything since he'd left his room that morning.

"No, and I'm certain my parents intend for it to stay that way. Even still, our friend makes me a bit edgy. I thought additional eyes might put me at ease."

True enough, Freya thought. She'd been turning over her conversation with Reginald in her mind most of yesterday, and despite the instances where she knew he was being untruthful, nothing about him rang false. While she was no mindreader, she'd always been a good judge of character—her father and mother wouldn't have allowed her not to be—and something told her he wasn't an enemy. If anything, he'd come off as just the opposite.

"He gave me no indication of animosity yesterday," she said.

"Which is all the more reason to be wary, I think. You are a good judge of character, certainly, but he could be just as good of an actor."

"Perhaps I'll strike up another conversation, then." When he didn't immediately reply, she sighed. "If our parents are insisting on putting us on a ship for Edhil tomorrow, we should know before we depart what political problems might await when we return. I don't doubt their ability to handle problems that may arise, but you and I should be as prepared as possible if there's the potential for anything to go awry."

"Oh, I agree, Valkyrie." The song ended and he smiled down at her. "Let's just see where the night takes us, shall we?"

47

W hile they received guests at the long head table set for each of the royal families, dozens of servants began to file in, each bearing plates laden with food to the guests' tables. Freya and the queen had decided on seven courses of Allanorian dishes—chestnut soup, roasted potatoes, carrots and squash steamed with lindberries, braised pheasant, and cinnamon and apple tarts, to name a few. Each would represent Freya's heritage.

As the spicy-sweetness of the roasted vegetables and savory smells of chestnuts and game wafted through the room, Freya was transported back to Watoria and her childhood home just on the outskirts of the city.

By the time plates were set before her, her throat burned after talking to one guest after another, several of whom would've sat and chatted all night if it hadn't been for Byrric hovering nearby, shooing off anyone who overstayed their welcome at her side.

When she saw the food the kitchens had prepared, she struggled to maintain the proper facade of a princess as it all but demanded she dive in.

From start to finish, dinner took nearly four hours, for which Freya was grateful as it gave her time to digest a bit between courses.

"You chose your menu well, Your Highness," Isadora said from beside her. She gestured toward her empty dessert plate. "I thought the apple tarts of Teid were the best to be had, but I've never tasted something so divine as this."

"I'm so pleased you're enjoying it," Freya replied, then leaned forward so she could speak to Willem. She'd hardly had a chance to converse with him since the humans had arrived, and whether it was intentional on his part or not, she wasn't sure. "How are you enjoying your meal, Your Majesty?"

He gave her a tight smile. "Delicious, Princess. I'm not sure my own chefs could hold a candle to yours."

Freya laughed. "Well, Maghda would be delighted to hear such high praise." Then, noting the empty chair beside him, she asked, "Is your brother unwell?" It was highly improper for anyone to leave the table before the monarchs had excused them.

"Reginald can't sit in any one place for too long," Willem said, hardly hiding his annoyance at that fact. He dabbed the corners of his mouth with his napkin. "He'll be along any time now."

Freya let her eyes drift over the room searching for Reginald's pale hair but saw no sign of him.

They talked lightly of other topics, of travel plans for the remainder of their stay in Lindoroth, and if they planned to make a return trip at any point. Despite Willem's aloofness, Freya couldn't help but be thankful she'd been placed beside the human monarchs instead of Lessia, who sat several seats down at Ordona's left. Willem might be standoffish and a bit odd, but it was far preferable to Lessia's calculated ways.

Once dinner was over and guests were encouraged to mingle, Freya and Aer found their friends and spent the next hour dancing. They'd agreed ahead of time that neither wanted to spend their wedding night intoxicated, so while Lea, Laz, Collin, Jonas, and several of their friends from Aldridge proceeded to drink themselves silly, Freya and Aer just let themselves enjoy celebrating.

After some time and citing pained feet, Freya stepped away from the revelers and took a seat at a nearby table, smiling as she leaned back in the chair and watched those around her as they enjoyed the party.

Someone sat down beside her.

"This is quite the party, Princess," Reginald said.

She blew out a breath. "It certainly is, although I don't quite know how I'm going to function tomorrow. I'm exhausted already, and no one seems to have any interest in making it to bed."

He laughed. "I take it you haven't been to a wedding in some time?"

"More than fifteen years. To the best of my knowledge, I spent most of the night asleep on my mother's shoulder."

"Well, the benefit of being the prince and princess is that you can both leave whenever you'd like and no one would bat an eye."

Laughing, she turned to face him. "Are you enjoying yourself?"

His answering smile was a bit wary. "I've heard rumors of Lindorothian revels but wasn't expecting something so... energized."

Frowning, Freya looked around the room, trying to see it from the perspective of a human and an outsider. The Linds were a raucous crowd, certainly, but aside from the amount of alcohol her people liked to consume at parties, she didn't see anything remarkable.

"There's a good deal to celebrate when a royal wedding comes around," she told him. "They only happen once every few centuries and it means a new king and queen will arise soon." She smiled softly as she looked at her guests, her future subjects, as they leapt about the dance floor and streamed in and out of the open veranda doors. Servants brought in several more casks of wine and mead, replacing the ones that had been emptied several times over already. No one seemed to have any plans of stopping soon.

"It's nice to have a reason to celebrate, isn't it?" he murmured.

Freya couldn't be sure, but it seemed as though a hint of sadness tinged in voice.

"You say that as if you don't often find cause for celebration in Dystone." She let the statement hang, hoping he might take it as a bit of bait.

He laughed. "Humans find a way to celebrate any damn thing,

Princess. Should you and your prince ever come to Dystone, I'll be happy to show you."

"His highness and I would appreciate that." she replied.

Lea appeared then, her cloudy eyes telling Freya she'd been at the wine table a fair number of times, and set her goblet down on the table, taking a seat beside Freya.

"My lady," Reginald said with a nod. He stood and gave Freya a bow. "Princess, it's been good talking to you. I hope you enjoy the rest of your evening."

After Reginald walked off, Lea turned to Freya, wide-eyed.

"So did you uncover a devious plot?" she whispered.

Freya rolled her eyes. "No, but perhaps if you'd come along a bit later..."

Lea waved off her insinuation with a huff. "You, my dear, look half-asleep on your feet. If you and Aer slip off now, you'll be long gone before anyone notices."

Freya scanned the room, then nodded. She'd felt as though she'd been holding her breath all evening, waiting for some invisible shoe to drop. They knew Reginald had ill intent toward his brother, but if he hoped to pull off anything tonight, devious or otherwise, it seemed poorly planned, as the casks had been replenished every half hour since they'd arrived and there wasn't an empty hand in the room.

No, it seemed if something nefarious was truly afoot, those plans would not be carried out here.

"Yes, I think that—Oh!" She jumped back in her seat, startled as Jonas, clearly more than half in the bottle, stumbled against the table.

"Apologies, Princess!" He flashed her a grin and held up his glass in salute. His smile shifted a bit as he looked at Lea. "My lady."

Freya's heartbeat slowed a bit, having sped up at his sudden appearance.

Lea gave him a cool look. "Was there something you needed from my princess, Lord Edrin?"

"Ah!" He held up a finger. "Yes! Princess, his highness has asked for you. I believe he wishes to depart, yet I can't seem to tear my aunt from his side." He rolled his eyes. "Someone mentioned the increased interest in Saithian silks in Jotunheim and the conversation went downhill from there."

Freya shot Lea a quick look and they both stood.

"Thank you, Jonas. I'll go give him a rescue."

He gave her a nod, then shifted his roguish grin to Lea. "And you, my lady, still owe me a dance."

Lea gave him an incredulous look. "You seem hardly able to walk, and you expect to lead me in a dance?"

He straightened and gave her a sharp nod. "For you, my lady, I promise to remain fully upright and the perfect gentleman."

Shaking her head in amusement, Freya left them, traversing the ballroom quickly, doing her best to smile and wave at her guests without getting drawn into conversation.

She found Aer with Lessia and a female that had come with her standing beside a set of open veranda doors, the female talking, Aer smiling politely and nodding. The female had black hair that was similar in style to Lessia's, and the same pale skin and narrow build, so Freya assumed some sort of familial relation.

Whether the female knew Freya was approaching or not, Freya wasn't sure, but just as Freya came upon them, she laid a hand on Aer's arm and tossed her head back in a laugh. At the same moment, Aer's gaze hardened, then shot to Freya's, instantly filling with relief as he took a step away from both females.

Freya couldn't help the flash of red she saw as another female touched her husband, but she forced down her fury as she quickened her steps.

When she arrived, she pasted on a bright smile and curled her arm through Aer's.

"There you are," Aer said, touching a kiss to her forehead. "This is Lady Effina Veldin, cousin to the empress. She's traveled from northern Jotunheim to share in the celebration of our marriage."

Effina, tall and even more beautiful up close, gave Freya a curtsy, then took a subtle step back, putting another foot of space between them. "I feel quite honored to attend such a joyous occasion."

"Ah." Freya inclined her head and gave her a smile tinged with condescension. "Out of curiosity, Lady Veldin, is it proper in northern Jotunheim to place your hands on married males?"

Effina's eyes widened in a pitiful show of shock, and Freya hoped Aer was focusing on Lessia's response.

"A-a-apologies, my lady. I—"

"It's Princess, and please don't stutter." Freya barely watched as Effina opened her mouth to respond before shifting her attention to Lessia. "Empress, I do hope you're enjoying yourself?"

Lessia blinked and her smile faltered slightly. "Why yes, Princess, this is one of the loveliest weddings I've been to in some time."

"The empress and I were just talking about the variations in fashion between our nations," Aer said, taking a sip of wine. "Quite a scintillating conversation, really."

Freya smiled at the hint of sarcasm in his words that only she could detect. "Well, I apologize for interrupting, but Jonas just stole Lea away for a dance, so I was hoping I might do the same."

"Anything for you, my love." He gave Lessia and Effina a polite smile. "Empress, Lady Veldin, it was wonderful talking with you. We'll speak again soon."

Lessia smiled politely. "Of course, Your Highness. You two go enjoy yourselves."

Aer curled his fingers through Freya's as they walked off. As they skirted the dance floor, Freya attempted to reason out why Lessia and her cousin would attempt something so brash in such a public place. Nearly everything the empress had done since her arrival went against the cold, calculating female she'd heard so much about. If anything, she seemed quite the opposite. Her attempts to bait, irritate, and belittle Freya this past week had been amateur at best. If Freya hadn't been trained by her parents to question everything, she might think Lessia had lost her touch.

Somehow, she doubted that was the case.

"Gods above," Aer groaned once they were well out of earshot. "What took so long? Jonas went for you ages ago!"

Freya laughed. "I came to you as soon as he told me you were trapped in conversation. It's not my fault if he got lost along the way."

She gave him a disbelieving look. "And please explain how you allowed yourself to get trapped in a discussion about textiles, of all things?"

"*Discussion*," Aer scoffed. Tightening his hand in hers, he led her across the room. "You know, I think they were trying to seduce me!"

"Your deductive skills have improved greatly, I see."

"Shall we escape, then?" He grinned as he tugged her toward the door. "It's nearly three, so I'm sure no one will notice."

Tossing a glance back toward the party, Freya nodded.

"Yes, let's go."

THE CORRIDORS LEADING AWAY from the ballroom to the royal chambers were blessedly quiet, a nice reprieve from the din of the reception. Their guards escorted them back, Rodrick and Perinald ahead, Rissen and Cecilia behind, all keeping a respectful distance as Aer swung Freya into his arms.

Laughing when he swept her off her feet, Freya wrapped her arms around his neck and touched a soft kiss to his jaw, more than happy to let him carry her the rest of the way. Her feet ached from hours of dancing and now she was all too eager to disappear into her chambers and forget about the rest of the world spinning along outside her door.

Her confidence that their wedding night would be fully enjoyable made her anticipation all that more intense. The feelings of apprehension she'd had no longer held the same weight as they once did, having been replaced by excitement. Her heart didn't thrum with nerves as her husband carried her to her room. Instead, it beat with his, eager to be behind closed doors with no one expecting them to emerge any time soon.

When Aer reached her door, he pushed it open and kicked it shut behind them.

Someone, likely Rini and Tyna, had prepared the room for them. The chandelier had been dimmed, sweet-smelling candles were spread about, and a bowl of sandalwood-infused water sat atop the mantel, filling the air with its heady scent. The bedding had been changed from soft wool to smooth, shimmering silk. Gossamer bed curtains were hung and tied to the posts, waiting to wrap them in a cocoon of gold.

With a flick of her wrist, Freya cast a soundproofing enchantment over the room, then toed off the soft slippers Kallan had given her.

Aer set her on her feet, leaving one hand at her waist. Tilting her chin toward his, he kissed her. "For the past few years, I've been wondering how this night would go. Whether you'd want me, whether we'd be happy." Another soft kiss. "What I might do to please you."

"Everything you do pleases me," she whispered.

His lips curved into a slow smile as he ran the back of his finger up her arm. Hooking it into the narrow sleeve that encircled her arm just below her shoulder, he gave a small tug. "Off with this."

Freya brushed her fingers along the short row of buttons that ran from the small of her back to the top of her thighs, instantly releasing them and loosening the gown. Stepping back, she let it puddle at her feet.

Aer's eyes darkened as he took her in. "What happened to those lacy underthings you were so fond of tormenting me with?"

Freya kicked her dress away and stepped toward him, then ran her hands up his chest, gently shoving his vest off his shoulders. "They itched."

"All day, you've had nothing on under your gown?" He slid his hands down to grip her waist, steadying himself as she began to unbutton his shirt. "You should've told me. I would've had you up here much sooner."

Freeing him from his shirt, Freya leaned forward and pressed a kiss to his chest, then dragged her fingers down his stomach to the laces on his pants.

"You needed to focus on our guests," she murmured. A tremble went through him as her fingers grazed the skin beneath his waistband, drawing forward a small, feline smile.

"Remind me to only buy you wretchedly uncomfortable under-garments from now on." He shuddered out a breath, resting his fore-head against hers as she loosened his pants and let them fall to the floor. Kicking them out of the way, he ran his hands across her hair, gently pulling away the pins and threads of gold that Tyna had used to hold it in place. As the rosy waves tumbled free, he smiled softly, his eyes saying more about the depth of his feelings than his touch ever could.

Elation poured over her as he carried her to the bed and gently laid her down atop the silk coverlet, then settled himself beside her.

"I believe," he murmured, sliding a hand across her stomach, "that I owe you something."

"Oh?" She tried to force a lightness into her tone, but the soft touch of his fingers was making her voice unsteady. "And what might that be?"

"A kiss." His lips hovered a breath above hers then quirked into a devious grin as he slowly began to walk his fingers down her torso. "Right... about... *here*."

She gasped, her back arching at his brazen touch. Her mind had hardly caught on to the sudden feelings of pleasure when he with-drew his hand and slowly kissed his way down her body.

"Wait," she said, putting a hand on his head, stopping him when he made to draw her legs over his shoulders.

"What is it?"

She shifted, gently nudging him off of her. Eyes hard on hers, he let her roll him to his back.

Planting her hands on the mattress on either side of his hips, she gave him a slow smile. "Me first."

48

Freya wasn't sure if it was a sound or a feeling that woke her with a start some time later, but something had her sitting up in bed, her hand instantly shifting toward the nightstand where she kept her sharpest dagger. The night was dark, the moon hidden behind a curtain of clouds, so the only light was the dwindling fire Dina had lit in the hearth earlier. Glancing at the clock on her mantel, she saw that dawn was hardly an hour off.

Still drowsy, she waited several tense moments, straining her ears for anything that might've woken her, but all she heard were the soft crackling of embers and the quiet, rhythmic breathing of her husband.

A dream, then, she thought to herself, allowing her body to relax a bit. *Only a dream.*

Glancing down, she watched Aer as he slept beside her, his arms wrapped around the pillow, and the blanket slung low across his hips. Smiling, she brushed her thumb across his full lips, savoring the memory of how they'd felt earlier as he'd run them across her skin.

Laying on her side, she'd just begun to contemplate waking him when she heard a muffled cry followed by a soft *thud*.

She sat up again, this time pulling her dagger from the drawer and quietly slipping out of bed, not wanting to disturb Aer if it was just a servant with a stubbed toe.

Heart pounding, she picked up the first articles of clothing she found that wasn't a gown—a pair of fur-lined leather pants and a red tunic she'd tossed over a chair the previous night—and pulled them on, then tiptoed to the door and cracked it open. The chilly night air hit her, awakening her senses a bit more as she stepped over the threshold. When she saw that the torches that normally lit the corridor had been extinguished, her heart sped up.

Tightening her grip on her dagger, she stepped a bit further into the corridor and squinted in each direction, letting her eyes adjust to the dim light. Warily, she looked toward the darkened mouth of the hallway directly across from her room.

A breeze came through, bringing with it the scent of blood. Her wings flared out behind her as she shifted her gaze to the marble floor beneath the shadowy archway, more visible now that her eyes had adjusted to the dim light.

The lifeless eyes of a Jotunheim guard stared back at her, his body almost completely concealed in shadow. Beside him lay the crumpled forms of her and Aer's guards. As she let her eyes slide upward, she found several more bodies strewn down the corridor. She drew in a breath, inhaling their scents. All bore the scent of Jotnar warlocks.

Frozen in place, her mind warred between stepping forward to help or escaping through the tunnel in her room.

Help, she thought frantically as she slipped a feather from her wing. *You have to help them!*

She'd hardly parted her lips to sound an alarm when there was a commotion at the other end of the hall. Two figures, one tall, slim, and dressed all in black, were striking out at one another. The scream shriveled in her throat as she realized it might not draw the kind of attention she was hoping for.

Get back inside!

She stumbled back a step at the sudden intrusion in her mind, the voice that wasn't hers, then froze when the two figures down the hall ceased their fighting and one slumped to the floor.

There was a noise behind her, then a shooting pain went up her spine as her wings were suddenly forced to retract. Just as she opened her mouth to cry out in pain, a hand clamped over her mouth and pinned her arms to her sides. Her blade fell to the floor, clattering loudly against the stone as she struggled against her captor. She tried to scream against his hand, but no sound would come out. Stretching her canines as long as was possible, she tried to bite down on the hand that was still silencing her, then cursed their too-short reach.

She threw back her head, and a wet crunch, followed by a growl of pain sounded from whoever held her. His arms loosened a fraction, giving her more room to move. Throwing her hand back, she stabbed the feather into his thigh, then readied herself to spring the moment the venom took effect.

Only it didn't. Arms regained their grip and she was pulled back against her assailant's hard chest once again. Aiming for his instep, she lashed out with her foot, remembering too late that she'd neglected to put her boots on before investigating.

She hardly had time to register her idiocy when the male who'd just been fighting appeared in front of her. Florian, his long, curved blade dripping blood on the floor beside him, raised a single finger to his lips, then jerked his chin toward her bedroom door.

She tried again to scream as Florian crossed the hall, not sparing a glance at the slumped bodies on the floor beneath him.

"Shh," Jonas breathed, pulling her tighter against his chest. "I am not going to hurt you, Princess, I swear."

I will not be kidnapped on my wedding night!

Her struggles began anew as Jonas dragged her back into her room.

The sound of her flailing legs caused Aer to startle awake. When he took in the scene before him, he leapt from the bed, pulling a short blade from the bedside table.

"What—"

The words died on his lips when he saw Florian step into the room behind Freya and Jonas, shutting and locking the door behind him. Freya continued to thrash against Jonas, trying again to bite his hands as Aer leapt over the divan toward her.

Florian was on him immediately.

She felt a sharp prick in her arm, and the last thing she saw before her eyes drifted shut was Aer slumping to the floor.

FREYA WAS awoken by the scuff of boot on stone and the low murmur of male voices nearby.

Immediately, everything came rushing back.

Dead bodies in the hall.

Florian working with Jonas.

"Freya, wake up! Wake up, Freya!"

Freya eyes flew open and she bolted upright, then jumped when she felt a hand on her arm.

"It's me," Aer whispered. "I don't think—" His eyes hardened when he looked past her, then he leapt to his feet, pulling her with him.

"Good, you're awake," Byrric said as he strode toward them, followed by Jonas. "Get up, we haven't much time."

Someone had set orbs of light floating in the air, surrounding them with just enough illumination to see that her father's uniform was streaked with blood and there was a fair bit of spatter across his face.

She stared at him, incredulous, her hands clenching into fists as she tried to force away the lingering burn of poison in her veins. "*Good?* That's all you have to say?"

She wouldn't—couldn't—believe that her father had done anything that would truly harm her, but to simply say "Good" after she'd been attacked, poisoned, and dragged from her bedroom in the middle of the night was wildly outside the realm of normal for him.

"Freya—"

"You dosed us with widow venom!" she shouted, her wings flaring out behind her. The shift nearly sent her staggering as the poison finished burning itself out of her system.

"Apologies, Princess, but we had to give you a slightly higher dose than the prince," Jonas said. Not a hint of remorse touched the male's features as he stood next to her father. "Your venom counteracts Florian's poisons quite fast. You should be fine momentarily."

Even as he said the words, the fog began to lift a bit more. Shaking off the last dregs of poison, she let her mind run over the last things she could remember.

"You were drunk," she said to Jonas. She realized it was likely the least-important detail to focus on, but her mind didn't seem to be working quite properly at the moment. "And I stabbed you with a feather. Why aren't you dead?"

"Florian had an antivenin at the ready," he told her. "He, ah, expected you might try something like that. As for my intoxication level... suffice to say I wasn't entirely forthright about how much I had to drink tonight."

"Where have you taken us?" Aer asked. "And why poison us to get us here?"

"Time was of the essence and I ordered Jonas and Florian to get you both to safety by whatever means necessary," Byrric said flatly. "We're in the tunnels beneath your rooms."

Aer chuckled darkly. "Your version of safety and mine seem to differ quite a bit, Commander."

Jonas opened his mouth to add something to the conversation, perhaps defend Byrric, but was cut off when Freya wrapped a hand of magic around his throat, tightening dangerously. He fell back against the wall, his hands scrabbling uselessly against her power. It took all her willpower to hold him there as her body still felt beaten down, but she forced herself to hold steady. She let out a quiet sigh of relief when she felt Aer's power join her own, bolstering her magic.

"We just...needed you to stay...silent!" Jonas rasped, his voice falling into a dreamy murmur under Aer's magic. "She...was about... to scream—"

"Because there were dead bodies in the hall! My guards were out there—"

"Alive," Byrric said calmly, as though she wasn't currently strangling someone just beside him. "I assure you, they are quite alright."

"What dead bodies? What's happened?" Aer demanded, stepping forward, then faltered as he took in the expression on the commander's face. Freya saw it the moment he did—dread, mixed with a small amount of fear.

Byrric exhaled a sharp breath, steeling himself for whatever he was about to say. "Empress Lessia and King Willem have staged a simultaneous coup. The humans and Jotnar joined forces not thirty minutes ago to take over the Lindorothian throne. The governors of all four realms have been killed. Isadora and Reginald Ristner have fled. Soldiers in the Jotunheim and Dystonian armies have overrun the city and begun taking prisoners." He inclined his head toward Jonas. "Lord Edrin has defected."

The words, clipped and matter-of-fact, hung in the air like lead. Each statement fell like stones in water, each one heavier than the last.

Freya felt sick as she reached out and grabbed Aer's hand.

Aer paled as he clung to her hand. "My parents—"

"I took them out through the passageways," Byrric told him. "We couldn't risk escaping together and having all four of you in one spot, not until we were sure no one was following."

There was a beat of silence as Freya and Aer digested the news they'd just been given.

"You can release Jonas now," Byrric said quietly. "We are all on the same side."

Struck dumb, Freya released her hold and leaned back against the wall. Aer did the same.

"What of the governors' families?" *Don't let them be dead,* she begged silently.

"The governors' wives have been taken captive, along with any children who were present when the coup went on. The eldest son of Emric Bryton and the first daughters of Allanor were the only children who remained behind. The other sons and daughters had already left. Ana, as well," he added, anticipating Freya's next question.

"How did this happen?" Freya asked, clinging to the fact that her friends and aunt were alright.

"Lessia and Willem seem to have been colluding with one another for some time now," Byrric replied. "It appears Willem has a strong desire to regain lands that were lost to the humans after the war with Jotunheim. Lessia has agreed to split the Lindorothian lands with him in exchange for his assistance eliminating the Harridan line."

"It's a farce, to be sure," Jonas said. Warily, he stepped away from the wall he'd fallen against, rubbing his eyes as he shook off the remnants of Aer's magic. "If she gives the humans any bit of Lindoroth, it will be the hottest parts of the Edhilian desert and nothing more. As yours was the first royal wedding since our three nations split entirely, I can only assume she saw it as an ideal opportunity to join forces with them. It is only because Lessia hasn't yet suspected my intent to take her throne that we were able to come warn you."

"Taking her— what are you *talking* about?" Freya demanded.

"Explain." Aer's expression hardened as he looked first at Byrric, then Jonas. "Now."

Jonas and Byrric exchanged a quick look. When Byrric gave Jonas a small nod, Jonas took a deep breath and turned to face Freya and Aer.

"Freya, do you recall when I told you about my sister?"

"Yes, of course."

"What I didn't tell you at the time was that the male she'd been married off to was not a Jotnar. Lessia—" He paused, then closed his eyes and exhaled. "Isadora is my sister, Your Highness. Part of the reason I've come to Lindoroth is to find a way to get her back without drawing the suspicion of my aunt or the humans. If they knew what I was attempting to do, I'd be tossed in the dungeons of Madrya and left to rot."

"But she's human," Freya replied dumbly. She chanced a look at Aer, who looked just as stunned as she.

Jonas shook his head. "Ten years ago, after my parents were killed, Lessia contacted Willem's father, Christopher, under the guise of forging a stronger alliance with Dystone. She said she'd gotten word that the elves in the eastern lands had been more active than usual, leaving their shores and visiting other lands, and was concerned they might be planning to attack."

"How would she know that?" Aer asked. "The elves have no contact with anyone outside of Avorell and sending scouts to spy on them is nearly impossible."

"Which is why I should have seen it as a ruse from the start," Jonas replied. "Alas, I did not. Unbeknownst to Christopher, she'd replaced the human Willem had been betrothed to with Isadora, glamouring her appearance to make her identical to the girl she'd replaced—a glamour so thorough she would appear to age just as any human would. When I questioned Lessia, she said she didn't trust the humans, wanted someone on the inside. As Isadora is family, Lessia assumed she could be trusted to do just that." He ran a hand across his jaw and shook his head. "My aunt has always been cunning, so I requested the position of emissary so I could attempt to keep an eye on Isadora during my legitimate visits to Dystone. Isadora and I connected the dots and came to the conclusion that Lessia had no intentions of allying with the humans."

"Lessia wanted to conquer Dystone," Aer murmured.

Jonas shook his head. "When I questioned her on it, she allowed me my misconceptions. I may be her family, but she trusts no one. After speaking with her tonight, it would appear this plan—ally with the humans to take over Lindoroth—had been in the works for some time now."

"That is..." Freya shook her head, unsure of what words fit what she was trying to say. "Absurd."

"My aunt is nothing if not thorough," Jonas replied. "She's had this plan in the works for decades and the human crown was all too willing to see it through."

"You are Lessia's nephew," Aer said quietly, dropping Freya's hand and stepping toward Jonas. "And you expect us to believe you had no knowledge of her true intentions before tonight? Not an *inkling* that she might have been colluding with the humans?"

"Whether you believe me or not is purely up to you," Jonas replied. "All I will tell you is that Lessia and Willem are now in control of Lindoroth and your deaths and those of anyone who share your blood are currently their primary goal."

"So your aunt doesn't know you're a turncoat?" Aer smirked. "Pity for her."

"And lucky for the two of you," Jonas snapped. "At this moment, she believes I and her guards are subduing you both so you can be brought before her and Willem for execution. We have very little time before she finds the trail Florian left behind and comes looking for us."

"Wait." Freya held up a hand. "You said Isadora fled. Why? If she was to be Lessia's spy, if she was to take part in such a complex scheme, why flee when Willem and Lessia attacked? Wouldn't it have been safer for her to stay behind?" Freya asked. That fact was sticking in her mind as something that was illogical for someone who was supposed to be ensuring a thing happened, especially after she went out of her way to seek out Freya's alliance when Lessia was upsetting her in the palace. The thought of the pretty, delicate queen being so thoroughly deceitful that she'd made Freya believe they could be friends was difficult to reconcile with the woman she'd spent the last week with. Something about it simply didn't ring true.

"In short?" Jonas huffed out a sigh. "She and Reginald fell in love."

"Of course they did." Freya rubbed a hand across her forehead, pressing away the last of the throbbing pain left behind by the widow venom.

"Isadora wanted nothing to do with Lessia's scheming, so each time I visited we tried to come up with a way to get her out of the betrothal. It was only after I heard news of your wedding that I thought it might be possible to hide her here. Reginald knew of our plight and had also been suspicious of his brother for some time. He agreed to help me get my sister to safety *and* take Lessia's throne in exchange for helping him overthrow his brother."

"He knew Willem and Lessia were conspiring?" Aer asked.

Jonas shook his head. "He had good reason to think Lessia had enthralled Willem and was attempting to take Dystone."

Aer held up his hand. "Just so we're clear, Reginald Ristner wants to take his brother's throne *and* his wife, but in order to do so he must help *you* overthrow Lessia, yet in all of your scheming you missed the fact that Dystone and Jotunheim were colluding to *take over my country?* How—" He shook his head as words seemed to fail him.

"Why should we believe you?" Freya asked quietly. "The fact that you've allowed yourself to become so ensnared in this web of deceit makes me more than a little hesitant to trust what you have to say. As Lessia's nephew, why wouldn't she have told you her plans?"

"She trusts me only enough to gather reports from Isadora, all of which are mostly fabricated. It would be another decade at least before I gained a seat at her table."

"I will vouch for Lord Edrin's loyalty," Byrric said.

"Because you're all in on this together," Aer said flatly, not bothering to hide his disdain.

"Not as thoroughly as you might think, but we'll discuss the rest soon enough," Byrric said sharply. "For now, we must get you both as far from Iladel as possible."

"What of Isadora?" Freya asked. "You don't seem to think she's betrayed you, but do you know where she's gone?"

"We believe Reginald managed to get her to safety, although we won't know for sure until we rendezvous," Byrric replied.

"Which will be where?" Aer asked.

"There's a place deeper in the tunnel system, farther into the mountain, that the first king of Lindoroth designed as a safe room, of sorts. A very small group of the palace guard know its exact location."

"King Eroan built this palace five thousand years ago," Freya said. "How secure could it possibly be?"

"Those who are told of its location are forbidden to speak of it,"

Byrric said. "I can tell you only that it exists, but I cannot tell you where. Those who are taken there and leave have no memory of their path to or from."

Freya dropped her head to her hands, then leaned gratefully against Aer when he squeezed her shoulder. Her mind spun as disbelief and fear began to well up inside her, so much so that she felt her brain begin to fuzz over.

Byrric cleared his throat. "We need to go, so if it's all the same to you both, I will answer the rest of your questions along the way."

Freya and Aer looked at each other, and the fear and concern that swirled within her was clearly visible in his eyes.

Her prince placed a hand over her heart. "It will all be okay," he whispered.

She nodded, then looked at her father.

"Lead the way, Commander."

The four of them started forward, Byrric leading the way while Jonas brought up the rear. They walked in silence for a few moments, Byrric navigating them rapidly down one tunnel, then the next. Freya tried to focus on other things, on the fact that she and Aer were safe, that her family and friends were alive, but it was fruitless. She'd sworn to do right by Lindoroth, to be a strong queen who would protect her land and its people at any cost. She'd hardly been crowned princess for a night and already her life, her future, and her kingdom were threatened. All of the training she'd done with Byrric, Cina, and Ana, all the work she'd done with the marshals and the other students at Aldridge, suddenly seemed like child's play in comparison to what they were facing now.

49

As they walked through the darkened tunnels, Freya did all she could to keep her fear at bay, hating how thoroughly it was beginning to suffocate her.

Fear is healthy, she told herself over and over. *It will keep you alive. We just need to regroup. Assess the damage and come up with a plan.*

But despite knowing the logic behind those thoughts, she couldn't help but feel as though she was failing some test she didn't know she'd been given.

Sensing her distress, Aer slid his arm around her shoulders and touched a kiss to her hair.

"Stop that," he murmured. "I see that look on your face, Valkyrie. You've done nothing wrong."

"He's right, Freya," Jonas said from behind him. "You were hardly born when this plan began to unfold. Lessia waited until the revelers were nearly all intoxicated to the point of inebriation, about two hours after you both departed, and the guard was overwhelmed within moments. Nothing you could've done would've changed the outcome. That you'd already left is the reason you're both still alive."

"I taught you better than that, Freya," Byrric added, not slowing his pace or even turning to look at her. "The smartest thing you could've done had you stayed at the party was flee."

"Is that what you did?" Her words came out more accusing than she intended, but she found it hard to believe that the king's commander would've fled a fight in his own castle.

"Yes," he said without an ounce of shame. "We were overwhelmed, Freya. My duty is to this land, as you well know. Keeping its leaders safe and alive is my top priority and remaining to fight a battle that my soldiers and I would not have won was not an option."

While she couldn't ignore his reasoning, Freya still struggled to reconcile the male before her, the one who'd raised her with a blade in her hand with the one who hadn't stayed behind to fight for the safety of those who remained in the palace. She looked for another way, something she might've done differently had she been in his shoes, but no alternate solution came. She let that thought soothe her a bit, allowed it to make her feel a bit better about leaving now.

Byrric led them around a few more turns before the tunnel began shifting downhill. Several more minutes slipped past in silence before they came to a dead end. Byrric touched a spot in the center-right of the wall before him and pushed. A moment later, the wall swung inward, revealing a gaping hole. Freya could just barely make out a lichen-covered wall on the other side.

Byrric waited until they were all through before closing the door and leading them toward a fork in the path.

"Wait." Freya paused as the scent of nitre and dirt reached her. "This is the garden tunnel. How—?"

"I believe you two may have missed a few doors in your meanderings," Byrric said dryly.

"So it would seem," she murmured, sliding a look to Aer. They hurried after Byrric as he strode briskly down the tunnel, then down the path they hadn't explored on their previous trip through, the one that smelled like iron and rot. Freya wrinkled her nose against the assault as she was overcome with a sudden desire to flee to the gardens and suck in precious breaths of fresh air.

The cave walls and floor grew slicker and the smell more putrid as they walked. She began to hope her father had a better plan than having them hide out in a sodden underground passage until their enemies were dealt with.

The mixture of fear, anger, and annoyance that had been percolating within her since the appearance of Florian and Jonas began to boil over the further they walked. The space was becoming smaller, more narrow, forcing Aer to release her hand and walk in front of her instead of beside, his head ducked to avoid knocking against the slick stone ceiling. Byrric's stiff uniform scratched softly against the walls as his broad shoulders took up almost the width of the passage. Lifting her hands, she let her fingers drift on the stone as she walked, feeling the distance, reassuring herself that she still had room to move.

She could hear Jonas' ragged breaths behind her, so she could only assume he was struggling with the close quarters as well.

"There's a thing I do, Jonas, when I begin to feel cooped up. Would you like to see?"

"Yes, I believe I would," he said shakily. "I've never been one for tight spaces."

"Nor have I," she replied. She reached up and gently brushed her fingertips against the roof of the passage that was now hardly a foot overhead. She pushed her magic against it, using more force than she normally would now that they were deep within the mountain, until the stone seemed to dissolve and only the lavender, pre-dawn sky stretched overhead.

Byrric gave a startled grunt while Aer reached back and brushed her hand gently with his. Jonas let out a quiet breath of relief, one she was sure he intended to conceal.

"Not much further," Byrric grumbled. "There's a chamber just up ahead."

Moments later, Freya heard the murmur of voices. An opening appeared in the corridor ahead, and a space, faintly illuminated with flickering light, lay beyond.

When they stepped through the archway into a wide cavern,

Freya instantly scanned the faces in the room, needing to see for herself who'd gotten out.

There were about thirty people by her estimate. Laz and Collin were sitting against the wall leaning against one another, hands clasped between them. Their eyes, filled with devastation, stared blankly ahead. Lea and Myria sat nearby, tears flowing silently down their cheeks as Lea held Myria in her arms. Isadora sat beside them, her pretty pink dress mussed with dirt and blood, her hair hanging limply at her shoulders. Reginald stood sentry above them, arms folded tensely as he surveyed the room. Ervic, Rissen, Cecilia, Rodrick, and Perinald hovered about with a dozen other palace guards. Her and Aer's guards still looked a bit worse for wear after being attacked in the hall, but they were alive, which was all that mattered. About two dozen others were also present, but Freya couldn't tear her eyes from the small cluster of people at the back of the room.

Ordona, her back to the door, stood beside Florian and Ana, who were crouched over a still, blanket-covered form.

"No," Aer breathed, his hand tightening in hers.

Byrric strode past them, so they followed him as he made his way across the room toward the queen.

When Ordona saw Aer, she let out a sigh of relief. "Thank the gods," she murmured, her eyes instantly welling with tears as she reached for him. Stepping back, Freya looked to her father, then down at Salazar's still face, his body covered by his mantle.

"What happened?" Byrric demanded. "He was fine when I left!"

Aer turned accusing eyes on Byrric. "You said they were safe!"

"A delayed reaction to something in his food," Freya's aunt said quietly, standing to face them. "Based on his symptoms and the rapid way in which he is... deteriorating, my guess would be ore powder." Ana's wide, sad eyes looked at Ordona, then back at Aer. "I'm sorry, but there's nothing I can do, other than make him comfortable."

Freya frowned and shook her head. "Can't Florian—"

"I've exhausted all of my remedies," Florian said quietly, then looked at Ordona who was staring, devastated, at her husband. "And we've both used up nearly all of our magic attempting to heal him."

"If we'd known sooner..." Ordona said, her voice quavering with grief. "It's possible, but we didn't notice anything was wrong until we reached the caves."

"Could I try?" Freya asked. "Perhaps there's something—"

Ana shook her head. "If it were a magical malady, I would say yes, but Freya, we all know the damage ore powder causes."

Yes, Freya thought. *We certainly do.*

"How—how long?" Aer rasped, his jaw tight and rigid.

Ana sent Byrric a look, then looked at the prince, her eyes full of pity. "Not very," she replied. Another look toward Byrric, then to Florian, before she returned her attention to the prince and queen. "Your Highness, Your Majesty, I would recommend saying your farewells."

Ordona's face crumbled under the weight of Ana's words as she reached out for her son. Freya released his hand, brushing her own down his arm as he stepped forward to be with his mother. She felt her father come to a stop beside her, hovering silently as a heavy lump formed in her throat.

The queen and prince knelt beside Salazar, Aer at his side, Ordona at his head.

Aer rested a hand on his father's slowly rising chest. "Father? Can you hear me?"

Freya closed her eyes, forcing back tears when she heard Ordona's muffled sob.

Salazar's dark, cloudy eyes drifted open slightly. He stared up at the ceiling blankly for a moment before he looked to his son. No words came, but his eyes, full of a fatherly love Freya had only rarely seen, took him in. His fingers fluttered against his stomach, stilling once he touched his other hand, where the heavy golden ring set with a single, large ruby encircled his thumb. He gave it a small tap, then blinked.

Tap tap tap.

Blink.

"You have to take it, Your Highness," Florian said.

Aer sent him a shocked look. "My father—"

"Is the king and he is dying," Florian said. "Lindoroth cannot be without a king, even for a moment. You must take his ring."

Freya opened her mouth to defend Aer, but Byrric clamped a hand down on her shoulder, silencing her. "I am truly sorry, Your Highness, but Andreus is right." He inclined his head toward where Salazar was still tapping his thumb. "It's time."

Aer looked to Freya, then his mother, who pulled him into an embrace.

"I'm so sorry, darling," Ordona said, her voice thick with unshed tears. "This is not how I intended things to be."

Aer stared dazedly down at his father. Salazar gave a nod so small it was no more than a twitch of his chin, but his hand stilled when Aer reached out and slid the ring from his finger.

"I will serve your memory well," Aer whispered, his fingers curling around it as Salazar's eyes drifted shut. "I will be the king you raised me to be."

Ordona rested her golden hands against Salazar's cheeks as she pressed her forehead to his, weeping.

"We've only moments, Your Highness," Florian murmured. "His heartbeat slows."

When he made no move to rise, Freya knelt down beside Aer and covered her hand with his. A shudder ran through his body, emotion that he refused to make visible to everyone who was looking on. Salazar's breathing became more labored and shallow.

Aer's eyes were wide with shock when he looked at her. "Can we do this, Freya?"

"Without question." Her own heart was thundering as the gravity of the situation slowly sank in, but she shoved back her own fears. She'd deal with herself later. Right now, this was about him. "Stand with me?"

He gave a short nod, then let her take his hand. When they stood, she cupped his face in her hands and stared into his eyes. "We can do this, Aer. *You* can do this."

"Aerelius, please," Ordona whispered, slipping off her own ring and pressing it into his hand along with Salazar's. "Now is not the time to doubt yourself."

He exhaled a heavy breath, then nodded.

As one, he and Freya turned to Florian, who stood beside Byrric.

Raising his voice, Florian addressed everyone in the room. "I will need all witnesses to come forth for the transference of power to Prince Aerelius and Princess Freya!"

Freya thought she might be sick.

Numbly, she watched as the others in the cavern began to come forward, surprised murmurs rippling throughout the room. Once everyone had settled into a circle around them, Florian spoke to Aer and Freya.

"I will transfer the king's power to you, and from you to your bride," he told Aer, slipping a thin dagger from his sheath. "Commander Balthana and I will then pledge our service to you both." He inclined his head toward their hands. "Your hands, please?"

Together, Freya and Aer held out their hands, palms up. Quickly, Florian scored the flesh of Aer's palm, then Freya's. Then, holding Aer's hand in place, he closed his eyes. His lips gave a small twitch, then magic, pure and white, began to flow from Salazar's failing body upward to swirl around the pair of them, hovering expectantly.

"Take her hand, Your Highness, and allow your blood to mix."

Aer's eyes were unfathomable as he wrapped his hand around hers, pressing their palms together just as they had done the night before.

Freya felt the kick of power immediately as it speared through Aer and straight into her. It swirled within her, touching her own magic like an old friend, twining around each other as though they'd been waiting for this day for some time.

The magic began to swirl faster, forming a cyclone around their bodies, the light nearly blinding as Florian spoke again.

"On this day, I Andreus of House Florian, Master Warlock and Spymaster of House Harridan, declare this male and this female the king and queen of Lindoroth, bound by the magic of their prede-cessors."

Freya's eyes widened, and she sent a shocked look at Aer, but he didn't seem at all surprised to hear Florian's true titles.

With a final burst of light, the power that had come from Salazar finished binding its new king and queen to the land.

"I present you with your king and queen, his majesty Aerelius Harridan and her majesty Freya Harridan. Long may they reign."

And then, the answering call.

"Long may they reign."

The words had hardly been spoken when Salazar's heart gave one last heavy beat, then went silent forever.

50

F reya and Aer hardly had time to squeeze each other's hands in a show of support before Byrric started barking orders. Ana and Florian covered Salazar's body, then Florian and Ordona magicked him away, hiding him somewhere no one would find him until his family could return and properly put him to rest in the palace catacombs. The rest of the occupants of the cave were quiet, most still a bit dazed, but all at attention as Byrric told everyone what their next steps were.

Still reeling from the new magic that was settling itself inside her, Freya listened as her father handed out assignments, sending individuals and small groups here and there across Lindoroth to spread the news of what had happened and to gather forces.

She knew she should be doing something, anything, that was more... *queenly* than waiting for her father, but all she could do was stand beside Aer as they, Byrric, and Ordona pored over a map of Lindoroth to determine where best to send people. As they had no idea how far Lessia and Willem's people had gotten into Lindoroth, they were running on the assumption that infiltrators could be anywhere, meaning small groups were the safest way to travel.

The plan so far was for Freya and Aer, along with a handful of others, to head west, aiming for Iston, where the rest of the Valkyrie would be waiting for her. Jonas, Isadora, and Reginald would travel with them part of the way before splitting off to find those groups of Jotnar who lived along the border between lands and wanted to live as far from Lessia's rule as possible but had no way of ensuring their own safety if they continued south. Ervic, the former king's most trusted guard, was assigned to spirit Ordona as far from Iladel as they could get. Not a word was spoken about where that might be.

Once all orders had been delivered and everyone began gathering supplies from the stockpile the cavern seemed to be filled with, Byrric handed her and Aer two heavily-laden rucksacks.

"You'll go on foot," he told them. "Ana has been ensuring allegiances in Iston and the nearby regions, so you'll be welcome there."

Aer jerked the bag from Byrric's hand. "How long have you known this might happen?"

"This?" Byrric shook his head. "We had no indication *this* would happen."

"We heard you colluding with Reginald," Freya said flatly, sending a look at the man who stood nearby.

"You heard a man justifiably concerned about a relationship forming between Willem and Lessia. He thought she was planning an attack on Dystone and brought his concerns to us. We agreed to assess the situation with Willem when he arrived, determine if he seemed to be under any type of thrall, which he didn't. In the interim, though, I sent out feelers to determine who else we might be able to call on, should the need arise."

Aer ground his teeth together as pure fury lit his eyes as he looked at both Byrric and his mother. "And yet you all saw fit to bring them here, gather them in one place? Regardless of Reginald's concerns—"

"Rescinding invitations to a royal wedding was not an option," Ordona told him wearily. "If Lessia didn't already plan to attack, a slight like that might have spurred her on."

"Florian will be going with you," Byrric interjected, no longer willing to debate. "Everyone in your party will need to be glamoured," he said, seeing the question on Freya's lips at hearing Florian's name. "You'll exhaust yourself within a week if you do it on your own, and his other skill sets will prove useful along the way, as well."

"Florian, the royal spymaster who somehow missed an impending coup?" Freya couldn't help the bitterness in her voice.

"Our concern at the time was Lessia's intentions with Dystone," Byrric said sharply. "By all accounts she's had her eye on the human lands for decades. Any plotting Willem and Lessia did was done long before we began watching." He sent her a level stare. "Don't question his methods, Freya. It won't get you anywhere."

As the rest of their party—Lea, Laz, Collin, and Myria, along with Reginald, Jonas, Isadora, Florian, and a handful of guards—joined them, Freya and Aer took a few moments to inspect their packs and converse in private.

Stepping away from the rest of the group, Freya gripped his hands.

"Are you alright?" She knew how stupid the question sounded, considering, but the queen's ring felt as though it weighed a hundred pounds on her thumb, so she could only imagine how much harder it was for him.

"No," he said, exhaling a heavy breath. "I'm not. But neither of us can take the time to dwell on that now."

Wrapping her arms around his neck, she drew him in for a hug. His arms tightened around her waist as he buried his face in her shoulder. For a few moments, they stood there as he got his emotions in hand and she tried to push aside all that was gnawing at her to make herself strong for everyone around her.

Her subjects. They really and truly were her subjects now.

When she turned back to face her friends, she saw Lea looking toward the entrance to the cavern. She'd changed her clothes and was now wearing a pair of black pants and a fitted black shirt with a sheath at her hip. She wore a hard look of determination.

"Lea, what is it?" Freya asked, glancing fearfully toward the exit.

Eyes hard, Lea faced her. "I'm going to stay."

"What?" Freya shook her head. "No, Lea, they'll kill you!"

"Absolutely not!" Aer said firmly.

"Hear her out," Ordona said calmly. The look she wore was similar to that of her niece.

Aer sent his mother a disbelieving look. "Mother, you can't— "

"They killed our fathers, Aerelius!" Lea shouted, tears filling her wide, dark eyes. "How can you ask us all to just *flee?*"

"It's the best option if we all want to live," Freya said calmly. "You know this."

"No." Lea straightened her shoulders. "I won't leave my mother here and you both know *someone* needs to remain behind." She sent beseeching eyes at Byrric, who stood not far behind Freya. "Commander, you know that I'm right."

"What's going on?" Jonas asked, coming up beside them.

Jaw tight, Byrric stared at Lea, then glanced at Jonas before finally looking at Aer and Freya.

"It's a good plan." He held up a hand before Freya and Aer could argue. "*Not* alone, though."

Lea frowned, then her faced relaxed when she saw Byrric looked toward Jonas again.

"Thank you." She nodded and sniffed, wiping the dampness of tears from her cheeks. "Yes, yes, that will work perfectly."

Aer caught on a moment before Freya. "You want her to stay behind as his *prisoner?* No. I won't allow it."

Lea looked as though she might spit.

"At the risk of getting stabbed again," Jonas began, eyeing them warily, "might I offer my opinion?" When Freya and Aer didn't respond, he nodded. "If my aunt believes I have not turned against her, I and, by proxy, Lea will be at an advantageous position in the middle of court."

Ordona put a hand on Aer's arm. "Darling, he isn't wrong. Believe me, I don't want to agree with them, but as neither of us can stay behind in such a beneficial position, it is the best option."

"How do you plan to keep her from getting tossed in the dungeons?" Aer asked, arms folded.

Jonas sent a quick look to Lea. "So long as Lessia believes I am on her side, I will be able to ensure Lea is not treated poorly in any way."

Lea's jaw tightened but she raised her chin in a show of confidence. "He can request that he be allowed to claim me as spoils of war." She lifted a brow. "Correct?"

He nodded tersely, seeming to be just as uncomfortable with the thought as she.

Freya's stomach roiled at the thought of what that might mean, what Lea would be expected to do.

"No." She shook her head. "Even if we could trust Jonas, what of the other Jotnar and humans who may try to take advantage?"

"I won't let that happen," Jonas said firmly. "I promise no harm will come to her."

"We cannot overrule your decisions," Byrric said, "but it would behoove you to reconsider."

Though she didn't want to admit it, Freya saw—and hated—the logic behind their plan, despite how hastily it had formed.

Aer looked down at Freya, and she saw the same conclusions in his eyes that she'd just come to. It was a simple plan and, if executed properly, could put Lea in a place where she could easily act as spy.

"I will keep her safe," Jonas said quietly. "I'll swear it, if you need me to."

"You say that as though you have another option," Aer said dryly, holding out his hand as Byrric gestured for Freya's blade.

Quickly and efficiently, Freya scored Aer and Jonas' palms, then recited the incantation that bound Jonas' loyalty to any who carried the same blood as Aerelius.

When it was done, she slid her dagger back into her sheath and turned to Lea.

"Are you sure about this?" She took her friend's hands. "This is utterly insane."

Lea took a deep breath and nodded. "We all have our roles to play, Freya. Let me do what I can to hold onto our family's throne until you return."

There was a loud *thump* some distance away, causing everyone in the room to go silent. She and Lea only had time to exchange a single, wide-eyed look before the lights winked out around them. Her eyes adjusted to the darkness almost immediately, but she could hardly make out more than the shapes of those around her.

Another thump, this time a bit closer.

"I'll take care of her, Your Majesties," Jonas said quietly, his voice suddenly closer than it had been a moment before. "Upon pain of death, you have my word."

"Come," Byrric said. "The way out is back here."

They only had time to exchange a quick embrace with Lea before Byrric had a hand on Freya's and Aerelius' backs and was leading them toward the back of the room.

The rustle of movement around her, of others gathering up the supplies they'd been given, increased as they all began to follow Byrric toward the back of the cavern. Freya had assumed it was a dead end, a solid rock wall with no means of exit or entry, but when Byrric took her wrist and pulled her to the side, she realized there was an opening hidden behind an overhang.

"Follow this all the way through to the forest floor," he told them. "It will let you out a good way into the mountains. From there, go west until you hit the Northern Road. Stay to the forest but follow the road until you reach Watoria. I've already sent word to the marshals that you'll be coming. Convene with them, then head to Iston."

"The marshals?" Aer asked.

"Allies to the crown are everywhere, Your Majesty," Byrric replied. "Even in the lands furthest from it." He stopped when the tunnel widened, then stepped to the side. "This is where I leave you."

"Where will you go?" A lump began to form in Freya's throat, and she was hit with a sudden urge to throw her arms around him and beg him to stay with her, to lead their group to wherever it was he wanted them to go.

"I'm going to check on the status of the individual realms." He pushed on a section of wall, and suddenly, the passage was filled with light. "If humans or Jotnar have taken over the governing houses, we need to take them back."

Freya squinted against the sudden light that filled the tunnel. Shadows still hung over the forest, but the sun was just beginning to touch the tops of the trees. A path, narrow and crumbling, wound down from where they stood, descending deeper into the dense pine.

She wanted to cry, but she wouldn't. Her heart ached at the thought of leaving her father behind. It was too soon, she thought. Too soon to put this on their shoulders.

Too soon...

Aer's hand slipped into hers and gave her a reassuring squeeze.

"How will we know if you've found anything?" he asked Byrric.

"I'll come to you soon," Byrric replied. He looked to Freya, his face hard. "I know this is not how you expected your reign to begin, but there's nothing we can do to change that now."

She took a deep breath, exhaling slowly, gathering herself.

No, this was not how her reign was supposed to begin. It was supposed to start with a lovely wedding followed by several months of travel around Lindoroth and a good deal of lovemaking in the interim.

And yet, here they were.

She gave her father a tight smile. "I know. We'll do all you've tasked us with."

He looked beside them at Ordona. "Ervic will take you to safety. We'll send word when it's time to return."

Head high, the former Queen nodded, her eyes brimming with tears. She looked at Aer, her only son, and opened her arms.

Freya turned away as they said their goodbyes, seeing it was a moment they needed to take together without anyone else interfering.

Byrric's jaw clenched, and the way he looked at Freya, as though she was a complete stranger standing before him, unnerved her.

He stepped forward and pulled her into his arms, wrapping her in a tight embrace. "Don't you dare give them the chance to shatter the person you've become, Freya," he whispered fiercely. Shifting back, he gripped her biceps and looked into her eyes, his expression hard. "You've grown into one of the strongest people I know and you cannot let this define you or your monarchy. Go, and when you come back, come back with a vengeance. Do you hear me?"

She nodded, shocked at her father's display of affection.

He's scared, too, she realized. *Big, strong, Byrric Balthana is afraid.*

Stepping back, he looked at Aer, whose eyes were red-rimmed and distraught, then her.

"Take care of one another. We'll see each other soon." He touched a hand to her cheek, then flared out his wings and took to the air. She watched as he aimed downward, tucking his wings tight as he disappeared into the trees.

Ervic stepped up beside Ordona and touched a hand to her arm. "Your Majesty? We must go."

Sniffing, Ordona nodded, then gave her son one last hard embrace before straightening her gown and nodding. "Lead on, sir."

Wordlessly, Ervic gestured toward her neck. Lifting her hair up, she allowed him to fasten on a thin golden chain with a large ruby that settled into the hollow at her throat.

"What—is that a transformation pendant?" Freya sent a frantic look at Aer.

"It's the only way, Your Majesty," Ervic said. "It will allow her to shift with me and we'll be able to travel more quickly."

"Who created it?" she demanded. Transformation pendants—objects that allowed shifters to transform non-shifters for certain periods of time, were rare and, if not created properly, incredibly dangerous.

"Your mother," Ordona said quietly. "Not long before she died, she gave it to me as a gift. Sal—" Her words stuck in her throat. "Salazar had one, as well."

Tears threatened to fall once more as Freya laid eyes on what had likely been the last talisman her mother had made before she was killed.

"It's alright," Aer whispered, kissing her temple. "Cina's charms were flawless, you know that."

Freya nodded numbly, then looked to Ervic. "That won't last more than a day before it will need to be replenished, so stop each night. Find a cave, something that will provide you enough cover." She looked at Ordona. "Cina showed you how to use it?"

Ordona nodded. "Yes, I know the spell." She placed a hand on Freya's arm. "Try not to worry, dear. Focus on your part, and Ervic and I will focus on ours."

With one last long embrace with her son, Ordona turned to Ervic. "I'm ready."

Wordlessly, the knight lifted Ordona into his arms. There was a flash as Ervic shifted into a giant seahawk, the only sign of Ordona a single red feather at his neck that was the same shade as the ruby she wore. Within seconds, they were gone.

Aer took her hand, then pulled her against his chest, seeming to need the contact just as much as she did. "We'll get through this, Freya."

Finally, and for just a few moments, she allowed herself to cry. She let tears slide down her cheeks and onto his shirt, hidden from all those who stood around them.

All she could spare was a few seconds, though, so she pulled back and wiped her eyes of tears, then exchanged a quick look with Aer before turning to face everyone else. All were at attention behind them, all the palace guards, their friends, Florian, Ana, and a handful she hardly knew.

"You've all received your orders," Aer said. "So we won't add to that burden. Just remember that, although we'll be traveling different paths in the coming days and weeks, our goal is the same. Travel safe and travel quick, as the fate of Lindoroth now hangs with us."

Freya slid her hand in his and squeezed. He looked down at her, his face still grief-stricken, but the strength his father's power had lent him added a sureness to his expression, a confidence in his role.

"We've got this," she whispered to him.

With a nod, he kissed her lightly on the forehead. "Yes, we do."

To get the latest updates, deals, and other goodies, subscribe to Lucy's newsletter here!

Continue reading for a preview of *The Valkyrie's Calling*, book 2 of the *Half-Blood Rising trilogy*...

LEA

There was a time in Lea Calliwell's life when she would've sworn to do anything for her family. It had always been easy to say she would lie for them if it meant keeping them safe, debase herself or die for them, even, because that's what family does.

Now, as she stared up at Lessia Edrin and Willem Ristner, the two royals who'd so swiftly usurped the thrones of Lindoroth, her hand clinging tightly to Jonas,' she couldn't help but wonder if that sentiment had been a bit too broad, a bit too naïve in thinking.

Lessia's elbow rested on the arm of the throne she was perched upon—Ordona's throne—as she eyed Lea and Jonas. The knights who were scattered about the room sat silent as they waited for her to speak. Finally, she tapped a long, pale finger on her chin and pursed her lips.

"Alright, Jonas. Let's say I buy this," she gestured toward Lea, "and allow her to live. Let's say I buy that you two are now... lovers. How are we to believe she won't turn on us at the first chance? This was her uncle's palace, after all. We *are* responsible for the deaths of a good number of her family members." She arched a perfect brow at Lea. "Including her father."

Lea swallowed but held her chin high as she met Lessia's piercing stare. "A cruel man, Empress. The main reason I insisted upon attending Aldridge was to get away from my home in Edhil." The words were like ash on her tongue, thick and bitter as she forced them past her lips. She set her mouth in a thin line and took a deep breath. "I can assure you, when Lord Edrin informed me of his death, I was not disappointed."

The corners of Lessia's perfectly red mouth twitched. "Interesting."

"And quite convenient," Willem drawled. "The cousin of the *former* prince of Lindoroth is happy with the outcome of tonight's events?"

Jaw tight, Lea shifted her gaze to the human king who'd taken up residence on Salazar Harridan's throne and made herself the picture of disdain. "I did not say I was *happy,* Your Majesty. My uncle was quite beloved, as is my aunt, and I love my mother dearly." She squeezed Jonas' hand and smiled up at him before looking back at Lessia. "But Lord Edrin has shown me a different side of the Jotnar people in recent weeks. He's told me things about your lands, Empress, that go against everything I've ever been told."

"And what *have* you been told, dear?" Lessia asked, leaning forward. Her eyes danced, as though this were a game and she was waiting for Lea to step into some trap.

"That you are a cruel and unforgiving people. That your rule is one of fear, not respect, and you only managed to stay in power after your husband died because you killed all who attempted to oppose you." Lea looked around the room at the dozens of Jotnar and human knights that milled about. "Yet your people are happy, according to Lord Edrin. I wouldn't expect that to be the case if people were living in fear of their ruler all the time."

"And this..." Lessia inclined her head toward their conjoined hands. "Why wasn't I informed of this sooner, Jonas? You seemed quite happy at the wedding, certainly, yet this is the first I'm hearing of any type of relationship?"

"It didn't seem pertinent," he replied. "You've never required me to report what I did during my spare time on previous trips and I saw no need."

"Even though this girl was so clearly unhappy here?" Willem asked. "It would've been nice to know of a potential ally before this."

"Had I known what you both intended, perhaps I would've seen a better use for this relationship," Jonas said through gritted teeth. "As it stands, she and I both think she could go a long way in solidifying your new rule, at least in the southern realm."

"I'm surprised you even took up with her in the first place," Willem commented. "The palace staff haven't been enough for you?"

Jonas sent the human king a bland look. "Do I strike you as the type to be amused by servants, human?"

Willem's face purpled, then his furious glare shifted to Lea. Something in his eyes nearly had Lea scrambling to hide behind Jonas, but she forced herself to meet them.

"Well, as tempting as this idea is, you'll have to wait," Willem told Jonas. His gaze dragged across Lea's body. "We have more important things to address, and I think there are a few here who might also like to make a case for her."

Lea froze, and Jonas' hand tensed in hers.

The look of pure disgust Jonas threw at Willem made it quite clear what he thought of the human king. "I don't recall asking your permission. What's mine is certainly not yours."

"You are not in charge here," Willem said calmly.

Jonas bared his teeth in a grin so cruel and so unlike the male she'd gotten to know, that Lea would've feared for the king if she wasn't so eager for his demise.

"Unfortunately, nephew, Willem is correct," Lessia said tiredly when Jonas took a menacing step forward. "I've had no sleep, and as it's now dawn, I won't discuss divvying spoils until I've had a few hours rest."

"I haven't asked to claim her as spoils," Jonas said evenly. "She is not my belonging. I've brought her to you as a potential ally."

"Indeed," Lessia said with a nod. "And while your stories are quite convincing, I'm not quite ready to allow the niece of Salazar Harridan loose in my palace without proper consideration first."

Lea forced back tears as she realized just how bad a turn this had taken.

"Yes, how are we to know she hasn't simply whored herself out to you in order to get a foot into our court?" Willem added, his gaze not leaving Lea. "You may not be the best judge of character in this instance. Someone else may need to bring her in hand, first."

"She will remain with me," Jonas growled. "If you so much as touch her—"

Lessia made a sound of disgust. "Enough. You can sort that all out later." She tilted her head in a small, predatory motion as she eyed Lea. "Not to worry, sweet thing. I find your story to be...tempting, and until Jonas' request has been granted or denied, you'll be kept perfectly safe."

Before Lea had a chance to look at Jonas for any measure of comfort, Lessia flicked a slender hand toward one of her guards. He was half-draug, by the looks of it, and smelled of death, with yellow teeth that flashed behind his bile-brown lips. Gnarled hands gripped her curly hair at the roots as he jerked her toward the door.

"Jonas!" she screamed. "Stop them!"

"Walk, witch!" the guard snapped.

"Lessia, this is unnecessary!" Jonas shouted. "Where are you taking her?"

With a scream, Lea rounded on the guard who'd grabbed her, shoved him to the floor, and ran toward the exit, knowing it was useless but needing to try all the same.

This had gone wrong, so horribly wrong.

She made it nearly halfway to the door before she was tackled to the ground by two human knights. When she lashed out with her magic, calling forward the thorny stems of the roses that still decorated the room to aid her, one of the knights slammed her head to the ground and set her world spinning. Jonas gave a shout, and the next moment, a powdery substance hit her face and everything went black.

~

WHEN SHE STARTED to come to, the gray-blue light of evening filtered through her eyelids, drawing her out of the fogginess of her mind.

A hissing sound brought her forward a little more. It was a bit like a cat, only not.

"Grevillea!"

No. Not a sound, a voice.

Her mother's voice.

Lea's eyes flew open, and her eyelids slammed shut at the sudden onslaught of light. Her body screamed in protest as she tried to shift her position on the damp and dirty dungeon floor, and her head swam with each movement.

Perida Calliwell let out a relieved breath when Lea stirred.

Lea carefully pulled herself into a sitting position and leaned back against the wall, pressing a hand to her forehead. "How…"

"They brought you in just past dawn," Perida said quietly. "It's nearly nightfall."

Lea drew her legs up to her chest and rested her forehead on her knees as she tried to find her equilibrium. Whatever they'd tossed in her face before bringing her here was making it impossible for her to focus.

"What did they give me?" she murmured. "I can't feel my magic."

"Powdered widow venom, most likely. It's being put in our food."

Several moments of silence passed as her mother waited for Lea to speak. When Lea finally turned to look at her mother in the cell across the way, Perida, who'd been thrown in the dungeons much the same way she had, only a few hours before her, looked as though she'd been there for months. Her soft, dark hair was a knotted mess, and her pretty golden skin and ice-blue gown were caked with blood. And, though her body seemed unbroken, the hollow-eyed look she wore told Lea her spirit was anything but intact.

Lea could only assume the blood was her father's, but that wasn't a truth she was willing to face just yet. No, she would tuck that away until she was in the proper setting for screaming out her grief. She would save that anger and sadness, bottle it up tight, and let it out the moment she had the chance on those who truly deserved it. Not now. Not when she couldn't properly grieve that loss, not when she couldn't watch her father be put to rest. As it was, whatever they'd used to knock her unconscious was making it hard enough to grab hold of the fact that her father was dead, that she'd never see him, nor her uncle, again. Dwelling on the wretched things so far outside her control would only make things worse.

"Where did they catch you?" Perida asked quietly.

"In the caves." Lea averted her eyes. "Jonas Edrin brought me back." She wasn't ready to tell her mother about the plan she and Jonas had come up with in the caves; a plan that had seemed nearly foolproof at the time, at least to her admittedly-inexperienced mind, that now seemed foolhardy at best.

They'd deemed the plan they'd made with Byrric—for Jonas to claim her as spoils—as imprudent, considering the circumstances. She needed to be able to act as a spy, and the length of time it would take for her to convincingly develop fealty to her captors was not conducive to helping Freya and Aerelius get their kingdom back.

So, they would pretend to be in love and she would pretend to be someone she was not.

She would spin the tale of a cruel father and an enabling mother. She would convince them how jealous she'd been of Aer, who'd had such an easy life in the palace with loving parents. And, most importantly, she would allow them to believe Jonas had convinced her that everything she knew of the Jotnar people, who were, in fact, cruel and unforgiving, was based on falsehoods and lies told by her parents.

Disgusting lies, all of them, but if she wanted to become privy to valuable information in a timely manner, they were a necessary evil.

"And the others?" Perida's eyes were vaguely hopeful. "Who else got away?"

Lea averted her eyes. "I'm not certain, Mother."

Perida slumped back against the wall morosely. "They killed your father."

Lea's hands curled into fists, her nails biting into her palms as she tried to halt the flood of tears that pressed behind her eyes.

Now is not the time, she reminded herself again.

"I know," Lea whispered, turning to pull herself closer to the prison bars. Her mother was no more than five feet away, but being trapped in this cell, where she couldn't even reach out to touch her hand in comfort, made the distance seem miles wide. "I'm so sorry, Mother. I wish I had been there."

Perida gave her a soft, pained smile. "No, Grevillea, you don't."

Lea stared at her, wondering how much she should tell her, or if it would be safer to just keep everything to herself.

"Have they harmed you?" Perida asked.

Lea shook her head. "No, Lessia said—" She clamped her mouth shut, but realization dawned on Perida's face.

"He—he's going to claim you as spoils, isn't he?" Perida rose to her knees and gripped her cell bars as something akin to hope lit in her eyes. "Is that what he said? Lea, do you know what that *means?*"

"He's not claiming—"

"It means no one can harm you until Lessia makes her decision," Perida pressed on, her words quiet and hurried. "And when she does, she will allow him to keep you with him, and he'd be a fool not to. The moment you get out of here, the moment he takes you to his room, you fight like hell, do you hear me? I don't care how you do it. You fight like mad and *get out.*"

Lea blinked. "Mother, I won't leave you here."

Perida let out a strangled laugh. "Oh, you most certainly will! If you get the chance, you leave and you *do not come back,* do you hear me? Don't spare me or anyone else here a second thought. I mean it, Lea. Promise me!"

But I came back for you.

Lea shook the thought off. It didn't matter what her mother said —she wasn't going to leave this palace without her.

"Alright, Mother. I promise."

DESPITE THE DISCOMFORT of the filthy pile of straw that acted as bedding, Lea managed to doze off now and then. Each stretch of sleep was fitful, fraught with nightmares and bursts of angry color. The cruel faces that haunted her, despite her waking knowledge that she was alive and not being tortured, brought on no small amount of fear.

It was two days before Lessia came to question her on the whereabouts and plans of Freya and Aerelius, who'd disappeared into the forest to head west toward Freya's home city of Watoria. It wasn't as vicious as Lea had expected of an interrogation with someone as feared as Lessia; the worst abuses being a few hard cuffs to the ear. Lea wasn't sure if Lessia decided she was lying or simply ignorant of her wayward monarchs' plans, but either way, Lea's relationship with Jonas seemed to keep Lessia from harming her too extensively.

On the fifth day, Lea had all but given up hope of Jonas coming for her.

By the seventh, as she looked down at the crude wooden tray on her lap that held a slice of moldy bread tainted with powdered widow venom, she'd decided she had made a terrible mistake in returning. Jonas either wasn't coming for her or...

No. She wouldn't think of any alternative.

She looked across the corridor to where her mother sat, staring down at her own meager meal, her face slack with grief, and sighed.

"He should've come for you by now," Perida said, setting aside her own tray. "I wonder why he hasn't?"

"I'm sure he will, soon enough."

She tried to be reassuring to keep Perida from losing even more hope, but she couldn't help but acknowledge just how little was left to cling to.

FREYA

Freya peered into the cave near the banks of the Selnor River that carved a path between Caelora and Allanor. Beads of frozen rain stung her cheeks and clung to her hair, the cold of which made the dry interior of the cave seem all the more welcoming. She conjured up a ball of light, then sent it drifting into the dim interior, illuminating the walls that stretched back several dozen feet.

She let out a quiet whistle, signaling to Aer.

He turned away from Florian and the others, then squinted into the trees, looking for her. When he caught sight, he tightened his cloak around his shoulders and made his way toward her.

"Our home for the evening?" he asked, eyeing the cave dubiously.

"There's no scent of anything living inside," she said. "It seems deep enough to house everyone, and getting out of this weather would be a good thing for all of us."

"Alright, I'll let the others know." He gave her a soft kiss on her temple, and she leaned into him, lacing her fingers through his.

"We should get a hunting party set up as well," she said. "It's been nearly a day since we've eaten anything substantial."

"I've already told Collin to organize it," Aer replied. He cast a glance over his shoulder, then stepped into the cave and drew her against his chest. "How are you doing?" he asked quietly. "I can feel your exhaustion."

She wrapped her arms around his waist and heaved a sigh. "I should be asking you that," she murmured. They'd hardly spoken of his father's death, or even had a chance to, since fleeing the palace a week ago. Their only goal had been to keep pushing their party of nearly thirty west toward the city of Watoria. There, they hoped to find word from her father, who'd promised to meet them, and a home base at the former home of her grandparents, Jora and Selinda Enrieth, a manor to the south of the city that had been in her family for centuries. It remained heavily cloaked with Selinda's magic—long-lasting spells that only allowed entry to those given express permission by Selinda's family—and would give them someplace safe to lay the rest of their plans. Their trek, a journey which would've taken, at most, four days by boat, was taking nearly thrice that on foot due to the circuitous route they'd been forced to take. Despite the glamours she and Florian had been weaving to obscure the appearances of their group, she and Aer felt a direct path to Watoria would be foolish, and Florian and their guards had agreed. So, they kept pace along the border between Caelora and Allanor, following the Selnor as it wended southwest, stopping each night as near a village as they would dare.

"I've got you," Aer replied after a moment, his words tense as he tightened his arms around her. "That's more than enough for now."

BY THE TIME they finished making camp an hour later, Freya wanted to do little more than collapse on the floor of the cave and fall asleep. The mounting exhaustion brought on by their exposure to the elements and the stress she bore due to the absence of her father, not to mention the burden she felt over the losses on her wedding night, had been wearing her down day-by-day. It wasn't something she cared to discuss with any of the others, whose losses had been just as great, if not more so. That she'd been draining her magic each day helping Florian wield an invisibility glamour over their party only made that exhaustion worse. She'd been hiding it quite well, in her opinion, but she'd noticed Florian eyeing her more than usual the last few days. When he'd offered to take on more of the share of magic-wielding so she could take a break that morning, she'd refused, but she was self-aware enough to know that that was more out of pride than a true belief that she didn't need a reprieve. The last thing she wanted was for anyone—her husband, in particular—to worry that she was struggling.

As she leaned against the cave wall and accepted the canteen of water that Aer had forced into her hand, she tried to ignore the twin looks of annoyance he and Florian had been casting her way.

"Your Majesty, I must insist on taking the larger share of this burden," Florian said, coming up to her. The tall, wiry warlock rarely held his tongue when he spoke to her or Aer and did little to hide his annoyance at her obstinance now. He knew far more than she did when it came to magic use, something she both appreciated and loathed at times. As he was currently trying to convince her to lessen her contributions to the well-being of her people, this was one of those times that leaned more toward loathsome.

She waved off his request and ignored her husband's glare. "It's fine, Lord Florian, truly."

"We still have three more days of travel, if we're lucky. I've been doing this far longer and don't tire nearly as quickly," he pressed.

Taking a sip from her canteen, she purposely ignored the unstated "as you" that was attached to the end of that sentence. "If I wanted to be scolded, Lord Florian, I would've insisted Byrric accompany us on this journey."

Florian sent her a level look, then glanced at Aer, who shook his head.

Before he could push further, Freya's aunt, Ana, appeared at her side, back from a scouting mission with Naedan and Amara, the hawk shifters that Byrric had assigned to act as scouts and messengers.

"Any news?" Freya asked, eager for the distraction.

"Some," Ana replied. "It's clear Lessia and Willem's knights know we're heading west, so we can only assume that they're expecting us to go to Watoria or perhaps Iston."

"How do you know?" Aer asked. They'd seen more than a few patrols the past week, some seemingly on the lookout for them, others rounding up any stragglers who may have escaped the towns and villages that dotted the countryside that had been attacked by the human and Jotnar knights. Now and then they'd witnessed a few prisoners being carted off, and as much as it pained her and Aer to stand by and not offer help, she knew they had little choice. Lindoroth needed their king and queen, and the only way they could ensure that end would be to get to Watoria undetected. The information they'd gleaned so far had been that Willem and Lessia were holed up in the palace in Iladel and had sent representatives to each capital, along with a small battalion of soldiers, to take control of the cities.

"There are more Jotnar and human patrols concentrated along the Selnor, and their numbers are increasing westward," she explained. "It would be my suggestion to veer away from the river, stick to the deeper forests for the rest of our journey. Let them split their troops between the north and south banks of the river."

Florian nodded. "Yes, that makes sense. Perhaps we'll detour south a bit before continuing west."

"If the patrols are expecting us in Watoria, Lessia and Willem must be as well," Freya murmured.

"Meaning, whoever they put there is likely one of their strongest and most trusted." Aer rubbed a hand across his brow. "Did you see any sign of Lindorothian soldiers?" Most notably absent on their journey had been knights from Lindoroth's five armies. Freya and Aer assumed they'd been directed toward the capitals, but when it became clear just how far-reaching Lessia's and Willem's attack had been, that assumption gave way to the knowledge that Lindoroth was likely on the verge of being completely overrun.

Ana shook her head, her expression grim. "None. My hope is that they're concentrated near the cities. But we'll learn more as we get closer. Lessia and Willem's plans might not be spread throughout all of their troops, but those who are closer to the city will know more. They wouldn't have placed a human there, at least not alone, no matter how skilled."

"Unlikely," Florian agreed. "Willem would've pushed for it, but Lessia is no fool."

"Debatable," Freya muttered.

Ana sent her a look before continuing. "I was hoping we'd receive word from Byrric by now, but it doesn't seem that'll be happening before we arrive. I overheard one of the Jotnar knights say Olthanas still seems salvageable, so I'm assuming that's where he's gone."

Freya's eyes automatically drifted to Myria Bryton, who was helping Isadora and a fox shifter named Amber sort out sleeping arrangements. Olthanas was the capital of Saith, Myria's home realm and the place her father, Emric Bryton, had governed for more than seventy years. Myria had been subdued this past week, her sharp tongue far more still than usual after the death of her father and brother. Freya assumed she was holding in her grief just as much as everyone else, but she could only imagine how Myria felt, being unable to get to her family's seat and knowing her mother was still held prisoner. The only thing that gave Freya cause to hope was that Olthanas was only considered salvageable to their enemies, which boded well for the rest of Saith and whatever Lindorothian soldiers had managed to make their way there.

As she watched Myria, who'd put on a brave face, despite it all, she could only pray that bit of news would give her some reason to hope, too.

"Freya?"

Freya turned her attention back to her aunt, who was looking at her with wide-eyed concern. "Yes?"

"I said that we'll need to sort out our plans tomorrow for our arrival in Watoria. I think it might make more sense for me to leave for Iston sooner rather than later, especially if we're going to detour south."

"How long will it take you to fly there from here?" Aer asked.

"Two days if I don't stop, three if I break for a few hours to rest. I'd prefer to wait another day or two to see if we get word from Byrric first, but I'd rather not delay too much longer. The Valkyrie need to be fully briefed and ready to launch an attack if needed."

"I'm sure we'll hear from him soon," Aer said.

His words were of little comfort to Freya, who knew her father's silence meant that he was either physically unable to send her a messenger or too occupied with enemy forces to take the time to.

"I have no doubts," Ana said. "My brother is nothing if not thorough, so if we haven't heard from him by now, it's because his focus is solely on the task before him." She gave Freya a pat on the arm. "Try not to worry, dear. We'll see him soon enough, and this isn't his first battle. In the meantime, rest. Give your magic a break for a day or two so you're at full strength when we reach Watoria."

Freya gave her a tight smile, then watched as her aunt and Florian walked away.

With a sigh, Freya cracked her neck and rolled her shoulders, still unable to shake her lingering discomfort, then sat down on the floor of the cave. Someone had gotten a fire going, and an air-user named Derrick had spread the heat throughout the space, giving the hard stone floor a soothing layer of warmth against the cold that had sunk into her bones.

"Freya," Aer said quietly, sliding down to sit beside her. He looked at her, annoyance clear in his eyes. "You should've told me it was your magic that was exhausting you, instead of letting me think it was just the travel."

She looked at him, searching his chocolate-brown eyes, and frowned. "Would you ask someone else to work harder just because you were feeling a bit peaky?"

Aer's brows lifted, but his answer was immediate. "If that someone was several centuries my senior and held far stronger magic than mine? Yes, without question. Just because you're the queen doesn't mean you have to exhaust yourself getting us to Watoria. It means quite the opposite, actually. Cast your glamours every day if you like, but there's no need to carry more of the burden than necessary."

Before she could reply, Collin appeared beside them, looking nearly as weary as Freya felt. "We managed to find a doe and a brace of rabbits. The doe should give us enough for tonight and a bit left for breakfast tomorrow." He glanced at Aer, then addressed Freya. "I saw a patch of witchbloom a few miles back, so I'm going to add some to your dinner. It will help with the fatigue."

She arched a brow. "For Florian as well, then."

"Florian doesn't need it," Aer told her the moment Collin walked away shaking his head. "You're being stubborn."

"My stubbornness is one of the many reasons you love me," she pointed out.

"Not when it's detrimental to your health." He huffed out a breath. "Please, Freya."

She heard the pain in his voice and could feel how much he hated asking her to limit herself. And yes, maybe she was being stubborn, but she couldn't help the feeling that she was—not for the first time —failing her people. To concede to her husband and Florian felt as though she were admitting defeat, admitting that she fell short in some way, even though the reasonable part of her mind told her that was patently false.

She met Aer's eyes and softened some when she saw the worry there. The gravity of it gave her pause as the weight of his own emotions mingled with hers. He'd lost his father, and his mother had been taken to an unknown location, someplace she'd only return from once they'd managed to eliminate the threats to their kingdom and their lives. Right now, they were nearly all the other had left. He'd forced a brave face this past week for their companions, but the pain was clear as day, both on his face and in the bond that ran between them.

Selfish. She was being selfish.

"I'm sorry," she whispered, taking his hand and lacing their fingers together.

"You can take care of yourself, Freya. I know that. But you need to know when to quit, when to accept help." He lifted her hand to his lips and kissed her knuckles, then brushed his thumb over the ruby ring that encircled her ring finger, a smaller, more delicate version of the one he wore. "You have nothing to prove to anyone, and needing to share a load like this doesn't make you deficient in any way. You and Florian might be the best here at casting glamours, but even the best of us need to pause from time to time."

She wrapped her hands around his and laid a kiss to his palm. "You're right. The last thing you need is to worry about me. If it will make you feel better, I'll take a break tomorrow."

"I think that would be for the best," he replied. "We all need to have our strength up when we near Watoria, and the last thing I want is a Valkyrie half-blood at diminished capacity." He grinned when she squawked out a protest and punched his side.

"I will throttle you, Aerelius Harridan! Don't test me."

"Ah, there she is," he murmured, putting an arm around her shoulders and kissing her temple. "What do you say, Valkyrie? Do you suppose with your waning strength, I'll be able to take down more Jotnar than you?"

"Why make a bet you know you can't win?"

He shrugged. "Under normal circumstances, that might be the case." He clicked his tongue and appraised her weary state. "Now, though... I wonder."

She rolled her eyes. "As much as I love you, I often find myself hating you."

"Impossible." He motioned for Rodrick, one of his guards, to come over before adding, "I'm going to make sure everyone is sorted. Go make up with Florian, will you?"

She smiled as he turned to speak with Rodrick. Then, tiredly, she looked around the cave, at the filthy faces of her companions, their clothing so sodden no mix of elemental magics could offer relief, and prayed they'd make it through the final days of their journey unscathed.

FREYA

It was well after sunset by the time everyone was settled in for the night, and a fire was crackling near the mouth of the cave. Once the guards were set and a watch scheduled, Florian and Freya combined their earth and air magic to barricade the entrance, obscuring them from passersby and ensuring no one came or left without their knowledge. Everyone took spots relatively near the fire as the game that had been caught were roasted and portions were handed out. Freya, Aer, Collin, Laz, and Myria sat toward the back of the cave, separating themselves a bit from the rest of the group but staying close enough to be present for the others.

Freya had just finished her food when Rini, the tiny palace pixie who'd taken a liking to her during her time at Aldridge, appeared at her side and clicked her tongue. Freya had been overjoyed when she saw that the pixie had been able to sneak out of the palace, only learning belatedly that Tyna had remained behind to tend to Lea, who, along with Jonas, was working out a plan to free the prisoners who'd been taken in the attack.

"Your Majesty, you must get some rest," Rini crooned, her brow furrowing as she flitted toward Freya and plucked a leaf from her hair. "Come, I've prepared a bed for you both—"

"In a bit," Freya told her, gently disentangling her hair from the pixie's small hands. "What news do you have?"

"Has there been any word from Tyna?" Aer asked.

Rini nodded, her shining lips set in a thin line. "This morning. I worry over her concerns regarding Lord Edrin and Lady Calliwell."

Freya and Aer exchanged a worried look. The most recent news Rini had gotten from her sister had been troubling. By Tyna's account, Lea had been thrown into the dungeons within minutes of returning to the palace with Jonas, despite their insistence that she was on their side. Meanwhile, Jonas looked to be going about his normal business, meeting frequently with Lessia and Willem to discuss plans to solidify their conquest of Lindoroth.

The only information Tyna had given of the other goings-on in the palace was that the other prisoners were alive, including Lazarus' mother, Collin's parents, his aunt and cousins, Lea's mother, and Myria's mother. But, sadly, their circumstances in the dungeons were quite dire. Aside from that, Tyna had only seen Lea once, and that had been just a brief glimpse as Lea was being dragged from the throne room to the dungeons by a Jotnar guard.

"Both were sent back with a part to play," Aer said, sounding as though he needed to remind himself just as much as Freya did. "Unsavory as it is, we should all assume they're playing those parts as planned. If nothing else, the blood bond Jonas swore will keep her safe."

Freya nodded, although she was becoming increasingly unsure that was the case. She struggled not to picture Lea sitting in the cold and damp dungeons with the other prisoners, receiving nothing but meager portions of stale bread and gritty water. The gods only knew how much longer Lessia and Willem would see fit to keep any of the prisoners alive. Blood-bond or no, without Jonas' immediate protection, Lea would be the perfect target for the Jotnar and Dystonians, and all manner of horrid things done at their hands.

She shuddered at the thought.

"What about Iladel?" Collin asked. "Has Tyna managed to get out of the palace and into the capital yet?"

Rini bobbed nervously in the air beside Freya. "According to Tyna, there's a bit of a stalemate at the indoor market, which is where the citizens who managed to escape have barricaded themselves. All entrances have been successfully blocked by a group of witches and warlocks, and Lessia and Willem haven't sent more than a handful of Jotnar troops to attempt to infiltrate."

Myria frowned. "That hardly makes sense."

Aer shook his head. "No, it makes perfect sense. Iladel is one city, and they've already taken the throne. The dissent will be easy enough to squash once morale has weakened more, and if the citizens have barricaded themselves, that means they have limited supplies."

"Which also means they're of little threat to Lessia's and Willem's cause," Collin said with a nod. "They're not worth expending the energy of the knights."

Freya sighed. "What else?"

"Caelora's capital is not doing well," Rini replied, sending a sympathetic look at Laz. "It appears Kildin was hit first when the Jotnar invaded from the north, then again the next day when the humans came in from the sea. The last report Tyna heard was that the Caelorian and Royal Armies were struggling to hold the city."

Laz's jaw clenched as he took the hand Collin offered in comfort. "How bad has it gotten?"

Rini sighed. "I'm unsure, my lord. I'm certain we'll know more when I speak to her next."

"Word from the Commander would go a long way in easing our minds," Collin said, giving Laz a sympathetic look.

Freya leaned back against the wall. She looked at Laz and tried to give him a comforting smile. "It'll be alright, Laz."

He shook his head. "You can't know that."

"We can do our best to ensure it's the truth," Aer told him. "Our hands may be tied while we're here, but once we get to Watoria, we should have more to work with."

"What about Saith?" Myria asked Rini. "Have you heard anything from the capital?"

"At last report, circumstances were still tenuous in Olthanas," Rini replied. "I'm sorry, I wish I had more," she added when she saw Myria's disappointment. "For all of you."

"You're doing more than we could've asked," Freya told her.

Rini's silver eyes inspected Freya's face and hair as she fluttered closer. "Come, Your Majesty, let me tend to you," she said pleadingly. The braided chignon Rini had put in Freya's hair that morning had taken on bits of forest throughout the day, and several stray locks had escaped, tickling Freya's neck. "You look quite dreadful."

Freya gave her a wry smile. "I'll be going to bed soon, Rini. Toying with my hair would be pointless."

With a small harrumph, the pixie vanished.

"It soothes her to have a task," Aer said quietly, lifting his arm for Freya to slide closer.

"I know." Freya tucked herself under his arm. "I just struggle with focusing on hairstyles when we're trekking through the wilderness."

"We all have things that help us through difficult times," Aer said. "It's important to remember that when dealing with a pixie who's spent her life beautifying the females of the court. Fighting, hunting, being on your guard—those things are second nature to you, but for the rest of us..."

Freya looked down at her hands and tapped her thumbs together absently. "You're right, I'm sorry. I'm just so focused on the next few hours that I can't think about much else."

He kissed her temple, then rested his head against hers. "It's alright. Let's just try to get some sleep, alright?"

Freya looked at their friends, each face drawn and distressed.

"Yes," she agreed. "We all should."

Collin met her eyes. "We only have a couple of days to go. Once we get to your grandparents' estate, we'll be able to regroup and find out more."

Closing her eyes, Freya rested her head against Aer's shoulder. "I certainly hope so."

∼

THE FOLLOWING EVENING, they came across the first camp of prisoners they'd seen in their travels. Freya was surprised they hadn't come across one sooner. It was far smaller than she'd expected. The number of citizens they'd seen being dragged off by patrols so far would've indicated that they were being held somewhere, but there'd been no evidence of such a place until now.

From their perch on the edge of a large depression in the earth, Freya, Aer, Collin, and Florian could just make out a group of Jotnar and human soldiers clustered around a fire. The wooden carts, each bearing an iron cage full of prisoners, were arranged in a curve around the fire behind the group of soldiers, who were mostly Jotnar with a few humans. Freya couldn't make out the prisoners' faces and they were too far away to identify by scent, but she could only assume they were all Linds who'd been taken after Lessia's coup had spread west.

Collin looked at Freya, confusion clear on his face. "Do they think themselves so invincible that they don't need to cloak their location?"

"That's certainly how it would seem," Florian replied.

Frowning, Freya glanced back toward the camp. "Or their master is far more fearsome than anyone out here might be."

Florian motioned for them to retreat, and the four slunk away from the crumbling edge, then made their way back to the small camp they'd set up for the night. Despite the undeniable effects of the witchbloom, Freya had grudgingly handed over her portion of the glamouring to Florian in order to rest up for a confrontation that would inevitably come when they reached Watoria.

"So, what should we do?" Freya asked.

"Nothing," Florian said brusquely. "We cannot risk exposing our location and we don't have the resources to take on that many more travelers."

"He's right," Collin said, seeming to take note of the look of an impending argument that had bloomed on Freya's face.

She shared a look with Aer, whose eyes held the same frustrated look she saw in Collin's. Shaking her head, she looked away, hating that there were people in danger, hungry, cold, and in pain, less than a half-mile away and there was nothing she could do to help them.

"Alright," she finally said. Without waiting for a response, she stalked off toward the shelter she and Aer planned to use for the night.

She relaxed a little when Aer fell into step beside her and took her hand.

"I'm sorry," he said quietly as they approached the small lean-to of branches Rini had helped set up for them. It wasn't much, but it would give them a small bit of privacy. A few other shelters had been set up for the larger groups, but she and Aer preferred to have their own space when they could manage it.

"They aren't wrong, so there's nothing to be sorry for," she said, resigned to the truth of those words. With a sigh, she rolled her shoulders, still unable to shake her lingering discomfort. "It doesn't lessen my aggravation that there's not a damn thing we can do to help those people."

Aer frowned at her movements. "You haven't stretched your wings since our wedding night. In the morning, you should try to get a quick flight in."

Although she had a strong desire to do just that, Freya shook her head. She'd never gone so long without releasing her wings and, until now, she'd also never had a need to keep them so concealed. The feeling of confinement had begun to shift toward claustrophobic.

"I've thought about it, but I don't want to risk being seen. Even with a cloaking spell, if there's a Jotnar patrol out there with magic strong enough to feel through mine, we'd be done for."

"An invisibility glamour—"

"—requires far more magic than simply changing my appearance," she snapped. "And if I'm to rest my magic, it doesn't make sense to expend extra energy just so I can stretch. That's not an option right now."

Hurt and a touch of aggravation flashed across his face. "I'm just trying to help," he said flatly. Shaking his head, he fixed his eyes on a point past her shoulder. "You're hurting yourself and taking it out on me, Freya. I don't appreciate it."

They stood silently for a moment as she stared up at him, waiting for him to look back at her.

"I'm sorry," she whispered. Hard eyes met hers as she stepped closer. "I just feel like I'm—"

"Failing? Welcome to the club. We've been crowned barely a week and already our kingdom has fallen."

Freya closed her eyes and leaned against his chest, not knowing what else to say. Ever since they'd left their parents and friends, she'd struggled to find the right words to express how sorry she was for the loss of his father's life and of his mother's constant, soothing presence. Freya felt their absence, along with that of her own father's, like a blow. But that didn't hold a candle to the feelings he was doing a very good job of hiding from everyone else.

After a moment, he wrapped his arms around her and kissed the top of her head. Tightening her arms around his waist, she tried hard not to cry.

"You're not doing this alone," he whispered, his breath soft against her hair. "I know you're used to being on your own, but that's not the case anymore. You need to let people help you."

"Once we get to my family's home and we're under the protection of my grandmother's magic, I'll do a few laps around the property." She lifted her face to his and smiled. "I promise."

"I'll hold you to that." He tilted his chin up and laid a soft kiss on her lips, then let his hand slip down to link his fingers through hers. "Come, let's get some sleep. Tomorrow will be a long day."

LEA

Lea had just managed to drag herself out of a particularly vile dream on the evening of her eighth day in the dungeon when a door clanged open and heavy footsteps sounded in the corridor. Groggily, she sat up and had only caught on to her mother's warning hiss when she saw the familiar white-leather-clad legs of Jonas.

She shoved her knotted curls out of her face and glared up at him. "Finally come to pay a visit, then?"

His lips twitched in amusement. Wordlessly, he jingled a ring of keys, the sound painful as it teased at freedom, then slid one into the lock of her cell. She exchanged a quick glance with her mother before scooting back a few feet, her hands curling into fists in the dirty straw on the floor.

Jonas crooked his fingers. "Lessia has deemed it acceptable to release you, so it's time to go."

"It's about time," Lea muttered as she pulled herself to her feet, wincing. The chill of the dungeon had caused her muscles to cramp, and standing was proving to be a painful feat. She stepped out of her cell, sending Jonas a scathing look as she passed him.

"Please, my lord, don't hurt her!" Perida sobbed, gripping the bars of her cell. "She's all I have left! *Please.*"

"It will be alright, Mother." Lea gave her mother a small smile. "I promise, it will be alright."

Perida stared up at Jonas beseechingly. "Lord Edrin, I beg you. Don't harm my daughter."

He smirked, and Perida let out a small, shocked whimper when she saw Lea slip her hand into his.

Lea wrapped her other hand around one of the bars of her mother's cell. "I will do what I can to get you released," she whispered. "But you must be patient."

"Come," Jonas snapped. "We have things to tend to."

Without giving her a chance to say a proper goodbye to her mother, he tugged Lea down the dimly lit dungeon hall, then up the stairs to the darkened palace yard, where the only entrance to the dungeons existed.

"Keep your head up," he murmured as they made their way toward the palace entrance. "Don't let any of them think you've been cowed by a week in the dungeon."

She didn't say a word as she followed him through the echoing palace halls, seething at the fact that he'd taken so long to come for her. Having their story questioned was bad enough; being thrown in the dungeon was worse, but understandable, at least from Lessia's perspective.

But for Jonas to take more than a *week* to free her from the dungeons...?

She huffed and sent him an irritated glare.

Jonas either didn't notice or pretended not to.

Two guards were stationed outside Jonas' door, both tall, slim, and donning the dark gray uniforms of the Jotnar royal guard. Jonas strode past them, giving them a muttered command to "take a walk," before slamming the heavy doors behind us.

He flicked the lock shut, then released Lea and took several steps back.

"Lea—"

She slapped him. Hard.

Eyes wide, he rubbed at his cheek.

"Do you have *any* idea how *disgusting* those cells are? What kind of food—if you can even call it that!—your prisoners are fed?"

"I tried—"

"Not hard enough, apparently!" She adjusted her dress and tucked her hair behind her ears, doing her best to look a bit more dignified than she felt.

There was the scuff of a boot in the hall, followed by a snicker and a vile comment from one of the guards.

"I told you to take a walk!" Jonas roared.

"Apologies, my lord," the guard mumbled. Fading footsteps quickly followed. Jonas narrowed his eyes, then dropped a silencing spell over the room.

"I wanted to get my mother out of there," Lea hissed. "Not watch her rot for an entire week, unable to do anything but cry and eat moldy bread!"

"As I said—"

"You tried." She put her hands on her hips. "Tried what, exactly? You're the Empress' nephew! Do you need permission from anyone but her to get what you saw as rightfully yours?"

"There has been a good deal going on here, and convincing Lessia that we're... involved was not an easy feat." He scratched his chin. "I'm still not sure she believes it. There was also a good deal of back-and-forth regarding the divvying of the 'trophies' of their coup, which Willem continues to insist you are. It took a good bit of time to get it through his head that I had no intentions of letting you slip away. Not to mention, I needed to ensure this room was secure, which took far longer than I anticipated." He rubbed the reddening spot on his cheek again. "I can't believe you hit me."

"Secure?" Lea looked around, suddenly wary as she stuck on that one bit of information. "There are passages connected to this room?"

He nodded. "Two, as well as nearly a dozen spy holes, which is presumably why Salazar chose this room for my quarters. Bringing you here without first ensuring all means of eavesdropping were blocked was not an option, and to cast a silencing spell over this room regularly from the start would raise suspicions. As Lessia requested my presence for more hours out of the day than I cared for, I didn't have much time to thoroughly examine the room." He shook his head. "There were spy holes in the ceiling, Lea, and Willem, along with half of his men, were hoping to catch themselves a pretty Lindorothian female to take to their beds. I'm sorry, but I had to be certain you'd be safe once here."

Lea's stomach went sour at the thought of one of Willem or his men taking her instead of Jonas. In the brief moments she'd been in the throne room after she had arrived, the humans had caused feelings of disgust nearly as deep as the Jotnar. Willem, in particular, made her skin crawl.

"I don't understand," Lea said slowly. "If you insisted our relationship began prior to Lessia and Willem's attack, why would he feel entitled to me?"

Jonas ran a hand through his pale blond hair and huffed out a breath. "I don't know, but for the time being, you will not leave this room. Is that clear?"

"So I'm a prisoner, then?" She scoffed. "Why not just leave me in the dungeon?"

"You're not a prisoner, not by any stretch, and Lessia has acknowledged that openly. But Willem is proving to be a bit more shrewd than I first believed him to be. I don't trust him."

Lea closed her eyes and leaned against the wall, suddenly overcome with exhaustion. While in the dungeon, the only thing that had kept the grief over the loss of her father and uncle at bay was the knowledge that she'd soon be out and hopefully working toward exacting revenge. But when three days turned into four, then four into five, she slowly began to lose hope that their plan would work. She'd truly become concerned that Lessia had discovered Jonas' deceit and had executed him. Or worse, that his deceit had been so thorough she'd allowed herself to be led right into a trap.

To be quite honest, she still wasn't sure that hadn't been the case. She lifted her eyes to his, suddenly wary of what he might expect of her now. What she saw when she looked at him was a bit of sadness mixed with aggravation. Whether that was with her or their circumstances, she couldn't be sure.

"How did you finally manage to convince Lessia to release me?" she asked quietly.

Jonas' jaw tensed, then relaxed. "I managed to convince her you would be fully amenable to switching sides, so to speak, and that there might be potential for getting the people of Errest to follow you. I assured them that was by no means guaranteed, but even the possibility of it helps you," he said when he saw her dubious look. "Now it's just a matter of sticking to our plan."

Lea exhaled quietly.

"I had one of the maids prepare a bath," he said quietly. "And Dina managed to salvage some of your clothing, although I wasn't able to retrieve the clothes Freya gave you in the caves."

She waved a hand tiredly. "I don't think pants would be appropriate, considering the circumstances."

Jonas opened his mouth, then let it fall closed in a tight smile. "Get yourself cleaned up, then we'll talk a bit more."

With a nod, Lea pushed herself away from the wall and walked toward the bathing room on the other side of the room. Jonas reached out to touch her arm as she walked past, but she shrugged him off, not wanting him to see how uncertain of him she still was.

She waited until she'd closed and locked the door before finally allowing her hands to shake. Clenching her fists, she slid to the floor and let her head come to rest on her knees. Then, slowly, she started to pick through her scattered thoughts.

Byrric trusted Jonas, and while Freya and Aer still didn't seem on board with allying with Jonas, they trusted Byrric, so Lea did, too. When they gave Lea and Jonas approval to go through with their plan to infiltrate Lessia and Willem's court, Lea assumed she would be safe. She'd become doubly sure once Jonas swore in blood not to harm her or anyone who shared blood with Aerelius.

Now, having spent more than a week in the dungeons, she begged to differ, although it was yet to be seen whether Jonas' account was true.

But... if what Jonas said *was* true, and he really *had* managed to convince Lessia that he and Lea cared for one another, then perhaps this plan wasn't as crazy as she'd started to think.

Heaving a sigh, she stood, then began to strip out of her dress, the same one she'd worn to Freya and Aer's wedding. What had once been a beautiful shade of red was now the color of mud. The silk-and-lace garment had been ripped and dirtied beyond repair, a thing that saddened her a good deal. The laces on the back had frayed and loosened, so it was an easy task to untie herself.

As she stepped out of the garment, she caught a glimpse of her reflection in the mirror above the washbasin, and the sight brought her up short. Her black curls were a frayed, frizzed mess, with the filth of the dungeons plastering portions to her cheeks. Her skin, a warm brown on a typical day, had taken on a grayish hue, which told her the poison that had tainted her food in the dungeon had done more than just suppress her own magic. It, along with the meager nutrition, had sapped her strength. All that looked back at her now was a hollow-eyed shell.

Gingerly, she picked up a washcloth that lay folded beside the basin and began scrubbing away most of the dirt and grime from her skin. Once the bulk of the filth was gone, she eased herself into the warm bath that had been prepared for her. The steaming water smelled sweet and felt soft, its heat a balm against the cold from the dungeon that still chilled her bones. After a few moments, she felt a bit of magic creep back into her body. It was faint, but the water seemed to be touched by some sort of spell—likely from Dina, the water witch who'd served Freya during her time at the palace.

She tried not to picture her mother wasting away in her cell while Lea soaked in hot water filled with rose petals and scented oil, nor did she dwell on the horrid thoughts that must be racing through Perida's head after watching her only child willingly walk off with an assumed-enemy. Her mother was smart—she knew Lea's best chance at escape was to allow Jonas to claim her as his, so if that's what she believed was happening, then Lea would allow her what small comfort that might offer.

She slid down and let her hair sink beneath the surface of the water, combing her fingers through the curls to loosen them. As the water eased her tense muscles and settled her mind, she thought of what her next steps should be. She could trust Jonas' intentions and see their plan through, hopefully glean some worthwhile information that would help strengthen their chances of taking back Lindoroth. Or she could take the first opportunity to flee, make her way to the Northern Road and follow the Selnor River across Lindoroth to find Freya, Aer, and the others. A trip that long on her own would be difficult, especially with minimal supplies, but it was possible.

Her confidence in their plan when she'd made the choice to stay had nearly shattered after her reception in the throne room, and it was becoming clear that admitting defeat and slipping away might be the better, albeit less desirable, of her two options.

"Oh, my lady!"

Lea startled, sloshing water over the edges of the tub as she moved to cover herself.

"What—*Tyna?*" Lea sagged with relief at the sight of the glittering silver pixie who'd attended her these past months. "Gods above, you scared me!"

Tyna fluttered over to the edge of the tub and sat, and Lea took a good look at her. The small female held the same silver gleam she always did, but there was something tarnished about it, as though it had dulled a bit. Her hair, normally twisted into an elaborate coronet, hung loose, and her iridescent wings drooped at her back when she sat down. The shimmer that normally surrounded her like a cloud of gossamer had all but vanished.

"Apologies, my lady," Tyna said, letting her feet sink into the water. She waved a hand, and the water that had become murky with the lingering dirt from Lea's skin was instantly clear as crystal. "I wanted to come see you in the dungeons, but Lord Edrin assured me you would be here soon enough."

"He did?" Lea sat up a bit straighter. "You've been speaking with him?"

Tyna nodded quickly. "A bit, my lady. The empress has had spies on him since you both returned. It's clear her trust in him has diminished a good deal, especially since you came back with him so willingly."

"How do you know?"

"I'm quite small and have ways of making myself unseen," she replied haughtily. "Has he caught you up on the goings-on of late?"

Lea shook her head. "I've only just been brought from the dungeons."

Tyna's silver brows puckered. "Well, there's been quite a bit happening, and I've been conversing with Rini when I can."

"Conversing? She hasn't stayed behind?"

"Oh, no, my lady! She left with Their Majesties. She and I thought it best I remain behind with you, so I'll be sure to update her shortly."

Lea let out a quiet sigh of relief. While the pixie might not be her closest friend, her familiar presence, not to mention her ability to travel from one place to another in the blink of an eye, gave her a small bit of comfort. "When did you speak to her last? What of Freya and my cousins?"

"I spoke with her a few days ago. Rini's last update was that they were halfway to the Enrieth family's manor outside Watoria, although she wasn't clear on where that was, exactly. They should arrive in three days' time." Tyna gestured for Lea to sit forward so she could tend to her hair. "Come, my lady, let's get you properly cleaned up."

After Tyna spent copious amounts of time combing the rest of the grime and tangles from Lea's hair and smoothing sweet-smelling oils over her skin, she twisted her hair into a long braid and helped her dress in a warm wool nightgown and matching robe.

Lea smoothed a hand over the soft fabric and frowned. "I expected silk... or something..."

Tyna smiled her understanding. "Lord Edrin wanted me to ensure your comfort on your first night out of the dungeons."

Lea's mouth tightened. "But not after?"

Tyna gave her a pitying look. "I can't say, my lady. He seemed to have your comfort in mind when he chose your wardrobe. You aren't his prisoner, so you'll have some freedoms, but it is quite typical for Jotnar males to dress their females. Whether Lessia will insist he do so with you is anyone's guess."

"'Dress me,'" Lea scoffed, tightening the belt on her robe with a scowl. "I suppose we'll see, then."

Tyna winced, a tiny, pointed tooth digging sharply into her lip as she fluttered closer. "A bit of advice, my lady?"

Lea sighed. "Of course."

"Choose your battles wisely. Your attire may seem important now, but you must remember—"

"That I'm here to play a part?" Lea finished. She sat down on the edge of the tub and pressed her fingers against her forehead. "Yes, I'm aware."

Tyna swooped down beside her and sat on the lip of the tub, then patted a tiny hand on Lea's thigh. "It will be alright, my lady. Lord Edrin is waiting to discuss how you both will handle things in the coming weeks, but just know...I do not plan to leave you."

Lea smiled wanly. "What do you think of..." she inclined her head toward the door to the bedroom where Jonas was waiting for her.

Tyna followed her gaze and her jaw tightened. "I trust him... for now, but there are many reasons why I plan to stay by your side, my lady."

FREYA

The former home of Jora and Selinda Enrieth and the place Freya had spent the bulk of her early years was just to the south of Watoria, about four miles into the woods on the western edge of the ravine that encircled most of the city. The road that came northwest from Errest ran along the large crevice for several miles to the east, while the long road from Olthanas stretched along the southeastern edge of the property, effectively sandwiching Freya's family home between two of the only means of entry to Watoria. Not only would the area be heavily patrolled, it would also be heavily travelled by Lessia's and Willem's soldiers, who they'd seen scouring the countryside in greater numbers since they'd encountered the camp of prisoners a few days earlier. Sometimes it seemed they were looking for something—presumably her and Aer—and other times they were driving more carts of Lindorothian prisoners to some destination Freya was unaware of.

They made camp on the final night of their journey in a thick copse of towering pines. Between them and the manor lay two more miles of forest. Based on the scouting Amara and Naedan had done, the woods were crawling with Jotnar and human knights. Whether they knew of the existence of Freya's family home was uncertain, but it became clear as they neared the convergence where all roads toward the city dovetailed into one, the need for stealth grew and Freya's hopes of crossing onto her family's lands unseen diminished. For now, the assumption they were working with was that the Jotnar and humans fully expected her, Aer, and a cadre of soldiers at their backs bearing down on Watoria intent on wresting it from the hands of whoever Lessia and Willem had sent in to take over.

After everyone had been fed, Freya, Aer, Ana, Florian, Reginald, and a handful of others sat down to discuss their plan of attack for the final leg of their journey. A map lay in the middle of their circle showing Watoria and the surrounding forest.

"We're outnumbered," Ana said briskly. "We've got barely thirty, many of whom have no experience in battle of any sort, and we counted nearly four dozen patrols between here and there, almost all Jotnar."

"Probably more," Freya added. "There are plenty of hiding places in these woods. It would've been easy to miss a few others, and far more of them have the ability to glamour than we do."

Amara, one of the hawk shifters, tapped her finger on a spot several miles to the southeast of Enrieth Manor where the forest was particularly dense and the ravine narrowed to barely a crevice. "This is the most sheltered section of the forest between here and your family home and the nearest point where we can cross the ravine on foot," she said. "We'll have the best chance of slipping across your property line with minimal detection here."

"It will also be the most heavily patrolled," Aer said, shaking his head.

"Agreed," Ana added. "Crossing at a place of convenience wouldn't be wise."

"They can't see the property, though," Reginald pointed out. "They don't even know it exists."

Florian looked at the human and shook his head. "No, Jotnar have powers far different from those of the Linds. They may not be able to see through Selinda's enchantments, but there's a slim chance they'll know *something* is there. If they see that our aim is to get to that *something*, they'll know it carries great significance."

"So you leave none alive," Isadora said. At Ana's surprised look and Florian's arched brow, her eyes widened. "I mean... I know little of battle, Lord Florian, but as they are the enemy, wouldn't that be the most prudent method of dealing with them?"

Florian nodded slowly. "Yes, I suppose it is."

Shifting forward, Freya eyed the map, then looked at the others. "I agree with Amara. Our best chance is a direct shot. My grandmother's enchantments protecting the property extend nearly to the roads on either side. Once we get over the ravine, it's barely a mile until we reach the property line, then we'll be obscured from sight for the rest of the journey. We'll get rid of any patrols and bring the bodies south toward the Saithian border. It won't be a stretch for anyone who finds them to assume there was a skirmish with Saithian soldiers."

Florian gave her a steady look. "Then I would implore you to rest for the night, because a direct shot would mean glamouring everyone, including the shifters, if we want to ensure maximum loss of life for our enemy."

"I don't think glamouring the shifters will be necessary," Freya told him. She glanced up at her guard, Rissen. "What are your thoughts?"

He shook his head. "We don't have many magic-wielders with us, and you two are the only ones who can effectively cast invisibility glamours for the amount of time we'd need them. I don't find it worthwhile to spread your magic so thin when it can be wielded defensively against our enemies. Naedan and Amara will have plenty of coverage in the branches. Amber as well," he added, referring to the fox shifter that accompanied them. "The rest of us can rely on our senses to guide us through."

"We were able to slip through the woods unseen easily enough when we were scouting," Laz said when he saw Freya's hesitation.

"Wolves are native to this part of Lindoroth," Freya said, nodding. "Seeing one here or there wouldn't be considered odd, but there are six of you. Considering things are the way they are, a pack of wolves would certainly raise suspicions."

"Then we spread out as much as possible," Collin said. "To the north and southeast of the manor. It's the most logical plan and will expose fewer weaknesses than if we spread the magic of two over nearly thirty people."

Aer nodded. "Alright. Naedan, Amara, do one last sweep over the forest. Amber, you take the forest floor and stick to the trees as much as possible. Once we have more information, we'll finalize our plans on how to proceed."

Amber, the small fox shifter, gave a quick nod, then she and the two hawks shifted and took off into the darkening woods. After dismissing the rest, Ana turned to Freya and Aer, her brow slightly furrowed.

"A word, Your Majesties?"

Freya gave her a chastising look but nodded.

"I'd like to fly ahead to Iston," Ana said. "The charm Florian gave me will keep me concealed long enough to get to the sea, and from there it's hardly more than a day's flight to Iston."

"Why?" Aer asked. "It seems it would make more sense to remain here with us."

"I'm not sure how much the Istonians know about our current situation, as they typically keep to themselves. I spoke to a few old acquaintances when I was there to ensure allegiances for the new king and queen, but now that I've got something concrete to approach them with, I'd prefer to brief them as soon as possible."

Freya shook her head. "We should go together. Wait until we get Watoria in hand, until we've heard from Byrric."

"If they were any other people I would agree, but you know how the people of Iston are," Ana replied. "If we show up at their gates with a full battalion behind us, which we presumably will once we're done here, they'll immediately go on the offense."

Aer and Freya exchanged a look.

"Alright," Freya said with a nod. "What will your plan be?"

"My mother, for one," Ana replied. "Assuming she's there. She's been gone the last two months."

Freya didn't miss the bitter tone Ana's voice carried. It had been more than a decade since Freya had seen her father's mother, partly because Freya's trips to Iston consisted of two visits when she was a girl and partly because Vara Balthana spent most of her time traveling, rarely staying in Iston for more than a few months at a time.

"And if she isn't?" Freya asked.

Ana shrugged. "I have a few other acquaintances I can tap, but I'll need to go about getting her back to Lindoroth as soon as possible, which could take time. I'll try to do a fly-over of your grandparents' home," she said to Freya. "If anything seems amiss, I'll fly back."

"Do what you think is best," Aer told her. "Just be careful."

Ana gave him a sharp nod before looking at Freya. "You do the same?"

Freya's answering smile was tight. "Aren't I always?"

Ana snorted, then gave Freya a warm hug before slipping on the ring Florian had given her to conceal her presence. A moment later, Freya felt the brush of air as her aunt spread her wings and lifted off, disappearing into the night.

THEY CROSSED the road from Saith without being detected the following morning and came to a stop in the woods on the eastern edge of the ravine to make the final leg of their journey. Once they crossed the ravine, they would be within striking distance of Enrieth manor, but the forest was riddled with patrols, meaning this part would be their most treacherous.

The eerie silence of the forest that faced west toward the edge of the Enrieth lands set Freya's nerves on edge. No birds sang, there was no crunch of animals among the trees, and no breeze rustled the leaves. Jotnar magic, heavy and viscous, pressed against the cloak of magic Freya and Florian had laid over the small cluster of trees they'd taken cover in. There were no enemy patrols in sight, but considering the ravine had narrowed to only ten feet across, they could only assume the enemy was simply lying in wait.

Freya cast her eyes upward, watching as Amara and Naedan flew above, black silhouettes against the gray sky, swooping and circling lazily about as though hunting for prey. Her own wings tingled beneath her skin, itching to be let free after more than a week of disuse. The promise of a free sky to fly in above her grandparents' land beckoned her forward, and it was only logic, the cloaking spell she and Florian had cast around their small group, and their careful planning that kept her feet planted firmly to the ground.

Letting her gaze fall back to her surroundings, she looked around, searching for any sign of pursuit. She, Aer, Reginald, and Isadora walked silently behind Florian as Laz and Collin prowled the forest in front of them, sniffing out any tracks that might indicate nearby enemies. Every now and then their tails would brush, as though reminding each other they were still there. The rest of the shifters had spread out a half-mile to the north, but Laz and Collin had insisted on staying close. Reginald and Isadora, the only two who held no supernatural abilities, stood beside them.

"What is the likelihood their knights will see through your shielding?" Reginald asked Florian.

"Nil."

"I must say I disagree," Isadora whispered to Freya. "You and Lord Florian are strong, but I fear Jotnar magic might trump yours."

Freya averted her eyes to avoid laughing at the poisoned look Florian sent the human queen.

Aer gave Isadora a curious look. "Could you have seen through it when you still had your powers?"

She shrugged and stared ahead. "It's hard to say because it's been some time since I had any magic to wield." Her face turned thoughtful, as though she was trying to remember what her own magic had felt like before Lessia leached it away. "Lessia only ever had the strongest warlocks in her employ, no matter the rank, so it's safe to assume these knights are old and come from long lines of strong magic."

Freya couldn't help but feel a bit of contempt at the way Isadora spoke of the strength of Jotnar magic.

"It's no matter," Reginald said quietly, sliding his longsword from the sheath at his hip. "It's not far to the property line. If we run—"

"*You* may run, human," Florian interrupted. "*We* cannot leave any alive to report on our whereabouts. One sentry returning to whoever holds Watoria is all it will take to have these woods swarming with Jotnar and human alike. Selinda's magic is strong, but it is not infallible."

"Let's just hope that whatever luck has gotten us this far without detection holds out a bit longer," Freya murmured.

Her head jerked upward when Naedan called out a warning, then dove for the trees on the other side of the ravine, Amara on his tail. Freya watched grimly as an arrow sailed past, missing both but confirming that whoever was patrolling this area knew they were there.

"That's our cue," Aer said quietly. He looked at Freya. "Wings out, my love. Something tells me you may need to fly."

Grinning, she let her wings flare wide, relishing the freedom of movement as she gave them a slow flap. The moment the cold forest air hit her feathers, she felt a bit of her strength return. She sent Aer a grin. "If circumstances weren't so dire, I'd think you intended to offer me as bait."

"Only you would think I would use my queen as a means of drawing enemy fire."

"I'm certain Her Majesty could easily outfly their arrows if it came down to it," Florian said absently as he scanned the forest around them.

"You'd offer up your queen?" Reginald whispered, aghast.

When Florian didn't respond, Reginald looked at Aer in horror.

"My spymaster would never suggest such a thing." Aer tilted his head toward Freya. "I don't think I can say the same for my wife."

"Only as long as Byrric isn't around," she said, smiling. "He'd poison me with my own feathers for even—"

Crack!

The sound of a snapping twig caused Laz and Collin to halt in their tracks, their noses low to the ground as their eyes roamed over their surroundings.

"They're close," Freya breathed, the smile fading from her lips.

With a flick of his wrist, Florian sent out a small ripple of magic. "Ah, that's better," he murmured, smiling grimly at the handful of knights who he'd just relieved of their glamours.

They had the typical gnarled looks of Jotnar soldiers, tall and lanky with faces that seemed twisted in permanent scowls, but Freya could feel their power creeping along the forest floor. It didn't seem any had noticed that Florian had obliterated their shields, but Freya knew it was only a matter of time.

"Remember, keep them on this side," Florian cautioned. "We need to drive them south."

Collin and Laz growled out a warning and Florian widened his stance in front of Aer and Freya. Aer's spirit magic swirled pearlescent around his forearms and palms, and Freya slid two feathers from her wings, wincing slightly at the sharp pain as two immediately began to regrow in their place.

Freya cast a glance over her shoulder at Reginald and inclined her head at Isadora. "Stay back and keep her safe."

Reginald nodded grimly and tightened his grip on his blade. Isadora took a small step behind him, a look of resignation on her face. It had been ten years since Isadora had been in possession of her own magic, and while Freya was uncertain how old Isadora actually was, she could only assume backing down from a fight due to lack of power wasn't something Isadora had gotten used to. Jotnar females prided themselves on strength of both body and magic, both of which, once taken, would be difficult to regain.

Suddenly, Freya heard the yowl of a lioness in the distance followed by a wolf yelping in pain. Recognition flashed across the faces of the knights as they took in Freya's wings and the power that dripped from Aer and Florian's fingers, but their shock lasted only a moment before they launched their attack.

Florian flicked a hand, then spun his finger, calling whip-thin roots up from the ground, wrapping around the arms and ankles of two the knights before spearing them through and cutting off their shouts.

Collin and Laz sprung forward, taking two down by their necks and landing in a flurry of fur and snapping teeth. Freya took flight after four took aim at her and Aer. She flew above them as Aer sent out a heavy burst of spirit magic, instantly diverting their intentions away from harm. Giving the knights no time to recover, Freya did a quick lap around them, slicing the neck of each with her feathers. The feel of the wind and thrill of being in the air again instantly began to revitalize her, and the magic that had begun to feel stagnant awoke.

She conjured up a handful of daggers from the air and tossed them at another cluster of incoming knights, taking them down just as they would've converged on Laz and Collin below. The sounds of fighting from the north increased as almost all of the shifters who'd come with them drove the Jotnar patrols south, further away from Watoria, to where Freya and the others would be waiting. Florian dispatched the last two of the group that had attacked them just as Freya landed on the ground beside him, and they all ran toward the battle a half-mile to the south.

Aer, Laz, Florian, and Collin continued to fight beside her, fending off the Jotnar coming from other directions as Reginald protected Isadora. Freya spun, kicked, punched, and sliced as one after another came at her. Each movement, each hit, each flex of muscle was a balm to her frustrations and anger of the past week.

The other shifters appeared, fighting against the Jotnar and a handful of human knights as they aimed to close in on Freya and Aer. More came from the trees, dropping down all around them and popping into existence as the glamours hiding them evaporated.

There are too many, Freya thought as she sliced the metallic tip of her feather through the neck of a human who'd attacked from her side.

She tossed the body aside, and as magic and growls flew around her, a burly, broad-shouldered Jotnar bore down on her, singling her out above the rest.

Freya gripped her feather tighter, then flung three magical daggers straight at her attacker.

He deflected them with a single blow.

"Noble effort from the Valkyrie queen," the Jotnar soldier said with a sneer. He twirled his knife and took aim. "It's a shame—"

She silenced him with a flick of her wrist, cutting off his air and piercing his throat with her feather. Hardly a second of satisfaction passed before three others took notice of her and began to converge. Feigning bravado, she widened her stance and beckoned them forward. She knew it was an idiotic move, but she needed to keep them focused on her so the others could handle their own fights.

Just as they lunged for her, streaks of black, gray, and russet tore through the trees, aiming for the enemy knights. Freya stumbled back into a tree as the wolves joined the melee. A Jotnar who'd taken aim at Aer was dragged to the ground by one, while the soldiers who'd turned their attention toward Freya were taken down by two others. The late arrivals mixed with Freya's party, using magic and claws to shred into the Jotnar soldiers.

Minutes later, the woods were silent once again and the air was clear of enemy magic. The only sounds were the heavy panting of wolves, the gurgle of blood, and the crunch of pine needles and oak leaves underfoot as the newcomers cautiously approached.

Freya's heart pounded as she took in the destruction around them, reaching blindly for Aer's hand when she felt him take his place beside her.

The largest wolf, black as midnight with wide, gold eyes, lumbered up to Freya and butted her shoulder with his snout.

"Freya—" Aer said as he tightened his grip.

She held up her other hand and let out a relieved laugh as the wolf shifted into her old friend and former commanding officer.

"Freya Balthana," Ashton Carinald said with a grin. "Aren't you a sight?"

FREYA

There was little time for reunions as Ashton and Aer began to bark out orders to scour the woods for any surviving enemy knights and to dispose of the bodies as far south as they could. The other marshals—twenty-six in total—who'd accompanied Ashton helped Freya's party lug the wounded across the border of Enrieth lands. As soon as they crossed through the rippling magic that protected the property, Freya breathed a sigh of relief and hoped Haegin, the earth-wielding groundskeeper Byrric had continued to employ, was at least somewhat prepared for their arrival.

When they broke from the forest onto the rising green that held the main house, a sprawling stone structure fit with turrets and wide, arched windows, and multi-level gardens bursting with flora, Freya's relief increased. She hadn't visited since before her grandmother died, which was nearly ten years ago. It was the place she'd grown up in before Byrric had moved her into Watoria, and no matter how much she'd loved the house she and Ana had lived in, this would always be her home.

Haegin seemed to have been expecting them, because they were halfway across the lawn when the lumbering old male came out to meet them. He was tall with a ruddy face, a broad nose, and soft, wide brown eyes.

"Ah, Your Majesty!" he called. "Have you got wounded?"

"We do," Freya replied. "Is the infirmary stocked?"

"Yes, yes, take them in," he said, stepping aside as those carrying the injured rushed past.

Freya watched as Myria, Amber, Naedan, Rissen, and three marshals were carried inside by Rodrick, Perinald, and four other marshals. Once they'd passed, Aer came to stand beside her and put a hand on her shoulder.

"Cecilia and the rest are disposing of the bodies and doing another sweep for stragglers." His eyes ran over her face and a slight furrow formed on his brow as he took in the blood drying on her neck. "Are you alright?"

She nodded, then looked up at him. "I am, considering. No injuries. You?"

"Likewise." He inclined his head toward where the rest of the marshals were approaching. "I suppose there are introductions to be made?"

"Yes," she agreed. She couldn't help but smile as she took in the people she'd worked with for so long. "Let's make sure everyone inside is tended to first, then we'll handle that."

"So long as someone here can wield a needle and thread, your soldiers will be fixed up," Haegin said.

"Not to worry, Your Majesties, I'll take care of them," Florian said. He snapped his fingers at one of the marshals and motioned for him to follow. The marshal balked at the command but kept quiet at Ashton's silencing nod before following Florian into the house.

When they'd passed, Haegin gave Freya a sympathetic smile. "It's wonderful to see you, Freya, dear. I only wish it were under better circumstances."

"That makes two of us," she said, reaching out to give the warlock a hug. "But it's good to be home."

ONCE THE WOUNDED HAD BEEN TENDED to and Florian had done all he could to hasten their healing, everyone gathered in the large dining room at the rear of the house to catch up.

After the marshals were introduced to the rest of the group, Freya and Aer filled them and Haegin in on the status of Iladel and the rest of Lindoroth they'd seen during their travels.

"We didn't get near any of the larger towns," Aer said. "The patrols we encountered closer to Watoria looked to be gathering up prisoners and taking them away."

"We saw very few of our own people along the way," Freya added. "I don't know if it's because most are captive or if they're all hiding. I would've expected to come across more who were fleeing, though."

Ashton folded his arms and shook his head. "No, they're likely captive. If the other towns, at least the larger ones, are in a state like Watoria, the city limits were probably sealed."

"Magically?" Florian asked.

Ashton gave a sharp nod.

"How did you find us, anyway?" Aer asked.

"Ana came yesterday. She stayed only long enough to rest for a few hours before departing for Iston. She told us you would reach Watoria by today and that we needed to get to you as soon as possible to give you cover for the rest of the trip. We've been patrolling as discreetly as possible, but Gideon felt Lord Florian's cloaking spell the moment you neared the property. We knew you were there, but I couldn't detect your scent at all. The best we could do was follow the push of his magic."

Myria, who'd insisted on staying in her lioness form to help her wounded leg heal faster, let out a low hiss, conveying her annoyance at the lack of backup.

Ashton arched a brow at her, then looked at Freya in question.

"We're just thankful you all found us when you did," she said, shooting a silencing look at Myria. "I'm afraid things would've turned out much worse if you hadn't."

"Yes," Aer agreed. "Now, what can you tell us about what's happened in Watoria?"

Ashton blew out a breath and shook his head. "Ten days ago, approximately five hundred human troops were found marching toward the city. Our own army laid waste to them, of course, but while their focus was on the humans, one thousand of Lessia Edrin's soldiers seized Watoria from the north while another battalion of humans came from the east, taking out a very large portion of our knights along the way. By the time the Allanorian knights that remained were able to get closer to Watoria, it had been sealed off and was surrounded by enemy soldiers."

Ashton waved a hand, indicating the house before continuing. "Byrric told me long ago to use this as a safe house should anything ever warrant doing such, so I and the other marshals who managed to get out of the city came here. Then, a few days ago, Byrric arrived in the dead of night to tell us what happened at your wedding. He told us he'd gone to Kildin immediately after leaving Iladel and found Caelora's capital overrun, its army crippled, so he shifted his focus to the outer capitals."

"Kildin is overrun?" Laz asked quietly, his voice pained. Freya sensed he knew it would eventually come to that, but knowing your home would be lost and hearing that it had actually come to pass were two different things entirely.

Ashton gave him a sharp nod. "Yes, my lord. Unfortunately, Byrric's report does not bode well for Caelora's citizens, Kildin's, in particular, as it seems to have been taken before Iladel and is now held by a human male and a Jotnar female. Due to its proximity to Iladel, remaining behind instead of rallying the outer regions would've been a mistake."

"A mistake?" Laz's eyes widened. "To protect—"

"Laz," Collin said quietly.

Aer frowned at Ashton. "Did Commander Balthana leave forces behind in Kildin at least?"

Ashton nodded. "Roughly five hundred of the Royal Army's knights stayed to back up the Caelorian army, but their main purpose is to aid the outer villages and towns should the Jotnar or humans attack there. Byrric left five hundred additional troops to supplement to Allanorians here, who are currently blocked from entering Watoria by two thousand human knights. He also sent his lieutenant commander to Errest to assess the situation there. Byrric's plan was to go from here straight to Olthanas to offer assistance, should they need it, but the Royal Army took a large hit when Lessia and Willem invaded."

Freya's heart twisted a little at the pained look Laz wore as he listened to Ashton describe the current state of their land. She knew Byrric wouldn't have left Laz's home behind if he didn't believe the prospect of more aid could be found farther west, but knowing that Laz's people might be suffering a similar fate as those in Iladel was troubling.

"My father said he'd spoken to the marshals already," she said to Ashton, wanting to divert the discussion to their immediate circumstances. Kildin would be saved, but based on its proximity to Iladel and the fact that it was nearly two weeks' travel in the direction they'd just come, it would be foolish to go there now. "He said he spoke to you before our wedding, weeks ago."

"With all of the sitting governors hundreds of miles from their houses for your wedding," Gideon, Ashton's second-in-command, said, "Commander Balthana told us to be on the lookout in case anyone chose to utilize their absence to their advantage. Out of an abundance of caution, we started ensuring the city's guards and marshals were prepared. That's not unusual for any royal wedding, though."

Ashton nodded in agreement. "That was about four weeks ago. He told us to come here, should something happen, and await further instruction from either him or you. He had nothing definitive to tell us, but he had a concern that something 'didn't feel right,' so if you arrived seeking assistance, we needed to be ready."

"Byrric's assumptions are rarely wrong," Aer murmured, his mouth turned down in anger as his eyes slid to Freya. "Why wouldn't he tell us this beforehand?"

Freya dragged a hand through her hair and let out a frustrated growl. "Why let us go through with a damn *wedding*—"

"A failsafe, Your Majesties," Florian said patiently. "To reign, you must be wed. If, the gods forbid, there was an attack and the reigning king and queen fell, you both needed to be prepared to take your crowns at a moment's notice. Commander Balthana may not have known what, if anything, was coming, but his gut told him enough to lay preparations, just to be safe. And for the record, I agreed, as did your parents," he added, looking at Aer.

"Byrric said we may need your assistance," Collin said to Ashton. "What did he mean by that?"

"Ideally? Stabilizing Watoria," Ashton replied. "After seeing the state of Kildin, he knew Lessia would be sending someone to take the governor's seat and with it, the city."

"He expects us to do that without the support of an army?" Aer asked, aghast. "You said the Allanorians can't get to the city!"

Freya huffed out a laugh. "Yes, of course. 'Retake the city with a handful of marshals and palace guards and a boxed-out army that can't get within a mile of the city.' That certainly sounds like my father."

"I'd say it's more likely he'd hoped for us to collectively assess the circumstances once you arrived and come up with some sort of plan for a smaller operation, one that doesn't require a large military force," Ashton replied, annoyance beginning to show in his tone. "You know your commander better than I, but even I find it unlikely he'd want or expect a few dozen soldiers and civilians to attempt to take on two armies, head-on."

"More explicit instructions still would've been appreciated," Freya muttered.

"Did Byrric give you any numbers regarding losses?" Florian asked. "Soldiers, civilians, and so forth?"

Ashton sent a look at Freya and Aer, then met Florian's eyes. "Byrric estimated we'd lost approximately one-quarter of Lindoroth's forces by the time he arrived here. That was three days ago. The rest are being spread throughout the kingdom."

Freya's frustration with her father evaporated as she let that news sink in. When they'd left Iladel, they thought the attack had just been on that city and would spread from there. As they'd traveled west, it became clear the attack was more far-reaching than that. Now, as Ashton confirmed the fears that had begun to grow within her, she realized just how hard her kingdom had been hit.

For the next few minutes, she listened intently as Ashton described the events of the past two weeks. The marshals had done as Byrric asked, shoring up their defenses, checking weapon stocks and food stores inside and outside the walls, reinforcing the city gates and so forth. When Byrric returned a few days earlier and found the city surrounded, he'd come to Enrieth manor and found the remaining marshals had done as he'd directed and taken up residence there with Haegin. He'd instructed them to do what they could with the Allanorian troops, but to remain sequestered at the manor as much as possible in order to maintain secrecy until Freya and Aer arrived.

Ashton's voice caught when he spoke of the last few days.

"Watoria..." Ashton shook his head, then met Freya's eyes. "It's bad."

Freya tensed as she took in his expression. "How bad?"

"The brother of Lessia's late husband, a Lord Fredrick Edrin, came in not half a day after the commander left. He's taken over the governor's manor and has been systematically executing anyone he feels won't swear allegiance to him as their new governor." He swallowed hard. "Which is most of Allanor, it seems, including the human woman he arrived with. The central square has become home to a guillotine that is put to use at least once per day."

"He's executing the citizens?" Freya whispered.

"Why did he kill the human he came with?" Aer asked.

"*Humans,*" Ashton corrected. "Another woman arrived two days ago and he put her head on a pike beside the first within hours. From what we've been able to deduce, the captain of his guard is a vicious bastard that has a tight hold on his ear, and Frederick is quite impressionable. The assumption is that he doesn't feel the need to feign regard for human life this far from where his leaders are."

"Who were the humans he sent?" Reginald asked, dread settling on his face.

Ashton's eyes darted between Reginald, Isadora at his side, and Freya before responding. "I'm unsure, Your Highness. Both were executed within a day of arriving."

Isadora ran a comforting hand up Reginald's arm, her eyes full of pity as she took in his expression. "We knew Willem would use his own people to achieve his ends," she said quietly. "This should come as no surprise."

Reginald gave a quick, jerky nod. "Yes, of course. How do the other citizens of Allanor fare?"

Ashton's expression turned grave. "He's been bringing them in by the wagon-full. We attempted to call in reinforcements from the surrounding regions, but the enemy came in droves, seemingly out of thin air. We'd hardly formed a plan of attack when they first appeared over the ravine and at the harbor. Human and Jotnar knights, draugs, huldra. The city was overrun within an hour. We protected it as best we could, but once it became clear the city couldn't be saved, at least not by us, most of us retreated here."

"You just *fled*?" Myria exclaimed, outraged as she shifted out of her lioness form. Her blonde hair had come out of its braid and hung in a tangled mass at her shoulders, but her eyes still sparked with fury. "You're tasked with protecting the city!"

Ashton sent her a flat look. "There are forty-two marshals left, my lady, out of more than two hundred. Twenty-six of them are here; the rest remained in the city with their families. I made the call to retreat because we were vastly outnumbered and overwhelmed. Staying in the city would've done nothing, Ana would likely be dead, and you all would now be going in blind."

It took all of Freya's strength not to slump into a chair. Sensing her distress, Aer squeezed her shoulder.

"Have we gotten any word on the status of the other capitals?" Aer asked, still wearing a mild look of shock.

"A messenger from Olthanas arrived a few days after the Commander left," Ashton told him. "He said a human male and

Jotnar female now hold the governing seat of Saith. Byrric and the bulk of the Saithian army were in the process of ousting them and had been quite successful so far. We hope to hear from Byrric any day now."

Myria's outrage peaked again, this time mingling with disgust as she flicked a glare at Reginald. "I don't suppose *you* know who your wretched brother might have sent to take over *my* family seat?"

"Likely one of his allies in Caldel," Reginald replied, arms folded. "Knowing Willem, he wouldn't trust anyone outside his own circle to hold a seat as far from Iladel as Olthanas is." He looked back at Ashton. "Have there been any other humans in this region?"

"The humans assisted the Jotnar in breaching Watoria, but their encampments are outside the city. Frederick doesn't seem to want them inside the city walls, and as far as we can tell, the Jotnar have little use for them. They took the city and have been having their fun ever since," he said bitterly.

"Reinforcements, then?" Freya asked.

"That's what it appears," Gideon said. "Another marshal and I snuck down to their camps a few nights back and it sounds as though they're just waiting to be put to use."

"That seems a bit odd," Isadora commented.

"How so?" Freya asked.

Isadora looked at Freya. "Willem is no fool. He wouldn't send his men here to simply wait around."

"It seems that's exactly what he's done, Your Majesty," Ashton said.

Isadora blushed and looked up at Reginald. "Lady Edrin will do, Officer."

Freya saw Ashton's lips tighten as he gave Isadora a sharp nod.

"Perhaps we should all get some rest, reconvene a bit later," Freya said, sensing Ashton's irritation with the number of people in the room. "We'll regroup in the morning."

"Lord Florian, Prince Reginald, if you wouldn't mind hanging back?" Aer said. "The rest of you, there's food available in the kitchen, and if anyone needs further healing, Haegin will be able to assist you."

Once everyone had filed out, Ashton turned to Freya and Aer and smiled grimly. "Now, tell me about Iladel."

LEA

Jonas kept Lea under lock and key in his chambers for the first two days out of the dungeon. Lea wanted to protest, but common sense told her she was better off waiting for Jonas to do whatever it was he was doing to better ensure her safety before wandering around the palace on her own.

While Jonas was out performing whatever his daily duties were, Lea spent the hours doing her best to suss out the secret entrances and spy holes in his chambers he'd spoken of on her first night. All had been sealed up, according to him, but she wanted to see for herself. Tyna appeared twice to assist her with the higher places, indicating three spy holes in the ceiling, one of which was directly above the canopied bed.

When Lea questioned the purpose of spying from a vantage point where there'd be nothing to see but heavy fabric, Tyna informed her that the four-poster bed had only held a canopy for the last five days.

"Considering you are to be in a... relationship with Lord Edrin, he had the canopy installed," Tyna explained. "He wasn't certain who knew of the spy holes in this room, but it would look quite suspicious for you to be sharing a bed without... sharing it." Her cheeks flushed.

"Ah." Lea nodded. She and Jonas *had* been sharing his bed, but both had kept to their own sides, a thing that would, indeed, arouse a good deal of suspicion if someone caught sight of them from above. Even though the canopy consisted of a simple piece of fabric, it gave Lea a bit of solace when she lay down at night, knowing no one could see her while she slept.

Learning that Jonas had the forethought to install it ahead of time also helped ease some of her concerns about him, although the question of her trust in him still lingered.

On her third day of freedom, Jonas informed Lea that she would be dining with him, Willem, and Lessia that evening in the palace's main dining room. While the thought of leaving the room she'd been stuck in was tempting—and seeing as Tyna had a good deal of information to share about the passageways that were hidden throughout the palace—the implications that such a dinner carried left a pit of dread in her stomach.

"You'll need to show a certain level of subservience," Jonas explained. "Jotnar females are respected and are typically allowed their independence, but as you are not Jotnar, it would be... unseemly if I gave you the same latitudes I might one of my own kind. If Lessia or Willem become overly suspicious or think you're not adapting to our ways adequately, you're more likely to be handed off to someone they feel will have a firmer hand, and our main goal right now is for you to stay with me."

She inhaled slowly, then nodded as she set her fork down on the small window-side table where they'd just finished eating lunch. "Yes, I know. I only wish... Sometimes I wonder if this was a good idea or if we were foolish to rush into things."

Jonas set his napkin aside then leaned forward and took her hands between his, not noticing or ignoring the way she tensed at his touch. "If the commander of Salazar's Royal Army hadn't given his approval, I might agree with that sentiment. Byrric has faith in us, and because of that, so do Aerelius and Freya."

"Wherever they are," she murmured, slumping back in her seat and letting her hands slip from his. Tyna hadn't received word from Rini since the day after Lea had been released from the dungeons, and even then it was only briefly. Freya, Aer, Laz, Collin, and the rest had avoided detection so far and were hoping to cross the border to Freya's homeland within three days. Lea hoped to hear word today as to whether or not they had reached their destination, but as the hours stretched on, her concerns only increased.

"It's still early in the day," Jonas said soothingly. "Earlier on the other side of the continent. It's unlikely we'll hear anything for several more hours, possibly not even until tomorrow."

"Do you suppose they'll have to fight?" Lea asked quietly. Whether it was due to her lack of knowledge of its location or to limit the amount of information she shared at court, Rini hadn't told them the precise location of Freya's family manor. At first, Lea wanted to press, find out exactly where her friends and cousins had fled to, but both Jonas and Tyna stopped her, citing the less knowledge they had of the location of Lindoroth's monarchs, the better.

Jonas leaned back in his chair and folded his arms. "That all depends on where they cross into Watoria and how successful they are at maintaining their cover. With Freya and Florian with them, my guess is their chances of slipping in undetected are good, although that says little about their ability to stay hidden."

"I wish I was with them," she whispered. "I know what I'm doing here will help them. At least, I hope it will. But it doesn't change the fact that I wish we were all together."

"I understand, Lea. I promise, I do. I can't even begin to presume how you must feel, being told to feign attraction to a male you hardly know." He rubbed a hand across his forehead and sighed. "Let's finish going over how you'll behave at dinner this evening."

Lea rolled her shoulders and took another breath. "Okay. Tell me what to do."

THE INSTRUCTIONS JONAS had given her made sense. She would allow him to touch her, although she'd been very clear as to how and where. He'd promised to keep things within the realm of proper, considering their true relationship, which hardly bordered on friendship. Her main goal tonight was to show her contentment with him, to demonstrate to Lessia and Willem how happy she was to finally be out of the dungeon and back in her lover's arms. A small step, but hopefully one in the right direction.

But Lessia was sly, and while Lea knew little of Willem, she could only assume he wasn't lacking in intelligence, either. No, they wouldn't be easily fooled.

When they entered the dining room, still adorned in the gold accents the Harridan's were so fond of, Lea saw that the table had been set for five. Three of the seats were already occupied by Lessia, Willem, and a raven-haired female who sat at Willem's side. The two empty seats meant for her and Jonas were opposite Willem and the female, with Lessia at the head.

"Ah, Jonas, Lady Calliwell," Lessia said as they approached, her red lips curving into a smile. Her crown, a spidery thing made of sleek, black metal, sat atop her perfectly smooth hair. "So kind of you to join us." Her eyes narrowed a bit as she took in Lea at Jonas' side, the fitted charcoal gown Tyna had chosen that was so typical of Jotnar fashion.

"Lady Calliwell, I'd like you to meet my cousin, Lady Effina Veldin," Jonas said.

Lea gave her a shy smile. "It's lovely to meet you, Lady Veldin," she said.

The smile Effina offered back lacked both sincerity and any semblance of kindness.

Jonas brushed a thumb across Lea's cheek and angled his head toward a table on the side of the room. "Get us some wine?"

She itched to tell him to have a servant get it but knew this was one small way she could show Lessia and Willem that she wanted to care for her lover. So, she smiled up at him. "Of course. Go sit, I'll bring it right over."

As she made her way over to the table where a carafe of wine had been left out, she made a quick note of the guards in the room and committed their placement and numbers to memory. Then, she picked up the carafe and began to pour, keeping her ears peeled for the conversation she knew was about to begin.

"Has there been any news from the west?" Jonas asked as he slid into his seat.

"Nothing as of yet," Lessia said airily. "It's only a matter of time, though."

"It's been more than a week," Jonas pointed out. "Kildin is well in-hand. Should I pull some knights from there and send them toward Watoria?"

Quietly, Lea returned to her seat, setting a goblet of wine down at Jonas' place, then Jonas motioned for a servant to fill her plate.

"Anything in particular, my lord?" the servant asked, a male Lea recognized as one of the palace servants. His face was carefully expressionless, and if she wasn't mistaken, it seemed he was struggling not to meet her eyes.

"A bit of what we're having is quite alright," Jonas replied. "She is our guest, after all."

"Yes, my lord." The servant leaned forward and began spooning food from the various serving dishes on the table onto Lea's plate.

Jonas waited until Lea began cutting into her food before addressing Lessia. "Well? Should I send some of our knights west?"

Lessia pursed her lips and drummed her long, pale fingers against the table. "Perhaps. Although we can only assume Freya and Aerelius have reached their destination, whatever that may be." She angled her head to the side and gave Lea a coy smile. "I don't suppose you know where they're going, do you?"

Lea swallowed the small sip of wine she'd just taken and gave Lessia a bashful smile. "I just assumed they were going to travel straight for Watoria. That was Freya's home for so long, after all."

"Yes, that's what I've been told," Lessia said. "Have you any idea *where* in Watoria they might try to go? I can assure you, the city is locked down. They will not get in, and I would venture to guess they know that."

Lea shook her head. "I'm sorry, Empress. I heard very little of their plans when we were in the caves. We weren't there very long."

Lessia made a considering hum, but before she could say more, Jonas spoke.

"So has this become official?" Jonas gestured toward Willem and Effina. "Are you to wed?"

Lea shoved a large bite of chicken in her mouth to conceal her shock.

Effina preened at Willem and took his hand. "We are. In three days' time."

Ignoring her, Willem stared directly at Lea. "Don't bother hiding your thoughts, pretty girl. Say what's on your mind."

Lea swallowed her bite of food quickly. "My—Your Majesty?"

"Speak, girl!" Lessia snapped, causing Lea to jump.

"Apologies, Empress, Your Majesty. I was just surprised—"

"That I might cast aside that opportunistic whore who thought fleeing with my brother was a better option than ruling at my side?" Willem dabbed his mouth with a napkin and leaned back in his high-back chair. "I'll have you know that once I found out Isadora was a Jotnar spy, I thought we'd be a great match, perfectly poised to take over Lindoroth together." His eyes slid to Jonas, then back to Lea and his lip curled. "Clearly that was not the case."

"I—Jotnar?" Lea didn't have to feign her surprise at that bit of information.

"It's quite shameful," Effina said with a sniff. "Even Salazar's royal warlock didn't know the sweet human queen was none other than Jonas' sister, working with the humans. Some spymaster that Lord Florian is."

Lessia leaned forward and rested her chin in her hand, a challenge in her gaze as she looked at Lea. "Well? What are your thoughts on that, dear?"

Lea's lips parted, then closed as she carefully weighed her response. If chosen carefully, her words could go a long way in improving her position with Lessia. If chosen poorly, she could seem overeager, if not outright suspicious in her desire to please.

"I suppose... well, I would say congratulations are in order."

A perfectly groomed black brow winged up. "Oh?"

Lea cleared her throat and twisted her hands in her lap, quelling the myriad questions that ran through her mind as she held Lessia's gaze. "While I may be a bit unhappy with the outcome, I can't ignore the great level of intelligence and cunning it must have taken to achieve such results. To join forces with the human monarchy in such a way as to hide it from your closest neighbors... well, forgive me, but it's quite impressive."

"Yes," Willem said, his tone condescending. "My father may have been a fool to miss the Empress' deceptions but it was quite simple, once I married her, to see that Isadora was far from the human woman I had been betrothed to years before."

"You overheard a conversation between me and my sister," Jonas drawled. "It was hardly high-class espionage."

Willem scowled at him, then turned back to Lea. "So you admit you are unhappy here?" he asked, his tone both teasing and dangerous.

"No," Lea said firmly. "I am unhappy that so much blood was shed, especially at such a joyous occasion as a wedding. As for the rest..." She smiled up at Jonas, doing her best to appear happily enamored, before looking back at Lessia and Willem. "I am not unhappy with the rest."

Willem held her eyes, his cold gaze narrowing slightly before he looked at Jonas. "Impressive. I'd almost go so far as to say you should take this one as your wife, seeing as how loyal she's become."

Lea nearly choked on her wine.

"Oh, as though Jonas has ever had a hard time training a lover!" Effina said with a laugh.

Jonas hardly spared her a glance before going back to his meat.

"Frederick is planning on taking a Lind bride, after all," Effina continued, eyeing Lea consideringly. "And she *is* quite pretty."

Jonas gave a non-committal grunt. "What of the humans you sent Frederick after he took over Watoria?" he asked.

Lessia laughed and waved a hand dismissively. "Oh, those were doomed to fail."

"Yes, I believe I chose poorly on both accounts," Willem admitted with a sigh. "I can only hope he finds a suitable replacement."

Lea nearly frowned at the odd statement but forced her face to remain neutral.

"Has he had any luck quelling unrest to the south of Watoria?" Jonas asked.

"Byrric and the Saithian commander have been keeping us busy in the southwestern regions," Willem said. "Edhil and Olthanas are likely lost for now."

Lea's heart leapt at that news. Jonas' reports over the past two days had been scarce, especially as news related to her home realm. To hear that Edhil hadn't yet fallen gave her a heart a much-needed jolt of hope.

"We'll get it back," Effina said, patting Willem's hand. "Try not to worry, darling."

"Yes, our armies combined are no match," Lessia agreed. "Those Edhilian mines will be ours."

Willem sent Lea a chilling look. "Perhaps stringing up the bodies of their former governing family at the gates would sway them."

A lump rose in Lea's throat, but she kept her eyes locked on his. "I believe you underestimate the will of the Edhilian people, Your Majesty." She tensed when Jonas touched her ankle with his boot.

"Oh, leave the girl alone, Willem," Lessia said, waving a hand in annoyance. "It's not your job to threaten her or convince her of anything." She smiled sweetly at Jonas. "That's what my darling nephew is for, isn't it?"

GRAB your copy of *The Valkyrie's Calling,* book 2 in the *Half-Blood Rising* trilogy on Amazon!

ACKNOWLEDGMENTS

To Jelly Bean and Maddie-Mads (aka my rest-time editing team).

To my husband for encouraging me to "just write the damn book."

To my dad for his kick-ass map-making skills.

To the rest of my family for their unwavering support.

To my alphas, betas, and ARC readers. None of you told me what you thought I wanted to hear, and my work is better for it.

To Eric Peterson, my first ever beta-turned-alpha. Whenever I question a plot point or style choice, my first thought is, "What would Eric say?" You never sugar-coated anything, which I can't thank you for enough.

To Vegas.

To Denise Worisch for my gorgeous cover—thank you for putting up with my pickiness.

To Jenifer, my amazing editor, for putting up with my inability to write short books.

To the authors I re-read over and over that inspire me to keep going.

Finally, to all of the readers who took a chance on Tessa and have followed along to meet Freya. Writing started as a fun hobby but has become so much more, and I'm thankful for all of you who've taken the time to read my work.

ABOUT THE AUTHOR

Lucy grew up "down the shore" in New Jersey, where her love of the mythological was born when her middle school English teacher introduced her to the Odyssey. After high school, she received Bachelor's degrees in Psychology and English Literature before continuing on to her Master's degree in Library and Information Science. In her spare time, Lucy loves to read, cook, and go hiking with her husband and two daughters. Chaos is her debut novel.

Stay up to date! Hop over to www.lucyroyauthor.com to sign up for Lucy's newsletter, follow her on social media, and read up on news and other bookish things!

www.ingramcontent.com/pod-product-compliance
Lightning Source LLC
Chambersburg PA
CBHW020227110726
47898CB00004B/1177